Praise for

My Lord Jack

"A book to feast upon. Jack is one of the most unique—and intriguing—heroes in romance. He will most certainly steal your heart. Fresh and original . . . Don't miss this one."
—Patricia Potter

"Stunning in its emotional impact and historical detail, *My Lord Jack* is an enchanting tale of love, forgiveness, redemption, and passion . . . impossible to put down."
—May McGoldrick

A Rogue's Pleasure

"Sparkles with laugh-out-loud humor, a rare sensitivity to postwar trauma, touching emotion, thrilling historical detail, and exquisitely drawn characters . . . Run, don't walk, to your local bookstore, and don't miss out on this stunning new talent!"
—*Affaire de Coeur*

"Wonderfully written! This is an impressive debut from a bright new author. Readers will devour it." —Cathy Maxwell

"What a wonderful read. *A Rogue's Pleasure* [has] all the makings of a great novel: vivid historical detail, vibrant characters, and a fast-paced adventure—everything I look for in a historical romance." —Victoria Lynne

continued on next page . . .

"Hope Tarr's first novel is an overall winner. Fast-paced, intriguing, and loaded with sexual tension, *A Rogue's Pleasure* is a real page-turner. With one book, this author has already gone onto my 'must buy' list." —*The Romance Reader*

"Ms. Tarr's debut is a smashing success. Here is a new and fresh voice for the historical romance genre . . . A must-read for those who like sexy heroes, strong-willed heroines, and fast-moving plots. This one goes on my keeper shelf and Ms. Tarr becomes an automatic buy for me." —*Sime-Gen Romance Reviews*

"An impressive debut . . . I enjoyed *A Rogue's Pleasure* very much and plan on reading more of Hope Tarr. She can create very good characters and knows how to pace a story."
—*All About Romance*

Tempting

Hope Tarr

JOVE BOOKS, NEW YORK

If you purchased this book without a cover, you should be aware that this book is stolen property. It was reported as "unsold and destroyed" to the publisher, and neither the author nor the publisher has received any payment for this "stripped book."

This is a work of fiction. Names, characters, places, and incidents either are the product of the author's imagination or are used fictitiously, and any resemblance to actual persons, living or dead, business establishments, events, or locales is entirely coincidental.

TEMPTING

A Jove Book / published by arrangement with
the author

PRINTING HISTORY
Jove edition / September 2002

Copyright © 2002 by Hope Tarr
Cover photo by Wendi Schneider
Corset by Meschantes Corsetry
Book design by Julie Rogers

All rights reserved.
This book, or parts thereof, may not be reproduced in any form without permission. For information address: The Berkley Publishing Group,
a division of Penguin Putnam Inc.,
375 Hudson Street, New York, New York 10014.

Visit our website at
www.penguinputnam.com

ISBN: 0-515-13365-5

A JOVE BOOK®
Jove Books are published by The Berkley Publishing Group,
a division of Penguin Putnam Inc.,
375 Hudson Street, New York, New York 10014.
JOVE and the "J" design
are trademarks belonging to Penguin Putnam Inc.

PRINTED IN THE UNITED STATES OF AMERICA

10 9 8 7 6 5 4 3 2 1

For my dear "Little G," the inspiration for the fictional feline, Puss, and living proof that indeed sometimes soul mates come with four legs and fur.

Acknowledgments

To my husband, Earl Pence, for his unflagging patience, love, and support.

To my family, both two- and four-legged members, who keep me sane, honest and, above all, cognizant of my many blessings.

To my friend and research assistant, Julie Kendrick, without whose Internet expertise I would surely have been lost.

To my critique partners and fellow authors, Carole Bellacera, Lisa Arlt, and Elizabeth Sommer, for their feedback and support on the "dreaded" first draft.

To my editor, Cindy Hwang, for her unerring editorial insight, patience—and compassion.

To author Mary Jo Putney, who devoted the better part of an hour one snowy afternoon to patiently explaining the basics of the British Parliamentary system and then directing me to several invaluable research resources. I would also like to thank Mrs. Fiona Ward of the House of Commons Information Office, London who, through the magic of the Internet, answered my e-mailed questions with thoroughness and aplomb. Any errors that may have found their way into the final manuscript are, of course, entirely my own.

To Amy Roman and the other members of Fredericksburg's "Sip N Read" Book Club for being my biggest fans but, most important, my neighbors and friends.

To Sara Khurody-Downs for doing such a beautiful job with my website, thereby affording me one fewer distraction from writing.

And finally, to my friend and fellow animal advocate, Karen Derrico, whose insightful book, *Unforgettable Mutts: Pure of Heart Not of Breed,* provided the inspiration for my mixed-breed canine character, Jake.

Prologue

> I wander thro' each charter'd street,
> Near where the charter'd Thames does flow,
> And mark in every face I meet
> Marks of weakness, marks of woe.
>
> —William Blake,
> *Songs of Innocence and
> of Experience*, 1794

ST. KATHERINE'S DOCK, LONDON, 1848

His delivery made, Simon stepped out of the silk warehouse and into the warm June evening, a rare smile touching his lips. It had been hot earlier, but now the breeze rolling off the Thames was balm to his sunburnt face. He drew a deep breath, savoring the scents wafting from the spice factory on the river's south bank. Cinnamon and nutmeg and even black pepper were sweet perfume compared to the stench of raw fish and sewage that a dockhand usually breathed from dawn 'til dusk. Not that he planned on being a wharf rat for much longer. Mr. Rosenberg had been so pleased to receive the bale of picked rags a day early that he'd paid sixpence more than they'd agreed to. Free arms swinging at his sides, Simon broke into a whistle. Could it be that his life was finally taking a turn for the better?

"Simon, wait." Rebecca, his sister, sent him an apologetic

smile, then bent to unlace her right boot, her back braced against the charred brick wall of a brewery.

Tamping down his impatience, Simon turned to retrace his last few steps. Arms folded, he looked on as Rebecca, three years his senior, restuffed the bit of white rag into the hole in her sole. The sight never failed to fill him with shame, but he consoled himself that she wouldn't have to make shift for much longer. Last winter he'd swallowed what remained of his pride and joined a group of scavenging boys—mudlarks. Every evening after he finished his work on the docks, he joined them on the Thames towpath where, lanterns in hand, they raked through the washed-up waste. His share of their collective booty—a gold bracelet with a broken clasp, a pair of spectacles, and a pewter snuffbox—now belonged to the local pawnbroker. The man had likely cheated him royally, but he'd come away with enough to purchase Rebecca a real birthday gift—a fine pair of ladies' half boots made of buttery soft leather. Watching her retie her shoe, he could hardly wait for the look on her face when he handed her the gift after supper.

After supper. Holding in a sigh, he gave her a hand up, then started down the pier. Rebecca fell in beside him. Their destination, the cookshop that boasted the finest goose in all of East London, lay within sight, one of a stretch of single-storied taverns and warehouses that backed onto the water. As they neared it, the wind carried the fragrance of roasting meat just beneath their noses, triggering a low rumble in Simon's empty belly. Mouth watering, he couldn't help lengthening his strides.

Rebecca's light touch landed on his arm. "I think we should go home. This place at night frightens me." Her sober blue-gray eyes, a shade lighter than his, darted about the quiet pier.

It was late. All that remained of the westward sun was a sliver of orange against the graying sky and, in its place, the white moon was rising above the billowing clouds like a ship's sail. The sailors and stevedores had left off their labors for the day. Most would be sitting down to supper now, be it in a tavern or lodging. Simon was eager to do the same.

Turning to her, he heaved a sigh. Girls could be so silly, sisters especially. "I promised you a goose and all the trimmings for your birthday and that's what you shall have.

'Tisn't every day my sister turns eighteen." Taking her hand, he urged her forward. "Don't worry, Becca. You'll be safe with me."

Ahead a door swung open, leaching pipe smoke and burning tallow into the twilight. Two young men in elaborately folded cravats and rainbow-bright jackets stepped out. Cigars in hand, they lurched onto the narrow walkway, colliding with Simon and Rebecca.

The lanky blond looked down at his beaver hat lying on the ground, then back at Simon. "Pick that up."

"You heard him," seconded his companion, ridiculous in a goatee and silk-striped pantaloons.

Bristling, Simon looked from one sneering face to the other. He knew their sort, rich nabobs from the West End. No doubt they were on holiday from university, hot to spend their papas' coin on drink and women. And trouble. He judged them to be three or four years older than he was, not that he was worried. The soft white hands holding their smokes had never known a day's work, and they were both drunk as David's sow.

He squared his shoulders, which, owing to long days of unloading shipments of brandy, tobacco, and rice, were broadening by the day. "Why should I when 'twas you who ran into us?"

Out of the corner of his eye, he glimpsed the pale oval of Rebecca's face. "Simon, *please!*" she whispered, twisting a lock of her dark hair.

The bearded student pulled a silver flask from his pocket and tipped it to his lips. Swallowing, he said, "Better listen to her, or we'll call out McShane to teach you better manners, won't we, Reg?"

His companion nodded. "That we will, Jimmy." He looked Rebecca up and down, his bleary gaze settling on her small breasts.

Simon itched to smash his fist into their leering faces, but he had Rebecca's safety to think of. "Bugger off." Taking her damp hand, he started down the narrow set of planked steps leading to the street.

He'd just crossed it when a small, solid object glanced off his back. The flask clattered onto the cobbles. Fists clenched, he swung around, prepared to charge back across and give the two their comeuppance. The sight of a thick-necked bully with a shaven pate and a pugilist's biceps emerging from the pub stopped him in his tracks. The McShane they'd threatened him with? Fear trickled down his spine as the newcomer loped over to the two dandies loitering beneath a lamppost. Murmured words were exchanged and menacing glances were tossed in Simon's direction, then the trio filed down the steps.

They're coming after us! Chest tight, Simon turned back to Rebecca and shouted, "Run!"

They fled the now-deserted fish market, zigzagging through stalls and abandoned carts. Tugging Rebecca along, Simon headed for Rosemary Lane. Once across, they could lose their pursuers in the maze of winding alleys and abandoned buildings.

Panting, she tripped over a broken cobble and lurched forward. Simon caught her before she fell.

Clutching his arm, she tested the foot with her weight and winced. "My ankle, I twisted it. I do not think I can walk on it, let alone run." Her face crumpled. "Oh, Simon, what are we to do?"

He raked shaking fingers through his sweat-slick hair. "We'll have to hide in that alley coming up."

Leaning on him, she limped toward it. Inside the passage, he took stock of possible hiding places.

"Behind that bin. Quickly!" He shoved her to the back of the rubbish heap, then crouched behind a stack of rotting lumber just as their pursuers appeared at the entry to the alley.

"I smell a rat." Whistling, the blond started down first. He passed in a cloud of cologne, his coattail snagging on a beam from Simon's hiding place.

Trembling, Simon watched him turn back to release it just as his friend with the goatee came up behind. "And I smell a bitch."

They stopped in front of Rebecca's hiding place, leaving the Irishman to search.

"Egads, Jimmy, but it stinks in here." Leaning back, the blond pulled a scented handkerchief from his pocket and dabbed his nostrils.

Heart drumming, Simon held his breath. Perfume tended to make Rebecca sneeze.

"*Ah-choo.*"

The pair swung around in unison. "Eureka!" Each seizing an elbow, they hoisted Rebecca up.

Oh God, Oh God, Oh God . . . Simon clawed through rotten vegetables and rat carcasses, searching for something to use as a weapon.

"Please!" Eyes streaming, Rebecca tore free and backed away.

Like wolves rounding on prey, they advanced. She slipped, feet flying out from under her. Simon winced as she landed hard on her backside.

"I think she likes me, Jimmy. Look, she's spreading her legs already." The blond pulled a coin from his pocket. "But to be fair, we'll flip to see who gets to break her in."

Sweat rolled down Simon's brow, the salt stinging his eyes. Swiping at it with the back of his arm, he spotted a loose plank small enough to lift.

Wielding it, he sprang into the open. "Don't you touch my sister." The blond was closest to Rebecca. Simon drew back and whacked him hard across the face.

Howling, he fell back, blood spurting. Cupping his mouth, he yelled, "McShane, what the hell are we paying you for? Get over here."

Simon whirled just as the Irishman bore down on him, ripping the board from his hands. Before he could move away, a cannonball-sized fist blasted his gut. Another blow, this one to his face, sent the sky and earth spinning. He sank down on all fours, spewing blood and vomit onto the cobbles.

Screams, a girl's, lanced through the black sickness. *Becca?* He tried to lift his head, but it fell forward, heavier than the bale he'd born earlier.

Over the pain thrumming through his skull, he heard a taunting voice call out, "Bring him over so he can watch. We're not shy, are we, sweetheart?"

Rough hands slipped beneath his arms, yanking him upright, but his knees buckled. Limbs as wooden and limp as those of a marionette, he felt the Irishman dragging him. Hoisting his head, he glimpsed a double-bodied Jimmy hunkering, trousers bunched about his ankles and bare bum glowing white in the darkness.

"Who's next?" Not waiting for a reply, the twin Jimmies pulled up their pants, rose, and faded into blackness.

Peering around the white-hot sparks blistering his eyes,

Simon found Rebecca sprawled on her back atop the cobbles, skirts riding her waist and skinny legs splayed. They'd left on her stockings and shoes. The whiteness peeking through the penny-sized hole in the bottom of her boot brought the reality, the horror, slamming into Simon with an even greater force than the Irishman's fist had. He heard sobbing, but this time, he realized, the sound came from him.

Cheeks wet, he cried, "Rebecca!" and pitted the last of his strength against the steel-banded grip that kept him from going to her.

Staring up at the darkening sky, she lay still except for her mouth, opening and closing on a silent scream.

And inside Simon's hammering head, the same sentence shrieked again and again.

You'll be safe with me.

One

> Teach me to feel another's woe,
> To hide the fault I see;
> That mercy I to others show,
> That mercy show to me.
>
> —Alexander Pope,
>   "The Universal Prayer,"
>   1738

LONDON, OCTOBER 1867

Simon Belleville was no stranger to squalor. He'd passed his first sixteen years in Whitechapel, the worst of the London stews, among the moneylenders, whores, and grimy immigrants of Eastern Europe. The brothel's staircase was every bit as narrow, as filthy, as dank as the ones he'd played on as a child. Only now he was a man of four-and-thirty. A man of property and experience. A man who'd traveled to India and back—to *hell* and back—to make his fortune. A fortune he'd doubled, no, quadrupled, many times over since his return. In a country where wealth and position were bestowed at birth—or not at all—he was a self-made man. A legend. At East India Company headquarters in Leadenhall, directors and shareholders and countinghouse clerks all uttered his name in reverent whispers. When he walked into the Royal Exchange, a hush fell over the central court as investors strained to hear what stocks he would buy, what others he would sell. And now, owing to the past six months he'd spent in the service of Her Majesty, he was poised to add yet another jewel to *his* crown: a seat in the House of Commons.

So why, at times such as these, did he still feel like a grubby little mudlark from the docks?

His damned memory was the culprit. Even now, poised on the stairwell, he found himself fighting to hold head and shoulders above the rubble of dark recollections crashing down on him. Struggling to remember that this descent into hell, into the *past,* was the nascence of his political career.

When Benjamin Disraeli, Chancellor of the Exchequer in Lord Derby's Conservative government, had offered Simon the opportunity to head Her Majesty's Morality and Vice Commission, he'd accepted with alacrity. Not that he had anything against whores in particular. If women elected to forfeit their virtue for a few quid and a roof over their heads, what had he or anyone else to say about it? But the appointment was his chance to prove his worth to Disraeli, to the Conservatives, perhaps even to the queen herself.

Over the past six months, Simon had applied himself to doing just that, leading raids on twenty-odd brothels. Thankfully the present establishment, Madame LeBow's, was the very last on his list. Like the others, it offered the standard fare of flagellations, deflorations, and fellatio at working-class prices. Patrons liked their sex rough, their wine cheap, and their whores young. The close air stank of spilled seed and stale beer, and at least four of the eight prostitutes incarcerated in the police wagon outside were younger than sixteen.

One hand wrapped about the scarred newel post, Simon looked below to the four blue-suited police sergeants flanking the first-floor entrance. A fifth officer was posted outside to guard the women. Simon had been about to issue the order to pull out when he'd overhead two of the prisoners whispering about the new girl in the attic. His ears had perked up. He might regret accepting this post, but he was a thorough man. A clean sweep meant just that, and he had no intention of allowing even one rabbit to escape from its warren.

Inspector Tolliver, lantern in hand, stood a few steps below him. "Shall I light the way, sir?"

Simon shook his head. "That won't be necessary. I'll go

alone." He reached for the lantern, which Tolliver reluctantly handed up.

At the last whorehouse where he'd allowed Tolliver to lead an arrest, the madam had emerged with a black eye and split lip. Tolliver claimed she'd tripped and fallen on her way down the stairs. Simon had his doubts.

Tolliver twisted one waxed end of his handlebar mustache. "Are you certain, sir? It could be a trap."

Simon wasn't accustomed to having his orders questioned. His annoyance rose. "I believe I can handle it, Inspector. By all accounts, there's only one woman up there, and if she's anything like the others, she's little more than a child."

Tolliver lifted his narrow shoulders. "Have it your way, guv. We'll be downstairs if you need us." He glanced significantly at the club swinging from his waist, then started down.

Simon felt the sudden urge to laugh. With its bicycles and billy clubs and smart blue uniforms, London's eight-man detective department fancied itself a force to be reckoned with. But then Tolliver and his men rarely ventured into the East End. Those dark, crooked lanes with their stench of urine, rotting rubbish, and spoiled dreams were a foreign land to them. To Simon, they were home.

Home. He continued up the remaining three flights to the attic, rotting floorboards groaning beneath the soles of his boots. It was nearly twenty years, and yet it might have been yesterday that he'd listened for the landlord's footfalls on a set of creaking stairs much like these.

"This isn't a charity house," the landlord, Mr. Plotkin, had said, after delivering what amounted to a death sentence. The three of them—Simon, his mother, and Rebecca—had twenty-four hours to gather their belongings and quit the premises; otherwise, he'd have them all hauled to debtors' prison.

It was the first time Simon had seen his mother cry since his father's death. Wringing her work-roughened hands, Lilith Belleville had looked from one child to the next and then back at the landlord. Then she'd done the unthinkable. She'd sunk to her knees—and begged.

"Have pity, Mr. Plotkin. If you turn us out, where shall we go? How shall we live?"

"That is not my affair, Mrs. Belleville." Stepping past her,

Plotkin's shoe had landed on the hem of her worn dress, leaving a muddy footprint on the clean calico.

The scene, like so many painful episodes from his past, remained branded on Simon's brain. Now someone else, some other cringing scrap of humanity, waited behind a closed attic door for him to deliver the edict that would result in her being dispatched to Newgate Gaol or, worse still, one of the prison hulks moored along the Thames.

Like grinding an insect with his heel, Simon moved to squash the pity surging inside him before it could rise any higher. "That is not my affair," he repeated, stepping off the landing and into a nest of cobwebs.

The eaves hung low, and he was obliged to remove his beaver top hat and hunker down. He lifted his lantern. The attic door was a narrow planked archway bolted on the outside and barely broader than his shoulders. He slid back the hasp and pushed. The warped wood moaned on rusted hinges, but it opened. Angling his body sideways, he ducked beneath the low-hanging lintel and stepped over the threshold.

The air inside was as foul as any draining ditch, the heat as stifling as Calcutta at midday, the darkness unrelieved by any light save the one Simon carried. Wishing he might shed his wool greatcoat, he held up the lantern and took stock. An old chest, a slop bucket—full, judging from the stench. Wedged beneath the slanted roof was a narrow rope bed, a bundle of rags piled atop. But where was the girl? Surely she didn't think to fool him by hiding under the bed?

He pulled the door closed behind him and walked inside, his footfalls on the bare floorboards sending mice scuttling. Dust motes danced like snowflakes before his eyes. The rags shifted. As his sight began to adjust, the mound assumed the shape of a small female huddled beneath a pile of castoffs.

He centered his light on the bed. "You can come out now."

She gasped. Flinging the clothes aside, she sat up and wiped hair from her damp forehead with the back of her hand. "Ye keep away from me, d'ye hear?"

"Easy now. No one will harm you."

He shone the light on her. She blinked owlishly, her little face puckering. This girl looked to be the youngest yet, but then those in the "maiden trade" were adept at the art of illusion. The childish night rail she wore—white cotton and buttoned to the neck—made her appear innocent, almost *virginal.*

Whatever her age, she was no beauty. Her eyes were too large, her breasts too small, and her waist-length hair of undeterminable color hung in greasy strands about her pinched face. That any man would pay to lie with such a pathetic waif was almost impossible to fathom. But then London was rife with men who found it diverting to prey on the young and innocent. He thought of Rebecca, and the familiar dull ache in his chest throbbed like an open wound.

He carried the lantern to the bed. She cringed when he came up beside her, squinting as though the light hurt her eyes. There was a dark blotch on her forehead that could have been a bruise, a birthmark, or simply more of the same filth that stained the front of her night rail. But there could be no doubt that the small reddish crescent on her left cheek was anything but a fresh scar.

Anger surged through him. No woman, be she a lady or a whore, deserved to be struck. Resolved that the manacles he'd brought would remain in his coat pocket, he said, "I've come to take you away."

She lifted her face, pinning him with her wide-eyed stare. "Truly?"

Before Simon could answer, she did the one thing for which he was completely unprepared. She snatched his gloved hand and pressed her lips to his palm.

"Oh sar, I've prayed and prayed that someone would come and just when I were a'most ready to give up, 'ere ye are."

Simon almost dropped the lantern. A praying prostitute? Nonplussed, he stared down at her upturned face. Was this show of gratitude some sort of scheme, a whore's trick to win his sympathy—and her freedom? Or had confinement and abuse unhinged the poor creature's mind?

He pulled his hand away and set the light atop the broken bedside table. "How long have you been here—in the attic, that is?"

"A'most a week, I think, though 'tis terrible hard to tell night from day."

Whoever she was, she was no Londoner. The twang of the Midlands was plain in her trembling voice. Mentally adding that bit of intelligence to his mounting stockpile of observations, he followed her sad gaze to the small casement window, the glass painted over with blacking. For a country-bred girl, being shut up thus would be an earthly hell.

Leaden pity weighed anchor in his chest. Knowing he must cut himself free of it or else sink, he summoned a brisk tone and said, "Yes, well, you must dress and gather up your things. The others are waiting for us below. *Outside*," he added as an enticement.

She beamed at him. "Oh, lovely. Are ye rescuing 'em too?"

Simon stared. The poor girl must indeed be mad. Looking into her dirty face for some sign of derangement, he saw that her eyes—brown, he thought—were clear, her cheekbones high, and her mouth full. Her top and bottom lips were near mirror images, and he found himself wondering how it would feel to kiss her, to match his own lips to those soft, full ones.

It was then that he gave himself a sound mental shake. Perhaps he was the one in danger of losing his reason? This girl was no sheltered innocent but a skillful actress. Her feigned naivete had, no doubt, coaxed many a fool to part with his coin.

Simon was no fool.

He folded his arms across his chest. "From here you and the others will be taken to Newgate. You will pass the night there until tomorrow morning when you will be brought before the Central Criminal Court."

Her smile fled, replaced by indignation—and fear. "The Old Bailey! But I've done naught wrong."

The tension that had been building at the base of his skull since he'd discovered her cinched another notch. "On the contrary, prostitution is a serious offense." *Hypocrite!* his inner voice crowed. "But, given your youth . . . How old are you, by the way?"

"Nineteen."

Nineteen. Not a child, but young. Simon thought back to how he'd felt at that age—callow and confused and so very alone.

He cleared his throat to smooth the sudden thickening. "The judges may be prepared to show mercy . . . provided you surrender yourself quietly."

Mercy? The workhouse instead of prison? Or perhaps if she were really fortunate, she'd be set free to . . . starve?

That is not my affair. He had only to carry out this last

arrest and write up his report to Parliament, then his obligation would be fulfilled. And then he, Simon Belleville, former street urchin and ship's stowaway, would be poised to seize his heart's desire: membership in Parliament. And with it power, respect, *acceptance*.

Provided he remained strong, stayed the course. Stayed strong. He focused his gaze on the girl, who was staring up at him with that curiously affecting union of terror... and hope.

Determined to squelch the soft sentiment rising inside him, he reached for her. "Come, they are waiting for us. Get up and get dressed."

Slippery as an eel, she wrenched free and scooted to the bottom of the bed. "I won't." A steely look replaced the raw vulnerability he'd imagined he'd seen.

But she was trapped, and they both knew it. The window, assuming it could be opened, was too small to crawl through and, even if it weren't, they were four flights above the ground.

Simon unfolded his arms and reached into the pocket with the manacles. How he'd hoped to avoid this.

"You are coming with me. Whether you do so of your own accord, clothed or unclothed, matters little to me."

"Oh please, sar, I've done nothin' wrong. Can't ye set me free?"

With her steepled hands and guileless eyes, she was the very image of a supplicating saint he'd once seen in a stained-glass window of St. Paul's Cathedral. His conscience, long buried, began to niggle. Why not simply go below and say he'd found the attic empty?

Don't be a fool, his damned inner voice bellowed.

Disraeli rewarded those who served him well. He was equally lavish in punishing those who betrayed his trust. Without his endorsement, Simon's dream of holding a seat in the Commons would remain just that. A dream.

"Regrettably I cannot." Leaning over, he grabbed her sharply boned wrists in one hand, pulling her up onto her knees. "Get up... *now!*"

"I ain't goin'—" She hesitated. "—leastwise not wi'out Puss." Her regard lifted over his right shoulder.

He released her and swung around, gaze searching. Puss?

Could there possibly be a second woman sharing this black hole?

Then he saw it. A black-and-silver tabby cat curled up in a wicker basket set in a corner. Apparently unconcerned that its fate hung in the balance, the feline stretched a striped paw over the side and yawned. Rebecca had kept a cat like that once. His heart, if indeed he still possessed such an organ, lurched.

Steeling himself against the rush of painful memories, he turned back to the girl. She twisted a lock of lank hair round and round her forefinger, all the while fixing those damned innocent eyes of hers on his face.

"Out of the question." He felt as though his darkest, ugliest secrets were emblazoned on his forehead for all to see. For her to see. Self-loathing roughened his voice. "And stop looking at me like that."

He slid his hands to her upper arms, scarcely wider than his wrist, his fingers biting into flesh-veiled bone. She cried out and somehow the sound, her pain, anchored him.

Gentling his hold, he said, "You'll do as you're told. Now get up."

No longer beseeching, she glared. "Your arse I will." She turned her head and sank her teeth into the side of his left hand.

Pain shot up his arm from fingertips to elbow. Eyes watering, he pulled back and stared down. Blood welled where her teeth had managed a small tear in the kid leather. He reached inside his breast pocket for a handkerchief to sop the blood. The linen wrapped about his throbbing palm, he grabbed for the iron cuffs.

But when he turned back to the girl, he saw that the restraint would not be needed after all.

She'd fainted.

Holding his bleeding hand aloft, he probed her with his right. She didn't stir. To be sure, he tickled the bottom of one callused foot. Nothing. Collapsed in a crumpled heap, she was completely senseless. Completely vulnerable. Completely at his . . . *mercy?*

His gaze settled once more on the raw mark of violence marring her cheek. He'd spent years armoring his soul until he'd thought it had become as callused and thick as once his hands had been. But somehow, Devil take her, this slip of a girl had found the one remaining chink and slipped inside.

Hell and damnation. With the resignation of a man who'd lost not only the battle but also the war, he rolled her onto her back and slipped an arm beneath her knees.

"You're a plucky little thing, I'll grant you that." He lifted her into his arms and started for the door.

Newgate Gaol would have to make due with one fewer inmate.

So this was heaven.

Christine awoke to find herself floating on a downy soft cloud. A late-afternoon sun bathed her in its mellow rays, and a woman with a round, kind face and gentle hands sat beside her, holding a cool cloth to Christine's forehead and humming softly. Her caretaker's brown hair was tucked beneath a starched cap frilled with white lace just like the one Christine's mother had worn on Sundays.

Christine looked up. "Mama?"

"Poor mite," the woman said beneath her breath. In a louder voice, she answered, "No, love, I'm Janet—one o' the maids 'ere. Master sent me to tend to you."

Janet smiled down at her, then pressed a spoon against Christine's bottom lip. Christine obediently opened and savory broth dribbled down her throat. Her limbs felt pleasantly heavy, the cloud beneath her wonderfully soft.

Swallowing, she asked, "Am I in heaven?"

Janet chuckled and spooned up more of the soup. "Not heaven 'xactly, though those o' us who works 'ere likes it well enough."

Christine's lips closed over the spoon. Vague memories of being carried in strong arms, of two men arguing—the one man's voice rising above the other—trickled through her muzzy mind.

"This girl goes with me, Inspector." The angry, determined voice had belonged to the man from the attic, the dark angel with the fierce scowl and the sad eyes. The one she'd bitten although now she couldn't recall why.

"Now see here, sir, with all due respect... By Jove, what's this—attacked you did she?" The second voice skirted a smirk.

"A scratch, Inspector. I caught my hand on a nail."

"Of course you did, sir. Now about the girl..."

"She's coming with me. I shall answer for it."

Then she'd been lifted and set on something stiff and leathery and curved—a horse's saddle? Warm, soft wool enfolded her and once more she'd found herself held against a hard, male chest. Seated behind her, her rescuer shifted and they shot forward. The late October air, crisp as a tart apple, tousled her hair and nipped at her nose and cheeks, stealing her breath. She and the dark angel were flying, but she'd not been afraid. For the first time in what felt like forever, she'd known she was safe.

But safe with whom?

Her rescuer hadn't looked like any angel she'd read about in the Bible. Backlit by the lantern light, his face appeared long and lean, his dark eyes fixed beneath a high, jutting brow. He was clean shaven—no whiskers or mustache to soften that strong nose and chiseled mouth. His hair, the blue-black of a crow's wing, grew low on his forehead in a V, and he wore it slicked straight back as if to flaunt the oddity. With his black greatcoat hanging from his broad shoulders, he'd reminded her of the vampire tales that Mr. Barnes, the smithy back in Nantwich, told on All Hallows' Eve.

Nantwich, the hamlet in southern Cheshire where generations of Tremaynes had made their home and availed themselves of the rich red marl to pasture their dairy cows. Home once but no more. Jumbled recollections of sharp threats, a fireplace poker sticky with blood, of Hareton lying ever so still at her feet, and the terrifying certainty that nothing, *nothing,* would ever be right again pushed to the forefront of her mind. The warm safe feeling curdled inside her, and she shivered beneath the blankets.

This time when the spoon descended, she shook her head and pushed herself up on her elbows to look about. The "cloud" on which she lay proved to be a mahogany four-poster, the mattress so soft it could only be stuffed with feathers, the bed curtains and counterpane the same pretty floral print—yellow roses, morning glories, and daisies woven into cunning bouquets. Surely neither hell—nor earthly prison— could be this bright, this *cheery?*

Leaning back against a bank of pillows, she asked, "Where am I?"

Janet set the bowl and tray on the bedside table. "Park

Square, miss. Number Five. Mr. Belleville carried you in himself nigh on three hours ago."

So it wasn't a dream. Christine pressed a hand to her throbbing temple. "Mr. Belleville?"

"Aye, miss. Mr. Simon Belleville."

So the dark angel was a flesh-and-blood man after all. "Simon Belleville." Christine said the name again, testing it on her tongue, liking the sound of it. "Is this his house, then?"

Janet's capped head bobbed. "One of 'em, anyhow. 'E's a country house in Kent, but mostly he stays 'ere in town, close to 'is work."

Christine started to ask after his work, then stopped herself when it occurred to her that she knew its nature all too well. Deciding silence was her best course, she gazed beyond Janet to the window, which overlooked a park of some sort. She'd never had a bedroom with a window before, let alone one as long as a door with gold velvet curtains that swept the floor, and smooth glass panes that let in the sunlight. So much light. And how welcome it was after the past week of darkness with only Puss for company.

Puss. Panic seized her. She searched the bedclothes, but no warm, furry body snuggled beneath. She might be safe but her cat had been left behind.

She threw off the covers and swung her legs over the side of the bed. "I have to go."

"Feeling that much better, are we?" Rising, Janet tucked a meaty arm about Christine's shoulders. "Easy now. The necessary's just down the hall, but you're weak as a kitten. Your cousin'll have me head if you should fall."

Cousin Hareton, here! Christine swayed and would have fallen if not for the maid's arm tucked about her.

"Aye, your cousin. Mr. Simon Belleville," Janet repeated, as patient as if she were schooling a child. "Poor mite. Starved as you are, 'tis small wonder you don't even know your own relation."

Christine sagged against the side of the bed. "There's been some mistake. I'm not . . . I don't 'ave—"

A knock on the door cut her off. Janet left her to answer it, the starched skirts of her black dress and white apron rustling.

Christine sank down on the edge of the bed, watching

Janet fumble in her pocket. Metal jangled, then Christine heard the click of the lock turning.

So, I'm a prisoner still.

Two sweaty-faced young men appeared in the open doorway. Huffing, they leaned over an enormous copper bathtub the likes of which Christine had only dreamt. Its claw feet were set on casters. Even so, it took both of them to roll it inside.

Because it was full.

Staring at the rising steam, imagining the water closing in on her—covering her face—Christine felt the prickly pangs of a different sort of panic rise inside her.

The men straightened, and Christine forced her fraught mind to focus on them rather than on the past. Close to her in age, they both wore gray cloth coats with striped waistcoats and matching trousers. Their shoes, she noticed with a vague sort of wonder, were polished to a high gloss. Was everyone who lived here rich?

"Where do you want it?" the older of the two asked, eyeing Christine with open interest. His gaze fell on her bare ankles, and he winked.

Cheeks warm, Christine looked away. He didn't seem unkind, but the past weeks had taught her that people weren't always what they seemed.

Janet stepped in front of them. "Here'll do just fine. Now off wi' the pair o' you."

One hand planted on either chest, she pushed them out into the hallway.

Closing the door on their gaping faces, she chuckled. "Don't mind that lot, miss." She turned back inside and walked over to the bath. Heart pounding, Christine watched her bend over the side and trail one hand in the water. "Water's lovely warm. Climb in and I'll wash your hair."

"I don't care for a bath just now, thank 'ee." Clammy sweat broke out on Christine's forehead, but Janet didn't seem to notice.

"Rubbish." The maid marched toward her, a towel draped over one sturdy arm. She lifted a limp strand from Christine's cheek. "I'll wager you 'ave pretty hair when it's clean. Now off wi' that grubby nightgown. We'll 'ave to wash that too or, like as not, burn it."

The bottoms of Christine's feet found the set of mahogany

bed stairs. She climbed down on wobbly legs. "I won't, and you can't make me."

"Surely you b'aint that modest?" A steely look replaced Janet's crooked smile. "The master's terrible particular about baths and such. It won't do to be seen at supper wi' dirt behind your ears."

"I'll no' have my children seen in church wi' dirt behind their ears. Set the others ta help ye draw the water, Chrissie, whilst I go fetch the tub."

On Saturday nights, Christine's father had hauled in the old hip bath, the metal dented and rusted, and set it before the kitchen hearth. It was small and narrow, barely big enough to crouch in, but all the same it had taken the better part of an evening to pump and heat enough water to fill it. With two little brothers and a sister to bathe, the water was always cold by the time Christine's turn came. In the summer months, after she'd tucked the children in, heard their prayers, and sung them to sleep, she'd head to the stream with a bar of Windsor soap and a towel. Once there, she'd bathe quickly, then spend an hour or more floating on her back. Staring up into the star-bright sky, listening to the crickets' humming, she'd think on all the generations before her that had bathed and swam and mayhap even made love in these waters. Her mother had often said that her firstborn had learned to swim before she'd learned to walk. Christine didn't know if that were exactly true but there was no getting around it—water spoke to her soul.

Until that August night when her cousin, Hareton, decided to join her. Her father had died the June before and his nephew had arrived a week later to run the dairy until Christine's brothers came of age. But the twins were only nine, and Hareton had come to regard the dairy—and his four cousins—as his personal property.

Thinking herself to be alone at last, Christine bent to sluice the fresh gash on her cheek when she heard a splash sound from the embankment. By the time she'd dashed the water from her eyes and turned about, her cousin was beside her.

"So this is where ye sneak off to nights?" His thick lips stretched into the drunkard's foolish grin, but his pale eyes were hard as stones as they fixed on her.

It was the same hard look he'd worn just before he'd kicked their cow, Tilly, when her milk wouldn't come. The same hard look as the time he'd sworn to drown Puss unless Christine kept her in the barn. The same hard look he'd given Christine at supper that evening when he'd accused her of overcooking her beefsteak and had hurled his heavy pewter mug at her from across the room, laying open her cheek.

Seeing that look now, in this lonely place, panic plowed her in the belly like a fist. Beneath the shoulder-high black water, her legs started to tremble. Even so, she hoisted her chin. Pride might not amount to much, but it was one of the few possessions she still had to hold on to.

"How many times must I tell ye, Hareton Tremayne, I want no part o' ye. Now leave me be."

Telling herself that, with his weak eyes, he wouldn't be able to make out much of her in the dark, she turned and swam for the bank, the night air brushing her bare backside. Halfway there, hands wrapped about her ankles. Hareton's hands. She kicked, but it was no use. He had her. And he was dragging her down. She managed to fill her lungs just before she went under, palms and knees scraping silt and pebbles. Something hard and heavy clamped down on the back of her skull. Hareton, holding her under? Her burning chest tightened until she thought it would explode, until she stopped clawing at the water and went as limp as the reeds curling about her legs.

Only then did he grab a fistful of her hair and haul her up. She choked, water scoring her throat and nose.

"Still think yerself too fine for the likes o' me?" His fingers took bruising hold of her upper arms. "Well, Chrissie, me girl, we'll just see about that."

Through stinging eyes, she saw him angle his face down to hers. She pulled back just before his mouth landed on hers. "L-lemme g-go."

Praying for strength, she dragged water-weighted arms up to his sunken chest and shoved. He let go and flopped backward, raising a fountain. Christine drew a deep gulp of air and swam for shore. By the time he surfaced, nose spouting water and hair plastering his scabby forehead, she'd scrambled up the embankment.

"Ye'll pay for that, bitch." Teeth chattering, she looked up from pulling on her shift to see him heft a fist. "D'ye 'ear me? Ye'll pay."

And how dearly she'd paid! More than a month later and

dirtier than she'd ever imagined being, she still couldn't look on water, couldn't bear to let so much as a drop touch her, without feeling as though she were strangling.

"Come, miss. Water'll be cold in no time and, by the looks o' you, we'll need it good and 'ot to do any good."

The maid's voice, tinged with impatience, brought Christine back to the present. She looked down to see Janet step forward, her nimble fingers going to the top button of Christine's night rail. Panic shot through Christine like a bolt from an electricity machine, enervating every muscle, every nerve, every instinct. She reached out and dealt Janet a mighty shove. The maid toppled backward into an empty chair, starched skirts riding up to her garters. She stared up at Christine, mouth agape like a fish's, lace-edged cap fallen over her brow and one eye. Seeing that she was shaken, not hurt, Christine whisked about the chair and made for the door. Panting, she reached for the knob and turned it.

Or tried to. Janet must have relocked the door, for the smooth metal rested motionless in Christine's damp palm.

Trapped, shivering, Christine took a step back. Then, she did what she hadn't had sufficient breath or strength to do that night with Hareton.

She filled her lungs with air and screamed.

Two

"Begin at the beginning," the King said, gravely, "and go till you come to the end; then stop."

—Lewis Carroll,
Alice's Adventures in Wonderland, 1865

"Bit you, did she?" Chuckling, Trumbull tossed the cloth inside the basin of bloody water. "I'd 'ave liked t'ave seen that."

Ensconced in an armchair in his bedchamber, a glass of his finest brandy cradled in his uninjured hand, Simon lifted his gaze from the fire crackling in the hearth to scowl at his valet. Obviously enjoying himself, Trumbull was taking his bloody good time winding the strip of linen around Simon's throbbing, swollen thumb. Salve covered the angry red puncture wounds left by a truly impressive set of incisors.

"Just bandage the blasted thing, would you?"

Trumbull had been his valet for ten years, his friend for almost eighteen. They'd cemented their friendship in Calcutta when Simon was a nineteen-year-old countinghouse clerk and Trumbull was one of the East India Company's most seasoned boatswains. With his twinkling blue eyes, leathery brown face, and endless sailors' yarns, Trumbull had seemed terribly swashbuckling and sophisticated. The plucky little Cockney had sailed to Singapore and Siam, even as far east as the Molucca Islands—places that Simon then had only dreamt of. In the course of their mutual travels, Trumbull had saved Simon from more than one near disaster, including an encounter with a member of the *Thuggee*, a secret Indian murder society whose members preyed on travelers, especially Europeans. Simon owed him.

And Simon always paid his debts.

When he'd left India in '57, just days after the sepoys had captured Delhi and put most Europeans in the city to the knife, there'd been no question of leaving his old friend behind. In the ten years since, he'd never regretted giving Trumbull a place in his household.

Well, almost never.

Trumbull hoisted the scissors and snipped the end of the bandage. "The word belowstairs is she's your cousin, fallen on 'ard times." He shot Simon a canny look. "By the by, what's coz's name?"

A fiend. The Devil incarnate. Simon rested his elbow on the tufted chair arm, and propped his cheek on his uninjured palm. "I'm still deciding."

In truth, he still didn't know it. Neither her real one nor the more flamboyant moniker she likely used with her customers. In the attic, he hadn't bothered to ask. Outside he'd been too intent on getting her past Tolliver—and himself home before he bled to death—to quiz the other girls.

Over the past few hours, he'd come to think of her as simply The Creature. If he'd had a grain of sense, he'd have deposited her at the nearest almshouse. Fragile as a hothouse blossom, she'd not last a fortnight on her own. That she'd survived thus far was nothing short of a miracle. And a testimony to her courage.

A survivor himself, Simon couldn't help but admire her spirit. A week locked in that attic would have broken any ordinary girl. Once again, he wondered what infraction she'd committed to warrant such a harsh punishment. He recalled the scar on her cheek. The calling card of one of the brothel's more brutish customers? Perhaps the girl had objected to the brutal handling—even bitten the culprit—and been imprisoned for her pains? But no, that scenario wouldn't wash. Her wound, while fresh, was older than a week.

The larger and more interesting question was why the hell

he should care. He'd seen poverty and despair aplenty in Calcutta, had known it firsthand growing up in East London. Why save this girl? And why choose now to act the Good Samaritan, when he had everything to lose and nothing to gain?

It was a question best kept for another day. For now, all he knew was that he had to get her out of his house and quickly. Servants were notorious gossips. Trumbull he could trust as well as his housekeeper, Mrs. Griffith, but the others? All it would take would be for one London matron to catch wind that he, a bachelor, was harboring a prostitute, and he could forget about holding public office. Even as dogcatcher.

What *had* gotten into him? His last spontaneous act had been to leave England eighteen years before. His mother had wed the neighborhood tailor, a good kind man of her own faith, who treated poor shattered Rebecca as his own. Having seen his mother settled and his sister cared for should have brought Simon some slight peace, but if anything the relative ease of his new life spawned a new restlessness, a disquiet so deep as to border on despair.

He had to get away.

He shunned his stepfather's tailoring shop; somehow the looms and cutting tables and big bolts of cloth made him feel that much more hemmed in. By day he hung about the docks. By night he haunted the waterfront taverns in the hope that he might encounter the objects of his hatred. If he had, a score of "McShanes" couldn't have stopped him from taking his revenge.

But no Reggie or Jimmy or even McShane ever crossed his path and, after a time, he acknowledged that in all likelihood they never would. He turned to brawling. Any brute big and stupid enough to take him on would serve. But all fighting earned him was a strong arm, knuckles shiny with scars, and a reputation for a temper that bordered on madness. The satisfaction of pounding his opponent to the ground was all but gone by the time he put his shirt back on.

One night his desperation drove him to the water's edge where the temptation to cast himself in had been enormous. Somehow he'd found the strength to resist, to go back. Later that night, lying sweating and quaking on the clean sheets of his snug little cot, he'd acknowledged that there was no help for it—or for him. Hatred and guilt and frustration were eating away at him like a pack of hungry hounds, and if he didn't get away soon he'd end up as hollowed out, as dead, as Rebecca was.

And so a few weeks later, he found himself crouched inside the bowels of an East Indiamen bound for Bombay, the sum of his few pitiful possessions poured into a pillowcase. Miraculously, he'd managed to stay hidden for the first full week out to sea before one of the sailors—Trumbull—had discovered him. The captain had dealt him a good cuffing, but he also wasn't about to lose a week from his voyage to return one scruffy lad who refused to tell him so much as his name. He set Simon to work, scrubbing the ship's decks, repairing damaged rigging, and tending the animals brought on board to serve as sustenance for the long journey ahead.

But Simon was no stranger to hard labor and filling his lungs with the clean, coal-free air and feeling the sun burning into his back took the hardship out of even the meanest of tasks. As he worked, he listened to the sailors' yarns, tall tales, for the most part, but spun from past journeys to India and other exotic lands. One day rolled seamlessly into the next, and Simon began to plan. And dream.

Steamy India was the graveyard of many an ambitious young Englishman, but poverty—and hatred—had toughened Simon and his demonstrated facility with numbers earned him a place in the company's countinghouse where he quickly climbed the ranks. While so many of his fellows tossed their money away on whores and liquor, he'd used his to buy stock in the company's mercantile fleet and sundry shipping interests. Frugality had paid off. After ten years, he'd come back to England a wealthy and far wiser man.

But today he'd not been wise.

Contemplating his own weakness, his own *stupidity*, was beyond depressing. He reached for the brandy decanter on the edge of the marble-topped wine table and poured another glass.

" 'Old still," Trumbull chided.

Simon set the glass aside with a low curse.

"There's a good lad." Trumbull tied the two ends of the bandage into a neat sailor's knot and then stood back to admire his handiwork. "Done," he pronounced, and then picked up Simon's full glass and tossed back the contents in one lip-smacking swallow.

Simon leaned back, stretching his long legs toward the fire's warmth. "I trust Mrs. Griffith has seen her settled?"

He'd ordered the creature installed in the yellow room, the nicest of the four guest bedchambers his town house boasted. With its eastern exposure and light, airy furnishings, the room would seem like paradise to a girl starved for sunshine and air—two commodities sorely lacking in Madam LeBow's attic. That it happened to be just down the hall from his own room was pure coincidence.

"I don't know as I'd call it settled."

Jarred, Simon snapped upright. "Meaning?"

"Like to 'ad a fit when the bathtub rolled in. A proper hellcat for all that she's a little thing. Swore she wouldn't take no bleedin' bath and gave poor Janet a proper shove when she tried to coax 'er in." He cocked a sandy brow. "Wi' that temper, she must be your relation after all, eh?"

Simon slammed the glass onto the marble with such force that the remaining brandy lapped the rim. The girl was trouble. Why hadn't he listened to his better judgment and had Mrs. Griffith find her a bed in the servants' quarters? Instead he'd invented the falsehood that she was his foundling cousin, thereby backing himself directly into a corner. Having owned her as a relation, he was obliged to treat her as such.

"Where is she now?"

A grin split Trumbull's tanned face. "Janet, why she's—"

Through clenched back teeth, Simon ground out, "Not Janet. The Creature."

"Oh, 'er. Why, locked in, to be sure."

Simon fisted his bandaged hand, ignoring the throbbing, and shot to his feet. "Why wasn't I told?"

Well used to his employer's dark tempers, Trumbull only grinned. "Why, sir, I do believe I'm tellin' ye now."

Simon gripped the brass knob with his good hand. Rotating it, he found himself imagining it to be The Creature's long, slender—and fragile-looking—neck. This was his house, the one place on God's green earth where he and he alone ruled. He wasn't about to let some ragamuffin set his carefully ordered domain on its ear. Even if he had been the one to give her the key to the kingdom.

He strode down the hall, Trumbull trailing.

"Steady as ye go, sir. It don't do to overheat the blood after ye've, well, lost so much o' it."

"You can tuck me in with a beefsteak and a glass of sherry later. For now . . . Good Lord—"

He halted in midstep. Half his household staff congregated outside the door to the yellow bedchamber, including Mrs. Griffith, his housekeeper, and the maid, Janet. The latter, it seemed, was busy recounting the details of her grisly encounter.

"And then 'er eyes went all round and wild like. The next thing I knowed, she were on me, like a jackal."

Simon folded his arms and listened, confident the maid had never set eyes on a picture-book jackal, let alone a live one.

" 'Twere like the Devil got right inside 'er and—"

"That will do." Simon pushed toward the front. "The exhibition has concluded. Back to work, all of you."

Trumbull materialized at his side. "Ye heard him. Chop-chop."

Simon whirled on his valet. "That includes you."

It was Trumbull's turn to scowl. Lifting his squared shoulders, then letting them drop, he addressed the dispersing crowd. "A fine thanks, this, and after I saved 'is life, no less." With a theatrical huff, he turned and made his way toward the stairs.

Turning his back on his staff, Simon tried the door. It was locked, of course. Behind him, he heard a faint, "Ahem." He spun about to see Mrs. Griffith, liver-spotted hand outstretched, a ring of house keys dangling from the tips of her crooked fingers.

" 'Tis the small silver one, third from left." Rheumy eyes twinkling, she handed him the keys, then turned to join the procession filing downstairs.

Face warm, Simon turned back to the closed door. He didn't bother knocking but fitted the key in the lock and turned it until it clicked home. Pushing open the door, he girded himself to dodge any number of projectiles, fingernails, and those sharp, sharp teeth. What he hadn't prepared for was silence.

The Creature sat on the edge of the bed, sniffling into one grubby, open hand. Judging from her running nose and scarlet-rimmed eyes, she'd been crying for some time.

Simon hated few sights as much as a woman's tears. The righteous indignation he'd draped about himself like a mantle upon leaving his bedchamber dissolved into dust. He closed the door behind him and walked toward her.

Coming up beside her, he pulled a handkerchief from his pocket and handed it to her. "Here, Miss uh—" Damn, but he still didn't know the chit's name.

Looking up, she snatched the crisply ironed square. "Christine. Christine Tremayne." She buried her nose in the cloth and blew. Mopping pink-rimmed nostrils, she demanded, "Why did 'ee tell 'em belowstairs that I were your cousin?" Tears streamed her flushed cheeks, yet she managed to glare.

"Well, I had to tell them *something*, now didn't I? The truth would hardly do." He swiped a hand through his hair, helpless as she scoured fresh tears from her face. "My name is Simon Belleville. I am Her Majesty's vice commissioner and, for the time being, your benefactor."

She wadded the handkerchief inside a tight, determined little fist. "I don't need a benef—"

"I beg to differ. You've already launched two vicious, unprovoked attacks, and we've yet to reach the supper hour. Women have been committed to Bedlam for less."

She scooted off the bed, landing with a thump. It was the first time he'd seen her on her feet. Slender as a tulip stem, she was tall for a woman, somewhere around five feet seven, he surmised. Standing at six feet two, Simon still towered over her, a fact that for some reason pleased him inordinately.

She fisted her hands on her narrow hips. The wadded handkerchief, forgotten, floated to the floor. "I want my cat. What've ye done with 'er?"

Cat? What cat? He opened his mouth to ask what the Devil she was talking about, then closed it, recalling the tabby from the brothel attic. The one that had looked so much like Rebecca's of nineteen years before that the sight of it— and its waiflike mistress—had been like a razor gouging his heart.

She stamped an impatient—and exceedingly grimy—bare foot. "She were wi' me in the attic."

"I'm sure it's fine," he said but only to placate her. In

truth, he hadn't given the feline a thought since they'd left the brothel—and it—behind.

"So, ye *did* leave 'er to... to starve." The treble in her voice, the naked yearning in her eyes, her quivering bottom lip made him feel petty and mean-spirited and, above all, ashamed.

Ashamed, him? Ludicrous. Preposterous. He'd have nothing more to do with such soft sentiments. Only witness in what trouble they'd landed him already.

He shrugged. "No doubt it... *she* is feasting on a nice fat mouse even now. But it's you I've come to talk about. Have you any family? Someone I can contact on your behalf?"

At his mention of "family," her face paled beneath its patina of filth. She shook her head. "Mother died in childbed five years ago, and Father's heart gave out last year. Since then 'tis been the little 'uns and me."

"The little ones?" he echoed, the words sticking like toast crumbs in his dry throat. Good God, had he stumbled upon not just a prostitute but one with a brood of illegitimate offspring?

She paused from wiping her nose on the sleeve of her nightgown to nod. "Aye, my brothers and sister. I promised the farmer who took 'em in I'd send money 'ome for their support."

Simon released the breath he hadn't realized he'd been holding. "I see."

Tapping a finger to his jaw, it occurred to him that he and Christine Tremayne had rather a lot in common. Like him, she was an orphan with a dependent sibling—in her case, *siblings*. Feeling his sense of kinship grow, he contemplated her with fresh interest. In full light, she was prettier, albeit filthier, than she'd appeared in the shadowed attic. If she cleaned herself up, fed her flesh, and learned to speak a bit more genteelly, there was no reason she couldn't find a place in a respectable household as a lady's maid. Or perhaps some well-off tradesman or shopkeeper might take her to wife. Her expectations might be far from grand, but at least she could keep herself and her family free of the workhouse.

Still studying her, he said, "I have a friend. Her name is Margot Ashcroft. She runs a school, an academy for young ladies."

Christine's dejected expression darkened to a scowl. "I've

a'ready been to parson's school, thank ye very much." Eyes flashing amber sparks, she stuck out her chin. "I can read and write and cipher. I kept the dairy accounts for Father when he were alive and for Hareton after that." At the mention of the latter, a blush stained her cheeks, leaching through the grime.

Derailed, he found himself asking, "Who is Hareton?" A brother? A sweetheart? A husband, perhaps?

Four impeccable white top teeth emerged to rake her bottom lip. "My cousin. He came to live wi' us and to manage the dairy after Father passed on."

Growing up in Whitechapel, Simon had known men who'd sold their sisters and wives and even daughters into prostitution. Striving for delicacy, he asked, "This cousin of yours, was it he who brought you to London?"

She shook her head. "Not exactly."

He rocked back on his heels, reaching for patience. "And precisely what does 'not exactly' mean? He either did or he did not. Kindly tell me which one it is."

Her head snapped about. Defiant amber brown eyes fixed on his face. "I ran away, if ye must know. I took the little 'uns to a farm in Shropshire where he'd not get 'is grubby hands on 'em, and then I left too."

"For London?"

She nodded. "Aye, I thought to find work. *Honest* work," she clarified, voice rising and eyes daring him to refute her. "I didn't know what sort of place LeBow's was until after I'd got there. She let me think she ran a decent household and that I'd work in the scullery or some such. By the time I saw what it was I'd come to, it was too late. She wouldn't let me leave though I tried to, truly I did."

Simon blew out a heavy breath. "I see."

And so he did, for hers was both a tragic and an all-too-common story. The cousin—Hareton—was a brute. He'd driven the girl to flee to London along with the hordes of other country youths seeking sanctuary, excitement, or simply a change from the drudgery of field labor. Like most of them, Christine had looked for honest work—at first.

Reminded that what she needed from him was help, not pity, he forced a brisk hopefulness into his tone. "Madame LeBow is in Newgate Gaol at this very moment. She'll not bother you again." Her gaze still held a certain wary skepticism, but the shoulders she'd all but hoisted up to her ears relaxed visibly. Heartened, he continued, "What I am offering you is the chance to wipe the slate clean, to better yourself and make a fresh start. At my friend's school, you'd acquire a different sort of education than you received at the parson's school or your father's dairy."

She arched a golden brown brow. "What sort, exactly?"

Simon cleared his throat. "Well, the sort of accomplishments a woman—a *lady*—needs to get on in life."

She wrinkled her nose. "Such as?"

"Well, uh, let's see." What *did* Margot teach in that blasted school of hers? "What to say in polite company, what *not* to say, how to choose a cigar."

She made a face. "I don't smoke."

"For a *gentleman*," he snapped, wondering if she were toying with him or if she truly might be that thick. "How to walk—"

"I've been walking all my life!" Hands on her narrow hips, she tramped to the window, the bottoms of her feet beating the carpet and bare floorboards. "See!" She pivoted and marched back to him, heavy-footed as an elephant.

"Lovely." Simon steeled himself to ignore the dull ache that had taken up residence in his temples. "But, as is the case with most activities, there is a desirable and an undesirable way to execute it."

Folding her arms across her breasts, she huffed. "If I go to this school, will I learn what I need to find work?"

"I'm sure Miss Ashcroft will explain the curriculum to you when you meet her." *If she agrees to take you on.* "Suffice it to say that, if it happens she has an opening, you'll have a bed of your own, three meals a day, and clean clothes."

Her face fell. She hugged herself tighter. "Madam LeBow promised fair near the same."

Simon stiffened, for Margot had indeed been a courtesan though her protectors all had come from the top drawer of society. But she'd retired from that life some years before and her school was just that: a school and nothing more.

"Miss Ashcroft is a different sort of person entirely. Her establishment is thoroughly aboveboard. Should she agree to admit you, you shall count yourself very fortunate."

He'd met Margot his first week back from India. Sick to death of bank managers taking one look at his faded broadcloth suit, frayed shirt collar, and checkered cravat and concluding he must not have one penny to rub against the other, he'd set about getting rip-roaring drunk. Hours later he'd barged into the supper room of the fashionable Claridge Hotel and demanded a bottle of their finest champagne and a table by the window. The maitre d' had been about to turn him over to two bull-necked doormen when Margot had risen from her table to intervene.

He'd awakened the following morning in her bed. Later that morning, she'd made him a man. But first she'd made him take a bath.

"Where are my clothes?" Head reeling, he yanked the satin sheet up to his chin.

From across the room, Margot's violet gaze met his in the gilded dressing mirror. "I gave them to my housekeeper to burn." She put down her hairbrush and rose. On the way to the bed, she untied her scarlet silk dressing gown and slid it off her creamy shoulders. "You're welcome to this." Smile wicked, she tossed him the robe. "You've never been with a woman, have you?"

He looked up from the crimson puddle on his lap, face warm. Training his gaze *above* her shoulders, he stammered, "W-why, of c-course . . ." He met her knowing eyes, and the denial died on his lips.

"It's nothing to be ashamed of." She lifted a full breast in each hand, her thumbs flicking over nipples so berry bright they must be rouged. "Would you like to do this for me?"

Beneath the covers, Simon felt the familiar achy stiffening. Only this time there was no need to deny himself. "Y-yes."

"I'd like that too." Leaning over him, her blond hair brushing his cheek, she unfurled his fingers from the sheet. "We'll begin your first lesson just as soon as you've bathed."

As always, the recollection of that morning filled him with a mixture of gratitude and shame. Giving himself a brisk mental shake, Simon returned his attention to Christine. "My friend is very fastidious." At her blank look, he clarified, "Fussy. One of the things she insists upon is that all her students take regular baths."

She eyed the tub, then him. "In that case, I ain't goin'." She darted to the other side of the tub.

Enough was enough. He took a step toward her. "We can

do this the easy way or the hard way. I can strip you and throw you in—"

"Ye'd like that, wouldn't 'ee, *prevert!*"

"That's *pervert*," he corrected. "Or you can be a good girl and bathe on your own."

"I won't!"

But she was trapped, and they both knew it. Behind her was the bed, in front of her the bath. To reach the door, she'd have to go through him. And Simon had no intention of moving.

"Very well, then. You leave me no choice." He flexed his fingers, hiding a wince when his forgotten wound throbbed.

Gaze trained on his hands, she swallowed hard. "Baths ain't good for a lady's 'ealth."

Following her regard, he allowed that his hands were large and powerful. Frightening even, he supposed, although the calluses that once had thickened his palms were long gone. While he abhorred violence against women, he had no qualms about exerting his superior strength to take a firm hand when the situation warranted it—which this singular situation most certainly did.

Determined, he closed the distance between them. "Since you are not, by any stretch of the imagination, a lady, you needn't worry."

Her mouth fell open and her eyes narrowed. "Why, ye—" Her gaze flew over his shoulder to the door.

She darted around the side of the tub, but he'd expected that. He caught her easily, his hands closing around her upper arms, fragile as a sparrow's wings. Slipping an arm beneath her knees, he swung her up into his arms.

"In you go." He hefted her kicking and screaming over the side of the tub.

She rose up almost immediately, spewing water and oaths foul enough to make a sailor blush.

Dashing water from his eyes, he stepped back barely in time to avoid the tidal wave. Wet hair clinging like seaweed, she dropped one skinny, bared leg over the side of the bath and scrabbled out, sloshing more water onto the carpet. Onto *him*. As determined as she, he started forward, then stopped abruptly, dropping his hands . . . along with his gaze.

The drenching had rendered her grayish-white night rail all but transparent. It molded to her like plaster, casting every outline, every nuance in stark relief—the pink areola of her small breasts, the well of her sunken belly, the knife-sharp shelf of her hips. And the dark V between her thighs.

Simon knew he should turn his back, at the very least look away, but he couldn't seem to summon the will to move. Instead he stood still, transfixed, even as a small, still-working part of his brain posed the question, *Why?* He'd always fancied full-figured females, the antithesis of the scarecrow-thin matrons of his childhood. Women like his mother who'd gone without so their children might have an extra potato, a second slice of bread.

But despite her lack of flesh, Christine's legs were long and lovely, her small breasts rose-tipped and nicely proportioned, her skin smooth and unblemished beneath the grime.

No stranger to being the object of lascivious thoughts, she crossed one arm over her breasts and cupped her free hand over the triangle of brown fleece between her thighs. Eyes aiming daggers, she hissed, "Ye'll be sorry for that. Someday I'll make ye sorry, see if I don't."

She was certainly the most modest whore he'd encountered, so maidenly in her outrage that, improbably, he found himself perched on the precipice of an apology. Thinking blood loss must have rotted his brain, he said, "I'll leave you to your bath then."

"Sod off." Still hugging herself, she turned her back on him.

He could see every vertebrae of her spine, but that wasn't what caused his breath to catch in his throat and his temper to unleash. Beneath the drenched drapery, cuts, bruises, and sundry weals made a patchwork quilt of her pale, bone-stretched flesh. Starting at her left shoulder, they trailed the length of her to the backs of her thighs. Some of them had healed to angry red scars, others bore scabs still.

Without thinking, he came up behind her. She jumped when he laid a hand on either of her shoulders. "Strap or whip?"

Without turning, she answered, "Strap, mostly. Sometimes a switch. The belt were the worst. Whatever was handy." The tone of her voice dared him to pity her.

And how he did. He felt every mark as though it were emblazoned on *his* back. On his soul. But she wouldn't thank him for his pity, didn't want it, and he'd be damned if he'd show it.

Slowly, carefully, he turned her toward him. This time he trained his gaze on her face—the lush lower lip jutting forward ever so slightly, the pointed chin raised, and the eyes—large, luminous, and unspeakably sad—staring beyond him.

"And this?" He touched the gash on her cheek with light fingers, marveling that someone so dirty could have such soft skin.

She flinched. He dropped his hand, hoping he hadn't hurt her, wondering if she'd thought he meant to.

A sad smile whispered across her mouth. "An ale pint. After that, I learned to duck."

Poor girl, it was small wonder she'd run away. "You didn't get these at LeBow's, did you?"

Beneath his palms, he felt her shoulders tense. She set her jaw, and glared, the perfect picture of injured female pride and queenly disdain. "What's it to ye?"

A fine question. What *was* she to him? A foundling he'd known just a few hours? A lifeline to that other Simon, the vulnerable part of himself he'd tried so hard to bury.

He shrugged off the question, best kept for later when he could ponder in private just what this strange girl was coming to mean to him. "This cousin of yours, he did this to you, didn't he?"

She shivered. "It were him. Madam started t'ave at me once but—" Her voice trailed off. He waited, then realized she didn't plan to finish.

"But?" He lifted her chin on the edge of his good hand and used the stiff fingers of the other to brush the hair from her eyes. Though wet, it felt fine, silky, and Simon was suddenly impatient to discover the color beneath the grease-streaked brown. But first things first.

She fretted her bottom lip, twisting it beneath her front teeth. "When she saw my back, she said there weren't no point. I weren't worth the effort. That I were damaged goods a'ready, best kept for the dark and them that had drunk too much to see clear enough to notice."

Simon's throat thickened. Since assuming his commission, he'd listened to many a woebegone tale. Tears, pleas, the occasional offer of sex were the usual accompaniments. But this girl was like no other whore he'd yet encountered. She didn't beg or cry—except for her cat. Neither did she cajole or seek, in any way, to win his sympathy.

Not that she didn't have it already. That she recounted the madam's cruel words without so much as a single tear increased the force of them tenfold.

Simon was torn. He didn't know what to make of her, let alone himself or, more properly, the strong emotions churning inside him. He wasn't sure what he wanted more—to board the next train to Christine's home, seek out the cousin, and flay him alive. Or to ride to Newgate where he could arrange for a private "interview" with the LeBow woman—and beat her bulk black and blue.

Shaken by the intensity of his anger, the vividness of his imagined revenge on behalf of—good God, a *stranger*—he dropped his hands and backed toward the door. "Soap, miss, see you use plenty of it."

He'd just fitted one palm to the knob when he heard a soft splash. "Oh, sar?"

He turned about. Her night rail lay in a wet ball on the carpet along with the imprint left by her wet feet. The curved sides of the tub hid all but her head and shoulders from view but that didn't alter the fact that she was naked. Naked and but a few feet away. She leaned back to wet the rest of her hair, and he found himself staring at the smooth, elegant arch of her long throat and the water lapping the flushed tops of her breasts. He felt his pulse quicken. And his sex harden, causing him to consider that perhaps she'd not been all that far off the mark when she'd called him a *prevert*.

Her voice, maddeningly matter-of-fact, pulled him from the realm of fantasy back to practical concerns. "D'ye think I might 'ave another copper o' that lovely warm water? This has gone cold."

He swallowed—hard. "I think I might be able to arrange that." He'd also see she received a generous measure of Trumbull's special salve for some of the more stubborn cuts on her back. Though he'd make sure that one of the maids, not Trumbull, applied it.

"Sar?"

The knob was slick as grease in his sweaty palm. Giving up, he released it and turned back inside. "Yes, what is it now?"

She smiled at him. A true smile, beguiling in its apparent

innocence, it illuminated her pinched face, even unearthed a dimple in the lower corner of her mouth. Suddenly Simon understood why a man—any man—would surrender his last farthing just to have her look at him as she was doing now.

"Baths make me mortal hungry. Might 'ee have summat to eat other than broth? I'm terrible partial to meat pies," she hinted broadly. "And tanzy tarts and plum pudding."

Simon nearly fell over. The cheeky chit was giving him her dinner order! Charmed in spite of himself, he said, "I suppose I can find you something to, uh, *sink* your teeth into. Will that be all?"

She tapped a long finger to the corner of her lush mouth, considering. "I'll be needing some clothes, I suppose, 'though I can't say as what size I am."

Small. Impossibly small.

"Shoes too." She hauled one foot out of the water, flexing fine-boned toes. "I've big feet for a woman."

But Simon's attention already had trailed upward to her shapely calve, glistening with droplets. He dragged his gaze away when he realized he was staring—and sweating. "The shops are all closed for the evening, but I'll have my housekeeper find a nightgown or something for you to wear in the interim. You'll take supper here in your room, so footwear will not be essential."

Her face fell, and he choked back something that tasted vaguely of guilt. The girl was being shuttled from one place to the next like a bucket of coal, and it wasn't in the least fair—but then what in life ever was?

He was on the precipice of apologizing when she shifted her bony shoulders in a shrug. "Suits me well enough. Truth be told, shoes is always more of a nuisance than not." Her rich, chicory-colored gaze settled on the hallway beyond him. "Now, Mr. Belleville, I believe I'll 'ave my bath in private, if 'tis all the same to ye."

Why, the imperious imp was showing *him* the door. A strange tickle, a sensation he hadn't experienced in years, tugged the corners of his mouth. "How fortunate, then, that I am on my way out."

It wasn't until he stood alone in the hallway that he let down his guard. Collapsing against the closed door, he tossed back his head.

For the first time in what felt like forever, Simon smiled.

Three

> We are sure to be losers when we quarrel with ourselves; it is a civil war, and in all such contentions, triumphs are defects.
>
> —Charles Caleb Colton,
> *Lacon,* 1825

Think, Simon. Think.

Simon turned weary eyes on the roman numerals of the small clock set on the edge of his writing desk. A quarter to twelve. For more than two hours he'd hunched over the marble-topped escritoire in his bedchamber, struggling with his note to Margot as though it were his inaugural address to Parliament. This was only a note, for Christ's sake, a few lines scribbled across the front of a sheet of foolscap. How hard could that be?

Bloody hard when one was trying to explain to one's former mistress why she should take on the feeding, housing—and education—of a stranger. A female stranger. A female stranger with long legs and lovely eyes.

A female stranger with long legs, lovely eyes, who happened to be a prostitute. Former prostitute.

Even so, it was a tall order, which accounted for the dozen or so balls of wadded foolscap lying fallow on his Oriental carpet. And for why his thoughts kept wandering from the paper to his "cousin" sleeping a mere four doors down the hall. At least he assumed she slept. No one had heard a peep from her since she'd wolfed down the contents of her supper tray, asked for a second tart, then gobbled it as well.

How would Disraeli handle the situation if he were in Simon's place? Not that Dizzy would ever, under any circumstances, be in Simon's place. It was his rival Gladstone who trolled the East London streets for prostitutes to reform, the sanctimonious old fool.

Benjamin Disraeli was no fool, sanctimonious or otherwise. And until—Simon consulted the clock once more—ten hours and twenty minutes before, he hadn't thought himself a fool either.

But he'd committed to this course, this foolish course, and now there was nothing to do but see it through. Resolved, he picked up his fountain pen and struggled to marshal his scattered thoughts.

Margot, the oddest thing happened to me earlier today. I found a girl locked inside a brothel attic and was hoping you might see your way to taking her off my hands for, say, the next year.

Margot, this is Christine. Seeing as she's a prostitute—ex-prostitute—and you're a demirep—ex-demirep—you're bound to be fast chums. I'll just step out—for a year or so—and let you two get acquainted.

Margot, you've always said you'd like a daughter, and it occurred to me this girl I found in a—gulp—brothel might just fill the bill. No, of course you're not actually old enough to be her mother, but . . .

Margot, I'm dying. I only have a year to live. Will you honor my final wish and take this ragamuffin on as your pupil?

Out in the hallway, the grandfather clock belted out the midnight hour. Rubbing his forehead, Simon allowed it was no use. The written word had failed him. He would wait and present his case tomorrow, in person, relying on the element of surprise—and whatever tender feelings she might still harbor for him—to win her over.

So much for having a strategy. He stabbed the pen back in its stand. Pain sang through his thumb.

"Blast!"

He clutched his injured hand to his chest. Leaping to his

feet, he gave his chair a good kick. Even with fresh blood seeping through the bandage, he battled to blot out the images of The Creature—Christine. Christine in the attic, eyes narrowed and glittering, just before she sunk her teeth into him. Christine in the bath, the nearest thing to naked, that full bottom lip of hers trembling in such a way that he'd wanted to kiss all her cares—all her pain—away.

The latter image stuck to his thoughts like wheat paste. Despite his hurting hand—his swollen, bruised, stiff flesh— he felt his manhood thicken and rise. If he were a superstitious man, he'd blame the full moon, which was casting quite a brilliant beam through his windowpane. Uncomfortably flushed, he turned down the desk lamp and drifted over to the window, threw up the sash, and peered down onto the boxwood-bordered square. Barring the church commanding the opposite street corner, the windows of the terrace of stately Georgian mansions facing his were uniformly dark. Uniformly silent.

He closed his eyes and listened, ears pricked for sounds of traffic from nearby Regent Street. All around him silence thrummed, the absence of sound becoming a sound in itself. How different it was from the boisterous Whitechapel neighborhood of his boyhood. In those days he'd fallen asleep to the Gaelic bickering of the old Irish couple who lived upstairs; to the mewling of the cats in the alley beneath his window; and to the sweet, slurred ballads of the drunks congregating outside The Three Nuns.

He opened his eyes. How did anyone manage to sleep in the midst of all this *quiet?* To his left lay Regent's Park, but even the park's Outer Circle was deserted at this hour. Except for a pair of lovers shivering on a wrought-iron bench at the York Gate, his neighbors appeared to have retired to bed.

Which is precisely where he should be.

He was about to move back inside when a crunch sounded above his head. Squirrels, at this hour? He fell back inside the dark room just as a slight silhouette landed on the ledge a few feet from his window. A housebreaker? Limned by moonlight, the figure slithered across the slates to the corner of the house where the drainpipe met the upper branches of an old oak tree. To get there, he would have to pass Simon's window. Arms out, Simon prepared to lunge. Caught unaware, the thief would find himself hauled inside, bound, and awaiting the police before he even realized he'd been seized.

Another step brought the culprit dead center of the patch of moonlight. Simon blinked. No, it couldn't be. A gust of wind whipped gauzy skirts about a pair of long and now familiar legs, and he dropped his hands to his sides.

It was The Creature. Miss Tremayne. Christine.

He opened his mouth to call to her, then clamped it shut. Earlier it had rained. The slates would still be slick, the gutters clogged with shed oak leaves. If startled, the little fool could easily lose her footing. A fall from the top of a three-storied house would almost certainly be lethal. Even if she somehow managed not to break her neck, there were arms, legs, and a spine to consider. He could almost hear the newspaper boys barking out the headlines: "Vice Commissioner abducts lady of the evening for day of dalliance . . . Prostitute plunges to her death at home of aspiring M.P."

His heart seemed to plummet with Christine's every wobbling footfall. Sweat trickled down the collar of his robe as he mentally calculated how long it would take him to wrench the sheet from his bed and twist it into a rope to cast out to her. Too long, he decided, forcing himself to watch her edge her way toward the tree. She'd almost reached it when . . .

"Ahhhhh . . ."

She skidded on her belly, feet flying and hands clawing at air and bricks. Simon's heart leapt into his throat. He was halfway out the window before he saw that an empty window box and the second-story ledge together had broken her fall. Chest heaving, he stilled. Below him, she found her footing in the bricks. Hands wrapped about the pipe, she started to climb back up. Indecision paralyzed him. If he tried to go to her, to meet her halfway, he might very well make matters worse. But, if he did nothing, and she fell again . . .

Panting, she gained the ledge. She sagged against the house, and so did Simon. Feeling a good ten years older than he had a few minutes earlier, he crawled back inside the window. The tree—her obvious destination—was less than a foot away. The upper branches were sturdy, as he recalled, and Christine couldn't weigh more than eight stone, if that. But, dear God, it was dark. And wet. And slippery.

She disappeared from his field of vision. He tensed, ears pricked. A moment later, he heard a soft thud, then the rustling of tree branches and a muffled "ouch." The timepiece in Simon's robe pocket ticked out the seconds as she navigated her way down the tree. A second thump and a low groan announced she'd made it to the ground, likely in one piece and reasonably ambulatory. Simon flew to his armoire. By the time he stripped off his robe, threw on clothes, and rushed back to the window, she was gone.

He scanned his front yard and, beyond it, the silent street and now empty park. Blast. The weather, it seemed, had finally driven indoors the only two persons who might have witnessed Christine's flight and told him her direction.

No matter. He had a good hunch where she'd headed.

Christine opened the door of the hansom cab and stepped down, gritting her teeth as the bruised arches of her bare feet connected with the cobbles.

From his seat on the box, the driver called down, "Sure ye want me to leave ye *'ere,* ducks?"

Here was Madame LeBow's former establishment. The clapboard town house with its bright yellow columns and purple gingerbread trim seemed even seedier with the windows boarded and a wooden placard, "V-A-G-R-A-N-T-S Will Be Prosecuted," nailed across the front door. Certainly not the destination the driver must have expected when Christine had hailed him from the corner of Regent Street.

Glancing up to the driver, she caught him giving her the once-over, and an unpleasant shiver ran through her. "Aye, I'm sure."

Given the state of her—her torn dress, the scratches on her face and arms, the leaves in her hair—he was probably wondering if he'd get his fare. She dug into her pocket, praying the coins she'd found in the bottom of a dresser drawer were still there and not lost to Mr. Belleville's lawn.

Miracle of miracles, they hadn't fallen out. She sighed, her relief only mildly tinged with guilt. She'd never stolen before but, with a precious life at stake, theft had seemed a small sin. Besides, if Mr. Belleville had allowed her to bring Puss in the first place, she wouldn't be in her present fix.

Steeled by that thought, she carefully counted out the coins. Six pence nine. Miraculously they were all there.

"How much?" she asked, then considered she probably ought to have found out the fare before producing the entirety of her fortune in broad view. If she'd been alone, she would have smacked the side of her empty head. Had the past two weeks taught her nothing?

The driver scratched one side of his stubbled jaw, an ugly leer cracking his mouth. "Ye tell me," he answered in an oily voice, wiggling his brows.

She'd seen that look on enough men's faces to know it spelled trouble. Backlit as she was by the streetlamp, she could only hope he couldn't see through her thin summer dress, a castoff from one of the Belleville housemaids. Unfortunately neither shoes—nor undergarments—had been part of the donation.

But she'd given up on modesty, along with pride, weeks before. Let him gawk all he wanted, so long as he didn't touch.

The only time she'd felt ashamed, truly ashamed, was the bathtub episode when she'd felt Mr. Belleville's dark, cool gaze gliding over her. "Strap or whip?" he'd asked in the same matter-of-fact tone one serving afternoon tea might ask, "Lemon or cream?" But the look he'd leveled her, somewhere between pity and disgust, had made her wish she were a little less dirty. A little less thin.

A little less scarred.

Not that it mattered, she reminded herself, since she'd never see him again. Once she found Puss, she'd camp out here for the night. At first light, she'd make herself as presentable as possible and then start walking. This time, she meant to go only to the "nice" neighborhoods. She'd knock on every door, if need be, until someone agreed to give her honest work. No matter how lowly the task, she'd do it, so long as it didn't include "that."

"That" was what Madame LeBow had meant to make her do and even now Christine cringed to think of what a green country girl, what an idiot, she'd been to believe for a moment that the heavily rouged and garishly dressed woman could be the housekeeper of a respectable household. But the woman who'd run the boardinghouse where Christine was lodging had pushed her to accept, assuring her that her "friend" ran a very fine house indeed. Down to her last farthing and with a stomach as empty as her prospects, Christine had finally given in. The two women had exchanged smug looks, and a cold trickle had run down Christine's spine.

By the time she saw just what sort of house it was Mistress LeBow kept, it was too late. The drugged soup she'd gulped down upon first arriving was taking rapid effect, and when one of the madam's bullies scooped her up and slung her over his beefy shoulder, her limbs were as limp as a rag doll's. She'd awakened in the attic with a splitting head, a cottony mouth, and the madam looming over her. She and her "mangy animal" would stay locked up, she was told, until she either came to her senses, or rotted.

Weak from hunger and half-crazed from days and nights passed in unrelenting darkness, Christine had been on the verge of giving in when the Dark Angel, Mr. Belleville as she now knew him to be, had come upon her. Despite his high-handed manner, and the way he'd simply dismissed any further mention of her cat, she couldn't help but feel grateful to him. He had, after all, saved her from becoming a fallen woman. And, had circumstances been other than what they were, she might have liked going to that school he spoke of. Gratitude, that must be it, the reason that the thought of never seeing him again, of never even having the chance to bid him a proper good-bye, caused her already low spirits to sink even lower.

Shifting on the seat, the driver reached under his cloak to adjust himself. "I b'ain't got all night. Make up yer mind. What's it to be?"

Fear churned her full stomach, but she girded herself to divvy up half the coins and hand them up to him. "Take it. 'Tis all ye'll get from me."

He snapped up the coins and made a grab for her wrist, but she pulled back before his fingers could close about her.

His black gloved hand disappeared beneath his cloak. "'Ave it yer way, then." Picking up the reins, he muttered, "Lousy whore. Ye'd think 'ee were the friggin' queen o' England for all the airs . . ."

Once Christine would have been shocked, but now she only turned away. Sidestepping garbage and broken glass, she headed up the brothel's cement steps, praying for the courage—and the strength—to break in. And, if she did, would she be lucky enough to find her companion still inside? Luck had never been a Tremayne trait, unless you counted the bad.

Before Hareton's arrival, Puss's five years of earthly life

had consisted of regular meals, a daily dish of cream, and nights curled up on Christine's pillow. Even after banishment to the barn, there had been warm straw, fat mice, and Christine's nightly deliveries of the choicest table scraps. Her cat hadn't any more of a notion about how to survive on the London streets than Christine had.

She reached the top step and surveyed the ground-floor window, nailed tight as a coffin. To break through, she'd need a metal prod or something to serve as a crowbar. Backing off the steps, she looked up. The upper-level windows were boarded as well. Someone—Mr. Belleville, no doubt—had been very thorough. Mounting the stoop once more, she felt almost relieved. The earlier episode on the roof had rattled her; she doubted she'd be able to bring herself to undertake such a steep climb for some time if ever. No, the door was the only way.

Yanking at the plank, she focused her every iota of strength on pulling the nails free. Light from the streetlamp on the corner dribbled her way, but not enough. Mostly she worked by feel, concentrating on the end that seemed to have fewer nails.

She toiled on, pulling and prodding and shoving fingers and thumbs into any conceivable space that might serve as a leverage point. It was cold enough that she could see her breath, yet sweat slid between her shoulder blades. A drunk loitering nearby came to inspect her handiwork, blowing gin-fouled breath in her face and asking her name. When she asked for his help, however, he moved on. A carriage passed. She started, fearing the hansom driver had returned. But it was a private conveyance and it stopped only long enough to deposit a foursome of well-heeled young men on the doorstep of the gaming hell across the street. Christine held her breath, but they didn't seem interested in her, so she turned back to her work. After that she didn't bother to look up, not even when the dampness gave way to a cold drizzle.

"One o' clock and all is well."

Swallowing a gasp, she ducked into the shadowed doorway. Pressed behind a pillar, she waited, heart hammering, for the night watchman to pass. Blood drummed her ears. All she needed was to be picked up for housebreaking. Or loitering. Or whoring.

The watchman passed, bell clanging. She watched, mouth

dry with fear, until he turned down the opposite street. Shaking with relief, she stepped out from her hiding place to inspect the door. The board hadn't budged. She'd worked for nearly an hour, and still it hadn't budged. Her fingers were a hacked, splintered, bloody mess; her body felt as though she'd been run through a threshing machine, and still the bloody thing hadn't loosened one bit. Without tools, it never would. She slumped onto the top step, head in her hands.

You're not going to cry, Christine. No, you're most definitely not.

Sucking her scraped knuckles, she looked about. Perhaps she had it all wrong. Perhaps, in all the earlier confusion, Puss had gotten out. Even on the farm, she'd never been much of a wanderer. Maybe she was hanging about out back, waiting to be let in?

Christine stood, reaching inside her pocket for the box of matches and candle stub she'd found earlier. Thank God she'd had the forethought to wrap the matches in a handkerchief; otherwise they'd be as sopping as she was. She lit the candle, then tucked the matches back into her pocket.

"Here, kitty, kitty, kitty . . . Puss, love, where are ye?"

Cradling the precious light, she picked her way through the rubbish toward the back of the brothel, thankful for the calluses that protected the bottoms of her feet. Hoarse from calling, she searched the narrow patch of yard, then the adjacent alley, then the yard again. She found several cats, including an entire litter of kittens burrowed beneath an overturned bushel, but no Puss.

Then her candle died.

Hot wax sputtered onto her hand. Dropping the burned-out stub, she felt the angry tears mingle with the rainwater rolling down her cheeks. She turned back to the house, gaze resting on the top gable. Beneath that evil, hulking peak was the attic. And in the attic was Puss.

The kitchen door was nailed shut too. Throwing herself upon it, she pounded the wood. "Damn, damn, *damn!*"

She thought she heard crunching gravel, but she was too lost in misery to even look up. Out of the corner of her eye, she glimpsed a sliver of light. Too golden to be the moon, it seemed to grow nearer and brighter with her every ragged breath. *Let 'em come and get me,* she thought, hardly caring whether *them* was a brigade of rats, the night watchman, or the mad drunk she'd encountered earlier.

As if on cue, a strong arm coiled about her midsection. She opened her mouth to scream, but a gloved hand clamped down on her mouth.

"Be quiet, you little fool, or I'll turn you over to the authorities myself."

It was him. Her Dark Angel. Mr. Belleville. An absurd gladness, a relief so powerful she felt her legs go weak, surged through her.

"If I release you, will you promise not to run?"

Sniffling into his glove, she nodded.

He started to pull back, then paused. "And no biting, understood?"

She nodded again, and this time he let go, although one hand rested lightly on her waist.

She pivoted to face him just as he bent to retrieve his lantern. "What are ye—"

"What am *I* doing here?" Brows crossed and mouth tight, he left the lantern lying and straightened to his full height. Looming over her, he demanded, "What are *you* doing here? Don't tell me you're missing your old life so soon?"

Christine had never felt so torn in all her life. Part of her wanted to beat her fists against his chest as she had the kitchen door. The other, weaker half wanted nothing so much as to throw herself on that very same chest and cry her eyes out.

She did neither. Swiping at the wet hair sticking to her cheek, she said, "Ye know full well why I come back."

He wasn't wearing a hat and his hair, just as wet as hers, gleamed like polished jet from its widow's peak. "I suppose you're just stubborn and pea-witted enough to risk lung fever to retrieve that mangy scrap of fur."

She stuck out her chin. "Mangy scrap . . . Why, Puss's the best mouser in Nantwich, the smartest, sweetest cat in the world, and ye're just too bloody stupid and hard-hearted to own it."

"Nantwich, is it?" For an instant, white teeth flashed in the midst of his shadow-darkened face.

Too miserable to care that she'd just let slip her home, tears flowing unchecked, she sank onto her knees in the mud. " 'Elp me, please." Her shoulders shook. Her whole body shook. The wretched sobs came so fast, so hard, she was sure the very earth beneath her must be vibrating.

Eyes wide, he dropped down beside her. "Miss Tremayne... Christine, please..." He reached for her hands. "Christine, you mustn't... Good God!" Looking down, he inspected her cracked and bleeding thumbnail, a splinter lodged below the quick. Turning her hands palms up, he demanded, "What have you done to yourself? Why on earth..."

"S-she's all I h-have. Oh p-please, won't y-ye... help me?" She dragged watery eyes up to his face, but her vision was too blurred to read him. "I'll d-do anything y-ye ask. *Anything*."

Pulling back, he let her hands drop. "Stop this, this... hysteria at once. You will make yourself ill."

Christine had no idea what hysteria was. All she could do was shake her head, wave her arms, and whimper, "Please," between sputtering, aching breaths.

He got to his feet, his lips curling downward in what could only be disgust.

But Christine was beyond shame. Beyond pride. She hurled herself forward and clasped his knees. "Please."

He started to back away, stopping when he saw he was dragging her with him. "Release me... *now*."

He drew back his hand, and suddenly all Christine could see was his glove, which seemed to grow bigger and blacker before her very eyes.

Her sobs stopped as though some unseen hand pulled an invisible lever to the "off" position. She let go of his legs, her arms flying up to shield her face.

She held herself stiff, waiting. Nothing happened. A few yards away, a dog barked. Still nothing happened. The rain slowed to a pitter-patter and still nothing happened. She lowered her hands and cracked open one eye, then two.

Mr. Belleville stood watching her, brows crossed, arms folded, and one booted foot tapping a cobble into powder. "Good God, did you really believe I would strike you?"

Murder her was more like it judging from his glare. Gaze trained on his face, she said, "You raised your hand to me."

"To lift you out of the mud."

"Oh."

"*Oh*, indeed." He thrust out his hand, his eyes daring her to refuse it.

This time she took it. "Thank 'ee."

Shaking his head, he let go and started on the buttons of his greatcoat. He took it off and handed it to her. "Put this on before you catch your death."

She started to refuse, but he was already reaching around her. The wool landed on her shoulders with a soft thud, swaddling her in the comforting scents of bay rum and cigars. Despite the rain, the inner lining was still warm from his body. Drawing it closer, she felt something long and solid clank against her right hip.

Reaching inside, she pulled the metal crowbar from an inside pocket. Hope swelled within her. "Does this mean ye'll help me get inside?"

He shoved his hands into his jacket pockets and stomped the ground. "Yes, yes, I suppose it does. If the beast's within, we'll rout it out."

Fresh tears—these of gratitude—sprang to her eyes. "Oh, thank you. Thank you. I'll do—"

"Don't beg," he cut in. His hands found her shoulders once more, and he looked long and hard in to her eyes. "Not to me, not to anyone, not ever again. Understood?"

She nodded, struck dumb by the passion, the *power,* of his gaze boring into hers.

He breathed deeply and released her. "Good. Let's begin with the window, shall we?" He took the crowbar from her, stepped up to the window, and set to work.

The ease with which he dislodged the plank was almost sinful. Christine had just slipped her right arm into his overcoat sleeve when she heard the telltale splinter. Another heave, and the board broke in half. He ripped away the rest of the fragments with his gloved hands.

"Keep back," he barked when she drew closer.

Pulling off his jacket, he wrapped it about the bar. Then he turned to the side and swung at the glass.

The coat muffled the crash but only somewhat. Christine pulled her hands away from her eyes and saw him knocking away the last remaining shards of glass and splintered wood. Tossing the tool aside, he cleared the ground below the window with the edge of his boot.

Looking back, he frowned at her bare feet. "There's certain to be glass on the inside as well. I'll go first, then lift you over."

The thought of being pressed against all that masculine strength for the second time that day—and this time with her conscious—was too much. Panicked, she started to protest, but he didn't seem to hear. He pulled off his ruined gloves, then picked up the lantern and turned back to the window.

Ducking beneath the transom, he climbed inside. Watching him throw one powerful leg, then the other, over the threshold, Christine felt her face heat and her pulse race. Even in semidarkness, she could appreciate how broad his shoulders were, how trim his waist, how his muscular thighs molded his trousers to him like a second skin. And what she couldn't see, she could well imagine.

Once inside, he moved away from the window. "Wait there. I need to set down the lantern."

Retreating into the gloom, he turned his back on her. Light bloomed, and Christine's gaze fixed on the muscles rippling beneath his shirt as he worked to clear the floor inside. Wetting dry lips, she asked herself how far one waistcoat and shirt could possibly stretch.

Abruptly he swung around. Christine nearly jumped out of her skin, which was flushed all over. Had he caught her gaping like some slack-jawed schoolgirl? Praying he hadn't, she hurried toward his outstretched arms, his heavy coat brushing her ankles. In her haste, she tripped. Her hands went out to catch herself.

Mr. Belleville's head and shoulders shot through the opening. His hands locked about her waist; her own hands landed on his upper arms. Beneath the damp linen of his shirt, biceps bulged.

He rolled his eyes. "You won't be satisfied until you do yourself an injury, will you? Here, grab hold of me."

He must think me the clumsiest girl in the whole world. Feeling as awkward as a newborn calf, she looked down to where her fingers were leaving dark prints on his white shirt. Even soggy, he smelled so fresh, looked so clean, it felt wrong to touch him. She pulled back.

"I won't let you fall," he snapped, apparently misreading her shyness as mistrust. Scowling, he slipped an arm beneath her knees and lifted her. "You have only to put your arms about my neck and mind your head. I'll do the rest."

Christine obeyed. His other arm locked about her shoulders. Tucking her head, she found her cheek pressed against the side of his neck, close enough that she could feel the pulse striking the corded muscles. Rainwater and sweat dampened his skin, the musky aroma mingling with the bay rum and shaving soap that clung to him as well. Christine inhaled, heart beating with a strange sense of excitement. Until now, she hadn't realized just how muscular he was, how solid. How strong.

She knew an odd sense of disappointment when he set her down on the other side of the passage and stepped away. "Its name is Puss?" he asked, lifting his lamp from a peg on the stucco wall.

"She's a *she,* not an *it,*" she corrected, fighting to find her legs after the weightless, flighty feeling of being held so close against him.

"Absurd." Holding the lantern aloft, he reached for her hand, catching the limp coat sleeve instead. "I suppose this is a bit overlarge." He reached inside and found her hand.

She looked down. His palm was square, the fingers long yet thick. Even though his nails were clipped and clean, somehow his hand wasn't what she'd expected of a gentleman. Yet his grip, the light pressure on her elbow, as he guided her through the pantry and downstairs were shockingly gentle. He held her as if she were made of the finest Dresden china instead of flesh and bone—and common flesh and bone, at that.

She was just getting used to it—and to the tingling sensation climbing her arm—when they came to the front hallway.

He released her and turned his light on the stairs. "Here, cat. Here, Puss," he called, the boards creaking beneath him as he started up. "Come here, you."

Hiding a smile, Christine lifted her sodden skirts and followed. Midway to the top, she couldn't resist observing aloud, "Ye don't know anything about cats, d'ye? The way ye're bellowin', ye sound like ye're orderin' 'er to come to ye."

He turned back to glare at her. "I *am* ordering her to come to me."

Christine shook her head. "That'll work wi' a dog, but not wi' a cat. Them only answers when ye call 'em gentle, like this." She demonstrated, crooning, "Here, kitty, kitty," until she caught him rolling his eyes.

"Hm, quite a science, I see."

She blew out a sigh. "Poke fun if ye've a mind to, but just ye wait."

They found Puss on the third floor, curled up beneath one of the abandoned beds. Purring, she stood, stretched, then strolled over to Christine.

Christine nearly collapsed with relief, the grateful tears squeezing out the corners of her eyes. "Oh, Puss, love, I'd a'most given up on ye." She reached down and scooped the tabby into her arms. "Warm as toast," she said, rubbing her cheek against the silky fur. Looking over at Mr. Belleville, she couldn't resist a smug smile. "See, I told ye she were smart."

Frowning, he chafed his upper arms, the gooseflesh all but visible through his drenched shirt. "That makes one of us."

Four

> Amongst the changes introduced by modern taste, it is not the least striking, that all the daughters of tradespeople, when sent to school, are no longer girls but young ladies.
>
> —S. S. Ellis, *The Women of England: Their Social Duties and Domestic Habits,* 1839

The following afternoon, Simon ferried a reluctant Christine through the entrance hall of the Mayfair Academy for Young Ladies.

He released his hold on her elbow and pointed to the deacon's bench set against one elaborately stenciled wall. "Sit."

Beneath the sheltering brim of her new poke bonnet, Christine's face was mutinous. "But I want to go wi' ye."

One hand fisted about the handle of Puss's basket, she used the other to bat the ostrich plume that insisted on drooping over her face. Simon held in a sigh. He knew next to nothing about women's fashions, yet he was almost certain she had the bonnet on backward.

"You'll join us presently. For now, *sit!*" He all but shoved her into the seat, then turned back to Margot's housekeeper, who'd followed them from the front door. "If she moves a muscle, you have my full permission to tether her."

Mrs. Fitz's jaw dropped. "Good heavens, Mr. Belleville! What a caution you are. If I didn't know better, I'd think you were serious."

"I *am* serious." Out of the corner of his eye, he glimpsed Christine half risen from the cushion. He turned on his heel and, laying hands on her shoulders, pushed her back down. "Sit." Casting a final glare in her direction, he turned and started up the carpeted stairs.

He found Margot in her drawing room. Seated at her piano, she was too lost in the Haydn sonata she was playing to notice him standing in the open doorway. Not wanting to disturb her, he leaned against the door frame and let the strains of sweet melody wash over him, easing the tautness from his neck and shoulders.

After he'd conveyed Christine—and her cat—back to his house, he'd spent the rest of the night picking glass and wood splinters from his hands—and replaying the evening's events in his mind. Even now when he knew Christine to be safe, warm, and dry, he couldn't shake the horror he'd felt when she'd gone down on her hands and knees in the mud. Hair hanging in wet ropes, face twisted in anguish, she'd somehow managed to dredge up memories and feelings he'd thought he'd buried. He felt battered, bruised, and altogether more vulnerable than he had in years.

He focused his gaze back on Margot. The delicate white hands moving deftly over the ivory keys held the solution to his problem.

He waited for the movement to end before making his presence known. "Brava! That was magnificent as always."

She whirled on the bench, lavender skirts swishing. "Simon! What a surprise!" Smiling, she rose and crossed the room toward him.

He hadn't been by for more than a month, not since they'd celebrated her forty-fifth birthday with champagne and caviar. Today he'd only come to beg a favor. Of all people, Margot deserved better from him.

Uncertain, he took off his hat and set it on the marble-topped pedestal table. "A welcome one, I trust?"

"Tsk-tsk. You should know better than to even ask such a question." Reaching him, she offered her cheek.

He bent to buss it. "I'd hoped you'd say as much. Your door knocker was up."

"And even if it wasn't, I always have time for you and you bloody well know it. Actually you're just in time. I was about to pour myself a sherry, and you know how I hate to drink alone." She took each of his hands in hers and led him inside.

Simon winced as she squeezed his right hand.

Margot frowned. "Is something the matter?"

He folded his hands behind him, grateful she hadn't suggested he remove his driving gloves. "It's a rather complicated story. I'll tell you all the sordid details later if you like." *Assuming you're still speaking to me.*

"Sounds delicious. I shall look forward to it." She left him and went to the small mahogany and rosewood liquor cabinet. "Cognac?"

"Perfect. Thank you."

She reached for a frosted crystal decanter and poured three fingers' worth into a snifter, then a small sherry for herself. Handing him his drink, she motioned him toward an armchair covered in peach damask and took her own seat on the piano bench. At a loss as to how to begin, he swirled the spirit in the crystal chinked goblet.

Perched on the bench, she regarded him. "If you'll pardon my saying so, you don't seem quite yourself. You look troubled. Is your new appointment not all you'd hoped?"

The irony hidden in her question prompted him to laugh. "Actually it's proving to be far more."

Her pale brows lifted. "I'm afraid I don't understand."

Wondering how Christine was faring out in the foyer, he lifted his glass and took a fortifying swallow. Setting the drink aside, he admitted, "Margot, I've a favor to ask."

She sipped her cordial. "You know you have only to name it."

He dropped his gaze to his tightly laced fingers. "Perhaps you should reserve any promises until after you hear me out."

In as few words as possible, he told her how he'd found Christine in the brothel's attic, how he'd taken her back to his house, and how, having committed to that rash course, he was at a loss as to what to do about her. In a shameless bid for Margot's sympathy, he made it a point to mention that the girl had turned up in London because she'd fled her cousin, who'd used her most cruelly.

"How dreadful," she said the very second he'd finished. "What the poor girl must have endured."

"Under the circumstances, I'm loathe to take her to the workhouse."

"To the workhouse! How could you even consider such a thing?"

"Well, I must do *something* with her."

She spread her elegant hands. "Surely you can find her a situation? A domestic position, perhaps?"

He shook his head. "Without references, I think not. Even if I could, she hasn't the training. She's a simple country girl. A dairymaid."

"Perhaps your housekeeper, Mrs. Griffith, could take her in hand? Find her something to do about the house?"

He stared into Margot's violet eyes. "She's young, she's pretty, and she is, or rather was, a prostitute. It's no secret I mean to stand for Maidstone in the next general election. Surely you can see why I can't keep her in my house?"

She regarded her wineglass, her fingers clasped tightly about the fragile stem. "You're perfectly correct, of course. I wonder you risk being seen here."

God, he was making a hash of this. He, who one day soon hoped to rise from his seat to address his fellows in the Commons, couldn't even approach his best friend without giving offense. Or pain.

He rose and crossed the room to sit next to her. Slipping an arm about her shoulders, he said, "Margot, that's not the case and you know it. The campaign, this business with the Vice Commission, the search for a competent estate manager to oversee Valhalla—all are taking more of my time than I'd anticipated. Don't you know you're my dearest, my oldest, my only *real* friend in London."

She turned to him. "Oh dear, did you have to say *oldest?*" When she pulled a face and tugged his collar, he knew all was forgiven. "Back to your Miss Tremayne, does the favor you need concern her?"

Simon shifted on the bench. Margot had done so much for him already; he hated to presume on their friendship. And yet what choice did he have?

Steeling himself, he said, "I was hoping you might consider admitting her as a pupil. Your winter term is just about to begin, is it not?"

Eyes wide, she admitted that was so. "Yes, but you know most of my girls come from monied families, even if they are from the trades or but one generation removed. Sometimes I think they are worse snobs than are those to the manner born. After all poor Miss Tremayne has endured, I'd hate to see her become the object of their ridicule."

A picture of Christine navigating his roof flashed through his mind. Now that she was out of danger, he found himself smiling at the memory. "I think you'll find Christine well able to hold her own, but I'll gladly pay double the usual tuition to compensate you for keeping the peace."

Margot's gaze narrowed. "As I told you the day you handed me the deed to this house *and* the bank draft to start this school, I won't accept another farthing. You've been far too generous already."

He shrugged. "That's only money. 'Tis I who am in your debt."

It was Margot who'd taught him how to dress, which wine went with which course, how to judge good horseflesh from bad—the genteel façade he'd needed to enter society. Dare he hope she might perform a similar miracle for Christine Tremayne?

Margot pursed her lips. A good sign, for it meant she was considering his proposal. "Well," she said at length, "I suppose there's no harm to be done by giving her a try."

"So you'll take her?"

Her sigh was theatrical. "I have ten girls enrolled already, so I'm full up, but I suppose I can squeeze another bed in somewhere. Bring her by at the end of the week. We'll be ready for her then."

Simon cleared his throat. "Actually, she's here already. Waiting below," he added, in response to her winged brows.

"Simon! Do you mean to say all this time you've left her standing about the front hall like so much baggage?"

He shrugged. "Perched on your deacon's bench, actually."

"Well, that won't do." She set aside her glass, rose, and swept across the room to tug the tasseled bellpull. Moments later a maid appeared in the doorway. "The young lady in the hallway is my newest pupil. Please show her up at once."

"Yes, mum."

Minutes later, Christine appeared in the doorway, feather sagging and basket in hand.

Cursing himself for not insisting she leave the beast in the foyer, he turned back to Margot. "Margot, allow me to present Miss Christine Tremayne. Christine, Miss Ashcroft."

Christine shuffled inside, the hem of the brown silk carriage dress trailing. Like the bonnet, the gown and matching pelisse were hasty purchases from that morning. Simon had guessed at her size and, as a result, the garments swam on her.

Turning from Simon to Christine, Margot summoned a warm smile and extended her hand. "Miss Tremayne, what a pleasure. I'm Margot Ashcroft, the headmistress of the Mayfair Academy for Young Ladies, and I am so happy you shall be joining us this term."

When Christine's only response was a sullen nod, Simon nudged her in the ribs. "Ouch!" Scowling at him, she took Margot's hand and ground out the words, "Thank ye, ma'am."

An awkward silence descended. Introductions behind them, Simon decided there was no point in postponing the inevitable.

He turned to Christine. "Well, I should be going."

She worried her hands. "Must ye leave a'ready?"

Margot's brows lifted, and her violet eyes narrowed as she fixed her gaze on Simon. "Yes, really, Simon, must you dash off just now? Stay for tea at least." Tone laced with vinegar, she added, "Surely you'll want to stay and help Miss Tremayne become better acquainted with her surroundings?"

He glanced from Margot to Christine. She was even paler than she'd been that morning when he'd handed her the brown-paper wrapped clothing parcels and told her to gather her things.

Tamping down the dangerous urge to touch her, he started backing toward the door. "I'm afraid I can't. I've a great deal of work to do."

Christine followed him. "When will I see ye next?"

Deliberately avoiding the question, he replied, "Miss Ashcroft will keep me informed of your progress, and I'll visit as my schedule allows."

"Promise?" Large, soulful eyes stared directly into his.

"Of course." Addressing himself to Margot, he added, "Whatever she needs—clothes, books, anything—have the accounts sent to me."

Margot nodded. She laid a hand on Christine's arm. "We'll be having our commencement ceremony at the end of the term, the thirty-first of March." Her gaze shifted to Simon. "I am sure Mr. Belleville, beleaguered by professional responsibilities though he is, will find the time to attend. May we expect you, Mr. Belleville?"

"We shall see." Simon regarded Christine for a long moment, then said, "We must say our good-byes now. Will you shake hands, Miss Tremayne?"

She held out her hand. "Good-bye then and thank 'ee, sar, for all what ye've done for me."

Simon enclosed her small hand in his, wishing he could smooth out the tremor. In his haste he'd forgotten to buy her gloves. Even wearing his, he could feel how cold her little hand was.

Voice deliberately firm, he said, "Study hard and do as you're bid, and you'll be a credit to me and to the institution."

She looked up at him, brown eyes suspiciously bright. "I will, sar. I promise."

Suddenly he felt as though the walls were closing in on him. Desperate to escape, he released Christine and stepped out into the hallway.

Following him, Margot called back over her shoulder, "Take a seat, Miss Tremayne. Mr. Belleville and I have a few last things to discuss, but I shall be back presently." She closed the door to the drawing room with a definite slam. "You beast! You insensitive, insufferable brute."

Nonplussed, he turned back. "I beg your pardon?"

"To desert that poor child and walk out without so much as a backward glance."

The rebuke hit home. Simon bristled. "I've known her scarcely more than twenty-four hours. We've hardly formed an attachment to merit protracted farewells." Wishing that were true, he stomped into the foyer, Margot hot on his heels.

"Perhaps that's true for you, but can't you see she's formed an attachment to you?"

He snorted. "I promise you, the only attachment she feels is to that mangy feline of hers. Last night I risked lung fever and housebreaking charges to fetch it from the brothel."

Keeping pace beside him, Margot brightened. "You don't mean to say you broke into a *brothel?*"

He nodded. "Thanks to the orders I'd left, the blasted place was bolted tighter than Newgate."

To his chagrin, her eyes lit until she positively beamed. "Why, Simon, that's . . . that's *marvelous.*"

"Marvelous, is it? I'm so glad you think so." He scowled. "Had I been caught, not only would my career be ruined, but we'd likely be having this conversation through the bars of my prison cell."

Shoulders shaking with suppressed laughter, she asked, "Is that how you hurt your hand?"

He shifted, gaze falling to the black-and-white parquet tiles. "More or less."

"More or less?"

"The little savage bit me, if you must know."

"Bit you! That's—"

"Marvelous, so you've said."

Sputtering, she dashed watery eyes with the back of her hand. "Oh dear, now I've made you grumpy."

Simon started to protest, then stopped. He was in a foul humor, but it had nothing to do with Margot's reproach or her teasing. Leaving Christine behind, even in Margot's capable care, was proving to be far more difficult than he'd imagined.

"I'm being a perfect ass yet again. I don't know why you put up with me, I'm only glad you do. And I appreciate your help more than I can ever express." He kissed her cheek. "Thank you."

She stepped back, fixing him with a wicked smile. "I suppose you say as much to all your former mistresses?"

He squeezed her hand. "Of course, but in your case it also happens to be true."

"A truthful politician?" She winked. "Dare I—"

Footsteps bounded down the hall toward them. Flushed, Christine emerged into the front hall, basket in hand.

Setting it down, she flung herself at Simon. "Please, sar, take me back wi' ye. I don't want to go to school." She gulped more air. "I don't want to be left."

"I'm afraid that is out of the question." He tried to pry her loose, but her little hand fastened on his sleeve like a vise.

She lifted pleading eyes from his coat front. "Can't I work for ye? I shan't be any more trouble, I swear it."

She was begging yet again, swallowing vowels and gulping consonants with the same desperation he and Rebecca once had applied to their charity school gruel.

Aghast, he attempted to disengage her, but she stuck to him like glue. "Miss Tremayne...Christine, I can't..."

Over the top of her head, he sent Margot a silent appeal.

She stepped forward to drape an arm about Christine's shuddering shoulders. "No attachment, clearly." To Christine, she said, "There, there, dear. It's only natural that you feel frightened—" She looked back at Simon. "—and *abandoned*, but once you've settled in you're going to have a lovely time here. You'll see." Gently but firmly she drew Christine away.

Looking across the foyer into Christine's stricken face, Simon felt as though a brick wall had just toppled on his chest. "It's for the best, really. Here you'll make friends your own age, learn all sorts of wonderful new things."

He backed to the entrance. Margot's housekeeper, Mrs. Fitz, materialized at his side to hand him his walking stick.

Mechanically he turned to take it. "Good-bye then."

He shoved on his hat and quickly stepped out into the gray drizzle. The feeling of terrible finality caught him unawares, exploding inside his skull like a ship's boom. It took all his resolve to force one foot in front of the other, down the town house's front steps, across the stone walkway, through the wrought-iron gate to the spot on the street where he'd stationed his brougham. Climbing inside, he told himself there'd been no other way. He'd had no choice. It was for the best.

And yet even as he settled into position on the bench and reached for the reins, Christine's plea pealed in his ears. *Please, sar, take me back wi' ye.*

Steeling himself against temptation, he took up the reins and urged his team of blacks out onto the street.

Margot and her housekeeper exchanged meaning-charged glances. "Tea in the drawing room, if you please, Mrs. Fitz. And tell Cook not to scrimp on the scones and clotted cream. I'm famished," she added with manufactured cheer.

"Yes, mum." Mrs. Fitz bobbed a curtsey. "Poor mite," she added under her breath, shooting a sympathetic look at Christine, who still stood in the open doorway.

Poor mite, indeed. The way Christine was looking after Simon reminded Margot of the little lost spaniel she'd found wandering Hyde Park, leash dangling. Cast aside. Confused. Abandoned. In the spaniel's case, Margot had known the satisfaction of reuniting him with his mistress. As for Christine...

"Come away, dear, before you catch a chill." When the girl didn't budge, she added, "We wouldn't want to give Mr. Belleville any more of an exaggerated sense of self-importance than he already has, now would we?"

This time Christine complied. Taking up her basket, she followed Margot back to the drawing room. As soon as she crossed the threshold, she set the basket carefully down on the carpet and flew to the window overlooking the street.

Seated on the sofa, Margot studied her charge. She was on the tall side, but a clever modiste knew how to turn height into an advantage. Provided Christine learned to hold her shoulders back instead of folding in on herself like a beast beaten down one too many times. But then Simon had told her about the marks on her back. Tapping a manicured fingernail against her chin, Margot wondered whether he'd seen them firsthand or was relying on a maid's report. The former carried with it all manner of delicious possibilities. She hadn't missed how his regard had riveted on Christine from the moment she'd entered the drawing room. Nor that, when he'd taken his leave, he'd looked nearly as miserable as Christine had.

She sighed. Knowing Simon, even if he cared for the girl, he'd be too stubborn to admit it—even to himself. *Especially* to himself.

"Miss Tremayne, won't you come away from the window and join me?"

Chin tucked, Christine pulled away and walked to the sofa.

Margot summoned a sunny smile. Time to see just what she had to work with. "You must be warm in that bonnet and jacket. Why not take them off and make yourself comfortable?"

Obediently Christine untied the strings and lifted off the hideous headgear. Margot seized the opportunity to take inventory. A fine pair of eyes, even if they were a bit bleary at the moment. Good skin, high cheekbones—always an advantage—and a full, rather dramatic mouth. The girl might not be a conventional beauty, but she had definite possibilities. Margot felt her spirits rise.

Christine held the bonnet aloft. "Where shall I put it, ma'am?"

"That empty chair should do," Margot replied, thinking that the girl's hairstyle wouldn't.

The tightly coiled bun was far too governesslike. The hair itself, a pleasing if unfashionable color of honey, looked silky and abundant.

Christine set the bonnet down with great care, then started on the cloth-covered buttons of her jacket. The garment shed, Margot studied her new protégée with a professional's eye. Small breasts, but then some men preferred more modestly endowed women, and the gown's basque did hint of a lovely long waist. Much too thin, of course, but regular meals would remedy that.

Encouraged, Margot patted the cushion next to her. "Come sit beside me."

Christine hesitated, then rounded the tea table and sat.

"Now dry your eyes and blow your nose."

The girl looked over at her and slowly shook her head. "I ain't got a hankie."

"*Haven't* and fortunately I do." She reached into her pocket.

Christine accepted the pressed linen square. "Ye've pretty things," she said, touching one lace-edged corner with a reverent finger.

Before Margot could reply, she buried her nose and blew. The result brought to mind a bugle blast. Margot winced. The raw material might be present in abundance, but fashioning Christine Tremayne into some semblance of a lady would still be an enormous challenge. And, if she succeeded, her greatest triumph since opening the school.

Mrs. Fitz arrived with the tea tray, an elegant arrangement of heavy silver, starched linen, and delicate bone china. Humming, she set it down on the table before them, then waddled out without breaking tune.

Christine surveyed the tray of sandwiches, scones, and biscuits with open appreciation. "Blimey, this tea is so high, I won't need to eat for the rest o' the week."

Margot held in a groan. "Ah well, after we've had our tea, I'll show you about. Then I'll send my maid, Marie, upstairs to help you unpack. We're a small school, ten pupils in all." She caught herself and added, "Eleven, now that you've joined us."

The girl, Christine, ventured a glance about. "Awful quiet."

"Indeed, the girls are touring the British Museum this afternoon, and so we have the house more or less to ourselves. It will be far from quiet when they return, I assure you. You'll share a room with one other girl, but you'll each have your own bed and a wardrobe to hang your things. Now, dear, where is your baggage?"

"Ma'am?"

"Yes, dear, your valise, your portmanteau, your . . ."

Christine answered her query with a blank stare.

"That basket over there, is that all you've brought?"

"Yes, ma'am."

The house tour would have to wait. Shopping, it seemed, would be their first priority. "I'll call a footman to carry it up."

The girl's eyes rounded as though she'd just been asked to relinquish the Crown Jewels. "Oh no, I can carry it myself."

"Don't be ridiculous. No one will steal it. It will be on your bed, waiting for you, when you go up."

"But I—"

Following the girl's horrified gaze, Margot glimpsed the wicker lid lifting. She blinked, thinking this was no more than she deserved for being too vain to wear her spectacles. Opening her eyes, she saw the basket begin to move, ever so slightly, from side to side.

The tabby sprang free and bounded toward them. Bracing its white front paws on the table edge, it stood on its hind legs and took stock, nose working. Its slanted green gaze alighted on the dish of clotted cream, and Margot would have sworn she saw its black lips smack.

She turned back to Christine, who'd leapt to her feet and was looking down at her cat in frozen horror. "Your baggage, I presume?"

Cheeks bathed crimson, Christine nodded. "She won't be a bit o' trouble, I swear it. I'll keep 'er in my room, and ye won't even know there's a cat in the house." She reached over, scooped the tabby up, and sat with it on her lap.

"What rubbish. She'll have the run of the house, of course, provided she learns to get on with Madame de Pompadour and King Louis."

"Madam o' what—"

"Madame de Pompadour and King Louis are my Persians. Normally they shadow me, but Pompie's just had a litter. They're all holed up in my bedroom closet, quite the close-knit little family. You can go up and see the kittens after tea, if you'd like. For now—" Margot broke off to glance at the tray. "Would you care to do the honors?"

Christine stared down at the tea service. Gnawing her bottom lip, she admitted, "I'm afraid I ne'er learned—"

"No matter," Margot interrupted. Determined to spare the poor girl what embarrassment she could, she poured the tea herself, adding liberal quantities of cream and sugar according to her charge's shy replies. "Teatime etiquette is one of the many accomplishments you'll acquire here." Hoping she sounded more assured than she felt, she handed Christine her tea.

Christine hesitated, then reached out. With equal parts fascination and horror, Margot watched her set the saucer aside, wrap both hands tankard-fashion about the delicate bone china cup, and draw a noisy slurp.

Oh dear. Margot quickly took a small sip of her own tea to hide her dismay. As she did, an unwelcome suspicion stuck in her throat. Almost afraid to ask, she said, "How much has Simon, Mr. Belleville, told you about my school?"

Licking her thumb, glossy with currant glaze from the pastry she'd all but inhaled, Christine admitted, "Not much. Mainly that ye're the lady that's to teach me what I must know to find work." She hooked a finger in the clotted cream and held it down to her cat.

Pretending not to notice, Margot asked, "What type of position have you in mind?"

Christine lifted her thin shoulders in a shrug. "One that pays fair decent. You see, I've two little brothers and a sister back home. Come spring, I've to start sending money for their support."

"I see." Simon had said Christine was orphaned and Margot had assumed that, barring her brute of a cousin, the girl was alone in the world. Now it seemed she had a full family to support. The situation was growing more complicated by the minute. *Oh, Simon, when I get my hands on you . . .*

"Will ye, ma'am?"

Still seething, Margot looked back at Christine, busy using

her thumbnail to pry a sliver of bun from a bottom tooth. Well, at least her teeth were good—white and straight and, most importantly, all present.

"Forgive me, I must have been woolgathering. What did you just ask?"

"Will ye teach me what I need to know to get on in the world? To earn my keep and my family's?"

Margot looked from Christine to her cat, trying to decide whose mouth wore more cream. The girl was undoubtedly rough-hewn but, with a bit of polishing . . .

Turning a dairymaid—this dairymaid—into a diamond of the first water would require enormous energy, but Margot was determined. When she'd finished turning out Christine Tremayne, Simon wouldn't know what had hit him.

And it would serve him right.

Five

Our hours in love have wings; in absence crutches.

—Colley Cibber,
Xerxes, 1699

THREE MONTHS LATER, JANUARY 1868

Simon was entertaining Benjamin Disraeli and a half dozen lesser Conservative Party officials when Margot's note arrived by messenger.

Standing outside the dining room doorway, his housekeeper twisted her liver-spotted hands. "I'm that sorry to disturb you, sir, but he did say it was urgent." She bent to his ear and whispered, "It has to do with Miss Christine."

Tidings of Christine—and urgent. Was she ill? Injured? Might Tolliver somehow have traced her to Margot's? Or perhaps her cousin? A myriad of grim possibilities churned inside his head, obliterating the foreign policy issue they'd been discussing. All his fine arguments for the importance of raising funds to purchase controlling shares in Egypt's Suez Canal fled from his thoughts like geese flocking south for winter.

"No, you did right, Mrs. Griffith. I shall attend him presently." He turned back to his guests, gathered about the map of the Far East unfurled over the cleared dining table. "Gentlemen, if you'll excuse me, I shall be but a moment."

From the head of the table, Benjamin Disraeli set down his pointer and looked up, pinning Simon with his hooded gaze. "Nothing amiss, I hope?"

Careful to compose his features into a bland mask, Simon shook his head. "No, sir. A trifling matter, but one that requires my attention."

Turning his back on the room of curious eyes, he followed Mrs. Griffith into the hall. Margot's footman awaited him in his study. Simon snatched the note, breaking the seal on his way to the desk.

Simon,
A new development regarding our little Galatea's prospects. We must arrive at a decision as soon as possible. Can you call tomorrow? Do say yes.

Margot

Weak with relief, he sank into the chair behind the desk and regarded the note. Galatea, Pygmalion's marble effigy of the perfect woman. Unlike the mythical sculptor, Simon had no need of divine intervention to bring Christine to life. She'd hovered in his thoughts for three months now, a lovely wraith with haunted eyes and full, trembling lips that pled, "Please, sar, take me back wi' ye, sar" at the most inopportune times until he could no longer ignore the truth. She moved him. To a man for whom emotions were a liability; who didn't dare pause to feel, let alone *remember;* who owed his success to his ability to operate with the smooth, rhythmic efficiency of a well-oiled machine, she was a very dangerous young woman.

So he'd kept away from her, hard though that had proved to be, relying on Margot's weekly letters for news.

Christine's piano has progressed from scales to "The Wraggle Taggle Gipsies." I expect the playhouse managers to come knocking any day now. Postscript: Seriously, you really ought to come hear her play.

Christine led our practice tea party the other day. She was doing splendidly until she passed the toast and one triangle slipped onto the floor. Maddie Johnson laughed and, lo and behold, the plate landed in her lap—upside down.

I thought Pompie must be breeding again, she'd grown so fat, then I caught Christine slipping her bits of ham beneath the breakfast table. I didn't have the heart to upbraid her— she cried so when I gave away the kittens.

Precious tidbits that had left him hungry to know more, to know *all*. Nothing, however, to hint of a "development." Whatever it was, Margot obviously was loath to commit it to paper.

He scribbled a brief reply, saying he would call the next day at noon, and handed it to the liveried messenger posted by the door. After tipping the man for his trouble, he returned to his guests. The conversation had shifted from Egypt to India and the relative merits of declaring Victoria as empress. A footman circulated with a decanter of port, replenishing glasses and emptying ashtrays.

Disraeli broke away from the circle of men still congregated about the table. "All is well, I trust?"

Simon chose his words with great care. "It seems a friend of mine is about to realize his expectations."

"Ah, splendid news. Anyone I know?" The heavy black brows drew together.

Simon retrieved his glass and held it out to be refilled. "I don't believe so. My friend is young and has been in London but a few months." Eager to put the subject to rest, he circuited the room with his gaze. "Gentlemen, shall we adjourn to the study?"

It was another two hours before the party dispersed. One by one, the guests took their leave until only Disraeli remained. It was a marked sign of favor and, under normal circumstances, Simon would have relished the opportunity to bend Dizzy's ear on a topic or two. Yet left alone with his distinguished guest, reposing opposite him in a leather armchair and cradling a snifter of cognac, Simon was hard-pressed to keep thoughts of Christine from invading his brain. Would he find her greatly changed from the scrawny, grubby girl he'd rescued? The one who hadn't given a second thought to throwing herself in his arms. Who'd gone down on her hands and knees in the mud to beg for the life of a *cat*. Odd, but the more he thought of seeing her on the morrow, the more he began to hope she hadn't changed *too much*. Not that he didn't look for her to have put on some weight. Certainly he would be glad to see her attired in decent clothes that actually fit. But the essence of her character, what he had come to think of as the beautiful simplicity of her soul, he hoped to God she hadn't lost *that*.

Disraeli fingered the shoe-black curl plastered to the center of his forehead. "You looked rather far away just now. Reliving your glory days in India, no doubt."

Simon snapped his thoughts back to the present. "What . . . uh, no, sir. And they were rather *in*glorious days, frankly, not to mention hot as Hades."

He smiled to cover his nervousness, but inwardly he was afraid. It wasn't like him to wool-gather, especially in such august company, but lately he'd become powerless against the pull of his thoughts. Thoughts of Christine.

"Balderdash, you're too modest." Voice dropping to just above a whisper, Disraeli said, "I have something I'd like to share with you, Belleville. A tidbit of information you might find of interest. You strike me as a discreet fellow."

Simon straightened in his chair. "You have my word of honor that anything you confide will not go beyond this room."

"Good, then I am not misled." He leaned forward as though the very walls had ears and confided, "Lord Derby means to retire. He will make the announcement next month. Naturally I will step up to take his place as prime minister."

Simon sat back, digesting the news. In his seventy-third year and on his third ministry, it came as no great surprise that Lord Derby should wish to step down before the triumphant tide he'd ridden for so long could reverse itself. Still, he was honored that Disraeli had singled him out to receive such a confidence even as he couldn't help but wonder why.

"Congratulations, sir. Britain could not ask for a better man to take his lordship's place."

Disraeli bowed his head in acknowledgment. "I've heard you've followed in my footsteps and joined the Church of England."

"It seemed the prudent course," Simon answered, for once thankful that his Jewish mother was not alive to witness his betrayal. Lilith might have walked away from her people to wed an Anglican, but that didn't mean she would have accepted her only son relinquishing his claim to her faith. As it stood, his stepfather, Mordechai, would be none too pleased with him.

"I take it then that you're serious about standing for Maidstone in the next general election?"

"That is my intention. I've recently acquired an estate midway between Maidstone and Ashford, which more than meets the property requirement."

Disraeli smiled his all-knowing smile. "My dear boy, I could not be more delighted. We need more like you in Parliament, men who understand the complexities of foreign affairs, the dictates of progress. But getting elected can be a tricky business." He sat back, dark gaze locking on Simon's. "Did you know I ran *five times* before I managed to win my seat?"

Simon did, of course, but he feigned surprise.

Seemingly satisfied, Disraeli went on, "If it hadn't been for Wyndham Lewis, my Mary Anne's first husband, taking me under his wing, I might not have made it even then. But times have changed. With Gladstone forging alliances with the Whigs, the Radicals, the Nonconformists and, God help us all, the Irish, our minority continues to dwindle. Several of our historically safe seats are in peril. We need you positioned so that, when your seat comes up, you are poised to take it." He paused to draw a wheezy breath. "Which is precisely why I've taken the liberty of writing William Harrison on your behalf."

Headquartered in the county town of Maidstone, Harrison was the party agent for Kent, traditionally a Conservative stronghold. That Disraeli had requested he give Simon's campaign his personal attention was a high mark of the future prime minister's favor. Simon was at a loss.

"Thank you, sir. You do me great honor. I only hope Mr. Harrison won't feel his talents wasted on a backbencher."

"Balderdash. Once you're in, you'll not languish on the backbench for long. You're ministerial timber if ever I saw it."

Out in the hallway, the grandfather clock struck. Disraeli cocked his head, listening.

"A quarter 'til midnight. I must be leaving. My wife still insists upon waiting up, and I dislike keeping her from her rest." He rose, one hand clutching the chair arm for support, the other wrapped about the knob of his ebony walking stick.

Simon stood as well, resisting the urge to offer a steadying hand. "Please convey my regards to Mrs. Disraeli."

"I shall." Disraeli nodded, harsh features softening. "Splendid woman, Mary Anne. Best wife in the world. Though I confess to marrying her for her money, had I to do it again I'd marry her for love."

Simon responded with the obligatory smile, but inwardly he scoffed. Money was easy to learn to love and, although Dizzy liked to think of himself as the last of the great Romantics, he was a pragmatist at heart. And a consummate politician, Simon mused as he led his visitor into the foyer where a footman materialized to help the chancellor on with his greatcoat.

At the entrance Disraeli turned back. Pinning Simon with his canny stare, he asked, "May I offer a word of advice?"

Simon's heart leapt into his throat. Had Disraeli somehow learned of Christine? It was rumored he had spies planted all over London, even in Buckingham Palace.

Heart pounding, he inclined his head. "I would be privileged to hear it, sir."

Disraeli's talon-like fingers curled about the gold knob of his cane. "Take yourself back to Maidstone, show your face at the local events, start building your constituency. If possible, get yourself a wife, preferably *before* the election. Not some flighty beauty, mind you, but a solid, practical woman. A wife like my Mary Anne, who will be a credit to you—and to the Party."

A wife. A woman Simon would be duty bound to not only honor but also to *protect*. He crossed his arms behind him, concealing clenched hands as the memory, the anger and the *pain* of his failure, rushed him with the violence of a monsoon. "With all due respect, sir, I fail to see what my private life has to do with my qualifications to sit in the Commons."

Disraeli shook his head, the corners of his thin mouth twitching. "My dear boy, you astound me." He smiled, but there was no mistaking the warning glint in his granite gaze. "Once a man stands for public office, he has no private life."

Ignoring her two smirking schoolmates seated across from her at the breakfast table, Christine snatched a still-warm blueberry muffin—her third that morning—from the silver basket. Smothering one half with honey and the other with sweet butter, she couldn't help but wonder what kind of breakfast Liza and Jake and Timmy were having. As a dairymaid on the Oates's farm in the county of Shropshire, Liza would be well fed. But the twins were too young to be of much use, as Farmer Oates's wife had pointed out when Christine had begged her to take them as well. The housewife had demanded fifteen pounds for their lodging—a straw pallet in the barn loft—and board through winter. Desperate, Christine had dipped into her small savings and paid. That had left just enough for a third-class train ticket to London and a cheap room once she'd arrived. She shuddered to think what would become of them all if she failed to find work after graduation in March.

Preoccupied with her worries, she didn't see the butter streaking down the front of her bodice until Maddie's braying laughter sliced through her silent thoughts.

"Some folk don't belong at table." Maddie elbowed her roommate, Bea, and the two tittered.

Christine felt her face flushing to match Maddie's rat's nest of copper-colored curls. She put down the muffin she'd been holding at half-mast and snatched the napkin from her lap.

From the head of the table, Miss Ashcroft's stern voice cut through the giggling. "That will do, ladies. I wish to speak to Christine in private. You two may join the others awaiting Monsieur Aristide in the music room. I believe today's dance lesson is the waltz which, as I recall, is not an accomplishment to which either of you can lay claim."

Eyes aiming daggers at Christine, Maddie and Bea set their napkins aside and rose. Passing behind Christine's chair, Maddie hissed "teacher's pet" and Bea yanked Christine's braid.

Teeth gritted, Christine dipped the corner of her napkin in her water glass and began rubbing furiously at the stain.

Miss Ashcroft waited until the door to the breakfast room closed, then said, "Christine, you have a visitor this afternoon." She gently tapped her poached egg with the back of her spoon. "Can you guess who?"

Christine could do better than guess. She'd met The Honorable Mr. Basil St. John three weeks before at the musicale Miss Ashcroft held on Sunday afternoons. With his golden good looks and finely tailored suits, he stood out from the other "gentlemen" in attendance, most of them the sons of prosperous shopkeepers and tradesmen. At first she'd been flattered to be singled out by such a distinguished person, a nobleman's son no less. But she'd quickly come to hate the way he remarked "how quaintly droll," or "so charmingly rustic" whenever she said something to amuse him, which seemed to be everything and all the time. Lately even his ready laughter had begun to set her teeth on edge.

Simon Belleville didn't laugh readily or, she suspected, much at all. In the fewer than forty-eight hours she'd spent with him, he'd never even smiled. Lines, no doubt brought on by scowling, bracketed the corners of his brooding dark eyes and stern mouth. And yet she found his face, his physique, his sharp manner even a thousand times more agreeable than St. John's, who seemed almost too pretty, too gay in comparison...

"If I must guess, ma'am, I'd have to say 'tis Mr. St. John." It was all Christine could do to stifle a groan, for even the thought of him made her mouth turn down. And the hot look in his eyes every time he cast his gaze her way told her in no uncertain terms just what it was he wanted from her.

Miss Ashcroft picked up her cup of chocolate and moved to occupy the chair across from Christine's. "Tell me truthfully, Christine, what are your feelings toward Mr. St. John?"

Christine traced the rim of her glass of milk. Thinned with water and sugared to make it palatable to city folk, it nonetheless reminded her of home. "I'm honored by the favor he's shown me. He's handsome and rich and a gentleman and yet..."

"And yet?"

Screwing up her courage, she blurted out, "If I ne'er laid eyes on him again, I'd not be sorry of it."

To Christine's surprise—and relief—Miss Ashcroft tossed back her head and laughed. Dashing a hand over her watery eyes, she said, "In that case, I trust you won't be too disappointed that your caller is *not* Mr. St. John but Mr. Belleville, your benefactor."

Christine gripped the table's edge as a sudden muzziness, equal parts disbelief and delight, swept over her. After all this time, three long months, Mr. Belleville was coming to see her? That first week she'd kept watch for him, racing

Mrs. Fitz to the front door every time the knocker clanged. By the second week, she'd relaxed her guard, but still she'd jumped from the table when the morning post came, hoping for a letter, even if someone would have to help her puzzle out the longer words. By the third week, she'd made peace with the terrible truth: Mr. Belleville had washed his hands of her.

But now it seemed that wasn't the case. Twisting her braid round and round her hand, she looked to the headmistress, almost afraid to believe. "Mr. Belleville, he's to come here?"

"Yes, he sent word last night that he would call today at noon. Oh dear . . ." Brow puckering, her violet gaze focused on Christine's right hand.

Christine looked down, heart plummeting. In her nervousness, she'd worked off the bow and now her undone hair streamed over one shoulder. "Deportment?" she said weakly, folding her hands in her lap where they could do no more damage.

"Deportment," Miss Ashcroft confirmed with a nod and a smile, setting her cup on its saucer. "Now run along and find Marie. Tell her I said to heat the curling rod and—" She frowned at the grease streaking Christine's bodice. "—to help you change your gown. The rose silk, I think, and perhaps just a touch of powder."

Along with honesty and loyalty, forthrightness was a quality that Simon both insisted upon and admired. And so later that day, standing in Margot's private drawing room, he should have had cause to be grateful that his friend lost no time in coming directly to the point.

Seating herself on the edge of the apple-green divan, she announced, "Christine has received an offer. Or, rather I've received one on her behalf."

"I see." Feeling his stomach drop, Simon walked over to the piano and lifted the keyboard case. Gliding his fingers over the ebony and ivory keys, he admitted, "I must confess to guessing as much." He reached out to strike a melancholy chord, fighting the surge of cold, sickly emptiness mounting inside him. "I presume the fellow has the funds to keep a wife in some comfort?"

Margot cleared her throat. "It's not that sort of offer. The gentleman, or rather *nobleman,* in question has a different sort of 'keeping' in mind."

Raw fury ripped through Simon. He whipped about. "What the devil . . . How dare . . . *Who* would dare—"

"Basil St. John. He's the second son of Viscount Rutherford, who—"

"I don't give a tinker's damn who he is, he's not getting his bloody mitts on Christine." Blood boiling, he shoved away from the piano and started to pace. "Why didn't you tell me?"

"He only broached the topic a few days ago," Margot answered reasonably. "And I must say you seem less than pleased. You must admit a girl of Christine's background could do far worse." A slight smile touched her lips. "Why, if memory serves me, being the adored mistress of a handsome and wealthy man is not without its merits."

He halted in midstep, reaching for a reply that wouldn't make him seem like a total prude—or, worse yet, a total hypocrite. "I brought Christine to you thinking you would prepare her to marry or to take a position as a lady's maid, perhaps. Never, *never,* did I intend . . . *this.*"

He swiped a hand through his hair, belatedly remembering he'd applied macassar oil. Extracting a handkerchief from his jacket pocket, he asked, "An aristocrat like St. John can have his pick of the most accomplished demireps in London. What could he possibly see in Christine?"

The moment he'd released the words from his mouth, he regretted them, but it was too late. Margot's eyes narrowed and her tone took on an all but forgotten edge. "Christine may have some rough edges in want of smoothing, but she is lovely and sweet-tempered. She also possesses a keen and lively mind, a trait you might have noted had you bothered to visit her so much as once these past months."

She had him there, and they both knew it. Guilt, that most uncomfortable of emotions, began to whittle away at the righteous indignation in which he'd been about to bask. Feeling like a pompous ass, he stuffed the handkerchief back in his pocket and rounded on the fireplace.

Needing something, anything, to occupy his hands, he jerked the poker from its brass rack and used it to stir the banked fire. "What does Christine say to this . . . this proposal?"

"I haven't told her yet. But St. John makes no secret of his preference. He calls nearly every afternoon and showers her with gifts and compliments."

Gifts. Compliments. Afternoon calls. While he had not so much as scribbled a note.

"And of course he's quite good-looking," Margot added. "Why, if I were ten years younger, I might be tempted to—"

"Enough. I take your point." Stabbing the prod into the piled coals, he asked, "And what are Christine's feelings toward this . . . this paragon of the manly virtues?"

"Hm, I'm sure I wouldn't presume to say, but as she's just arrived, why not ask her yourself?"

Bloody, *bloody* hell. He returned the fire iron to the rack, straightened, and slowly, very slowly, turned about. Christine—or rather, the new powdered and perfumed version of her—stood in the open doorway.

Simon caught his breath, his heart kicking from a canter to a full gallop. She was delicate still, the leg-of-mutton sleeves of her rose-colored gown falling back to reveal upper arms scarcely broader than his wrists. But her face was fuller, her cheeks less hollow. And her hair, elaborately dressed and immaculately clean, was the color of toffee.

She was, in a word, lovely. And for the first time in years, Simon felt completely at a loss.

"Christine . . . Miss Tremayne." He started toward her, praying his suddenly wobbling legs wouldn't drop him to the ground.

"Mr. Belleville, how nice to see you again."

She cast a coolly polite nod his way, the perfect image of ladylike refinement—and about as lively as a figure from Madame Tussaud's Waxworks. The transformation stalled Simon in his tracks.

Margot, however, had risen and was making brisk progress toward the door. "I'll just leave you two to entertain one another while I see how our luncheon is progressing. I asked Cook to prepare a few special dishes, but I don't believe she's entirely comfortable with the receipts."

Simon felt something akin to panic closing in on his chest. "No!" he said, surprised to hear Christine join her voice to his. "I mean, must you?"

One foot already in the hallway, Margot turned back. She looked from Simon's heated face to Christine's pinkening cheeks and a small smile touched her lips. "Nonsense, my dear," she said, addressing herself to Christine. "Surely you don't need me hanging about, not when you are the very person Mr. Belleville has come to see. I'll just be off and let you two catch up."

With that, she pulled the door closed behind her but not before Simon detected a slight chuckle.

Left to themselves, Simon and Christine faced each other across the expanse of rose-patterned carpet, tension churning the very air about them.

"Will you sit, sar?" Christine asked, her gaze fixed on some spot beyond him and her slender hands folded in front of her in a single tight little fist.

"No thank you. I mean, not just yet. But please, if you'd care to . . ."

He started to draw out a chair for her, but she shook her head, sending a toffee-colored strand bouncing free of its hairpins. The silky thread brushed the side of her face, touching just below her chin, and Simon had the almost irrepressible urge to coil the tendril about his finger.

But touching her, the *new* her, under any circumstances would be an enormous mistake, and so he wrapped his right hand about his left wrist like a manacle, and blundered on, "Miss Ashcroft informs me you've become quite the pianist."

"I play . . . a little," she conceded, and Simon was torn between tenderness and relief at the familiar little lost look her lovely face now wore.

"A little, is it," he repeated, hard-pressed not to smile. "Well, play something for me now and we shall see just what a *little* constitutes."

She shook her head, and another soft strand slipped free to frame her flushed cheek. "Oh no, I mustn't. I'm not nearly good enough."

"Come now, allow me to be the judge of that. Besides, false modesty is not modesty at all," he teased and before she could refuse again he took light hold of her elbow and steered her over to the piano.

He dropped his hand from her arm with reluctance and stepped back to make room for her to take her place at the keyboard. Even though she gathered in her skirts, she couldn't help but brush against him, and when she did, the scent of her washed over him like an olfactory wave. She smelled nice, delicious even, though he didn't think she wore perfume. Just the bouquet of the soap she'd bathed with, the fragrance of clean hair—clean *woman*.

Seated, she took a moment more to settle in. "What is it you fancy?" she asked, not bothering to look back at him.

You, he wanted to say but of course that would never do.

Instead, he said, "Play whatever it is you play for the other gentlemen who call here. Mr. St. John, does he have a particular favorite?"

Was it his wishful thinking or did her slender shoulders stiffen at his mention of the cad's name? Yes, he thought so, though whether due to guilt or dislike he could not know.

"I wouldn't know, sar," she answered at length. "I've only played for him the once."

She reached for the thick volume of musical scores and began to page through, her fragile-looking fingers with their bitten down nails lifting each vellum leaf and turning it with reverent care.

Gaze on the lovely line of that long, long neck, he leaned closer and poked a finger toward the open book. "What the devil, play whatever score it is you turn to next," he said, when she still couldn't seem to decide.

The gods must be laughing at him indeed, for his *selection* proved to be the plaintive folk song, "Lady Maisry." Listening to Christine's sweet, quavering voice singing of the heroine's illicit liaison with an English nobleman, Simon felt his blood begin to bubble. Damn St. John, whoever he was. He'd see Christine in a convent before he'd hand her over to some spoiled, flighty aristocrat, who would use her and then toss her aside like so much soiled linen.

The idea, the *solution*, came to him in a blinding rush, so brash, so impetuous, so far removed from his normal mode of thinking that just contemplating it made him dizzy. He needed to return to the country to begin courting his constituency. Christine, whether she realized it or not, needed to get away from London—and temptation—as soon as possible. Why not satisfy both objectives by taking her with him? The few London servants he'd bring with him already knew her as his cousin and, once in the country, he could make shift with his housekeeper as a chaperone.

All the while he plotted, his gaze never left Christine's slender hands moving over the keys—the fingernails chewed to the quick, the cuticles and surrounding flesh as raw as freshly butchered beef. Nor could his mind leave off imagining those small, endearingly battered appendages moving over St. John of the good looks, pleasant manner, and impeccable pedigree. Simon had never laid eyes on the man and yet he hated him already—with a passion.

When she came to the part where the English lord bends to kiss his ladylove's lifeless "red ruby lips," Simon's temper had spiked past boiling. "That will be quite enough," he snapped, swiping a hand across his damp brow.

Swinging her skirts over the bench, she shot to her feet, her lithe little body quivering like an arrow released from its bowstring. "I told you that you wouldn't like it. That I wasn't ready to play."

Alas, so much for ladylike sangfroid. Despite himself, he felt another smile tickling the corners of his mouth. "Not above pride, I see, but it was the piece I didn't care for, not your playing. And your voice was, is, very sweet." A horrible thought punctured his temporary good humor and he added, "Is that the ballad St. John had you perform?"

Beneath its fine dusting of powder, her face flushed. He could just make out the healed scar on her cheekbone. "I can't recall what it was I played for him. Nor can I think why you're making such a fuss o'er it," she added, voice rising.

Oddly satisfied, he felt his own temper cooling. Hiding a smile, he observed, "Argumentative, too."

Hands fisted on her hips, Christine glared at him. "I am not argu— Whatever it is you say I am."

"What you are is an impertinent baggage, even saucier and more willful than when I brought you here. Without proper supervision, it will be only a matter of time before you land yourself in similar straits to those in which I found you."

"W-what are you saying?" Her brown eyes, bright with welling tears, searched his face.

Determined to land the blow as kindly as he could, he said, "It is evident that your tenure here has done you considerable good, Christine, and for that I applaud both your diligence and Miss Ashcroft's capabilities. But, that said, I am no longer convinced that London, or indeed this school, is the best environment for shaping your mind—or your morals."

"My morals! But I've done naught wrong," she protested, her thickening dialect some measure of her sincere distress. "Mr. St. John, why except for the dancing, I've not so much as let him hold my hand."

Simon swallowed a sigh of relief. "If that is true, Christine, then I'm heartened to hear it. Even so, I can only imagine how flattering the attentions of a man such as Mr. St. John must seem to a girl in your position. But I assure you," he forged on, brushing aside her sputtering protests, "his intentions toward you are far from honorable."

Crimson pooled on either of her cheeks, reservoirs for the blood draining from the rest of her suddenly pale visage. "And what of *my* intentions? D'ye not think even t'ask me how I feel on the matter? Or," she added, a sadness stealing in to her voice, "is it that you still think of me as you found me? As . . . as a whore?"

He should have upbraided her for so much as speaking the word—she was supposed to be molding herself into some semblance of genteel womanhood after all. But then he saw the first tear fall, and then the second and the third, and the sight was enough to make all his logic, all his reserve, come undone.

Bloody hell. He pulled his handkerchief from his pocket and took a step toward her. "Christine, please. I—"

"Lunch is served," Margot called from the doorway. "I hope you're both hun—" She stopped, switching her gaze from Simon to Christine. "Whatever is the matter?"

Christine lifted her tear-streaked face to the doorway. "He says he's taking me away." As though suddenly sapped of strength, she dropped to the edge of the bench.

"Simon, can this be true?" Margot asked though it occurred to him that her expression was more in keeping with placidity than shock.

"I no longer feel that it is in Christine's best interest to remain in London."

He stole a quick glance at Christine. She looked so miserable, so pathetic, and so very young and lost that he felt the last of his anger turning inward.

"I see," Margot answered, sounding suspiciously calm in Simon's estimation when by rights, she should be furious with him. Could it be that, despite her previous glowing description of St. John, she didn't want Christine to end up with the cad, either?

Coming to stand beside Christine, she settled a hand on her pupil's slumped shoulder. "In that case, may I ask what your plans for Christine's future are? And, more to the point, whether or not you've bothered to discuss them with her?"

Gazing on Christine's stricken face, Simon felt a trickle of shame run through him. But a trickle did not a stream make and even that bit dried up when he reminded himself that it was his duty to save Christine from herself.

He sat down beside her on the bench. His shoulder brushed against hers and she flinched away from him as though she'd been burned. Clearly, she hated him and that he couldn't in good conscience blame her only increased his misery tenfold.

Hoping that someday she'd come to see that he had only her best interest at heart, he said, "Miss Ashcroft informs me that you have a 'keen and lively' mind," he began, pressing the hankie into her hand. "If that is indeed the case, then it's time we turned it to more serious pursuits than waltzing and watercolors."

Margot stalked toward him, and this time there was no doubting that her displeasure was genuine. "You sound as though you mean to turn her into a nun."

Simon tore his gaze from Christine's taut profile with its little red-tipped nose to look up. "Not a nun, Margot. A governess."

For Christine, the rest of that awful afternoon passed in a blur. Perched on the piano bench, she looked from Miss Ashcroft to Mr. Belleville, who'd risen to pace. Although she'd never seen a tennis match, she imagined it would be very much like watching these two lobbing arguments back and forth.

Hands on her hips, Miss Ashcroft repeated, "*You* mean to train her for a governess? *You,* Simon?" Christine couldn't be sure if the headmistress was about to laugh or cry.

Mouth dipped in a scowl, he shot back, "Yes, as a matter of fact, I do. When I built Valhalla, I made certain the library would be extensive. In addition to the several thousand volumes I've purchased over the past year, I have pens, paper, a desk."

"But, Simon," Miss Ashcroft said as though striving for patience. "A classroom is more than simply the raw materials. You know absolutely nothing about teaching."

"I expect I know as much as *some person* did when *she* first began."

Christine turned back to the headmistress, whose porcelain cheeks wore a slight flush. "Well, unlike *that person*, you haven't a grain of patience."

Apparently he couldn't argue there. *Point to Miss Ashcroft.*

"And what about the gossip you were so worried about three months ago?" she demanded, pressing her advantage.

That threw him, but he recovered quickly. "In Kent, she's unlikely to encounter anyone who might know her from—" He coughed. "—From *before*. I can say she's a poor relation, my cousin, and no one will be the wiser. My servants here in town already know her as such."

Miss Ashcroft tossed back her head, sending golden curls swishing over one silk-sheathed shoulder. "Hah! If you think that will satisfy your neighbors, then you obviously haven't spent much time in rural hamlets."

"There are no neighbors, no society, to speak of. At any rate, no one will expect a bachelor to entertain much. By the time the polls open—" He stopped to look down at Christine.

Her cheeks felt stiff as leather from where the tears had dried and she was sure her face and neck were as mottled as a Christmas quilt, but she forced her eyes up to his. "I'll be long gone? Is that what you meant to say?"

"I trust we will have found you a situation by then, yes." He picked up his bowler from the top of the piano and set it on his head. "I should like to leave on Saturday morning. That gives you nearly a full week to settle your affairs and say your good-byes." To Miss Ashcroft he added, "I'll send word regarding the specific arrangements." With a stiff bow to each of them, he turned on his heel and left.

"Well, I suppose that's that," Miss Ashcroft said as his retreating footfalls sounded down the corridor. "I'm sorry. I tried." She sank down on the bench beside Christine.

"I know, ma'am, and I'm grateful for it, truly I am. But, if 'tis all the same to you, I'd like to go to my room now."

Miss Ashcroft lifted her head in a weary nod. "Of course."

Christine spent the rest of that afternoon and evening in her room. Moping might not solve anything and yet there was something inordinately comforting about throwing herself onto her bed and howling into the pillow at the bloody, *bloody*, unfairness of it all. Just when she'd come to think of the school as her home, just when she'd made friends, just when she'd finally learned how to pour the tea through the strainer without spilling half of it, she was to be uprooted.

Things didn't get any easier as the week wore on. On the evening before she was to depart, Miss Ashcroft asked to see her in the drawing room after supper. Christine had planned on retiring early to pack, a chore she could no longer put off given that Mr. Belleville would come for her at eight the next morning, but she could hardly refuse after Miss Ashcroft's many kindnesses. She dragged herself inside, expecting to find the headmistress alone. Instead she crossed the threshold to shouts of "Surprise!" and girls popping out from behind chairs and drapery. A rousing chorus of "For She's a Jolly Good Fellow" followed; an iced plum cake and punch rounded out the festivities.

Misty-eyed, Christine looked about the room, decorated with streamers and brightly colored balloons. Aside from Maddie and Bea, who wore their usual smirks, everyone looked genuinely sorry to see her leave. Certainly she wouldn't miss those two but there were others whom she would miss. Clara, her roommate, a rawboned brewer's daughter, for one. And then there was her other friend Bette, whose mama was a dressmaker but called herself a *modiste* because customers paid more if you sounded French. Most of all, Christine hated the thought of saying good-bye to Miss Ashcroft. Over the past months, she'd come to think of the headmistress as a second mother.

She turned to her now with a tremulous smile and murmured, "Thank you," wishing she could offer more in the way of a speech, but already her throat was closing with emotion.

A plate of cake and a glass of punch in hand, Christine followed Miss Ashcroft over to the seclusion of the sofa set in the far corner.

Seated, Miss Ashcroft said, "I know things haven't turned out as we planned, but we must try to make the best of them. Simon is a hard man, but he's also a very good one. I'm sure he has your best interest at heart."

Christine wasn't convinced Mr. Belleville even had a

heart, but rather than voice her skepticism she took a sip of punch. Madame de Pompadour, who'd been lounging on the velvet sofa cushion, rose and walked onto Christine's lap, sniffing at her untouched cake.

Setting the plate down to the cat, she confided, "The truth is, I've always dreamt of being a teacher."

Relief smoothed the tension from the older woman's lovely face. "Really, Christine. That's marvelous. But why didn't you say so before?"

Christine looked away, shy about confiding something so near and dear to her heart. "Well, I suppose I hadn't thought much about it 'til now. After Mum passed on, there was only me to keep house and to take care of my little brothers and sister. Between that and helping in the dairy, there wasn't time to study for the certification examination."

Miss Ashcroft smiled, but her violet eyes were sad. "Well then things really have turned out for the best."

"Yes, ma'am, I suppose they have."

In more ways than one. Christine had spent the better part of her afternoon perusing the Places Wanted section of *The Times*. The employment listing had confirmed what she'd suspected: a governess earned nearly triple the salary of a village schoolmistress. And with room and board included in the arrangement, she'd be able to send most of her wages to Liza and the boys.

Moreover, losing herself in London was proving to be a more difficult enterprise than she'd ever imagined it would be when she'd first set out. Just that afternoon she'd stumbled across her childhood mate Tommy Fielding on her way back from the newsstand. Wearing a white smock and puffy white cap, he'd been sweeping the pavement outside a bakery. She was fairly certain she'd managed to dart across the street before he'd seen her. Even so, with more and more folk coming into London for work, there was no telling whom she might meet on the bustling city streets. By now all of Nantwich, if not the whole county, would know she'd killed Hareton. It was likely there was a reward for information leading to her capture and arrest. As much as she hated to think about leaving the school, she knew she'd be safer tucked away on Mr. Belleville's private estate. And, assuming she was trainable, afterward she'd take a position as far away from England as she could find.

Miss Ashcroft's voice brought her back to the present. "Train stations have a way of turning me into a watering pot, so I think it's best if we say our good-byes now instead of tomorrow morning." She reached over and gave Christine's hand a squeeze. "You'll write from time to time, I dare say?"

"As best I can." Feeling the pressure building behind her eyes, Christine set the cat aside and rose. Better to go upstairs now before she too turned into a watering pot. She bent to give her mentor a farewell hug. "I'm not much with words, at least not yet, but I'd just like to say thank you for all you've done for me." Throat tight, she pulled out of Miss Ashcroft's embrace and straightened. "I'll never forget it, or you, ma'am, though I live to be as old as my granny did." She thought she'd cried herself out, but a tear slid down her cheek.

A lace handkerchief materialized in Miss Ashcroft's hand. She used it to dab at the corners of her own eyes. "And I'll never forget you, my dear. In fact—" She hesitated. "—Since you're no longer my pupil, I'd like it if you'd call me by my Christian name. Margot."

Lungs tight, Christine backed to the doorway. "I'd be honored . . . Margot."

She turned to go, but Margot's voice stayed her. "If things don't work out with Simon, if you should decide you want to return to London, please know you have a friend here in me. And a home, if you're ever in need of one."

Six

> There's nothing of so infinite vexation
> As a man's own thoughts.
>
> —John Webster,
> *The White Devil,* 1612

Simon spent his final week in town immersed in meetings with his banker, broker, and man of affairs—and doing his utmost to banish Christine from his thoughts. Every time he recalled the look of abject betrayal in her tear-bright eyes when he'd announced his decision to withdraw her from the academy, he felt like an ogre. Work became more than a duty; it was his solace, his *refuge.* Yet no matter how late he remained at his desk, how exhausted he was when he finally sank into bed, like a capricious spirit refusing to be cast out, Christine flitted in and out of his conscious and unconscious brain.

But Simon was long accustomed to being haunted; guilt, after all, had been his boon companion for nearly twenty years. On the eve of his departure, there was yet one ghost with whom duty and the ties of familial affection compelled him to commune. One on whose behalf he had far greater cause for contrition than he need feel for Christine Tremayne. His sister, Rebecca. Dreading the evening ahead, he called for his town coach and set out for his stepfather's house in Whitechapel.

Mordechai lived in Goodman's Fields, a middle-class community of tailors, weavers, and glassmakers. When a sixteen-year-old Simon had first clapped eyes on the three-storied brick town house where his new stepfather had brought the three of them to live, he'd exclaimed, "Blimey, Ma, we're rich!"

Back then, the house and its surrounds had seemed a veritable paradise. Brushing back the leather window curtain as his carriage turned onto Leman Street, Simon marveled at how age, experience—and money—had tempered his perception of the place. Even lit by a brilliant sunset, the façades of coal-blackened brick seemed squalid rather than grand; the postage stamp–sized front yards were weed-riddled and pathetic.

His driver drew up beneath the leafless branches of a mulberry tree. Dread dropping anchor in his breast, Simon stepped down from the coach. The cooking fumes of boiled cabbage and grease hovered in the chilly winter air, clinging to the folds of his greatcoat like oily ghosts from a past that refused to stay buried. *What would Christine Tremayne think of me if she saw me now?* he mused, turning sluggish footsteps toward the end house where propped inside the thick glass of the bowfront window a sign proclaimed, "Tailoring done here." Steeling himself, he climbed the sagging brick steps to the front door and lifted the knocker.

Mordechai's shop manager and chief cutter opened the door. "Shalom, Master Simon."

Stepping inside to the jingling of the shop bell above the lintel, Simon doffed his hat. "Good evening, Rubin. I hadn't thought to find you still here."

"Not for much longer." Rubin reached for the black hat hanging on a peg by the door. "I am just on my way home. Master Mordechai is above." He waved a hand to indicate the wooden staircase at the back of the house, then hurried out the door.

Six days a week the ground floor of Mordechai's house buzzed with activity from dawn until dark. Simon knew this because his mother, Lilith, had found work there as a seamstress. It was not long before the attractive widow drew the notice of the bachelor tailor. Mordechai's proposal of marriage had been the saving of their fractured family, and his gentleness toward Rebecca eventually earned Simon's grudging acceptance. Being able to once more practice the rituals and traditions of her faith had seemed to bring Lilith, if not happiness, a measure of contentment.

Tonight was Friday, and the tailors and seamstresses had been released early to celebrate the Sabbath. Simon filed past the silent machines and deserted cutting tables toward the back of the shop. Doffing his hat, he mounted the set of narrow wooden stairs leading to his stepfather's second-floor living quarters.

He stepped off the stairs and passed through the short, open gallery that overlooked the shop floor to Mordechai's private apartments. The door stood ajar, a clear sign that Simon was expected. Drawing a deep breath, he crossed the threshold. He tossed his hat upon the surface of a scarred console table and shrugged free of his coat, then made his way through the comfortably cluttered parlor to the dining room.

Seated at the head of the round cloth-covered table, Mordechai looked up from his prayer book as Simon approached. "So you've come after all?"

"It would seem so." Slipping into his customary seat, Simon glanced across the table to the empty chair on Mordechai's left. Dreading the answer, he nonetheless asked, "Where is Rebecca?"

Mordechai closed the worn leather volume and laid it aside. "Our Rebecca had a bad night last night. I am not certain she will be joining us."

Simon's spirits, already low, sunk another notch. "I see." He reached for the decanter of red wine and filled his glass.

"Do not look so downtrodden. I administered the laudanum, and she slept peacefully most of this afternoon. She may awaken before too long."

Mrs. Milstein, one of a handful of neighborhood matrons who cooked for Mordechai since Simon's mother was carried away by the cholera epidemic of '53, emerged from the kitchen.

She hefted a huge soup tureen onto the edge of the table. "Shalom, Master Simon," she said, ladling soup into Simon's bowl.

"Mrs. Milstein." Simon passed the full bowl to his stepfather, then handed her the empty one to be filled.

The obligatory prayers said, Simon waited until she'd returned to the kitchen before dipping his spoon into the pottage. He took a cautious sip.

Pleasantly surprised, he shot a backward glance to the kitchen where the matron busied herself with carving the lamb. Leaning toward his stepfather, he whispered, "I'm glad this one can cook."

Mordechai sent him a conspiratorial wink. "And she's not bad-looking either."

Simon grinned. "A widow, I take it?"

Buried in the folds of his gray beard, Mordechai's mouth lifted in a smile. "And rich. Her husband owned one of the finest bakeries in Spitalfields. Most mornings, there is a line from the door all the way to the Tower."

A baker's widow. Simon almost snorted his contempt for what passed for wealth in this narrow world. "I'll never understand why you insist upon staying here. Why not retire and let me buy you a house in Knightsbridge or Richmond?"

Mordechai's high brow wrinkled. "This is my home. Your mother's grave is here. My *shop* is here. I have no wish to leave either, thank you very much."

Stubborn old man. Simon shook his head, torn between respect and annoyance. "Next you'll be telling me I belong here as well."

His stepfather's scowl softened, then disappeared into an expression akin to pity. "No, my boy, you belong out there, in the wider world. I only wish you would find happiness in it. This restless ambition of yours, these dark thoughts of revenge, they are a scourge to your soul. You will never find peace until you put them aside."

Sensing the onset of the same tired old argument, Simon pushed his bowl aside and reached for his wine. "I will know peace the day the deed to The Priory is mine. The day I approach the Speaker and take the Parliamentary oath."

Mordechai's eyes narrowed. "And this oath, you will take it 'on the true faith of a Christian'?" He lifted a brow, waiting.

Simon stiffened. "Disraeli did."

"I'm not asking him, I'm asking you."

"Very well then, yes, if I must."

Mordechai opened his mouth as if to reply but whatever reproach he'd intended withered to a sigh. "In so many ways you are your mother's child. You have her passion, her fire."

Simon glanced down at his right hand. The onyx signet ring he wore on his middle finger was his sole legacy from the family that had exiled him. "Better I take after her than after a weakling like Father."

Mordechai shook his grizzled head. "He was human, Simon. It was a different life he was bred for. Your mother knew this. She never faulted him for it."

Simon clenched the stem of his goblet. "She never saw him clearly."

"When you love someone, you overlook their failings. She loved him with all her heart as I loved her. Love, it is the greatest gift—and the greatest lesson—life offers us. Sometimes it seems as though it will cleave us in two, and yet we can never be whole without it. I only pray you find it someday before it's too late."

Simon was about to tell him to save his prayers when Rebecca drifted in. "Simon!" Eyes alight, she rushed toward him, long black hair flying like a windswept sail. "I am so happy to see you."

"And I you, Becca." He summoned a smile, although the sight of her always sliced his heart to ribbons. On her next birthday she would be thirty-seven, yet the face she turned up to his was guileless as a young girl's.

She pulled back. As if suddenly recalling the doll in her arms, she shoved it toward him. "Simon, look at Miss Lucy. Rubin sewed her a new dress. See, it has real seed pearls on the front. Doesn't she look pretty?"

"Very pretty," he replied, pretending to admire the doll's bashed and peeling face. As Rebecca's sole confidante since the rape, Miss Lucy had weathered many an emotional storm over the years. A few years ago, he'd bought a lovely replacement, but Rebecca would have nothing to do with it.

"Rebecca," Mrs. Milstein called from the kitchen. "It is time to put Miss Lucy aside and have your supper. I have some lovely soup for you. You must eat it while it is hot."

Rebecca's brow creased. Her gray eyes, a mirror image of Simon's, turned stormy. "I'm not hungry, and I won't eat your horrid soup. I want my mama. Where is my mama?"

Clutching the doll, she burst into tears. Mrs. Milstein hurried from the kitchen. Casting an apologetic look at Simon, she put an arm about Rebecca's thin shoulders and shepherded her toward her bedchamber at the back of the house.

Mordechai broke off a piece of challah bread and handed it to Simon. "You still blame yourself." It wasn't a question.

No longer hungry, Simon laid the bread on his plate and reached for his wine. "Why shouldn't I when it was my fault?"

Mordechai slammed his fist upon the table. In the wake of rattling cutlery and glassware, he thundered, "It was the fault of those evil men. When will you see you were not to blame?"

Simon couldn't help it. He slammed his own glass, sending wine lopping the sides. "Not to blame? When she begged me to take her home, I should have listened. Instead I insisted we deliver the cloth that night."

Mordechai shook his grizzled head. "You were fifteen years old, a boy trying to fill a man's shoes. Perhaps if you could forgive yourself, you might learn to forgive others?"

They had waged the same argument even before Simon had left for India. Suddenly too weary to travel that well-trod path, he pushed back from the table and rose. "I should go."

Mordechai followed him through the apartment to the door. "Simon, do you think to run from this the rest of your life?"

"I'm leaving for Kent early tomorrow morning. I expect to remain there through spring." He retrieved his hat and tossed his coat over his arm. "Tell Rebecca I'll write."

On the other side of town, Christine was wrestling with demons of her own. Jittery with nerves about her next day's journey, she spent the evening packing her greatly multiplied belongings into the three traveling trunks Margot had donated. The daunting task at last complete, she retired at nine only to lie awake for hours listening to Clara snoring from the little cot across from hers. It was only after the hallway clock chimed one that she finally fell into a fitful doze.

"Ye've been a bad girl, Chrissie," Hareton spat, backing her up to the cottage's fireplace grate until the leaping flames nearly licked her skirts.

Fueled by fear, Christine's body took on a will of its own. She reached behind, and somehow the poker found its way into her sweating hand.

Raising the iron high, she said, "Liza and the boys are somewhere where ye'll ne'er lay hands on 'em as soon I'll be. Now stand aside."

But instead of moving away, he closed in on her, a silly grin splitting his face. "Now we both knows 'ee ain't got it in ye to use that thing. Better give it o'er, luv, before one o' us gets hurt."

Before one of us gets hurt.

As always, fact and fiction, reason and fear, blended to produce the dream's terrifying finale. They'd found Hareton. Found him as she'd left him, lifeless on the cottage floor, the bloody poker lying beside him where, in her panic, she'd cast it. There'd been no getting around the damning evidence, for hadn't she gone missing that very night, her cousin's blood blotting the front of her frock? Convicted, she saw herself standing on the open scaffold, hands bound, a raw wind whipping her hair about her face, the noose biting into her neck. Congregated below, the men and women, boys and girls of Nantwich raised their voices in a single chant: *"Murderess, murderess!"*

Then the dream altered. The crowd fell away, leaving only one dark figure silhouetted against the gunmetal gray landscape. Simon Belleville stared up at her with his dark, sad eyes, a softer wind whispering through his raven-colored locks. She called to him that she hadn't meant to kill Hareton, only to stun him. That she wasn't a murderess, not really. But the hemp about her throat was cinched tight, and none of her words came out above a croak.

"It was an accident," she tried again even as she wondered why, at her life's end, she should care that Simon Belleville of all people knew the truth. But she did care. Deeply. She was still calling to him when the trapdoor beneath her gave way. Suddenly she was kicking air, fighting for breath, fighting the rope. Fighting to hold Mr. Belleville's gaze, to make him understand, even as he shook his head and mouthed the word, "Murderess."

"I'm not a murderess!"

"Christine, love, wake up!"

Christine bolted upright, nightgown clinging to her damp skin. Blinking against the bright light that streamed the room, she turned to Clara.

Already dressed in day clothes, her roommate stood between their two beds, concern knitting her freckled forehead. "You were having another a nightmare."

A nightmare. Christine started to shake her head, thought better of it, and managed a nod instead. The dream's terrifying conclusion might not have happened—yet—but the episode in the cottage was only too true. A permanent mark on her soul, it was as much a part of her as the color of her hair or the shape of her too-wide mouth.

Shivering, she dragged a hand through her tangled hair and looked from Clara's concerned face to the clock on her bedside table. The small hand pointed to seven, the large to six.

Good Lord, it was seven-thirty! And Mr. Belleville was coming for her at eight. She leapt from bed and flew past Clara to the washstand. Counting herself fortunate that a footman had hauled her trunks downstairs the night before, she splashed water on her face, then dressed quickly in the wine-colored carriage dress, fur-trimmed wool cloak, and sturdy half boots.

After bidding Clara a hasty and tearful farewell, she bolted down the hallway to the stairs, Puss's traveling basket in one hand and her carpetbag in the other.

She found Mr. Belleville in the front hall wearing holes in the carpet. One hand clenched about the handle of his writing case, he used the other to brandish his timepiece, rounding on her as she stepped off the stair landing. "You're late."

She glanced at the watch face, then back at him. "Only by five minutes. Puss didn't want to go into the basket."

"Late is late," he muttered, reaching for the carrier. "You and that blasted feline of yours will be the ruin of me yet."

"If that's the way you feel about it..." She pulled the basket out of reach and handed him the carpetbag instead.

Scowling at the needlepoint roses, he huffed, "Come along. The carriage is waiting." The baggage in hand, he strode toward the front door.

That interchange set the tone for the rest of the morning. On the way to London Bridge Station, they sat in hostile silence on opposite seats, every now and again bumping knees when the driver found a rut in the road. At the station, Mr. Belleville purchased their tickets, turned their luggage over to a porter, and then deftly steered Christine through the throng and up the stairs to the South Eastern Railway line—all while more or less ignoring her.

It wasn't until they'd boarded one of the smart yellow-and-black first-class coaches near the train's front that he deigned to address her.

"Have you taken breakfast?" It sounded more like an accusation than a question.

Settling into the plushly upholstered seat by the window, Christine considered lying, then remembered he'd seen her come downstairs. "No." And then, because she couldn't resist, she added, "There wasn't *time*."

"And now there is." He reached inside his coat pocket and withdrew a crinkled brown paper bag. "Consider breakfast, such as it is, to be served."

Eying the bag, Christine remembered that before boarding he'd excused himself to duck inside one of the canopied vendor's stalls lining the station side of the train platform. Her first reaction was to be touched that he'd gone to the trouble for her; then she recalled his earlier harsh words and her temper bubbled.

She folded her arms across her chest, lifted her chin, and speared him with her sharpest look. "No thank you."

"Suit yourself." He tossed the bag onto the empty seat beside her. "In the event that martyrdom loses its charm," he explained with a wink.

"Humph." She might not know what *martyrdom* meant but she knew when she was being made fun of. Face warm, she cut her gaze from the bag to him. "Whoever sits there can have it for all I care."

"Suit yourself." He reached for his fountain pen. He didn't look up, but she heard the smile in his voice when he said, "As there are no other passengers, you may as well swallow that pride of yours and eat it. No crow, I promise. Just an apple and some tea biscuits."

She opened her mouth to demand he stop teasing her when a question intruded. "You mean to say we have this great big car all to ourselves?"

He shrugged. "I dislike being crowded, so I purchased all six seats."

"Oh."

To have money enough to purchase an entire first-class compartment! Christine was still trying to get her mind around the notion when she heard the clang of the starting bell, the bellowing of the whistle, and finally the sudden, thrilling tug as the locomotive lurched forward. Heart pumping, she pressed her nose to the window, hungry gaze devouring every spire, every bridge. Only after the tall buildings gave way to familiar green fields did she settle back against her seat and return her attention to her traveling companion.

Sifting through the contents of the writing case he'd lifted onto his lap, Mr. Belleville didn't appear to share her enthusiasm. He sat next to the window, but not once had he bothered to look out. Studying his bowed head, she found herself shaking her own. Simon Belleville might have thousands, even *millions,* of pounds in the bank, but he hadn't a shilling's worth of fun shored up in his whole body.

A rumble issuing forth from Christine's empty stomach cut short further reflection. One eye on Mr. Belleville, she walked her fingers over to the brown paper bag next to her. Wincing at the crinkling sound, she was wondering how she'd ever manage to open the biscuit tin when, without looking up, he said, "Hungry after all?"

That was it, the final straw. She hurled the bag at him. It hit him squarely on the chest, then slipped to his lap.

He glanced down at the apple rolling on the carpeted floor between them. "Had I known you were inclined to throw food, I would have let you ride in third-class."

She stabbed a quaking forefinger at him. "I didn't ask you to buy me breakfast, I didn't ask you to send me to school, and I most certainly didn't ask you to take me with you to Kent. This is all your bloody doing, so don't blame me now that you've decided you're sorry for it."

He frowned. "Whatever makes you think that?"

The angry words came tumbling out and, along with them, the hurt. "What you said before about me and Puss bein'—*being*—the ruin of you."

For a moment, he looked at her in confusion. Then his gaze sharpened, as if only now recalling the cutting comment. "Still harping on that, are we? By God, you must be as thin-skinned as an onion."

"I'm not harping. And . . . and don't blaspheme."

He stared at her as though she'd just sprouted a third eye, then he threw back his head and . . . laughed! The rumbling came from deep in his chest, the sound husky yet rich. She'd never seen him smile before let alone laugh. The flesh crinkled at the corners of his smoky eyes, and the lines bracketing his mouth softened. He had a beautiful smile, his teeth strong and straight. Her gaze settled on the thin ribbon of his upper lip, and she felt her heart go *pitter-patter*.

Then she recalled he was laughing not with her but *at* her. Spine stiffening against the seat back, she lifted her chin. "What are you laughing at?"

He dashed a hand at the corner of one eye. "You," he answered without hesitation. "You're such a paradox." He must have read her confusion because he quickly added, "A puzzle, a contradiction in terms."

"I am not!" she snapped, wishing he didn't always have to use such complicated words.

"It's not an insult, you know." He took up his silver fountain pen and began scratching notations on the newspaper in his neat, tightly controlled script. A moment later, he was completely absorbed, their quarrel—and her—as good as forgotten.

Christine picked up the apple. Passing it from palm to palm, she pretended she was Salome and the apple was Simon Belleville's severed head. Considerably cheered, she chomped into the fruit.

They passed through a tunnel and the compartment grew dim. Bored because there was nothing really to see, around a mouthful of apple, she asked, "What are you reading?"

Gaze on the printed page, he answered, "the *Times* and don't speak with your mouth full."

Ignoring the rebuke, she asked, "Does it carry an installment from one of Mr. Dickens's novels?"

This time he looked over at her, the pen suspended in midair. "Hardly. In addition to foreign dispatches, the *Times* prints in full the latest parliamentary debates and papers."

"Oh." Personally Christine couldn't imagine anything more deadly dull. After a moment's hesitation, she asked, "And you *like* reading such things?"

His head snapped up. He dropped the pen and glared. "In addition to being a British subject, I mean to stand for Maidstone in the next general election."

"Oh, well then." Unwilling to let the conversation die, she asked, "Do you think you might win?"

This time when he glanced up his eyes were as hard as stones. "I *will* win."

Now who's being thin-skinned? "My, my but aren't we the confident one," she said with a smile, gratified to have the upper hand this once.

He answered with a snort and then returned to his paper. Her moment of glory at an end, she wrapped up the apple core and turned her head to the window. They'd cleared the tunnel, and the tall, imposing buildings of London had given way to thatched cottages, whitewashed churches, and frost-parched fields. The familiarity of the scene made her heart ache for home. For family. She squeezed her eyes shut as the homesickness, the longing to look upon those three dear faces, twisted her heart. But she'd rather die than endanger them, which, for the foreseeable future, meant staying far away. Blinking back tears, she glanced over to the man who was helping her do just that.

To her horror, he was looking straight at her. "What were you thinking just now?"

Startled as much by the question as the intensity of those gray eyes riveted on her face, it took her a moment to find her voice. "I was thinking of my family, sar."

"You miss them very much?"

"Yes. Yes, I do."

"And you're worried for them too I think?" Hoping to let the matter lie, she nodded and then turned back to the window. Instead he said, "You needn't be, you know. I am more than happy to provide for their needs until you secure employment."

She whipped her head about. "Oh, no, sar. That wouldn't be right. They're my responsibility, not yours."

He muttered something about her being mulish and a fool but in the end he said, "Call it a loan then, if you like."

"Once I get on my feet, I'll pay you back. Every penny," she added, because suddenly it was so very important that he not think her a moneygrubber.

"As you wish," he answered and then turned back to his work. Christine was minded she'd yet to say thank-you when the train whistle blew and the conductor bellowed, "Ashford."

A fine rain greeted them as they stepped out onto the platform. Mr. Belleville's coach awaited them on the other side of the entrance gate. Peering through the wrought-iron bars, Christine knew at once which vehicle belonged to him, for wasn't it bigger, shinier, and blacker than any of the others waiting in queue? A matching team of four black stallions stood in harness at the front, their plumed headgear waving in the chilly wind.

Sighting them, the driver climbed down from the box and hurried forward, a big black umbrella held aloft. "Good'ay, sir, miss. I'm terrible sorry about the rain," he apologized, as though the weather were his personal responsibility. "The sun was shining bright as a copper an hour ago." He doffed his hat and Christine glimpsed the roan-colored curls wreathing his cherub's face.

"No matter, Jem," Mr. Belleville assured him. "I don't pay you enough to hold you responsible for the weather."

Christine used her gloved hand to muffle a giggle for hadn't she just thought the very same thing. Might it be that the man had some sense of humor after all?

Mr. Belleville tipped the porter who'd carted out their trunks, then took the umbrella and positioned it over Christine's head.

"Shall we?" he asked, already steering her toward the carriage. He settled her inside, then took the seat across from hers.

Jem poked his head inside the window on Christine's side. "Shall I load that too miss, or will you be wantin' to keep it wi' you?"

Christine followed his gaze to the basket on the seat beside her. "Oh, this is my cat."

"A cat, you say?" Mischievous blue eyes slanting to his employer, he grinned. "Well, that's just dandy. I'm terrible partial to cats myself. What kind is he?"

A cat lover! Christine felt herself warming to him already. "Puss's a she, actually. A tabby. Black and silver with four little white paws just like—"

"I don't suppose we might leave now?" Leaning forward, Mr. Belleville settled his scowl on Jem.

"O' course, sir, we'll be off in a jiffy, just as soon as I finish loadin' your trunks."

The baggage loaded, Jem climbed up into the driver's seat and soon they were rambling over heavily rutted dirt roads. Christine propped her feet atop the warm flannel-wrapped brick and snuggled deeper beneath the plaid blanket. Smothering a yawn inside her glove, she leaned back against the plush leather squabs and let her eyes drift closed.

She'd intended only to rest her eyes but, when she opened them next, the coach was at a standstill.

"Welcome back," Mr. Belleville called from the opposite seat.

Blinking gritty eyes, she turned from him to look out the window.

And caught her breath. If Mr. Belleville's London residence had seemed a mansion, his country house amounted to a castle. A fortress of granite, its pinnacle-topped turrets seemed to strain to touch the cloud-banked sky. In keeping with the master's temperament, griffins and gargoyles snarled and snapped from every visible nook and cranny.

"I call it Valhalla."

She turned back inside. "Vale Hollow?" A queer name since they were neither in a vale nor hollow but rather on a vast expanse of flat, open land.

"*Valhalla*. In Norse mythology, Valhalla is the great hall where the souls of heroes slain in battle are received."

"Like heaven?"

"More or less."

Jem opened the door. "Easy does it, miss," he cautioned, helping her down the carriage steps as though she were of china made. " 'Twas ice on the path this mornin'."

Following her out, Mr. Belleville shot Jem a withering glare and then offered Christine his arm. She hesitated, then took it, and together they crossed the brickwork forecourt to the marble steps leading up to the entrance. Two liveried footmen appeared on either side of an archway guarded by two stone lions and held the massive oak double doors for them to pass through. Stomach fluttering, Christine stepped inside the entrance hall. Beeswax and lemon oil hung heavily in the air, and the dark mahogany paneled walls gleamed as though freshly polished. She tilted her head and backed up to better view the vaulted ceiling. It reminded her of a church as did the bank of stained-glass windows flanking the open, spiral staircase.

Mr. Belleville's London housekeeper, Mrs. Griffith, padded down the Persian carpet to greet them. "Welcome home, sir, miss. You had a pleasant trip, I hope?"

"*Restful*, to be sure." Stripping off his gloves, his dark gaze slid to Christine.

Feeling herself flushing, she set her basket down and started on the buttons of her cloak. Until now, her destination had seemed a vague dream. But standing by as Jem lugged her trunks up the steps and set them inside the doorway, reality bore down on her with the intensity of a rolling boulder. Suddenly everything—the journey, the house, the man standing beside her—struck her as frightfully *real*.

Mr. Belleville handed Mrs. Griffith his coat and hat, then looked to the brass-faced grandfather's clock. "Tea in the library, Mrs. Griffith, in ten minutes." He hesitated, looking back at Christine. "Unless, of course, you prefer to be shown directly to your room?"

"Oh no," she answered much too quickly, "I'm not at all tired. I should like to see your house." Her guardian might not be the warmest of companions, but she wasn't yet ready to face his great hulk of a house on her own.

He met her gaze. "Very well then. See it you shall."

She fancied she saw a twitching about the corners of his chiseled mouth, as though he were stifling an inner smile. Before she could be sure, he took off. Christine hung her cloak on one of the bowers of the massive oak hall tree and started after him. Puss's loud mewl prompted her to turn back.

"Not to fret, m'dear," Mrs. Griffith assured her, following her gaze to Puss's basket setting inside the door. "He'll be in your room waitin' for you. I'll send up a dish of cream and some water. And," she added, glancing significantly in her employer's direction, "a box of sand."

"Thank you." Christine sent her a grateful smile, then bolted after Mr. Belleville, who'd just turned left at the stairs and disappeared from view.

Following the sound of his footfalls down the sconce-lit corridor, she finally caught up beneath an elaborately carved archway.

"After you," he prompted, holding the door for her.

Peering inside, Christine's first impression was of velvet-shrouded windows, thick Oriental carpets, and dark, ponderous furnishings. As she stepped over the threshold, heart quaking, she was reminded of the nursery rhyme, "Will you walk into my parlour?" said the Spider to the Fly.

All too aware of her guardian's dark gaze boring into her back, she fancied she knew just how that poor fly must have felt.

Seven

A weed is no more than a flower in disguise,
Which is seen through at once, if love give a man eyes.

—James Russell Lowell,
"A Fable for Critics,"
1848

Simon was proud of his house. Every gabled niche, every soffit-nestled griffin and gargoyle, every traceried window bore witness to how far he'd progressed in his life. But he'd never been prouder than he was now as he stood back and watched Christine roam his library. Upon crossing the threshold, she'd barely taken time to remove her bonnet and gloves before rushing forward to the three shelves of floor-to-ceiling books. Running reverent fingertips over the tooled leather spines, occasionally calling out a familiar title, she wore on her lovely face the perfect blend of reverence and delight. Simon felt his chest swell just looking at her.

At last she dragged her attention away from the open book she cradled between her palms. Peering back over her shoulder, she exclaimed, "There must be hundreds of books in here."

"Thousands actually." Arms folded, he leaned a hip against the side of his pedestal desk and added, "I'm glad you like it."

"Like it! I've never seen so many books, and to think they all belong to one person."

She still pronounced *person* as *parson*, but at the moment he lacked the will to point out the error. Her praise, the look on her heart-shaped face reminded him of how little comfort she'd known in her life until now, of how much more he had than most people. That he'd earned it all by the proverbial sweat of his brow no longer seemed to signify. He'd hoarded it like the worst of misers.

He met her wide gaze through lowered lashes. "Yes."

"Have you really read all of these?"

"Some, not all." He unfolded his arms and picked up the small bronze figurine of Siva, the Hindu god of creation and destruction, set at one corner of his desk blotter. Turning it in his hand, he added, "I read a great deal more when I was younger."

Christine's astonished gaze shot to his face. "But not now?"

Was that censure he detected? Stiffening, he set the statue down and faced her. "I'm obliged to read a great deal—stock reports, account ledgers, political periodicals. There's little time left for leisure."

She pulled a face, a habit he made a mental note to break her of. "Sounds terrible dull. Don't you miss 'em, books, I mean?"

This time he didn't resist. "That would be *terribly* dull and yes, on occasion I do miss reading for pleasure. However, to progress in life, one must make sacrifices."

Harsh, Simon. You sound as stern as a Methodist minister. A God-awful thought if ever there was one.

He moved away from the desk. Coming up behind her, he glanced down at the gold-leafed volume she held open. *Alice's Adventures in Wonderland.* A pen-and-ink drawing of diminutive Alice standing before three closed doors and reaching for a cake marked "Eat Me" filled half of one page. Looking from the picture back up to her, he wondered if she grasped the parallels between Alice's story and her own. Both were little more than children, wide-eyed and dangerously eager to hurl themselves down the rabbit hole. Like Alice, Christine had known more than her share of misadventures but, in the end, she'd prevailed. Accompanying him to Kent was tantamount to her stepping through a looking glass into a bright new world of previously unimaginable possibilities.

Wondering if that made him the White Rabbit—or the Mad Hatter—he said, "But that doesn't mean *you* shouldn't enjoy my library. Take from it anything you like, starting with this if you fancy it."

She turned to him so fast she nearly dropped the book. "Truly?" She looked as though he'd just given her the keys to the kingdom—or at least to the tiny door leading to Wonderland's garden.

Feeling ten feet tall and fighting a ticklish twitching that threatened to lift the corners of his mouth, he answered, "Of course, provided you complete your lessons first."

"I will, sar, every last one. And I'll take very good care of your books, you needn't worry about that."

Looking into her big brown eyes, he said, "My dear Miss Tremayne, of all my worries in life, that is the very least."

She replaced the book on the shelf. After a long moment that, he suspected, she used to memorize its location, she turned to face him. "I never know what to think when I'm with you. How to tell if you're serious or . . ." She trailed off.

When she didn't say more, he lifted her chin on the edge of his hand and prompted, "Or . . . ?"

"If you're mockin' me."

He swallowed hard. She was so young, so open, and so very fresh. He thought back to his homecoming from India. In one sense he'd returned a man of the world, wealthy and well-traveled. And yet, as far as *civilized society* was concerned, he'd been painfully awkward, woefully inept. Even now, certain memories still had the power to make him cringe.

Feeling like the lowest of beasts for having inflicted a similar torture, he said, "Tweaking you, perhaps, but I'd never mock you."

The knock sounding outside the door caused them to break apart. Christine stepped back and Simon dropped his hand, which, he was annoyed to see, shook.

"That will be our tea," he said and then gave the call to enter.

A parlor maid entered with the tea service, a massive silver affair. She headed for the leather-covered sofa and suite of chairs that occupied one sheltered alcove and set the tray down on the gate-leg table.

Time to put Christine's hostess skills to the test. Simon shook his head. "That will be all for now. My cousin will do the honors."

"Very good, sir." The girl bobbed a quick curtsey, then backed toward the door.

"Well," he said upon hearing it shut. "Shall we?"

Face grave, Christine followed him to the chair he held for her. Reaching out, she touched the crocheted doily covering its back, her eyes lifting to him in question.

Throat suddenly thick, he admitted, "My mother made that."

She touched the yellowed scrap with the same gentle reverence with which she'd touched his books. "My mum was handy with a needle too. Me, I'm all thumbs." She held her hands up, tucked her four fingers, and wiggled both thumbs.

She was stalling, but she did it so charmingly that Simon found he couldn't be angry. On impulse, he crossed to the front of her chair and took her hands in each of his. "Hm, let's have a look, shall we?"

He held her hands up, then turned them over in his. The cuts had healed long ago and the calluses on her palms looked to have softened, but the insides of her little thumbs were still work-roughened, the nails of all ten fingers chewed to the quick.

"Pretty thumbs. Pretty fingers," he said, giving them back to her. "They'd be even prettier if you'd stop gnawing on them."

She gave a little laugh. "That's just what Mum used to say."

"Wise woman, your mother. I'm guessing she also told you to drink your tea while it's still hot." She grimaced and he added, "You've had your reprieve, Miss Thumbs. Take a seat and pour. And mind you don't spill on the carpet. It's Persian and worth a bloody fortune."

Her manners weren't precisely those of a lady but they were better than he'd dare to hope. She managed to pour their tea without major incident and once she'd handed him his cup and saucer, she seemed to relax. There was no doubt she savored her food. She ate heartily but slowly, her movements marked by a careful, measured grace. If she occasionally answered his questions before swallowing or slathered cream on an entire scone rather than breaking off a bite-sized bit, he was inclined to be lenient. From his own painstaking development, he knew social polish—even the thinnest of veneers—required considerably more time than the three months Christine had spent at school. Rome wasn't built in a day; neither were gentlefolk.

"Why do you go to this trouble for me?" she finally asked around a mouthful of poppy-seed cake. "To say you'll be my teacher, train me for a governess, when you're set to stand for Parliament?"

Surveying the smoked salmon and cucumber finger sandwich on his plate, he thought for a moment. It was an excellent question, one he'd asked himself many times over the past week. "Someone once went to a great deal of trouble to help me. I suppose helping you is my way of repaying that debt."

If it hadn't been for Margot, he'd still be eating cheese from his knife and wearing polka dots with stripes. But the deeper, underlying truth was that he was drawn to Christine. Why, he had yet to discover. Was it because she was young and lovely, brave but alone? Because helping her make something of herself would be his first unselfish act in almost twenty years? Not totally unselfish. Being with her, simply sitting with her over tea, helped to salve the dull, hollow ache inside him. He'd lived with that emptiness for years yet only in the past few months had he acknowledged that yes, something was absent from his life. From *him*.

Eyeing his sandwich, she leaned over and added one to her own plate. "Miss Ashcroft, you mean?"

Caught off guard, he nearly choked on his tea. Setting his cup down onto his saucer, he demanded, "Did she tell you that?"

Munching her sandwich, she shook her head. "No, it was just a feeling I got."

"A feeling?" he echoed, a whole host of alarm bells sounding off in his head.

She nodded again. "From seeing the both of you together."

What a canny little thing she was, dangerously so. Vowing to keep up his guard about her in the future, he set his cup and saucer aside and rose. A gentleman would have bided his time until she'd finished, but then he was no gentleman, just as Christine Tremayne was no lady with whom he need mind his p's and q's.

"If you've finished with your tea," he hinted broadly, "I'd like to show you the rest of Valhalla."

Swallowing, she picked up her napkin and dusted the crumbs from her lips. "I'd like that too."

Valhalla was so massive that, by the time they'd come full circle, Christine had a hard time believing it was one house. Going from room to room, each more lavish than the last, she knew the same spine-tingling sense of awe, the same certainty of belonging to something larger and grander than herself, as she had on excursions with Miss Ashcroft to the British Museum, the Houses of Parliament, and St. Paul's Cathedral.

"The master bedroom and the larger guest rooms all have fitted bathrooms," he told her, closing the door on a masculine sitting room with tooled leather walls, walnut furnishings, and heavy velvet drapery.

"How many rooms are there?" she asked, following him out into the hallway.

He had to stop to think. "Fifty-odd, if you count the kitchen and those in the servants' wing."

Fifty-odd. Christine was about to ask who, other than the royal family possibly, could need so many rooms when they approached an arched doorway. Stopping to gaze out the clear glass panes, Christine saw that the double doors opened onto a balcony overlooking the back of the house. Rooks roosted on the carved stone parapet, and Christine found herself envying them. To come and go as you pleased. To fly about wherever your fancy took you, free of want. Free of fear. Would she ever know even a measure of such liberty?

She looked back to where Mr. Belleville waited, taut with impatience, on the stairwell. "Can we go out there?" she asked, suddenly desperate for fresh air and light.

When she'd first arrived, she'd wondered that the lamps were lit while it was still daylight. She'd quickly learned the reason. Valhalla's many stained-glass and leaded windows were beautiful, but they made for a dark house. And, with the windows and doors closed against the cold, it was easy to feel stifled.

"It's the middle of winter. There's nothing to see but a great lot of withered weeds. Besides, you've left your coat below."

She spun around to protest. Too late she realized he'd come up behind her, so close she very nearly clipped him on the chin with the top of her head. Standing but a pace apart, she could feel the heat, the *power,* pouring off him. In Miss Ashcroft's parlor, he'd seemed frightfully dignified. Larger than life. At the train station in London, she'd seen how the ticketing agent and porters all jumped to do his bidding, how the other passengers automatically stepped aside to let them pass. Neither his height nor breadth nor obvious wealth could account for it completely, this sway he had over people. Over her.

Seeing him in his own surroundings, in his Valhalla, she could no longer brush aside the foolish fancies that popped into her head whenever they were close. Could no longer pretend the weakness settling into her knees was from hunger. When he lifted a dark brow and looked at her as he was doing now, she couldn't stop imagining what it would be like to kiss him, to feel his firm lips covering hers, to feel his big hands touching her in places she hadn't ever wanted to be touched. Until now.

She needed air. Now. And a touch of cold wouldn't come amiss either.

Focusing her gaze on the sapphire winking at her from his cravat pin, she said, "I don't mind the cold. I'm used to it. And t'would only be for a minute."

He rolled his eyes. Then, as if he were giving in to a child's silly whim, he said, "Very well. A minute, no more."

The door handles stuck at first. He yanked them open and, hunched against the cold, they stepped outside. A sharp gust caught the doors, tearing at the hinges, and Mr. Belleville had to throw his full weight against them before they'd stay closed.

Holding out one arm to keep her balance, Christine made her way over to the rail, sending the birds scuttling to the ledge below. Far away, a wan winter sun was beginning to dip below the barren treetops. In the fading light, she could just make out the set of gray stone steps leading down to the terraced gardens. A white painted gazebo occupied the first tier. On the second, a fountain stood chalky and dry along with several barren, brick-edged flower beds. The path continued downward to a third garden, now buried in clouds of heavy fog. He was right, it wasn't much to look at in the wintertime. Yet her hungry gaze drank in every withered bud, every browned blade of grass, her mind's eye conjuring a picture of how it must be in springtime. Bursting with color, alive with bees and birds and earthworms, the balmy air scented with honeysuckle and roses.

He came up beside her and rested one big hand on the wall. "There's an orchard as well but you won't be able to see it until tomorrow after the fog lifts. We have cherry and apple trees mainly, although I'd try my hand at pears if I could find a gardener worth his salt."

"Hm," she said, staring down at his bare hands—the dark hairs dusting the backs, the fingers thick but long. Despite the cold, she felt perspiration pricking her beneath the sleeves of her gown. Frightened by the turn of her thoughts, befuddled by her body's strange sensations, she found herself asking, "And roses, do you grow them too?"

"Yes, or rather I try. The bushes we planted last year suffered an attack from some sort of insect."

She thought for a moment. "Little green ones, no bigger than specks of dust?"

He nodded, making a face. "So I'm told."

She hid a smile. His acres might extend beyond her ability to reckon, but he was a cit through and through. "Aphids most like. Spraying with stinging nettle broth will kill the bugs but not the bushes. If that won't work, you might have your gardener try onion and garlic juice."

"I'm not much of a horticulturist, so I'll have to take your word on it. And, since my head gardener took sick last spring, I've been more or less at Nature's mercy. Perhaps you'd have a look sometime, advise me on how to proceed?"

To once again know the pleasure of digging in the rich, fragrant earth; to watch what she'd planted and nurtured spring to life—that alone would have been enough. But to think he'd asked for her help, for her advice, made her foolish heart swell tenfold. She didn't dare look at him for fear he'd see just how much his casual remark meant to her.

"If you like. I want to be useful whilst I'm 'ere."

"You're not a servant, you know." He laid a hand on her shoulder, turning her toward him. "While you're here, I'd very much like for you to think of Valhalla as your home."

She shook her head at the impossibility of that. "Oh sar, I couldn't ever—"

"Call me Simon. We're supposed to be cousins, remember?" A smile whispered about his mouth. His gaze resting on her face looked softer and warmer than she'd ever seen it. Losing herself in its smoky depths, she could have sworn it was the whole bleeding house—and not just her head—that twirled like a top.

"Simon," she said after taking a deep breath to clear it, her fingers tightening on the balustrade.

She'd already come to think of him as Simon rather than as Mr. Belleville, had repeated his given name so many times in her head since they'd met that she'd started to worry she might slip and call him by it. But naming him to his face was a horse of a different color. Now that she had, she felt her cheeks heat.

"Excellent," he said, looking at her so purposely that she felt her temperature spike another notch. "Then I have leave to call you Christine?"

Hearing him say her name turned her insides to pudding. His asking her permission to use it was only a courtesy, to be sure, but the gesture warmed her just the same. Hoping he'd chalk up her pinkening cheeks to the cold, grateful he couldn't overhear her drumming heart, she turned to stare out onto the barren gardens. "I'd like that."

"And now that we're calling one another by our given names, tell me, *Christine,* exactly what it is about my house that offends you so that you must risk lung fever to escape it?"

"Offends me? Oh no, sar, you've got it all wrong. T'isn't that at all. What I mean is . . ."

She stopped herself when she saw him break into a broad smile. This time it reached his eyes, which were positively glowing with mischief, reminding her of her little brother Jake after he'd dipped his arm elbow-deep in the honey pot.

But Mr. Belleville—Simon—was no boy. He had to be at least a decade older than she was. Undoubtedly he was her superior in education, wealth, and station. They weren't equals now nor ever would be and yet she had the sudden urge to deal him a good swat.

Exasperated, she accused, "You're... *tweaking* me again."

"Indeed, I am." Sobering, he added, "But I'm sincere when I say I want you to feel at home here."

Christine hesitated. How to explain it to him? Born to riches as he was, he'd never understand.

Biting her bottom lip, she began, "Despite what you might think of me, my folk weren't poor. Father made a good living from the dairy. On fair days, we were always one of the first families to sell out of butter and cheese. We had our own pew at church, and the cottage was big enough that we had a parlor we kept just for Sundays and a smaller one for every day. It wasn't fancy, mind you, but it was clean and neat."

Hands shoved into his pockets, he rocked back on his heels. "Yes, yes," he said, voice straining with the old impatience.

She paused to tuck a loose strand of hair behind her ear. "After what I've come from, after living rough as I did when I first came to London, I don't think I could ever grow used to a place this grand. At least not as a home."

"You'd be surprised what a person can grow accustomed to," he said, shoving away from the railing. Yanking the doors open, he called over the wind, "Now come inside before you turn blue."

His voice was as frosty, as biting as the wind tearing at their hair and clothes. For the first time since they'd stepped outside, Christine shivered.

Hugging herself, she turned and walked back through the glass door he held open.

Eight

> Good society uses the same language everywhere, and dialects ought to be got rid of in those who would frequent it.
>
> —Anonymous,
> *The Habits of Good Society,* 1864

Simon was not the sort of man who spent a great deal of time wrestling with self-doubt. Once he chose a course of action he generally stuck with it. Whether the decision made was as significant as selling his railway shares in Great Western or as trifling as choosing a hat from Locke and Company's, he rarely entertained second thoughts.

But his resolution to bring Christine to Kent, to tutor her himself, had cracked the very foundation of his self-trust. For the first time since adolescence, he found himself wondering if he were up to the task.

You know absolutely nothing about teaching.

Margot's words, which he'd managed to banish from his brain during the previous harried week of departure preparations, had shoved their way to the forefront of his thoughts from the very moment his head had hit the pillow.

And so he found himself, at a quarter past two in the morning, pacing his library in his slippers and black velvet dressing robe.

You're obsessed with her? an inner voice taunted.

"I am not," he answered to no one in particular, running a hand over the sandpaper roughness of his jaw.

He kept a few bottles of fortified wine and other spirits in a small bowfront cabinet by his desk. Going over to it, he took out a bottle of port and a clean glass from the uppermost shelf. The fire had gone out hours before, and he could see his breath in the chilly air. Resigned to sleeplessness, he set the bottle and glass on the edge of his desk, then withdrew the fireplace poker from its brass rack and bent to the grate. He'd just gotten a goodly blaze going and was reaching for another stick of kindling when the library door clicked open.

Christine, attired in a flannel wrapper and nightgown, poked her head around the open door. Slanting a puzzled look at the lit desk lamp, she closed the door quietly behind her and tiptoed inside. She looked very young and innocent with her hair pulled into a braid at her back. And very appealing.

"Trouble sleeping?" He rose from the shadows and stepped into the dome of light

"Uh!" Her slender feet, showing bare beneath the hem of her flannel robe, cleared the carpet by several inches. Recovering, one hand still pressed over her left breast, she blew out the breath she'd sucked in and said, "I hadn't thought to find you here."

That much was obvious. He'd have to be blind not to see the way her face fell now that she'd recovered sufficiently to realize he wasn't a ghost. His heart, which had leapt with gladness at the sight of her, dove. Stung, he started to retort that it was, after all, his library, but he stopped himself short of uttering the caustic comment. The last thing their budding relationship needed was more of his signature sarcasm. Dinner had been a strained enough affair, with him at one end of the long mahogany dining room table and Christine at the other. Between her awkward attempts to negotiate the cutlery and him calling down to her to explain its configuration, conversation had not come easily. It had, for the most part, not come at all. Silence had proven *not* to be golden. He hadn't missed the look of relief that had flashed across her face when he'd announced, halfway through the apple cobbler, that he meant to repair to his study.

But perhaps he should try again? "You aren't sleepwalking, are you?" he teased. Nearing her, he beckoned her inside.

She shook her head and began backing to the door. "I had a bad dream and couldn't fall back to sleep. I thought to borrow a book, but I can come back later."

Her left foot was already planted in the hallway when he gave in to the impulse to call her back. "Christine," he said, torn between amusement and annoyance. "You're being absurd. It's already past two o'clock in the morning. Just when do you propose to come back? Come in and warm yourself by the fire at least."

"A'right," she capitulated, crossing the threshold. "If you're sure I'm not disturbing you."

"Perfectly certain." He went to replace the poker in the rack. When he turned back, she stood beside him. "I was just about to pour myself a nightcap." He nodded toward the bottle and glass setting atop his desk. "May I offer you something? A cordial, perhaps? I seem to recall seeing some ratafia buried in the back of my liquor cabinet."

"Oh no. No, thank you. I'm afeared . . ." She swallowed hard and, even in the dim light of the solitary desk lamp, he could see her cheeks pinken. "What I mean to say is, I'm *afraid* I don't have much of a head for spirits."

Earlier at dinner she'd barely touched her wine, a fine French burgundy he'd selected to complement the roast. Normally he wasn't much of an imbiber himself, which was one of the reasons he'd tolerated the humid Indian climate far better than most of the other company men posted there.

"Very well," he said, glad he needn't worry about locking up the liquor. "But won't you bear me company while I have mine?" He dug deep within himself and added, "Please."

"If you like."

"I would like it very much." In truth, now that she was here he couldn't abide the thought of sitting up alone.

He brushed by her on his way to the desk. Her fragrance—the unique blend of flowers and sunshine that was Christine—struck his senses, and he poured the port with a less than steady hand.

Desperate to distract himself from his rising desire, he said, "Tell me about your nightmare."

Still standing before the fire, she traced the pattern of the

Persian carpet with her big toe. "I don't know as there's much to tell."

Bracing a hip against the side of the desk, he raised the glass to his lips and drank. "Had it to do with your time at Madame LeBow's?"

She looked up from toeing the carpet to shake her head.

"Then with that cousin of yours, the one who beat you?"

She whirled on him, face blotchy and eyes full. For a terrible moment, he thought she would cry. "Yes, I did dream of him. But how did you know?"

"A logical deduction given what you endured at his hands."

In his mind's eye, he saw her as she had looked on that first afternoon, dripping bathwater and injured dignity, her wet night rail plastered to the flayed flesh of her shivering shoulders like a gauze bandage. The memory alone sufficed to send fresh anger erupting inside him, threatening to spew forth like lava from an active volcano. The knowledge that she suffered still, albeit a torment of a different sort, dredged up protective instincts he hadn't known he still possessed.

"You've nothing more to fear from him, Christine. He'll never harm you again, I swear it."

Her tear-bright eyes met his from across the room, and he thought he'd never seen a more miserable face. "I know that, sar," she answered softly in what he'd come to think of as her solemn voice.

On impulse, he confided, "I suffer from the occasional dark night of the soul myself."

"You?"

"That surprises you?"

She answered with a slow nod. "Bad dreams come from bein' afraid. 'Tis hard to imagine you afraid of anything."

"You'd be surprised," he muttered, draining his glass.

She came to the front of the desk as he poured himself another. Surveying the contents of the leather top, she asked, "What are your bad dreams about?"

He concentrated on swirling the tawny liquid about the rim of his glass, afraid he might not be able to keep up the pretense if he had to meet that steady brown gaze much longer. "I'm sure I couldn't say," he answered, an outright lie if there ever was one. "They're a jumble of images, most forgotten upon waking."

"Then you're lucky."

"Lucky," he repeated, the word bitter on his tongue. He'd been made to watch the person he loved best in the world suffer an unspeakable act of degradation and violence. The memory—the guilt—had stuck with him through nearly two decades, two continents, and several fortunes. He didn't expect to ever be free of it. He didn't *deserve* to be free of it.

She picked up the statue of Siva he used as a paperweight and scrutinized it.

Only too willing to shift topics, he asked, "What do you think of Siva?"

"Siva?"

"The Hindu god of creation and destruction."

"It's an idol, then?" She set the figure down as though it might singe her fingertips.

He laughed. "You needn't fear for my immortal soul—at least not on account of that statuette. While many Hindus worship Siva as a god, to me he's a keepsake only, a memento of my years in India."

"You've been to India?" she exclaimed, eyes as wide and incredulous as though he'd visited the moon.

She pronounced India as though it ended with "er." Ordinarily he would have pointed out the error, but the brandy and being with Christine were a potent combination. He couldn't remember the last time he'd felt this languid and at ease.

"I lived there from the time I was sixteen until I was almost twenty-five." Drink in hand, he gestured her to the sitting area where earlier they'd taken tea.

Settling on the leather sofa, she asked, "Did you like it, living in India, I mean?"

Legs tucked beneath her, she reached down to pull her robe and night rail over her ankles. Very slim, very bare ankles. All too conscious that they both wore only their nightclothes, Simon took the armchair across from her, separated by a gateleg table.

Contemplating his port, he thought for a moment. "I suppose I liked it well enough. It's quite literally a world apart from England, as different as night is from day."

He'd assumed the subject would die there. To his surprise, she pressed, "How is it different?"

Setting his glass down, he spoke of his years in India, of

midday heat so intense that it drove Europeans and natives alike indoors to seek refuge from the searing sun. He told her of the bungalows that the company's officers and civil servants occupied, striving to paint a picture of their sloping thatched roofs, gleaming white walls, and open verandas where, during the worst of the heat, entire families might spend the better part of the day in cane chairs beneath whirring ceiling fans. Words couldn't begin to do justice to the jungle, but he tried to describe its raw, primitive beauty, explaining that, during monsoon season, trees that had stood for hundreds of years might be plucked from the earth by their roots like turnips. Even more tumultuous was the political climate.

"Some months before the sepoys rebelled, the native police in the north began circulating *chapatis*."

Throughout Christine had listened intently, stopping him periodically to pose interested questions. Now she asked, "What are cha-pa-tis?"

"They're flat, spicy biscuits. The Indians serve them with most meals. At any rate, the sepoys were passing them from hand to hand in great numbers. We all puzzled over it, but the significance was never determined. After the rebellion broke out, many recalled the chapatis and credited their distribution as being some sort of secret signal."

"I thought the revolt 'twas on account of the Indian soldiers' rifle cartridges being smeared with grease."

He wouldn't have expected her to know that. Impressed, he continued, "The thought of having to bite open the ends of cartridges treated with animal fats would be exceedingly offensive to Hindus and Muslims alike. In fact Canning, the governor general at the time, found out and issued an ordinance forbidding the use of such fats, but it was too late. After generations of living under the British raj, the sepoys had scant reason to trust our word. And, of course, their reasons for mutinying went beyond the matter of the cartridges."

"Did you see any fightin'?"

He shook his head. "Fortunate fellow that I am, I'd booked passage home months before. My ship set sail on the eleventh of May, 1857. The sepoys put Delhi to the torch the very next day."

She hugged her knees. "See, you really are lucky."

He smiled with taut lips. "So I am. It seems I'll have to keep you close at hand to remind me of it, though."

Her eyes met his for a brief, knowing instant, and he felt another shaft of desire shoot through him like a current of electricity.

"Close for the time bein'." Staring into the fire, she fingered the braid that hung over her shoulder. "Thank you for saying you'll help my family. You don't know what it means to me to know . . ." She broke off and shook her head as though the rest of the words eluded her.

"I think perhaps I do."

Her hair, limned by firelight, looked warm and soft and silky. He'd acknowledged his attraction to her some time ago, even thought he'd made peace with it. Yet the strength of his urge to touch her—her hair, her smooth cheek, the sleek column of throat peaking out from her high-collared night rail—shocked him.

The grandfather clock chiming from the front hallway called him back to sanity. If they sat up much longer, they risked being caught by the maid who came in early to sweep the grate and lay the fire. If she were to find them alone together and in their nightclothes . . .

With the fourth and final note still vibrating in the air, he said, "Breakfast is at seven-thirty. You should try to get some sleep."

"Oh, I'm used to rising early. During milking season, I'm often in the fields as early as this, earlier betimes. I don't need that much sleep, so you needn't worry on my account."

"But I do worry." Appalled that he'd spoken his inner thoughts aloud, he quickly added, "We fellow insomniacs must look out for one another."

Her brows fitted together in a frown. "You use such big words."

He hadn't meant to, but the time wasn't all he'd forgotten. It struck him that, for the past hour at least, the differences between them in age, rank, education had blurred to near extinction. They'd ceased to be master and pupil, benefactor and ward, and instead had become simply "Christine" and "Simon." Friends.

"Insomniac," he repeated. "It only means a person who has difficulty in sleeping."

"Oh, well, then I suppose that fits the both of us," she said with a little laugh, fidgeting with the belt of her flannel wrapper.

His gaze fell on the cinched waist, and he found himself willing it to come undone and, with it, the night rail beneath. He could only imagine how soft she would feel against his hands. His lips. His tongue.

He stood, grateful to be wearing a loose robe instead of trousers. "We should try to get some sleep."

She untucked her legs and rose as well. "Rest our eyes at least."

He followed her to the door. "Yes, that too."

On the open threshold, she turned back so quickly that their bodies very nearly bumped. "Good night, Simon."

"Good night, Christine."

He leaned against the door frame, watching until she turned the corner. When he could no longer hear the soft patter of her footfalls, he pulled the door closed and walked back to the sofa. There was no sense in his going back to bed at this hour but perhaps he would "rest his eyes" as Christine had suggested. The concave pucker in the leather seat cushion was still warm from where she'd curled up like a kitten. He took one of the decorative tasseled pillows for his head and stretched out. Feet dangling over one rolled sofa arm, he let his eyelids drift closed.

He slept so soundly he nearly missed breakfast.

"I have a present for you," Simon said later that morning at breakfast, lowering his newspaper to steal a glance at Christine. Seated to his right, she looked exceedingly fetching in a fresh morning frock of indigo blue wool trimmed with a lace collar and cuffs. She wore her pretty hair simply, pulled away from her face and tied with a lace bow. Aside from the faint smudges beneath her remarkable eyes, she bore no trace of her nocturnal wanderings. Certainly her appetite had not been dulled.

He'd had no idea what she liked, so he'd ordered his cook to serve something of everything. The marble-topped sideboard groaned beneath silver rashers of grilled kidneys, bacon, and sausages; eggs—shirred, poached, and scrambled; and a goodly assortment of breads, jams, and jellies. If there was a dish she disliked, he'd yet to discover it.

"A present! For me?" she exclaimed, then clamped a hand over her full mouth. Cheeks puffed out like helium balloons, she pushed her plate away and reached for the brown paper–wrapped parcel he slid toward her.

"It's nothing really," he demurred, her enthusiasm making him wish it were a real present, something frivolous and personal, and not merely a means to an end.

She held the package up to her ear and shook it. "It's a book, isn't it?" she asked, eyes bright.

Feeling like the proverbial heel, he closed his newspaper, folded it, and set it aside. "You'll have to open it and find out."

She did, tearing at the cording and paper until the latter fell away. "It is a book. Two books!" She picked the larger volume from the wrapper and held it up. "*Mind Your H's and Take Care of Your R's* by the Honorable Charles W. Smith." She looked back at him, expression puzzled.

"It's an elocution manual I picked up in London," he explained, avoiding her gaze by stirring more sugar into his coffee. "Smith is a noted grammarian, and this is his most recent work. I thought we might use it as a starting point for today's grammar lesson."

Flipping through the pages, she asked, "If I read this, will it teach me how to talk proper?"

He sipped his coffee. "If you mean will you learn to *speak properly,* then yes, this book should set you on the correct path provided you study it faithfully."

She picked up the second, smaller book.

Before she could ask, he said, "It's a pronunciation dictionary. Smith's manual focuses on the proper placement and pronunciation of h's and r's, but this dictionary provides guidance to sounding out all the letters in words."

"Oh," she said, closing it. "That'll be handy," she added though she looked far from enthused.

Simon couldn't really fault her. "Indeed," he mumbled, thinking back to ten years earlier when he'd found Mr. Charles W. Smith's previous work, *Hints On Elocution and Public Speaking,* very "handy" indeed. Margot had made him read it again and again—and yet again. Finally one Sunday afternoon, boiling with frustration, he'd shoved his way through her crowded drawing room, Smith's manual topping the stack clenched beneath his left arm. Amidst gasps and giggles, he'd thrown open the window and dumped the hateful little handbook into the alley below along with such soporific gems as *Errors of Pronunciation and Improper Expressions, Poor Letter R. Its Use and Abuse,* and *Etiquette for Ladies and Gentlemen.* Then he'd turned and stomped out. That evening, he'd found them all reassembled on his bedside stand along with a note from Margot that read: *I think you'd do well to begin again.*

In the ensuing years, he'd managed to master not only his h's and r's but also his temper. But it was still there, lodged beneath the surface, a caged beast that growled and snapped as it waited for its opportunity to escape. In tutoring Christine, he'd count himself fortunate if he managed to match even a modicum of the forbearance Margot had shown him. Of course he and Margot had been sleeping together at the time, a state of affairs that no doubt had made it easier for her to tolerate both his gaffes and his outbursts. In his case, he'd have his frustrated desire to contend with. Even so, Christine was a woman—a child in many ways—and he was a man. She was young and biddable, her mind as unformed as a lump of raw clay, yet the night before he'd seen in her a canniness, a clarity of vision, that both astounded and delighted him.

With all those factors in his favor, how difficult could it be to mold her into some semblance of a lady?

Seated beside Christine at the leather-topped library table, Simon snatched the open reader from her and reread the sentence that, she was sure, they'd both come to hate.

" 'Hairy Harry Hastings asked his aunt Hannah to Hold His Handsome Hat for Him while He went to Hail a Hansom.' "

"I tell you, 'tis the very thing I said," Christine insisted, stabbing her pencil behind one ear.

He rubbed the bridge of his nose. "What you said was *arsked.* The word is *asked.* Mark that it is a simple word of but one syllable and three letters—none of which happen to be *r.* Now begin again."

Face afire, Christine grabbed the book from him. Elbows planted on the table, she began to read aloud, straining each word through set back teeth.

"And stop your infernal fidgeting. Anyone who walked in right now would think you were afflicted." He aimed his gaze at her right hand.

Belatedly she realized she'd been winding a loose strand of hair about her index finger. Untangling it, she pushed back her chair and started up. "If you're expecting company, I can come back."

"Sit down. You aren't going anywhere."

A devilish thought struck her, but Simon was such a sobersides that she couldn't resist. All innocence, she asked, "Not even if I have to use the necessary?"

The tips of his ears turned bright as a cherry. "No lady would ever, under any circumstances, admit to such a thing in a gentleman's presence."

She hid a pleased smile. "What would she do then?"

"She'd ask to be excused."

"May I be excused?"

"No. Now sit up straight—elbows *off* the table—and read the passage once more."

Her bottom found the chair seat with a deliberate thud. For good measure, she let out a heavy sigh, but there was nothing feigned about her frustration. She'd expected her lessons with Simon to be difficult but also to be fun. Somehow she'd imagined herself reading her way through his library, the novels mostly, from dawn to dusk. Instead it was almost time for luncheon and so far she'd only read one sentence.

The light tap outside the library door provided her reprieve. It was Mrs. Griffith.

Christine looked over the top of the book and smiled as the housekeeper approached. "Time for luncheon already, Mrs. Griffith?"

"Not quite, Miss Christine, though I'll warrant you'll find Cook's pigeon pie well worth the wait." To Simon, she said, "I'm sorry to disturb you, sir, but there are several ladies to see you."

Simon slid back his chair and rose. "Ladies, Mrs. Griffith?"

"Aye, sir. Squire Priestly's wife and four others from the parish, all come to pay their respects." She handed him a stack of cream-colored vellum cards.

He took them and shuffled through. "Mrs. Charles Priestly. The Misses Dorothea and Daphne Priestly. Miss Frances Albright. Miss Faith Pettibon. *Blast*." Christine watched him drop the cards into his jacket pocket and look up at the housekeeper, a scowl creasing his brow. "Where have you put them?"

"In the east drawing room, sir, with a tray of refreshments on its way."

"Then I had better be as well." He reached up to cinch the cravat he'd earlier loosened. Slipping a hand inside his jacket, he took out his pocket comb and slid it through his dark hair. "I'm sorry, Christine, but this really cannot be helped. Priestly is a magistrate and well respected. Most of the other farmers will vote as he does. I cannot afford to offend his wife. Our lesson will have to wait."

So this was it, her moment of truth. Steeling herself, Christine pushed back her chair and rose. "I understand." She nibbled on her bottom lip, mentally rehearsing the proper sequence for dispensing the tea that, as Simon's *cousin*, she would surely be called upon to serve.

She was about to ask if she might have a moment to run upstairs and tidy her own hair when he turned to her and said, "We'll take up geography when we reconvene. Perhaps you could take your luncheon now so that you'll be prepared to begin when I return?"

Crossing the carpet, she froze in midstep, his meaning seeping in. *He doesn't want to be seen with me.*

"I'm not hungry." She managed to push the words over the lump in her throat. "I think I'll bide here and . . . and look up India." Not wanting him to see how much he'd hurt her, she started toward the giant globe. Mounted in its clawfoot brass stand, it occupied the windowed alcove overlooking the gardens.

Out of the corner of her eye she glimpsed the housekeeper's pitying face. "I'll have your luncheon brought in on a tray, Miss Christine."

She opened her mouth to protest, but Simon cut her off. "Yes, do that, Mrs. Griffith." From the doorway, he called, "Christine, I'll be back as soon as I can."

She didn't bother to answer but stood spinning the orb until the library door clicked closed. Only after their retreating footsteps died did she move away. Then, like a child picking at the edges of a scab, she gave in to the temptation to relive every word, every gesture, and every look of the night before beginning with the first magical moment when Simon had stepped from the shadows. Dressed in his nightclothes, he'd looked handsomer than any man had a right to at two in the morning, and genuinely *pleased* to see her.

Now, pacing the library, she searched for some sign that the night before had been real, not simply a lovely dream. But bleached by the stark winter's light, the well-appointed room seemed haughty rather than welcoming, the marble busts of philosophers and politicians disapproving rather than merely dignified. Even the shelves of beloved books seemed to suffocate her; she couldn't shake the feeling that they might crash down upon her... much like her hopes and dreams.

What she needed was to be out-of-doors where she could breathe the fresh air and think. She crossed the carpet to the door and slipped out into the hallway. Passing the parlor door, slightly ajar, she heard Simon's deep voice, followed by a chorus of high-pitched female laughter.

Flattening her back against the door paneling, she craned her neck and peaked inside. Simon was sandwiched between two women on a camelback settee intended for two.

"Oh, my dear Mr. Belleville," crooned the big-bosomed redhead seated to his right. "Had we known you were so amusing we would have called on you ere now." Her gloved hand found the top of his knee and squeezed.

"Now, Fanny, we must not forget that Mr. Belleville is a politician," put in the older woman on his left. She reached up to secure her pince-nez before it slid further down the bridge of her long, thin nose. "We must expect him to have a silver tongue and a ready wit. But seriously, Mr. Belleville, what is your opinion of all this fuss over parliamentary reform?"

Feeling ill, Christine shoved away from the door, giggles and trilling voices following her to the front hall. So these were the oh-so-proper ladies she wasn't fit to meet, let alone serve tea and biscuits? Angry tears tumbling down her cheeks, she ripped her coat from the hall tree, stuffed her arms in the sleeves, and started out the front door. The sight of an unfamiliar coach and four parked in the long circular drive sent her heading back inside to the opposite end of the house. Slipping out a back door, she found herself on a columned terrace overlooking the south lawn and gardens.

Stepping up to the rail, she lifted her face to the sharp wind. It was colder than she'd expected. The gusts stung her eyes, crystallizing the tears tracking her cheeks. But not even the cold cutting through her clothing could numb her to the pain of Simon's abandonment.

True, he meant to stand for public office. Not just public office but *Parliament!* He had a duty, a *reputation,* to uphold. And yet curled up on his library sofa listening to the melodic sound of his voice as he spoke of his years in India, she'd fancied they were on the path to becoming more than master and pupil. More than benefactor and protégée. Friends?

A midnight fancy, that was all it had been. That feeling of closeness, of sharing in something larger and grander than herself. As touchable as moonstone and about as reachable as India by train. Looking ahead to the barren gardens, Christine reminded herself that dreams no longer had a place in her life.

Hands shoved into pockets, she descended the marble stairs and directed her footsteps away from the house.

Nine

> "If everybody minded their own business," the Duchess said in a hoarse growl, "the world would go round a deal faster than it does."
>
> —Lewis Carroll,
> *Alice's Adventures in
> Wonderland*, 1865

"But seriously, Mr. Belleville, what is your opinion of all this fuss over parliamentary reform?" Eugenia Priestly asked from her place beside Simon on the curved-back sofa. Passing him his tea, she added, "Won't reducing the property requirement and increasing the number of seats open the House to all manner of scalawags and ne'er-do-wells?"

"That is one interpretation," he admitted, resting the delicate bone china on his knee. Were Mrs. Priestly to learn of his East End beginnings, no doubt she would consider his candidacy as proof for her point. "However, the counties have always been Conservative strongholds. Further increasing the number of county seats according to the provisions of last year's Reform Act can do us only good."

"But what of the townships, Mr. Belleville?" put in Faith Pettibon. The vicar's spinster sister, Miss Pettibon was a nervous sparrow of a woman, as lackluster as the oatmeal-colored settee on which she perched.

He leveled each of the five women, including Mrs.

Priestly's twin daughters, a penetrating look. "By way of a conciliatory gesture to our opponents, the present Reform Act does indeed provide for further extension of the borough franchise. And yet we would do well to ask ourselves just what our opponents have gained. It would be difficult to imagine the towns becoming more Liberal than they already are, now wouldn't it?" He cocked a brow, waiting.

Two bright spots of color appeared on either of Miss Pettibon's chalky cheeks. "Well, I . . . I suppose so."

Even Mrs. Priestly's grim mouth softened and her stiff back relaxed against the damask cushion. "You are a persuasive man, Mr. Belleville."

"Yes, he certainly is," seconded Fanny Albright, the mayor's red-haired daughter.

Miss Albright had seated herself on his left, albeit the sofa was built to accommodate only two. For the second time that day, her hand clamped onto his leg. Her smile left no doubt that she was his if he wanted her.

Only he didn't. Puzzled by his lack of interest, he stole a sideways glance, noting the rise and fall of her bosom beneath her snug-fitting bodice. She was a handsome woman, big-breasted and full-hipped, yet lately he'd come to appreciate a more lithe form. He'd come to appreciate . . .

Christine. Waiting for him in the library, she would be having her luncheon now, perhaps frowning over her reader as she forked up her pigeon pie. He hadn't missed the stricken look on her face when he'd told her to stay behind. Had he been wrong not to invite her to join them? The women seated about him were the proverbial pillars of the community—in short, predators. Given the chance, they would have raked Christine with their fangs, sunk their talons into her jugular, and then devoured what was left of her with far more zeal than they'd applied to their biscuits and watercress sandwiches. Even so, he couldn't seem to stay the sinking feeling that he'd failed not only her but himself as well.

A wicked smile lighting her green gaze, Miss Albright declared, "Pooh on all this talk of politics. Shall we be honest, ladies, and admit the real reason we've come?"

Simon felt the old wariness crawling up his spine. "And that is?"

Her triumphant gaze returned to his. "We're all positively

dying to know whether or not you're any relation to Lord Stonevale of The Priory."

"Really, Fanny," Mrs. Priestly hissed, setting her cup down on its delicate scallop-edged saucer with a clang. "Trust you to be tactless."

Shrugging, Miss Albright leaned forward and plucked a frosted biscuit from the silver platter, in the process plastering her full hip to Simon's thigh. "Well, his lordship's family name *is* Belleville as well."

Although he'd known it was only a matter of time before he'd be called upon to explain his warped family relationships, Simon had always assumed the question would come with him standing on an assembly hall podium, facing off against his opponent. Never had he dreamt he'd be called upon to air his family's soiled linens in his own parlor for the amusement of a pack of gossipy *women*.

"I am his grandson," he answered tightly, feeling the tension move into his neck and shoulders.

Shocked gasps, then a flurry of competing questions greeted his admission.

Eugenia Priestly's voice rose above the babble. "How extraordinary." Lifting a gloved hand, she signaled for silence. Addressing herself to Simon, she explained, "When we first learned that a *Mr. Belleville* had purchased this property to build upon, Priestly and I assumed you must be from a cadet branch of the family. We never supposed your connection to his lordship was so close as this. Good heavens, sir, why ever didn't you say so before?"

Spine stiffening against the damask-covered sofa back, he answered, "I have never made any secret of my blood tie to Lord Stonevale nor of the fact that we are estranged."

Nibbling on her biscuit, Fanny Albright's catlike eyes glowed. "Estranged! How delicious. Pray do not keep us on tenterhooks any longer, Mr. Belleville. What is the nature of your and his lordship's quarrel?"

"Yes, Mr. Belleville," chorused the Misses Priestly, "pray do tell."

"Girls," interjected their mother, "it is dreadfully ill-mannered of us to press our host to speak of a matter so personal in nature. Mr. Belleville should not be badgered into relaying his family history. That is . . . well, Mr. Belleville, should you care to unburden yourself, we would be happy to oblige you, wouldn't we, ladies?"

Simon's gaze swept the semicircle of bobbing heads, faces schooled to sympathy—except for the eyes. Noting the greedy gleam in all five pairs, he felt his annoyance flower into genuine dislike.

He shrugged. "As Lord Stonevale and I have no *personal* quarrel, there is nothing more to speak of."

A bald lie if ever there was one. Sitting up nights listening to his father's slurred stories of his bygone glory days had been personal. Shouldering casks of brandy, crates of tobacco, and sacks of rice until he thought his spine would crack had been personal. Watching his newly widowed mother grow lean-cheeked and gray-headed as she searched the post each morning for a reply from Lord Stonevale had been personal as well.

But no letter, no help, had ever arrived. Had it, neither he nor Rebecca would have been on the pier that night. But they had been and, as a result, his sister was a prisoner locked inside a little girl's mind. Of all he had to endure before or since, that proved to be the hardest to forgive.

Impossible to forgive.

Miss Albright made a show of dusting cookie crumbs from her bodice but her gaze was keen. "How can a quarrel not be personal?"

Choosing his words with great care, Simon answered, "Lord Stonevale did not approve of my parents' marriage." An understatement if ever there was one. The news that his only son and heir meant to wed the Jewish housemaid had all but brought on an apoplectic fit. "And so he had a new will drawn, one that disinherited not only my father but also any progeny he might sire."

His parents had wed in a civil ceremony that neither of their respective families had recognized. Rebecca had been born a few months later.

"But the *title,* sir," Mrs. Priestly went on, like a dog refusing to let drop a gnawed through bone. "Good gracious, you would be his heir, would you not?"

"My grandfather did not know of my sister's or my existence until my thirteenth year. By that time, he had conferred that honor on a cousin."

Fanny Albright spoke up, "But surely you may present

your case to the College of Heralds, petition Parliament if need be to redress that wrong?"

"If I so chose," Simon admitted though in truth he'd rather rot than beg in public for what was rightfully his. "But I far prefer to let sleeping dogs lie," he added, thinking he'd never before encountered quite such a pack of bloodthirsty bitches.

Reinstatement would require him to produce his parents' marriage lines, long ago lost. It might even go so far as to require the queen's approval. Admire Disraeli though Victoria might, it was well known that she had declined to raise even the great philanthropist, Sir Lionel Rothschild, above the level of a baronet because of his Jewish faith.

And more and more the true power of Parliament resided not with the Lords but with the Commons. All that power, all that control—Simon was determined to be at the heart of it.

"The sins of the fathers," Mrs. Priestly intoned, shaking her head. Turning her sharp gaze on her daughters, she added, "Dorothea, Daphne, mark Mr. Belleville's story well, for there is a moral in it. Only think, had his papa done his duty and wed where he was bid, Mr. Belleville would have his birthright and rightful place in the House of Lords."

"Indeed, only think." Hiding a grimace, Simon drained his teacup, wishing for something stronger.

Curiosity sated for the present, his callers suddenly seemed to grow bored with the topic. Setting aside her cup, Mrs. Priestly announced, "Well, I for one am anxious to see these famous gardens of yours before I take my leave."

Horticulture. A safe if uninspiring topic. Relieved, Simon replied, "Infamous is more like it. There's really nothing to see aside from a great lot of weeds and bare bushes. Simms, my head gardener, took ill last summer, and I'm afraid I've let the grounds go to rack and ruin." He had, in fact, kept the position open deliberately, not wanting to strip the man of his livelihood.

Mrs. Priestly's face expressed stern disapproval. "Have you looked into hiring a replacement?"

Simon thought back to the day before when he'd stood on the stone parapet with Christine and found himself in the unusual position of seeking advice.

A smile tickling the corners of his mouth, he answered, "I have begun to make inquiries."

But Mrs. Priestly was not so easily deterred. Already on her feet, she started for the door. "As the president of our parish garden club, I shall be only too happy to offer my advice."

Simon didn't doubt that for a moment. Dutifully rising, he made his way across the room to the tasseled bellpull. "In that case, ladies, I'll ring for a footman to fetch your coats."

Flexing benumbed fingers, Christine put down her pruning shears and surveyed the hill of loose leaves and compost she'd built about the base of each bush. Simon's shrub roses were a sorry lot, but hopefully her efforts to protect them from further frost damage had saved some of the sturdier bushes. Owing to the lateness of the season, she'd kept pruning to a minimum, cutting away only the dead and diseased canes to prevent snow breakage. Rising from the empty burlap bag she'd knelt upon, she took advantage of her thick work gloves to sweep up the debris. As she worked, a strange peace filled her. *This I'm good at,* she thought, and a smile lifted her cold-stiffened lips.

She might be a complete failure as a lady, she might not know what h's to pronounce and what others to ignore, but within the bounds of Simon's gardens she felt as calm and all-knowing as a queen.

She wasn't finished by any means, but the burning sensation flaring in her fingertips and earlobes told her it was past time to go in. Surely Simon's callers would have taken their leave by now? Valhalla might be the biggest house she'd ever been inside yet their presence had made it—and her—feel crowded. Choked.

And Simon? Might he have discovered her missing and set out to look for her? Despite the hurt and disappointment she'd felt—still felt—at his earlier dismissal, the possibility of meeting him on the path prompted a strange, fluttery feeling to take root in her breast.

Stiff-backed, she swatted at her skirts. Clods of mud and grass clung stubbornly to the crumpled creases, and her fine wool overcoat showed damp stains on the knees and cuffs. She hadn't meant to get so dirty but, as so often happened, her enthusiasm had carried her away, along with her better judgment. Once inside the house, she'd scoot upstairs to thaw and change, then meet Simon back in the library.

She collected her tools and the full bag and returned to the gardener's shed. The door secured behind her, she started back up the path, gravel crunching beneath her boot heels, frozen hands stuffed into her pockets. The wind had picked up during her short time inside; now it whipped her face and hair. Eyes watering, she pushed back a loose strand lashing her cheek, then realized she'd left on her muddy gloves. Too cold to even think of retracing her steps, she forged ahead. She'd just started up the terrace steps when a sharp female voice pierced the air above her.

"I can see I've come not a moment too soon."

Christine's head snapped up. Blinking bleary eyes, she saw the gray-haired matron from the parlor come out onto the terrace, four other women—and Simon—in tow. Simon's guests. So they hadn't left after all. Hoping to hunker beneath the stairs until they went back inside, Christine backed away. As she did, her left shoulder struck something solid. She whirled just as the empty stone flower urn plunged from its pedestal to the ground at her feet, splitting in two.

Directly above her, the matron shrilled, "Good heavens, whatever was that?"

Like the wind blasting her, Simon's voice triggered a chill that ran bone deep. "A squirrel, most likely. They sometimes bury acorns in the flower urns. This one seems to have knocked it over."

"Rubbish, someone's down there, and I for one intend to have a look. Ladies."

The battle cry sent a brigade of feet bounding single file down the steps.

With no choice but to surrender or be discovered, Christine stepped into the open just as the first woman descended. "Hullo," she said, forcing a smile.

"Good heavens, Mr. Belleville. Surely you haven't hired a *female* gardener!"

From the terrace, Simon grimaced. "In a manner of speaking." Setting his gaze on Christine, he started down the steps. "Keep silent and follow my lead," he ordered beneath his breath and then turned about to face the others, smile strained. "Ladies, allow me to present my cousin, Miss Christine Tremayne."

"Your cousin!"

"On my mother's side," he clarified.

The redhead Christine had caught groping Simon's leg pushed forward. "Oh, that explains it then." Looking Christine up and down, her mouth turned up in a smirk.

The introductions passed in a blur of halfhearted greetings and stony stares. Christine confined herself to a single word—hello—each time expelling the air from her lungs in order to give the all-important *h* its due.

"Charmed," murmured the squire's wife, her pinched expression conveying she was anything but. Glaring at Christine's muddied glove, she withdrew her hand just as Christine reached to take it.

"You really should look to that wheezing in your chest," suggested the redhead, Miss Albright, shoving both hands inside her mink muff.

The Priestly girls and the vicar's sister followed suit. Christine's cheeks burned as much from humiliation as from cold, but she kept her chin up and her shoulders squared in a way that would have made her father proud.

But Simon looked far from proud. Bearing the women's snubs was easy compared to the contempt she saw in his stormy gaze.

"As you can see, my cousin fancies herself something of an horticulturalist," he said, taking one of her gloved hands in his and lifting it for all to see. "When she learned of my plight, she kindly consented to make a study of my gardens." Turning back to Christine, he added, "My dear, you will take a chill if you do not exercise greater care. Go inside and warm yourself. I shall join you in five minutes ... *in the library*."

His tone, sharp as a butcher's knife, made it clear that her ordeal was far from over. Still, it was a reprieve.

Seizing on the excuse, she offered a final "good day"— mercifully there were no h's in either word—and dashed for the steps. She hurried toward the nearest door, feeling their stares like daggers in her back.

"What an extraordinary girl," Mrs. Priestly remarked, scarcely waiting for Christine to move beyond earshot. Her long, thin nostrils flared as though waiting for a noxious odor to clear.

Simon regarded her, feeling his dislike harden into something akin to genuine hatred. Pasting on the politician's smile he practiced in his shaving mirror each morning, he said, "My dear Mrs. Priestly, I do believe that is the wisest observation you've made all afternoon."

You're a rum fool, Christine, that's what you are. And a bloody mess, to boot.

Not about to argue, Christine's reflection nodded back at her from the beveled mirror topping her washstand. Small wonder everyone, including Simon, had stared at her as though she'd sprouted a third eye. Her hair hung about her shoulders in limp tangles, free from the ribbon she'd somehow lost. The tip of her nose was beet red, and the mud streaking her left cheekbone had started to crack and flake, putting her in mind of a snake shedding its skin.

Still thinking of snakes—one redheaded viper in particular—she splashed water from the pitcher into the basin and reached for the bar of lavender-scented soap. She'd just bent to sluice her face when heavy pounding sounded outside her door. Before she could move to answer it, the door rocked open on shuddering hinges.

Water dribbling down her chin, Christine swiveled to see Simon standing in the open doorway. He'd shed his jacket and his untied cravat hung loosely about his open shirt collar.

"I told you to meet me in the library." A lock of his normally tidy hair fell over one angry eye as he slammed the door closed and strode toward her. "Can you not even follow that simple direction?"

He ground to a halt in front of her, and she felt her explanation shrivel along with her courage. She looked down at his big hands dangling at his sides, the thick fingers opening and closing on air, and a shudder of pure, animal fear shot through her.

But no, this was Simon, the most civilized man she'd ever known. He might slam a door or two, but he'd never lay angry hands on her. And yet old habits died hard. Swallowing, she scanned the room for an escape route.

"Then perhaps you'd be so good as to explain what the *hell* you were doing tramping about the grounds in the dead of winter like some vagrant?"

Darting to the side, she barricaded herself behind a high-backed chair covered in chintz. "T'other day, you arsked—

asked—for my help with the roses." She drew a deep breath and focused on calming her breathing. "So, after you left, I decided to um, . . . help."

He followed her, stopping in front of the cushioned seat. "I asked for your advice. I never meant that you should perform *manual labor*."

Manual labor. He spat out the words as though they were dirty, as though they might soil him if he didn't put them behind him quickly.

Thinking of all the *manual labor* involved in working a dairy farm, Christine felt her foolish fear dissolve. In its place, anger blazed. Who was he to judge the worth of an honest day's labor? Barring the night he'd helped her to break back into the brothel, the heaviest thing she'd seen him lift was a pencil.

Gaze boring into his, she rounded the chair, obliging him to take a step back. "If you hadn't . . ." She stopped, racking her brain for a word big and complicated enough to express all she felt. "*Banished* me in the first place, I never would have had cause to go out."

For the first time since he'd stormed in, he looked less than sure of himself. "I never banished you. I simply requested you go on with your lesson while I attended to my guests."

She folded her arms across her breasts as if to cover the hurt. "You didn't want me to meet those women. You were afraid I'd do or say something to shame you."

He hesitated, a long swallow rippling down the corded muscles of his throat. Finally he said, "Good God, Christine, I'm standing for Parliament."

"So you are." Christine was glad she wasn't near the mantel because, had she stood within arm's reach of it, all the pretty little figurines arranged atop would have stood in serious danger. Fists clenched at her sides, she spat, " 'Tis all well and good for you, with your fancy house and fine friends, to poke fun, but I've a heart and feelings the same as you do."

He went positively white. Except for his ears, which were tipped in pink. Could it be that she'd finally struck some nerve, some weak vein of feeling, inside him?

"I don't mean to . . . that is to say, I wasn't poking fun, as you call it."

"My cousin fancies herself something of an horticulturalist," she mimicked, tears burning her eyes. "I'm not blind, you know. I saw the way those women looked at me. Like I was some sort of snake crawled up from the garden. But I didn't care one bit, truly I didn't, not 'til I saw you looking at me that way too."

Their anger spent, heavy silence descended. Needing to put some distance between them, she stalked toward the fireplace. Picking up the iron, she bent and poked aimlessly at the blue-orange flames, all the while listening over the crackling logs for the sound of Simon's footfalls heading for the door.

Instead, he came up behind her. "Christine."

Startled, she swung around. Standing before her, he was flushed still, but the anger had left his eyes and a smile hovered about his lips. "I hope you'll settle for an apology although a sound whack over the head might improve my manners."

Following his gaze to the poker in her hand, she felt the blood rush from her trunk and limbs to her head. Hands numb, her fingers about the iron went slack. Too late she realized what the ear-splitting clang signified. She stared down at the tiles between them, the ordered pattern of delicate blue flowers reduced to a fractured mess.

"I'm sorry. So sorry." She bent to pick up the larger shards.

"Leave it." He took hold of her elbow, staying her. "Broken tiles are a great deal easier to mend than injured feelings. Or a broken trust." He drew a deep breath and swallowed hard, throat working, and Christine couldn't help but think how nice it would be to press her lips there, just *there*, at the shadowed hollow. "I'm sorry I hurt your feelings earlier, sorry I didn't ask you to join in as I should have. I told myself I was thinking of you, that I wanted to make certain you were ready before I exposed you to . . . *them*. But now I realize I was only thinking of myself, my reputation. Can you forgive me?"

She'd expected anger, annoyance at the very least. Certainly not an acknowledgment of her feelings, never an *apology*. And yet here he was, Mr. Simon Belleville of Valhalla, making her the most heartfelt apology a woman might wish for. When he used the edge of his thumb to dry the tear she didn't remember shedding, the gentleness of the gesture nearly undid her.

A hairbreadth from casting herself into his arms, she lifted her face to his. "There's naught to forgive. You were right, I'm not fit for society. I may never be." Feeling scorched by the fire that leapt into his eyes at that statement, she let her own slip to his shirt collar. "The truth is, I ask myself every day just why it is you waste your time with me."

His hands closed over her shoulders, the powerful fingers clamping about the joints. He drew her toward him, closing what remained of the distance between them until her breasts all but brushed his chest. "I never waste my time."

His fingers flexing on her shoulders sent a delicious little shudder sliding down her spine. A funny tingling feeling settled low in her belly. Her gaze fixed on the pulse point at the side of his neck and again she thought what sweet heaven it would be to run her lips and tongue along the corded muscles.

His gray gaze speared hers, forcing her to meet it. "Haven't you any notion of just how special you are?" he demanded, firm mouth pressed into a determined line.

Startled, Christine couldn't think what to say. No one, not even her father, had ever told her she was special. Coming from Simon, the compliment was as startling as snow in June, as sweet as the season's first peach plucked from the tree.

"Oh, Simon," she managed, finding her voice at last.

He reached between them and slipped his hand over hers. Carrying it to his lips, he pressed a kiss into her palm. Warmth pooled in her belly; deep inside her woman's core, a small, trapped bird beat its wings, begging for release. She turned her face up to his, seeking. Wanting. More tempted than she'd thought it possible to be, she felt herself bending to him, with no more will of her own than a windblown reed.

Their mouths were but a hairsbreadth apart when her inner voice piped up, *You're a rum fool, Christine, that's what you are.*

Oh, dear Lord! Fearful of what she might do if she were to remain in his arms, she slipped her hand from his and shoved at his chest. "Please sar, leave me be."

Her puny push didn't budge him, but her plea must have. He dropped his hands and stepped back, running shaking hands through his hair. "Forgive me. I've offended you. I didn't mean . . ." He shook his head as if to clear it, and then backed to the door.

A wise woman would have let him go on thinking what he would, so long as he went. But Christine couldn't be wise where Simon was concerned. The anguished look in his eyes slashed through her; she felt her willpower giving way like field grasses beneath a scythe's blade.

She took a deep breath and blurted out, "Kindness can wound the same as meanness, worse betimes. When you talk gentle to me, when you . . . *touch* me, there's a pain that comes, the kind that won't just go away."

Spent, she dropped into a chair, rested her elbows on her lap, and let her head drop into her upturned palms. Quiet fell upon the room like a funeral drape.

"It won't happen again," he finally said, voice flat.

She didn't trust herself to look up. Seconds later she heard the door open, and then softly close.

Ten

> The secret thoughts of a man run over all things, holy, profane, clean, obscene, grave, and light, without shame or blame.
>
> —Thomas Hobbes,
> *Leviathan*, 1651

For Simon, the episode in Christine's bedchamber served as a reminder of how quickly a situation could go from bad to worse. It also served as a warning.

In the three weeks and a day since he'd charged into her chamber, he'd relived the scene countless times in his mind. Ample time to examine not only his actions, which were as disgraceful as they were pathetic, but also the motive driving them. Now that he could look beyond his anger, he saw that emotion for what it had been. A smoke screen. A sham.

From the moment he'd crossed the threshold and laid eyes on Christine, disheveled and dripping by the washstand, he'd felt his anger ebb. He hadn't been able to hold on to it any more than he'd been able to fight the surge of tender feelings nor the hot, heady rush of desire. Even now it amazed him to think how perfectly she'd fitted in his arms, how right it had felt to have her there. He'd been acutely aware of Christine as a woman, of himself as a man. And of the big brass four-poster that lay but a few feet away. Fortunately for them both, Christine had come to her senses.

When you talk gentle to me, when you touch me, there's a pain that comes, the kind that won't just go away.

How many sleepless nights had he spent mulling over that anguished declaration? How many meals had he pushed food about his plate, asking himself if she might possibly feel some small measure of the raw, restless yearning that gripped him whenever he found himself alone with her, an unavoidable state of affairs if he were to continue as her tutor. On that front at least, his plan was progressing better than he'd dared to hope. Christine did indeed possess a keen and lively mind. He'd been delighted to discover her reading and writing to be far more advanced than her rustic speech had led him to believe. A voracious reader, she'd already cut a blazing swath through his library. Novels mostly—the Brontë sisters, George Eliot, and Wilkie Collins were among her favorite authors. Simon considered most of what she read to be romantic tripe, but he refrained from saying so. The characters in her books were proving to be excellent teachers. It was apparent she derived more value from their example than she did from the sundry primers, pronunciation manuals, and etiquette books he'd first foisted upon her. Just the other day she'd asked him, quite out of the blue, if he didn't find Miss Albright "rather a haughty baggage." Cracking a smile in spite of himself, he'd admitted he did. Solemn-faced, Christine had commended him on his "sagacity," then gone back to her book. Astounding.

Seated at the library table, he lifted his gaze from the volume on ancient history he'd been reading from to the alcove. One hand resting on the globe—on Egypt, he hoped—she stared out the window, expression rapt.

Simon too found himself enjoying the view, but it wasn't the falling snow that captured, and held, his attention, but Christine. She looked particularly charming in a checkered frock of green, amber, and indigo; the yoked waist and full skirt complemented her lithe form to perfection. Even so, he couldn't help but imagine how much better the gown might look were the v-shaped neckline freed from its demure fichu collar.

Christ, he was doing it again. Deciding it was high time they both stopped pining over what they couldn't have, he said, "Our recess is past up. Come and take your seat."

Christine answered with a long sigh. " 'Tis ankle-deep by

now, surely." Pivoting, she turned pleading eyes on his face. "Mayn't we go out for a little while?"

"Go out . . . in this weather?"

" 'Tis falling ever so gentle and lovely. And we ain't had—"

"Haven't had."

She took a deep breath, obviously collecting her patience. "We *haven't had* a proper snowfall all winter."

A few months before he would have held firm. Instead he found himself relenting. "Oh, very well. I suppose ancient Egypt can wait until we get back."

Her eyebrows lifted. "We?"

It appeared she hadn't figured him into the bargain. He set his jaw. "I can hardly allow you to go out unaccompanied. Nor can I, in good conscience, order one of the footmen out in what amounts to a blizzard." When she made no further protest, he pushed back his chair and rose. "I'll fetch my coat and meet you at the south entrance in five minutes."

He left her for his bedchamber. Entering it, he found Trumbull lounging in one of the tapestry armchairs flanking the fire. The valet lifted his glass in a brief salute, then tipped it back and polished off the amber-colored contents. "Lovely stuff," he said, smacking his lips.

Simon eyed the open bottle at his manservant's elbow. "That's twenty-five-year-old scotch you're swilling."

"Not swillin', me boy. *Savorin.'* "

"Well, see you don't *savor* the entire bottle." Trumbull muttered something about Simon being no bloody fun anymore, but Simon was in no mood. "I'm going for a walk, so if you could bestir yourself . . ." He inclined his head toward the walnut wardrobe occupying the better part of one wall.

Trumbull set his glass on the side table with a heavy sigh, rose, and strolled over to the wardrobe. Opening the double doors, he ducked head and shoulders inside and began riffling through. Outer garments slung over one arm, he turned back to Simon. "But you hate snow."

What Simon hated was winter—period. Slate skies had made the crooked East End streets seem even uglier; the gusty wind had always seemed to find each and every chink in the plaster walls. No feeble winter sun could penetrate the clouds of coal dust that hung low above the vaporous air. Even now the sound of the wind gusting through the leafless trees outside brought to mind winter nights camped before the kitchen fire. Swathed in every stitch of clothing they owned, he and Rebecca hadn't been able to raise their arms for being so bundled yet it had been a struggle to stay warm. To stay alive.

"Perhaps I'm turning over a new leaf?" He bent his head to Trumbull, who wound an expensively scratchy wool muffler about his neck.

Grinning, Trumbull held out the coat. "If I was still a gaming man, I'd wager me last farthin' the lovely Miss Christine's behind this sudden urge to go gadding about. Am I wrong?"

Feeling as transparent as glass, Simon was only too happy to give Trumbull his back as he fed his arms through the coat sleeves. Rather than answer, he asked a question of his own. "Are you suggesting there is something wrong with Miss Tremayne and I walking together?"

Rounding him, Trumbull handed him his hat and fleece-lined leather gloves, then went to close the wardrobe. "I ain't suggestin' nothin' o' the sort, lad. I'd just 'ate to see ye hurt is all."

One foot in the hallway, Simon turned back. "What was that?"

The wardrobe doors clicked closed. Facing him, Trumbull shot him a sheepish grin. "I said be careful ye don't take a fall."

Minutes later, Simon joined Christine at the terrace doors.

"You look like a mummy," she giggled, gaze taking in his muffler that, owing to Trumbull's ministrations, covered his chin and most of his mouth.

He bit back a sharp retort as she opened the door and darted out onto the terrace.

"Oh, lovely!" she exclaimed, turning her face up to the sky to invite the snow and wind.

"L-lovely is it." He set his back teeth against a shudder. "I'll h-have to take your w-word on it."

"Oh, Simon, must you be such a curmudgeon?" Laughing, she flew past him and down the steps.

Curmudgeon, indeed. Shivering, Simon clenched the handrail and descended, boot heels slipping on the snow-sheeted steps. "Don't get too far ahead," he called after her.

But she was already sprinting down the snow-banked *allée*

toward a shoveling Jem, who stabbed his trowel into the snow and hailed her. Clenching his jaw, Simon quickened his pace.

Jem touched his forelock as Simon approached. "Good'ay, sar. Why, ye're the last person I'd have expected to see out and about in this muck."

Bristling beneath his many layers, Simon seized Christine by the elbow. "We're taking a walk." Anchoring Christine to his side, he ferried her forward.

The two lower gardens had yet to benefit from Jem's labors, and the snow climbed to Christine's calves. Once or twice Simon pulled down his scarf and, through stiffening lips, suggested they turn back, but Christine only laughed and urged him onward.

"I've a better idea," she announced as they approached the third and final garden. Had the wind not blown sharp enough to cut glass, the wild glint in Christine's gaze would have sufficed to make him shiver. She pointed to the woods that abutted the garden. "I'll race you to that oak tree."

Her challenge issued, she grabbed a fistful of her skirts and took off like an arrow. Simon had no choice.

"Infernal woman." Taking his hands out of his pockets, he bolted after her.

Chest heaving from gulping the razor-sharp air, he stopped at the edge of the woods. Snow carpeted the ground and feathered the branches of the leafless trees overhead. Squinting against the glare, he scanned the overgrown path twisting through the stand of trees. Where was she?

"Christine, this isn't funny," he called out, voice hoarse from shouting her name.

His annoyance had just given way to mild alarm when he heard a faint rustling from behind him.

"My, my, I thought I'd lost you."

He swung about just as a ball of packed snow hit him square between the eyes.

"She-devil!"

This is war. Taking cover, he dropped to his haunches and started scraping snow into piles.

Another wad of packed snow shattered against the trunk of his tree. Dodging the raining crystals, he kept on, not stopping until he'd lain in a goodly arsenal. Hands full, he stood and cautiously peered around the trunk. All was quiet. She must be out of ammunition.

Striving for his sternest tone, he called out, "Christine, if you don't stop this nonsense at once, it will be a month of Sundays before you see the outdoors again."

"Oh, all right." Empty hands at her sides, she stepped out into the open—and firing range.

Simon's snowball smacked her square on the chin.

"You tricked me!" she screeched, then turned tail to make a full-scale retreat.

"That's what the French call a *ruse de guerre*," he called back in a cheery voice, then lobbed another ball at her backside.

She dropped out of sight. Her mitten appeared and, dangling from it, a white hankie. Waving it, she called, "I surrender."

He grinned, palming his largest snowball yet. "How do I know this isn't a trick?"

"You'll just have to trust me."

So Eve had likely said to Adam. "Hm, I'll have to think about it."

"Please, Simon, I'm cold."

So she'd finally tired of her childish game. Half regretting she'd given in so soon, he dropped his snowball and stepped out into the clearing and into . . .

The missile, bigger and, if possible, colder than any of the others, smashed into his forehead, knocking the hat from his head.

"A *roose dew gare*," she yelled, then darted into the thicket.

He picked up his hat, knocked the snow from the crushed brim, and plunked it atop his head. Then he turned and ran like hell. Threading his way through the thicket, ignoring the branches clawing at his coat, he quickly caught up. As soon as she was an arm's length away, he lunged.

"Got you!"

Clamped to his chest, head tucked beneath his chin, she struggled for a moment more, then went slack. "All right, all right. Fair is fair. You have me. I give up."

Laughing, he turned her about in his arms. Snowflakes silvered the tips of her lashes and the cold had tinted her cheeks and lips a deep rose. Simon stopped laughing. He drew a ragged breath, scarcely noticing how the cold air cut his lungs. She was beautiful, part siren, part wood nymph, and she didn't even know it.

Telling himself that his quickened breathing owed to the chase, he said, "You're a worthy opponent, Miss Tremayne, but you appear to be my prisoner. Any suggestions for what I should do with you?"

One of her hands crept up to settle on his shoulder. "Seeing as how I've never been a prisoner of war before, I don't know as I can say." Her tongue darted out to moisten her bottom lip, thawing the pink flesh. "What would the French do?"

Oh, God, what indeed. Laying a hand on the small of her back, he drew her against him. Despite the layers of clothing between them, a thrill shot through him as he settled her firmly against his thighs. What he was about to do was tantamount to violating a sacred trust, but for the present he no longer cared.

Propping the leather-sheathed knuckles of his right hand beneath her jaw, he tipped her face up to his. "I imagine they'd do something like this." Their exhaled breaths melded into a single crystallized cloud as he lowered his mouth to meet hers.

A high-pitched hoot shattered the stillness. Disoriented, Simon stared up at the interloper: a snow owl perched on the branch directly above them. The creature blinked at them with wide, all-knowing eyes.

Christine backed away and began dusting snow from her shoulders. Directing her gaze beyond him, she asked, "What's on the other side?"

Humbled by how close he'd come to jettisoning all his fine resolutions, Simon stripped off his ice-encrusted gloves and slapped them against his thigh. "Only pasture land."

"Is it yours?"

"Yes."

"Then I want to see. Will you show me?"

"Yes, if you like though it's nothing to see."

They walked on in silence. The path was too narrow to accommodate them both, so Simon led the way until they emerged into the open snow-covered field.

His hope that her curiosity might be satisfied was dashed when she pointed to the chalk hill ahead and said, "That hill yonder. It overlooks the valley, doesn't it?" Without waiting for his answer, she hitched up her skirts and plowed toward it.

That hill and the valley it overlooked were Simon's least favorite places on the estate. On earth. If lying would have stayed her, he would have gladly done so, but already she'd moved beyond earshot. Panic seized him when he saw her take hold of a tree limb protruding from the hillside and lever herself up.

He reached her just as she found her footing amidst the snow-covered rock. "Determined to break your neck, I see."

"Rubbish, I'm as surefooted as a mountain goat." To prove it, she found a jutting rock with her right foot and started up.

Gritting his teeth, he reached for her hand. "Too bad you have the judgment of a peahen to go with it."

They climbed. Breathing hard, they reached the summit at last. Christine walked over to the ledge. "It's so beautiful here. It looks like a fairy land."

Reluctantly Simon followed her. "It's land, at any rate."

Looking down, she said, "It must be lovely in the springtime when the field flowers are in bloom."

Following her downward gaze, he felt his knees go weak. A nearly fatal fall from a ship's rigging had left him with a fear of heights. Even so, he knew that the memory alone accounted for only a part of the dread weighing anchor in his chest. This was the last place on earth he would ever seek refuge.

"I suppose so." He took a shaky step back, then covered the retreat by knocking snow from his boot heels.

Her gaze fell on his face. "You've never been up here before, have you?"

Feigning nonchalance, he shrugged. "Once, with the surveyor I hired."

But it had been long enough to ensure that his property line abutted that of his nearest neighbor. And that Valhalla, the house he was building, would be far bigger, far grander, and far more splendid than the sprawling granite structure at which Christine now pointed.

"What's the name of that big church over there?" she asked, looking back at him with wide, curious eyes.

Heart drumming, he hastened to satisfy her curiosity before it took root. "Not a church but a medieval priory. Stonevale

Priory. It's been a private residence ever since Henry the Eighth dissolved it, along with most of the wealthier monasteries and religious houses."

She turned back to him. "Have you ever been inside?"

He swallowed hard, feeling the cold creep into his bones. "No."

She turned away from him and looked back out. "It looks like a fairy castle."

"Don't be absurd," he snapped, feeling the old rancor rise. "It's just an old house. It has the obligatory great hall, a minstrel's gallery, and the requisite number of drafty bedchambers."

"Does anyone live there now?" she asked, still staring across the valley.

Inside his pockets, his hands fisted. "Yes," he ground out, his pleasure in the afternoon, in being with Christine, spoiled by her obvious fascination. "The old earl." More to himself than to her, he muttered, "He must be closing in on eighty."

She glanced back at him. "Perhaps we could call on him sometime?"

That did it. Before what he knew what he was about, he'd laid his hands on her shoulders and drawn her back from the ledge. Back to him.

"That house, you are never to go near it, do you understand?"

Eyes wide, she nodded. "Yes, but why not?"

His grip tightened until he could feel her shoulder bones beneath the layers. "Because I said not to. While you are living under my roof, you will abide by my rules. *All* my rules. Understood?"

He looked down to his hands, the powerful fingers bunching the wool of her cloak. The tenements in which he'd grown up had been fraught with men who thought nothing of beating their wives and taking their daughters to bed. What if, in the course of living among all that brutality, some of it had rubbed off?

Sickened by his inability to control his temper, he let go of her and backed away. "Forgive me. I don't know what came over . . . I only want you to promise to stay away." But suddenly it was he who needed to get away. Away from this place, away from Christine, as quickly as possible before he did something else he'd only live to regret. He swung away from her and started down the slope, not stopping even when he realized she wasn't following.

Innate wisdom urged him to turn back and see her down, but he reminded himself of her earlier boast about her climbing skills and told himself that she'd probably beat him to the bottom anyway.

He'd just reached bottom and stopped to wait for her when he heard it. A scream.

Fighting the sick lump of fear in his stomach, he started back up, pushing himself until he'd once more gained the summit.

Dragging great gulps of icy air into his burning chest, he shouted, "Christine!"

No reply.

Struggling to keep his balance against the buffeting wind, he staggered to the edge and looked below to the billowing whiteness. "Christine!"

"Simon!" From somewhere at his back, Christine's voice managed to carry on the wailing wind.

He whirled and ran to the other side. Blinking against the cold, he looked down and caught sight of a snow-covered mound caught in the bracken. Christine. Lying on her side and motionless, she was fast disappearing beneath the falling snow.

Heart in his throat, he raced toward her. Reaching her, he dropped down on his knees, furiously brushing snow from her face, her cloak. Ignoring the snow seeping through the knees of his breeches, he slipped an arm beneath her shoulders and lifted her.

Tears of relief sprang to his eyes when she blinked up at him. "Simon."

Mastering himself, he surveyed the damage. There were scratches on her cheek that didn't look serious, and an angry-looking bump above her left eye that did.

Throat tight, he demanded, "Where does it hurt?"

"My ankle, the right one." Features strained, she explained, "My feet tangled in my cloak, and I slipped." Brave creature that she was, she attempted a smile, but it ended as a wince.

He looked above them. The swath slicing through the otherwise undisturbed snow told the rest of the tale. She'd fallen, then rolled partway down the embankment. The gorse bushes that grew out of the hillside had broken her fall. They had, in all likelihood, also saved her life. Provided he got her indoors and soon. It must be closing in on four o'clock, and the temperature was fast falling. It would be dark—and freezing—inside of an hour.

He shifted his gaze back to Christine and forced a smile. "I'm going to have to carry you. Put your arm around my neck and hold on."

She nodded. As soon as she'd slipped her arms about his neck, he stood, his own arms tightened about her. Carrying her, he forced himself to take short, patient steps. Not that he could have gone much faster if he'd wanted to. Christine herself was light as a snowflake, but her sodden clothing felt like it weighed two stone.

He didn't speak to her until they'd safely reached the bottom. Then he asked, "How do you fare?"

She smiled up at him with blue-tinged lips. "I can't feel the hurt anymore."

What she meant was that she couldn't feel her feet. Fear welled inside him but he pushed it down and plunged into the thicket, hunkering low to protect his precious charge from the branches that seemed to rake his own limbs at every pass.

When they emerged into his gardens, the white flakes had turned to sleet. Simon's trousers were drenched to the knees, and his feet and hands were frozen beyond feeling. He held on to Christine through sheer force of will. Blinking watery eyes, he matched his footsteps to their previous tracks and forged ahead.

She shifted in his arms. He looked down. Her teeth chattered, and the waxy redness at the tip of her nose worried him. Frostbite? A myriad of nightmarish possibilities pushed through his mind. What if she contracted pneumonia? What if she lost a limb to gangrene? What if she died?

He walked faster. They passed the gazebo and pressed on until at long last he stood at the bottom of the terrace steps, the stone slabs glossy as glass. He ascended, ice splintering beneath the soles of his boots, the muscles in his calves and thighs quivering as he fought to keep his footing.

Mrs. Griffith must have been watching from one of the back windows. She opened the door just as they reached the terrace.

"My word, what's happened?" she asked, throwing her

weight against the door to close it behind them.

The warmth hit Simon like a blast from a baker's oven. Balancing Christine in his arms, he said, "My cousin has taken a bad fall. She may have broken her ankle." With that, he whisked around and started toward the front hall, leaving the housekeeper to follow. "Send Jem for Dr. Barker at once."

Christine lifted her head from his shoulder. "We mustn't send Jem out in this weather. For certain 'tis naught but a sprain."

But Simon would brook no argument. Jaw set, he mounted the stairs. "Dr. Barker shall be the judge of that. Send for him, Mrs. Griffith."

Christine's bedroom door stood ajar. Simon kicked it the rest of the way open and carried her inside.

A young housemaid stood before the crackling fire, applying her feather duster to the bric-a-brac lining the mantel shelf. Sighting them, she spun about.

Simon set Christine on the edge of the bed. Banking the pillows against the headboard, he eased her back, then turned to the maid who stood watching, mouth agape. "There's a bottle of scotch in my bedchamber. Fetch it and bring it here. And more blankets, too. *Now!*" he added, when the girl remained rooted to the same spot.

"Y-yes, sir," she stammered, then dropped her duster and bolted out the door.

He stripped off his gloves, then worked on freeing Christine of her wet cloak, his numbed fingers clumsy as he fought to unhook the queue of brass buttons at the front. Slipping an arm behind her, he tugged the garment down and off.

"Better?" he asked, whisking it away.

She answered with a groggy nod, and he left her to drape the garment over the back of a chair. Feeling the blood returning to his hands, he peeled off her gloves. "Are you in much pain?" he asked, chafing her icy fingers.

She shook her head, tendrils of wet hair plastered to her pale cheeks. "My ankle smarts some, but it's not too bad."

Now that she'd begun to thaw, her injury would throb. His own face and hands stung, the nerves resurrected by the fire's heat. But his discomfort was nothing compared to the pain she must be in.

"Let me make you more comfortable while we wait for the doctor."

He'd just started on the laces of her boots when the housemaid returned. " 'Ere, sir," she said, dropping the blanket on the foot of the bed and handing him the bottle. "Will there be anythin'—"

"No," he said, cutting her off. He put the bottle down and grabbed for the blanket, bundling it about Christine's shivering shoulders. Catching Christine's gaze, he remembered to add, "Thank you," then reached for the bottle on the bedside table.

He poured three-fingers' worth into a glass and pressed it into Christine's cold hand. "Drink this," he urged. "It will help dull the throbbing."

Sniffing the rim, she pulled a face. "It smells like medicine. What if the doctor should smell it on my breath?"

He couldn't help but smile. What a prim little thing she was, how preoccupied with appearances. Hard to believe he'd found her in a ... well, what did that matter now? "We'll tell him I forced it down you, all right?"

Solemn-faced, she nodded. "All right then but just a sip." She lifted the glass to her lips and tipped it back. A moment later, her face went up in flames and her eyes ran rivers. Sputtering, she held the remainder out to him. "T-tastes l-like m-medicine too."

He coaxed her into taking another sip, then took the glass and set it on the night table. "Let's have a look at that ankle." He reached down and slipped off her left shoe.

Christine cried out. She sank back into the bed. "You must think me a terrible baby."

He shook his head. "Hardly. But your stockings will have to come off as well. I can use my pocketknife to cut away the fabric."

Her horrified gaze flew to his face. "Oh no, don't do that. They're *new*. If you'll just—"

"Of course." He turned away. Standing with his back to her, he folded his hands behind him and waited.

Petticoats rustled. A moment later she whispered, "I'm decent."

He turned about to see her gown once more in place and her cotton stockings laid neatly at her side. Gently he hedged up her hem and probed the ankle. Already it had swollen to twice the circumference of the other and boasted a knot the size of a hen's egg, but he felt no obvious broken bones. In India, the nearest physician often had been several days' journey and, like most British expatriates, he'd become adept at treating minor injuries. Likely Christine's was a sprain but, even so, she'd have to stay off it for several weeks. He thought about how active she was, how much she loved being outside, and fresh guilt rose inside him.

He hadn't known such shame since he was nine, and his mother had caught him handing Rebecca the gingerbread he'd pilfered from a costermonger's cart. None of them had eaten since breakfast the day before, but she'd tossed out the treat all the same.

"You are my son. You are not a thief," she'd said, then whipped him soundly.

Despite his stinging backside and empty belly, he'd gone to bed happier. Relieved. If only Christine would berate him for his churlish behavior, how much better he would feel.

Instead she said, "I'm sorry to be such a bother."

Any other woman in her place would have hurled reproaches until her breath ran out, but this was Christine. Sweet, generous, *forgiving* Christine.

"God, Christine, are you trying to torture me?" He dragged a hand through his wet hair. "If anyone's to blame, it's me. I should never have left you to come down on your own. It could just as easily been your neck you twisted." Or broke.

Around a yawn, she said, "I'm just lucky I guess."

Her eyelids fluttered closed. It was the scotch. She wasn't used to it. Combined with the exposure to the cold, it was making her drowsy.

"Sleep well, love." He bent and kissed one closed lid, then the other. Her soft sigh wafted across his face. He brushed back her hair, and his lips found the bump on her forehead.

A cough sounded from the hallway. He straightened and swung about to see Mrs. Griffith, tray in hand, watching them from the doorway. Her open mouth put him in mind of a fish.

Color high, she entered. Her gaze darting from Christine's exposed ankles to the scotch on the nightstand, she set down the tray.

"Jem's gone for the doctor," she informed Simon in a low voice. "And Janet's on her way up with some cold cloths for her ankle." Rooting her regard to the slumbering patient, she added, "She really ought to get out of those wet clothes."

Attention fixed on Christine's sweet face, it took Simon a full moment to recognize his cue to leave. "Yes, yes, of course." He turned and started for the door.

Christine's voice called him back. "Simon." Beneath the bundle of blankets, she pushed herself up on her elbows. "Don't go."

He tried to smile. "I'll be just downstairs. Rest now."

She smiled back. "I'll try. You'll come back, won't you?"

Guilt—and something else—wrenched him. Rather than lie to her, he turned back to the housekeeper. "A word with you outside, if I may?"

"Of course, sir." She nodded and followed him into the hallway.

Pulling Christine's door closed, he said, "I don't want her left alone. See that someone—one of the housemaids—stays with her tonight."

She nodded, and Simon fancied some of the disapproval lifted from her lined face. "I'll sit with her myself."

"Thank you. Thank you, Mrs. Griffith."

Leaving his heart behind, Simon turned heavy footsteps toward the stairs.

Eleven

> If Winter comes, can Spring be far behind?
>
> —Percy Bysshe Shelley,
> "Ode to the West Wind," 1819

Simon knew firsthand that a month of hobbling about would test even the mildest of temperaments. In the two weeks following her accident, Christine bore her confinement with few complaints. A miserable bout of the sniffles accompanied her sprained ankle and, between the two ailments and the raw weather, she'd seemed content to bide indoors. Most of her free time she'd spent curled up on the library sofa, her nose stuck in a novel and her cat warming her feet. Simon had liked having her there. He'd liked it so much that he'd even given off complaining about her interloping cat. Personally he didn't care whether or not spring ever came. But of course it did.

Midway through the third week of Christine's convalescence the weather turned from lion to lamb. Gray skies gave way to blue, blades of green grass poked through the melting snow, and the wintry gales gentled to zephyr breezes redolent with the promise of spring. Christine grew snappish and restless, demanding to be allowed to take part in activities that, as she well knew, Dr. Barker had expressly forbade.

"You treat me like a child," she complained one Monday morning over breakfast, after Simon had told her she wasn't even to think of going near the stables.

"Hm?" Closing his ears, he unfolded his crisply ironed copy of the *Kentish Observer*. He'd just begun perusing the front page when the screech of cutlery grating against china set his teeth on edge. Lowering the paper, he looked over its top to Christine.

"I'm not, you know." She stabbed her fork's prongs into the mutilated remains of what had started out that morning as a shirred egg. Looking up from the yellow muck, she added, "I'll be twenty in four more days."

Concealing a smile, he folded his paper and set it next to his plate atop the week-old copy of the *Times* that had just arrived that morning. "Twenty," he repeated, striving to look solemn. "Quite an age. I suppose we should begin planning your retirement. Do you fancy Brighton or Bath?"

Eyes aiming daggers, she lifted her chin. "I'll not stay to be made fun of." She whipped away from him and reached for the crutches she'd lain across the seat of the adjacent chair.

"Wait." Reaching over, he touched her shoulder. "Please don't go off angry. I was only teasing."

She unfurled her fingers from the crutch and turned back. Raising repentant eyes to his, she admitted, "And I'm only cross."

He took back his hand, but fixed his gaze on her face. "And more than a little homesick, I suspect. Have you heard from your family?"

Her brown eyes widened for an instant, then she looked down. "I posted the money you gave me last week. I expect Liza will write when she can." Pushing the forked egg about her plate, she admitted, "This is the first birthday I've ever spent away from them."

"Wont to make something of a fuss, are they?"

She nodded. "Liza always bakes a cake, or *burns* one more like. Last year she fair near brought down the cottage." She put down the fork and whisked the napkin from her lap. Dabbing the corners of her eyes, she said, "Jake and Timmy gathered a bag of stones, and the four of us spent the afternoon playing ducks and drakes on the pond. But that must seem silly to you."

"Not at all." Simon had passed his last eighteen birthdays apart from his family, starting with his sixteenth spent retching in a ship's cargo hold. Well acquainted with the loneliness she was feeling, determined to cheer her, he said, "I'm a poor substitute, I know, but why not spend your birthday with me? We'll do something special, make it a real celebration. Now that the roads are clear, there's no reason we can't go out."

At the word *out*, her whole face brightened. "Oh, Simon, do you mean it?"

He glanced at her plate, the delicate floral motif at its center encrusted with yellow glob. Unable to resist, he said, "Provided you promise to never, under any circumstances, wreak such havoc on an egg again."

This time she smiled. He smiled too although, in the back of his mind, guilt rankled like heavy chains. How easy she was to please and how selfish he was not to have suggested an outing before now. He'd told himself he was waiting for her ankle to heal, for the roads to clear, but now he dismissed them as excuses and feeble ones at that. The unflattering truth was that he'd rather liked keeping Christine all to himself.

He reached for the silver coffeepot and topped off both their cups. "I thought we'd drive into Maidstone. The county chamber music society performs every Friday evening, and there's an inn near the concert hall that serves fairly decent food. We could have a late supper after the performance if you'd like."

Beaming, she pushed her plate aside. "It all sounds perfect."

His own birthday came at the beginning of April, only he would be five and thirty. Most men his age were married with a brood of children but that had never bothered him . . . until now. Looking into Christine's face, so earnest and so *young*, the oppressive possibility struck him that he'd already lived half his life, maybe more.

Sobered, he raised his coffee cup and took a bracing swallow. Returning it to his saucer, he mused aloud, "Would you believe I was twenty once?"

"Why, no . . . I mean, yes." She cast him a helpless look. "I don't know what you want me to say."

Lies. Sweet, beautiful lies. "Try the truth."

"Well, um . . ." She broke off and fiddled with her cutlery. Turning her teaspoon over and over, she finally said, "Sometimes, when you look at me stern-like or call me down for some mistake I've made, you remind me of Father."

Good God, it was worse than he'd thought. Chilled, he asked, "How so?"

Nibbling on her thumbnail, she thought for a moment. "Father was a reg'lar tartar in the dairy. Things had to be done just so. Only old linen for dryin' the pails, and the floors must be scoured twice a week with lime and skimmed milk. One time he caught me using soap instead. Even though I'd made sure to use cold water so it wouldn't stick, he boxed my ears just the same."

Feeling as though a mirror were being held up to his face, Simon stared down into his coffee. "If I seem critical or faultfinding, it's only because I want to see you improve. You must believe me when I say I have your best interest at heart."

Your best interest at heart. God, he *did* sound fatherly. And old.

She nodded, expression solemn. "I know, and most times I don't mind."

He cleared his throat, which suddenly seemed to have grown a lump the size of a hen's egg. "And the times when you do mind?"

She chewed on her bottom lip, a nervous habit he'd come to find too endearing to want to change. "When we're taking a turn about the garden or playing cribbage, you're a different person. You smile more, even laugh sometimes, and I get so caught up I forget to mind my p's and q's." She rolled her eyes. "That's usually when you catch me in some fox's paw. Afterward I feel so stupid, so foolish, I wish the earth would open up and swallow me like the whale swallowed Jonah."

She'd meant to say *faux pas,* but Simon was too shaken to correct her. He'd tried to be her mentor, but instead he'd become her tormenter. Appalled, he searched her face for some sign he'd misheard.

"You're neither stupid nor foolish but a bright, intelligent young woman. You know that, don't you?"

To his chagrin, she only shrugged. "I'd best get to that

mathematics problem you set me to last night, and we'll just see how sharp I am. I thought I had it all worked out but . . ." Pushing back from the table, she reached for her crutches.

Simon was on his feet in an instant. "Let me help you."

Holding on to the curved back of her chair, she waved him back down. "Sit and have your coffee. I'll manage."

Already leaden with guilt, he refused to take no for an answer. He came to her side and gave her his arm to lean on while she positioned the crutches. After he'd ferried her to the door and opened it, there was nothing left to do but step aside and watch her hobble through.

Heart plummeting with each *thump, thump*, he sagged against the door frame.

I wish the earth would open up and swallow me like the whale swallowed Jonah.

Little did Christine know just how well acquainted he was with that very sentiment.

Standing before the full-length dressing mirror in nothing but her shift and drawers, Christine faced her reflection with squared shoulders, fastened on a smile, and drawled, "Why, yes, Simon, another gla-a-a-ss of champagne would be glorious. How good of you to a-a-a-sk."

"Good heavens, miss, at this rate ye'll be on yer ear before yer even out the front door." Christine spun about to see a grinning Janet standing just behind her, arms full.

Christine gave her freshly curled hair a light pat. "Oh, Janet, you nearly scared the life out of me."

"Sorry, miss. I did knock, but I guess you was too caught up to hear." She glanced down to the golden silk spread over her arm. " 'Tis pressed and ready. I saw to it myself."

Thanks to Margot's taste and Simon's bottomless purse, Christine had a wardrobe of pretty clothes, but this gown she'd been saving for a special occasion. Tonight, her birthday, was it.

Antsy with anticipation, she could hardly hold still while Janet laced her into her corset, then helped her on with her crinoline and petticoat. Feeling like a princess from the pages of a Grimm Brothers fairy tale, she closed her eyes as the maid lifted the gown over her head and fed her arms through the armholes of the puffed sleeves. As soon as the hooks and eyes at the back were fastened, she opened her eyes and limped over to the mirror.

Gazing once more into the glass, she scarcely recognized the elegant stranger peering back at her. Certainly she'd never imagined that Christine Tremayne, the dairyman's daughter, would wear such a dress. Fit for a royal princess, it had a fitted bodice, deeply pointed waist, and a full pleated skirt. Intricate satin rosebuds edged the scalloped neckline; larger roses spilled from the bustle at back. At Janet's urging, she'd applied a hint of color to her lips and cheekbones and a light dusting of powder to her bosom. She looked sophisticated, pretty even. If Liza and the boys were to see her now, they likely wouldn't know her. And Simon...

In the midst of her excitement, a terrible thought struck her. Simon had bid her a happy birthday at breakfast, but he hadn't so much as mentioned their evening plans. Immediately after luncheon he'd called for his horse to be saddled and had left for town. What if he didn't return in time? What if he'd forgotten altogether?

Janet came up beside her and handed Christine her evening gloves. "Oh, miss, you look a picture."

"Thank you." Slipping on her evening gloves, she glanced at the ormolu clock atop the mantel shelf. Preparing for disappointment, she asked, "Mr. Belleville—"

"Rode in a half hour ago. I saw him on my way upstairs."

Relief washed over her. Simon was back. He hadn't forgotten. But she mustn't keep him waiting. She of all people knew how he prized punctuality.

She gave Janet a grateful peck on the cheek for all her help, then hurried to gather up her gold velvet evening cape, beaded reticule, and ivory fan.

Janet's eyes bugged. "You can't mean to say you're going down *now?*"

"Why ever not? We were to meet below at five o' clock. It's almost that."

Janet shot her a pained look. "Are ye sure ye won't wait a bit? I could send downstairs for a nice cup of tea."

A cup of tea, when she'd been sipping imaginary champagne all afternoon! Feeling as giddy as if she'd imbibed in earnest, Christine executed an awkward twirl, her ankle all but forgotten in the sheer delight of the moment. Her cloak draped over her arm, she headed for the hallway. "Wish me luck," she called back, one foot already out the door.

At the head of the stairs, she paused to gather herself. *Deportment,* Margot's voice reminded her. Sliding her hand down the polished mahogany banister, she started down slowly, not rushing as she was wont to do when she was nervous. Peering over the railing, she sighted Simon in the front hall below. Her heart skipped, her breath caught, her gloved fingers clenched on the banister. Dressed in formal black, he was the tall, dark, handsome prince of every girlish fantasy she'd ever entertained. Only Simon was real.

And for one night, *this* night, she would pretend he was all hers.

Simon paced from one end of the fringed runner to the other, white-gloved hands clenched behind him, gaze riveted on the carpet pattern. He was being foolish, he knew. Christine wouldn't be down for some time, he was certain of it. Even so, he couldn't seem to sit still let alone apply himself to the mountain of papers awaiting him on his desk.

A soft sound drew his attention to the stairs. Expecting to see Mrs. Griffith or one of the housemaids, he turned about. And found himself locking gazes with . . . Christine.

Garbed in a gown of saffron silk, her hair swept up into an intricate confection of ringlets, her bared shoulders held back to reveal every proud inch of her lithe frame, she seemed more a vision, a dream, than the flesh-and-blood woman he'd grown accustomed to.

Desire hit him with the force of a hammer striking an anvil. The hall was chilly but, inside him, heat rose, coiling in his chest, his belly, his groin. As he moved toward her, he felt every glib greeting, every clichéd compliment, flee his brain like geese flying south for the winter until only a single word remained. *Beautiful.*

"Christine," he said, barely above a whisper.

Drowning in the soft, welcoming smile she sent him, he reached out to take her offered hand as she stepped off the landing.

"I'm not late, am I?"

That made him smile. Despite her finery, she was so unspoiled, so *dear.* "When a gentleman escorts a lady to an event, unless he doesn't mind being very late indeed, he usually arranges to meet her well in advance of when he intends on leaving." When she continued to look puzzled, he added, "Put simply, to be truly fashionable, you should have kept me waiting for at least a half hour more."

For a second, she looked crestfallen. "I've gone about it all wrong again?"

Her words touched off an explosion of tenderness in his heart. "No, not at all. I'm glad you're here. So glad." Remembering himself, he took the cape from her and draped it across the bench. Turning back, he said, "I have a present for you."

Her eyes flew open. "You got me a present too!"

He nodded, feeling suddenly unsure. "It's not a whole bag of stones, I'm afraid, but I hope you'll like it." He led her to the pier glass. Stepping behind her, he said, "Close your eyes and don't open them until I say so."

"Simon, I—"

"Tut, tut, I'll brook no argument." As soon as she closed her eyes, he reached into the inner pocket of his cutaway jacket and withdrew the black velvet box. "No peeking," he said, flipping open the lid. Withdrawing the necklace, he wove the gold chain about her throat.

"Oh, it's cold." She reached up, her fingertips brushing the pendant dangling just above the swell of her breasts.

"Sorry for that. It was a long and rather bracing ride back from town."

"Your errand?"

"The very one." His evening gloves made him awkward, but he finally fastened the clasp. He lingered a moment more, inhaling her sweet lavender scent, then stepped back. "Now you may open your eyes."

She did, and their gazes met in the mirror. Hers slipped from his face to the necklace, and she uttered an exclamation of pure delight. "Oh, Simon, it's fair near the same color as my gown. How did you know?"

"My spies are everywhere." He winked, feeling light and gay and altogether freer than he had in years. "The stone is amber. Do you like it?"

She whisked around to face him. "Like it! Simon, it's the loveliest thing I've ever seen."

You're the loveliest thing I've ever seen. "I'm glad you think so," he said in a cool tone that belied his burning blood.

She took a small step back. "Well?" she asked, extending her arms from her sides.

He cocked a brow and folded his arms across his chest, pretending to consider. "Well what?"

Two bright spots of scarlet appeared on either of her cheeks. "Do I look—" She faltered, lips pursed, brow furrowed, causing him to suspect she was searching for one of the long, elegant words she'd likely shored up for the occasion. Apparently finding it, she drew a deep breath and blurted out, "Do I look . . . *ravished?*"

Accustomed as he'd grown to the practiced simpering of society beauties, Christine's guileless gaffe was like being handed a glass of iced lemonade after toiling for hours in the searing sun. Refreshing. Delicious. The perfect antidote to the sensual tension thrumming between them.

Laying a hand in the small of her back, he guided her toward the door. "Not yet . . . but then the evening is young."

Maidstone's concert hall was little more than a glorified assembly room. Owing to the beneficence of a select few private patrons, Simon among them, a larger stage and an orchestra pit replaced the former bare platform and curtained private boxes now graced the upper tiers of the audience. It was to one of these velvet-hung boxes that Simon led Christine.

They'd just settled into their seats when from behind them a woman's voice shrilled, "Oh dear, have they begun already?"

Simon looked back just as a plump, gray-haired matron in a purple taffeta gown and feathered headdress appeared at the back of the box on the arm of a distinguished—and by now very familiar—older gentleman.

Simon sprang from his seat and turned to greet the mayor and his wife. "Mayor Albright, this a pleasant surprise."

"Good to see you, Belleville. I didn't know you were a subscriber." He extended his hand and Simon shook it. Turning back to his wife, he said, "Martha, this is the young Tory firebrand I've been telling you about. The one Fanny's always prosing on about."

"*The* Mr. Belleville?" Squinting, the elder woman peered around Simon to Christine, who also had risen. Turning back to her husband, she said, "Good heavens, Horatio, Fanny led me to believe the fellow was a bachelor."

Mayor Albright scratched the grizzled sideburn covering the better part of his flushed cheek. "I didn't know you were married, Belleville. Really ought to spread that about. Married candidates always have the advantage in an election."

Feeling supremely uncomfortable, Simon turned to Christine, who hung back. Moving aside to draw her into their circle, he said, "Allow me to present my ward, Miss Christine Tremayne."

"Your ward." Brows lifted, the matron looked from Christine to Simon, then back at her husband. "I see," she said beneath her breath, and there was no mistaking the disapproving undercurrent in those two innocuous words.

An awkward silence descended. Simon was wondering how to dispel it when Christine piped up, "It's my birthday."

Three heads, including Simon's, snapped about to regard her.

Swallowing, she continued, "When my abigail took ill this morning and couldn't come with us, I wanted to cry off but Cousin Simon, well, he's such a dear old thing." She paused to send Simon a syrupy smile. "He couldn't bear to see me disappointed."

The mayor looked from Christine to Simon. "You two are cousins?"

Simon braced himself to tell the first lie of his political career. "Yes."

"First cousins, actually," Christine embellished, giving Simon's forearm a cousinly pat. "That explains the resemblance."

Squinting, Mrs. Albright leaned forward. "What resemblance?"

Turning to Simon, Christine dealt the bridge of his nose a smart crack with her closed fan. "Why the Tremayne nose, of course," she intoned with a knowing nod, then turned her face to the side to display her own profile.

Holding her quizzing glass aloft, the mayor's wife looked from Christine to Simon. "Hm." She handed the glass to her husband, who followed suit.

Fortunately the theater bell rang and the house lights flickered, signaling that it was indeed time for the audience to take their seats.

"Shall we?" Linking her arm through Simon's, Christine tugged him toward the front of the box. "Perhaps we can all have supper together after the performance?" She tossed a gay smile back over her shoulder.

Simon nearly choked on his own saliva. "Yes, by all means. We'd be honored if you'd join us."

"Lovely of you to ask, but we dined earlier, didn't we, Horatio?" Mrs. Albright's elbow found her husband's side.

Wincing, the mayor dutifully nodded. "Can't sup past six, or I'm up all night."

Pouching her lips into a pretty pout, Christine said, "Pity. Another time, then?" Raising her closed fan, she waved it gaily. "Well, cheerio. Perhaps we'll meet up at the intermission."

As soon as the musicians took up their instruments, Mrs. Albright bent close to her husband's ear. "If she's his cousin, I'll eat these feathers I'm wearing."

" *'Dear old thing!* The Tremayne nose'! Really, Christine, have you no shame?" Seated across from her at a window-front table in the dining room of the inn, Simon raised his champagne flute in a heartfelt salute.

Expression uncertain, Christine touched her glass to his. "You aren't angry with me, then?"

"Aside from that crack you dealt my nose, I feel nothing but heartfelt admiration. You were a marvel of quick thinking. You took a potentially disastrous situation and completely turned it about." Focusing on the champagne in his goblet, he voiced the compliment he should have paid earlier. "Graced with both brains and beauty, I dare say you won't remain a governess for long." In response to her quizzing look, he added, "What I mean to say is that you're certain to marry."

Setting her champagne aside, she went back to pushing the poached salmon about her plate. "But I'll be in the schoolroom with *children*. And taking my meals alone in my room, or so you tell me. I don't see how I shall meet anybody even to be friends with, let alone to marry."

"Oh, but you will. One day your employers will host a dinner party, and you shall be asked to join them in order to make an even number. There'll be at least one bachelor present, there always is. His eyes will meet yours from overtop the centerpiece, and six months thence you'll find yourself walking down a church aisle, carrying a clutch of orange blossoms."

Absurd to feel envy for someone who didn't exist. And yet, imagining Christine's future husband, Simon felt a sharp stab of jealousy and something else—regret?—twisting like a knife in his gut.

Grinning, Christine said, "And I thought *I* had an imagination. As if anyone with a grain of sense in his head would have *me*." Her amused gaze fixed on his champagne flute. "Perhaps you'd best not finish that, sar, for surely you're in your cups a'ready to be having such queer fancies."

"You'll see," he said, wishing that the champagne might indeed buoy his suddenly flagging mood. He glanced from her half-eaten meal to his own barely touched ginny fowl. "Shall we see about ordering dessert? It appears we've both left room."

They passed the ride home in companionable silence. For once, Simon was in no rush to reach his destination. Seated across from Christine in his coach's shadowed interior, he would have been quite content to travel the countryside until dawn, gazing at his lovely companion's shadow-swathed shape.

All too soon, they halted in Valhalla's circular drive.

Lantern in hand, Jem appeared to open the coach door. " 'Appy birthday, Miss Christine. And might I say again what a treat you look."

A treat, indeed. Glancing at his driver, framed in the open carriage door, Simon wondered whether or not his own visage registered a similar state of moonstruck worship. Hoping to God he'd managed somewhat more in the way of subtlety, he stepped out, and then turned back for Christine.

Light from the carriage lantern touched her face as she stepped down and released his hand. "This was a wonderful birthday. I wish it didn't have to end."

He thought of his bedroom, depressingly deserted. It was Trumbull's night off, so he couldn't even count on a game of chess to ease his restlessness. Loathe to play victim to the sleepless hours, he found himself saying, "Your birthday doesn't end officially until midnight. We've at least an hour more to celebrate."

A smile replaced the confusion knitting her brow. "Is it to be cribbage in the library, then? Are you sure you can afford to lose any more matchsticks?"

It was his turn to smile. "Unless my losing streak abates, soon you'll have enough lumber to build your own Valhalla. But actually what I had in mind was a stroll in the gardens." A strange look settled over her features. Seeing it, self-doubt seized him. "Forgive me. That was thoughtless. Your ankle—"

"Feels perfectly fine." She laid a hand on his arm, an innocent gesture that sent his heart tripping. "And I'm far too wide awake to sleep."

Until now, he hadn't realized how much he'd dreaded her saying no. Almost giddy, he called to Jem to bring them a light.

Holding the lantern aloft, Simon took Christine's hand and together they skirted the house. Leading a beautiful, desirable, young woman into his gardens after dark was tantamount to playing with fire, but he couldn't seem to bring himself to care. For this night at least, he would let himself live the fantasy that Christine was his. A harmless bit of self-indulgence provided he made sure matters didn't go beyond hand-holding.

Coming up on the gardens, Simon set their course for the path leading to the gazebo, freshly painted and festooned with gingerbread trim.

He held the light in one hand and Christine's in his other while she climbed the three small steps. Just inside he found a second lamp hanging on a peg by the door. Taking it down, he lit it as well, then joined Christine at the rail where she stood looking out. Silvered by the moon, her golden cape billowing in the breeze, she might have been one of Diana's nymphs or the moon goddess herself. As ethereal as a moonbeam and just as certain to vanish the moment he reached out to her.

"Formulating plans for the foliage?" he quipped, his shoulder brushing hers as he settled next to her and leaned over the side.

She nodded. "I love all the seasons, but spring is my favorite."

Apart from worrying how inclement weather would affect the train schedule, Simon hadn't considered the change in seasons in years. Now he found himself recalling how he and Rebecca had looked forward to spring as a brief, blissful interlude between the numbing cold of winter and summer's stifling heat.

A soft breeze caught at her hair, snatching a glossy curl from its velvet ribbon. She tucked it behind one shell-shaped ear, and Simon's gaze alighted on the small indentation marring her cheekbone. A thought struck him.

"Earlier tonight, when you refused to credit the notion that anyone would want to marry you..." Reaching out, he brushed the small scar with his thumb. "Don't tell me this is the reason." When she didn't answer, he found himself shaking his head at the folly of youth. "Christine," he tried again. "Don't you know it's the tiny flaw that makes the masterpiece?"

She turned to him. The raw vulnerability in her eyes made his chest ache. " 'Tis our deeds that mark us more than what others do to us. What I've done, it's marked me deeper than any scar ever could."

What an idiot he was. Of course she'd meant her time at the brothel. To be forced to take part in that most intimate of acts with any number of strangers—Simon was well acquainted with the mental damage that could result from enduring a single such experience. That Christine had lived the nightmare day after day and somehow had managed to hold on to her sanity, her sense of humor, and her *sweetness,* filled him with admiration.

Carried away on a flood of feeling, he reached for her. His hands found her shoulders. Very gently he turned her toward him. "You did what you had to do. You survived. That's all that matters."

She bit her quivering bottom lip. "Is it?"

"Yes," he vowed, a fierce protectiveness surging through him. It was then, in that precise moment, that he realized he never wanted to let her go.

But he must. If he didn't accept that inevitability, if he didn't begin to wean himself from his foolish fantasies, there'd be the devil to pay when it came time for them to part.

He dropped his hands and took a small step back. "You're

a survivor, Christine. I'm a survivor too. Perhaps someday I'll tell you..." He caught himself before the revelations could come spilling out. Instead, he ended with, "As a fellow survivor, I admire you more than words can convey."

She touched the pendant he'd given her, and Simon followed her hand with his gaze. "I thought this was the best present anyone ever gave me, but I was wrong. What you just said, the way you eased my mind, you can't know what it means to me." Bracing her hand on his chest, she turned her face up and brushed a kiss over his cheek.

At the touch of her lips, Simon felt as if the whole gazebo, and him with it, were spinning out of control. Recovering, he looked down into her bright, liquid eyes. "What was that for?"

"For making this a night I'll treasure the rest of my days." Before he could form a reply, she grabbed one of the two lanterns from the table and limped out.

"Christine, wait." He started down the steps after her, then stopped short when he saw her standing just below.

"It's all been so lovely," she said, her voice a quavering whisper. "Please don't ruin it by saying more." With that she turned and headed back toward the house.

Sinking down onto the bottom step, Simon pressed his fingertips to the spot where her soft lips had touched and watched as Christine became one with the shadows.

Twelve

Nothing is so burdensome as a secret.

—French Proverb

Simon was in the thick of his meeting with William Harrison, the party agent, when his library door flew open. Both men looked up from the papers littering Simon's desk as Christine, dressed in a riding habit of peacock blue, sailed in.

"Simon, I—" She drew up short when she saw Harrison by the desk. "Oh, forgive me. I didn't know you had company."

A month before Simon would have launched into a lecture on the vital importance of knocking before entering. Instead he rounded the desk and, with a foolish grin, said, "A welcome intrusion. We were due for a break, weren't we, Harrison?"

Behind him, Harrison plucked the pencil from behind one pointed ear and hurried forward. "Indeed, particularly when the intruder proves to be so charming a young lady."

"In this case, the charming young lady happens to be my ward, Miss Christine Tremayne," Simon said, striving to sound avuncular. "Christine, come and meet Mr. William

Harrison, the party agent from Maidstone. Mr. Harrison has ridden in from town to advise me on the election."

Simon couldn't quite conquer the stab of stupid jealousy that struck him when Christine offered the smitten Harrison a soft smile and extended her hand. "Mr. Harrison, I'm pleased to meet you."

From behind his wire-rimmed spectacles, Harrison's pale gaze brightened. He took Christine's hand in his and, in Simon's estimation, held it overlong. "Miss Tremayne, the pleasure is entirely mine." He squared his slender shoulders until he almost appeared to fill out his heavily padded jacket.

Taking back her hand, Christine turned to Simon. "I'd thought to ask if you might come riding with me, but I see you're working. I'll be off then. Good day, Mr. Harrison."

She bobbed a brisk curtsey in Harrison's direction, then turned about and started toward the door. Watching her go, Simon knew a sharp sense of regret. Today happened to be his birthday, his *thirty-fifth,* a secret he suddenly wished he hadn't kept to himself. How he wished he were spending the day with Christine instead of closeted with the party agent. Just when had pouring over parliamentary transcripts and party position papers lost its luster?

Stifling a sigh, he turned back to Harrison. "Now where were we?" he asked, mentally calculating the time it would take the party agent to ask the inevitable.

Harrison did not disappoint. Pale gaze fixed on the closed door, he said, "Pretty little thing. Your ward, you say?"

Training his tone to neutrality, Simon answered, "Yes. I brought her down from London in January."

Harrison's narrow shoulders slipped into their habitual slump. "You don't mean to say she lives *here*? With *you*?" The question skirted a plea.

Simon picked up a transcript and pretended to study it. Gaze glued to the meaningless black ink characters, he admitted, "With me and a dozen or so others."

"Servants, you mean?"

Simon hesitated. "Yes."

"I trust there is a chaperone among them?"

Ah, politics. The fine art of shading the truth without actually lying. "My housekeeper also fulfills that role, yes."

"An attractive unattached female living under your roof."

Harrison shook his head, expression dour. "Dizzy isn't going to like it."

Dizzy can go hang, Simon felt like saying but held back. Thrusting the report aside, he said, "There is absolutely nothing untoward between us."

The declaration was, strictly speaking, the truth barring the torrid happenings taking place in his mind. There were nights when he'd lie awake mentally making love to Christine three, sometimes four times before finally dropping into a fitful doze. Others he'd spend wondering what it would be like to trace the long, elegant column of her throat with a single finger or to kiss her softly, *slowly,* outlining her bottom lip with his tongue. And there was a little mole at the juncture of her left ear and jaw that was driving him to madness.

He'd come to await their daily lessons with the same hungry anticipation he'd known as a boy when, on Sunday afternoons, he'd trek to Billingsgate Market. Once there, he'd plant himself by the vendor carts and ogle the oysters and roasted chestnuts and savory meat pies until one of the costermongers either gave him something or chased him off. In retrospect, he realized he'd derived the most satisfaction from the latter. For, no matter how tempting the morsel, it was never so delicious as the idea of it in his mind.

And Christine? Were he to sample her, to make her his mistress, would she eventually lose some of her sweetness? It was a question that must remain unanswered. Even if he weren't about to embark on a career in politics, she was his dependent. Her every morsel of food, her every scrap of clothing, the very roof over her head—all were his to give or take away. But he didn't want her to come to him because she was grateful. If he were anything resembling a gentleman, he wouldn't want her to come to him at all.

Harrison's manufactured cough pulled Simon from the murky morass of regret. "Really, Belleville, you're shrewd enough to know that, in politics, appearances are everything. With Gladstone and the Liberals forever prosing on about morality and the plight of the poor, you're one of our party's most valuable assets. Not only are you a self-made man, a living testimonial to Tory Democracy, but your personal life is unassailable. If that were to change, if Miss Tremayne's presence here were to become widely known . . ." Harrison brought his ink-stained index finger to collar level and made a slicing motion.

I'll be finished, Simon supplied, and then wondered why that prospect didn't strike the toll of terror it would have but a few weeks before. In truth, the only feeling it prompted was mild disappointment. In contrast, knowing that all too soon he would have to bid Christine farewell—the terrible finality of it—brought a jolt of pain so harsh he found himself clutching the desk's beveled edge.

Determined to crush his weakness, he turned back to Harrison and forced a smile. "Not to worry, Will. By summer's end, Miss Tremayne will have left Valhalla. Her stay here will be as good as ancient history."

Fortunately for Simon, Harrison chose that moment to retrieve his copy of Mr. Forster's proposed Education Act; otherwise he might have reflected on the sudden huskiness marring his candidate's usual deep timbre.

Their conversation turned to the party's position on universal elementary education and to the latest figures for coal production. Simon managed the appropriate responses, but in truth he listened with only half an ear. His thoughts kept slipping back to Christine. He'd known he couldn't risk keeping her with him beyond the summer nor, given her impressive progress, would there be a need to. Yet until now, he hadn't allowed himself to contemplate how rapidly the days were slipping away. Like sands in an upturned hourglass, soon they'd be spent.

Staring beyond Harrison to the April sunshine streaking through the library window, he tried to close his mind to the image of Christine flying through his fields on the back of the cinnamon-colored mare. But he couldn't. He didn't want to.

From here on, he vowed, he'd not waste so much as a single moment of their precious time together.

In the thick of enemy territory, Christine dismounted and led Cinnamon off the gravel path to a stand of trees. After checking to make certain that no poisonous yew grew nearby, she left the mare to graze and started up the main walk leading toward the house.

Not any house but Stonevale Priory.

Each crunch of her boot heels drew her deeper into forbidden territory, but she told herself she'd come too far to turn back now. No one knew she was here, least of all Simon. She wouldn't be surprised if he forgot his birthday altogether and stayed closeted with Mr. Harrison until supper. She only hoped the surprise she'd hidden away would keep until then.

The sudden sensation of being stalked brought the hairs on the back of her neck to full attention. She whipped about. "Who's there?"

Shivering in the April sunshine, she studied the path, which branched off to connect carriage house, stable, and paddock. Deserted unless one counted a smattering of crows pecking away at the carcass of a less fortunate bird. She released a nervous breath and continued on. Nerves, she told herself, and guilt over breaking faith with Simon. And yet sensing that whatever tortured him had to do with this house, how could she stay away? The raw desperation in his eyes when he'd forced that promise from her had been impossible to miss. He was hiding something. But what could a man such as Simon, a pillar of the community, a future Member of Parliament, possibly have to hide?

Determined to find out, she cut through what once had been a formal garden and followed the main path toward the house. Viewed from across the valley, Stonevale Priory had appeared to be a magnificent white. Coming upon it now, she saw that moss and lichen veiled the ancient stones, several of which were crumbling into powder. Darkened windows, peeling window paint, and a broken shutter hanging at half-mast added to the general atmosphere of decay and neglect. Earl or not, whoever lived here must be pursepinched. If, indeed, anyone still lived here at all.

Just a quick look about, then I'll leave. She made for an octagonal turret jutting from the house's eastern side. Lifting her skirts, she stepped over the scraggly skeleton of a rosebush—really, it was all but a crime what these Kentish folk did to their roses—and sallied up to the mullioned window. Finding her footing on one of the bricks used to edge the bed, she stood on tiptoe and looked in. Or tried to. The leaded glass was wavy as water and white with dust. Pulling a handkerchief from her pocket, she mopped a small circle and, standing on tiptoe, peered inside. Squinting, she got a general impression of faded velvet drapery and furniture buried beneath holland covers.

She was about to move to another window when a shadow fell and a gravelly voice demanded, "What's this . . . housebreaking, are we?"

Heart in her throat, Christine whirled to find the butt of a walking stick aimed at her midriff. "I wasn't going to steal anything, truly I wasn't. The gate was open—well, not exactly locked—so I . . ."

"Rode straight through, bold as brass."

She nodded, and the cane was promptly withdrawn. Relaxing a fraction, Christine edged her gaze upward. The gray eyes that looked down at her from beneath bushy brows were no less steely for being clouded with age, the chiseled features no less impressive for being veiled in wrinkles, the broad shoulders beneath the greatcoat no less imposing for being a bit bowed.

Finding her voice, she admitted, "I only wanted to have a look about. It was wrong of me to trespass, but . . ."

"Right, wrong, you're here now." With that, he turned on his heel and started toward the front of the house.

He disappeared around the corner and Christine hesitated, not sure whether she should follow or make a dash for her horse. Given his bearing, he might have been the earl himself yet his threadbare coat and moth-riddled beaver hat indicated he was a servant, most likely the coachman. Still, she *had* come to see the house.

"Well, if you're certain your master won't mind," she called after him, hiking her skirts ankle-high to keep up.

He did an about-face so that she nearly crashed into his back. For a moment his rheumy gaze widened, then the mouth beneath the neatly trimmed white mustache curved into a vaguely familiar smile. "Oh, he's not such a beastly fellow as you may have heard." He turned back and, leaning on his cane and clenching the rusted railing, started up the first of several flights of sagging front steps, leaving Christine to follow.

The planked doorway shrieked open just as they reached the top. "I take it we've a guest?" a bald gentleman, attired from head to toe in immaculate black, called out from the open doorway.

The earl? Christine wondered and then reached up to make sure her bonnet was straight before she crossed the threshold.

The coachman nodded. "This is Miss . . ." He peered back at Christine and cocked a brow. "What the devil did you say your name was, gel?"

Behind her, the door creaked closed. Standing inside the dark, taper-lit hallway, gaze darting from the coffered ceiling to the rusted suits of armor lining both sides of the vast open hall, Christine felt as though she'd been transported several centuries back in time. She also felt well and truly trapped. Swallowing against the cobwebs gathering at the back of her throat, she tried to think of what Simon would do were he in similar shoes.

Lifting her chin and meeting both men's gazes, she replied, "I didn't say but, as you've asked, it's Christine. Christine Tremayne."

To her chagrin, the coachman let out a belly laugh. Dashing a hand across his watery eyes, he finally said, "Cheeky chit, ain't she, Jamison?"

"Indeed, milord."

Milord!

The "coachman" must have read her startled look, for he flashed a wicked smile. "I'm Stonevale as in 'Earl of'."

Lord Stonevale gave his back to Jamison, whom Christine now understood to be his butler, and shrugged out of his coat. Sweeping off his hat, he handed it to the butler. Unlike poor Jamison, whose pate was as shiny as a billiard ball, the earl had a full head of thick white hair that grew in a low peak on his forehead.

Handing over his leather gloves as well, he said, "Tea in the study as usual, Jamison."

Christine had hoped only for a quick look about. Tea was far more than she'd bargained for. "Oh, but I mustn't stay."

The earl's gnarled—and surprisingly strong—hand closed over her left shoulder. "Rubbish! Of course you'll stay, won't she, Jamison?"

"She shall, milord," the butler replied, expression as unruffled as the marble bust of Bach Simon kept atop his piano.

They both behaved as though she hadn't anything to say about it. Despite being in the wrong for having trespassed, Christine's resentment flared. Shrugging free of his lordship's clutches, she said, "I don't drink tea."

Two heads snapped around to stare at her.

"Don't drink *tea!*" The earl's square jaw dropped. "Then what *do* you drink in the afternoon? Not strong spirits, I hope."

"Oh, no, sar. Never, truly." Christine thought for a moment. "Milk, mostly."

"Milk." The earl pulled a face. "Sickly stuff. Can't abide it myself but if that is what you fancy then you shall have it. You heard her, Jamison. Fetch the gel a glass of milk."

With that, Lord Stonevale fired off down the hall like a shot, strides brisk despite the limp. *Why, he's as used to having his way as Simon is,* she thought, torn between amusement and frustration as she hurried after him.

Coming into a narrow corridor of modern origin, the earl finally slowed. Pulling open one of the many closed doors, he gestured Christine inside.

The strong smell of must hit her even before he nudged her through the open threshold. Books covered the walls, most of the furnishings, and the better part of the threadbare carpet. Christine picked her way through the path the earl forged to a suite of chairs by the fireplace.

"Sit." Motioning her to a straight-backed chair heaped with books, he swept a thick tome from the seat of an armchair and, stiff-kneed, lowered himself onto the cracked leather cushion.

Christine hesitated. Common sense bid her bolt for the door before Jamison returned but, as was often the case, curiosity got the better of her. Resolved, she set to work clearing her chair. She'd just lifted the last stack onto the floor when a dark shape flashed past, brushing her skirts.

Imagining a rat, she spun about to see a black cat leap atop the earl's knees. "There now, Tom, I was wondering when you'd show yourself."

Christine relaxed and took her seat. Looking on as the earl stroked his cat, cooing baby talk into the beast's ripped right ear, she felt herself warming to him.

"Have you lived here long?" she finally asked, wondering if he might have forgotten her.

He looked up from scratching the top of Tom's head. "Bloody mausoleum's been my family's seat for more than three hundred years. I grew up here, know all the local gentry." He pointed a crooked forefinger finger at her. "But I don't know any Tremaynes. And I'm equally certain I don't know *you*."

Christine wasn't sure whether she should feel flattered that he'd mistook her for a gentlewoman or foolish for letting him goad her into staying. She decided on foolish.

"My folk are from Cheshire."

"Ah-hah!" He slapped his thigh, startling Tom, who replied with a loud mewl. Soothing the cat, he explained, "I thought I detected a touch of the Midlands in your vowels."

She felt her cheeks heat. "I'm working to be rid of it."

"Really? Whatever for? It suits you."

Before she could decide whether he'd just paid her a compliment or an insult, Jamison entered with their tea. He set the heavy tray on the table-high island of books before Christine.

Stepping back, he asked, "Shall I be mother, miss, or shall you?"

Christine's gaze flew from the overwhelmingly arrayed tray—even her milk was served in a goblet of chinked crystal and covered with a linen cloth—to the butler. "I beg your pard—"

"He means do you want to pour the bloody tea," the earl intercepted, shooting her a wink. Then, as though the butler were not standing right at his elbow, he leaned forward to confide, "Jamison's been with me for fifty-odd years. Admirable fellow, best butler in the empire, yet despite all my efforts he's yet to master plain speaking. Ain't that right, Jamison?"

"Indeed, milord, albeit you are a constant example to me."

Pressing her lips together to hold in a laugh, Christine found her napkin and settled it over her lap. She managed to compose herself as Jamison performed the ritual with impressive ease, then bowed his way into the hall.

The earl reached for a slice of poppy-seed cake and crammed half of it in his mouth. Crumbs rained down onto his neck cloth and were promptly gobbled up by Tom, who then made it his business to oversee every motion from hand to mouth.

Wiping his chin with his napkin, Lord Stonevale said, "We don't get many visitors. With whom are you staying?"

She hesitated. Gentlefolk were mighty sensitive about what Simon called "propriety." From what Christine could tell, propriety amounted to a great lot of rules that kept a person—especially a *female* person—from doing what she wanted. One of the rules was that ladies, especially unmarried ones, never traveled by themselves.

Owning there was no help for it, she finally answered, "With my cousin."

"Then you must be from a cadet branch of one of our fine families?"

Christine looked away, fixing her gaze on a blotch of mildew staining the plasterwork ceiling. She'd never been much of a liar. Whether with a blush, clammy palms, or the sudden treble that crept into her voice at the worst possible moment, in the end she always gave herself away. With the earl's probing eyes on her face, she felt her heartbeats quickening to a canter.

"This cousin of yours, surely I must know her parents—your aunt and uncle?"

She looked down at the glass of milk clasped in her clammy hand and wondered if she would ever be permitted to drink it. "It's a he, actually. Mr. Simon Belleville . . . of Valhalla," she added, hoping he might be satisfied at last.

The earl's bushy brows shot heavenward, nearly meeting the vee of his hairline. "So you're Simon's protégée," he said more to himself than to her, and his thin upper lip disappeared beneath his mustache.

Protégée? Heat rushed her cheeks. She wasn't certain, but she thought it sounded French. She only hoped it didn't mean something dirty.

Hoisting her chin, she dared to pose a question of her own. "You call him by his given name. Might I inquire how you came to be acquainted with Mr. Belleville?" Feeling very sophisticated and grand, she paused to take a drink from her glass.

"You might." Frowning, he set his cup and saucer aside. "He's my grandson."

An arc of frothy spray was Christine's reply.

"*Oh, forgive me,* sar. I mean, milord."

Despite the milk dribbling down her chin, despite the fact that his lordship's cat was lapping the puddle atop her right boot, Christine struggled to recover her composure. She'd made a terrible mess, yet somehow had managed to swallow a good deal, the wrong way of course. The back of her throat smarted, but the sting was nothing compared to the wound to her pride. By now there could be no doubt in his lordship's mind that she was most definitely *not* a lady. When Jamison returned with a wet cloth and silently handed it to her, her shame was complete.

But, as she mopped the front of her gown, temper began to replace lost dignity. "All along you've know I wasn't a relation and yet you let me prattle on. Why?"

The earl seemed to have regained his equanimity. "I rather enjoyed it. It's been a long time since we've had a young voice to liven up these old halls, hasn't it, Jamison?"

"An eternity, milord."

"Finish your milk, Miss Tremayne, or at least what remains of it. My offer to show you the house still stands, although now more than ever it occurs to me to wonder why you came." His eyes narrowed into suspicious slits. "Simon didn't send you to spy on me, did he?"

Indignant on Simon's behalf, she squared her shoulders. "Of course not. In fact, he made me promise to stay away."

The earl's eyes dimmed. "And yet you came anyway?"

She shrugged. "I suppose I wanted to see for myself what it is about this place that upsets him so."

For the first time since she'd arrived, the earl seemed at a loss. His jaw sagged, and he looked away. "He's never so much as set foot inside the door." Clearing his throat, he turned back and reached for his cane. "But that doesn't mean you shouldn't look your fill." He rose stiffly, one hand braced on the chair arm.

He hobbled toward the door, shoulders bowed in the manner of an old man. Wondering at the abrupt change, Christine followed him out, the cat padding behind them.

The tour lasted at least an hour and during that time they covered only one of Stonevale's four wings. The other three had been shut up for years, the earl explained, ever since his wife had passed on. He had a daughter but she lived off in Cornwall and, when he left it at that, Christine gathered they didn't get on. There was a male cousin, thrice removed, whom he'd never met but once, but who had a reputation as a gamester and a fool. And of course Lord Stonevale's only son, Simon's father, had died more than twenty years before.

"It is immodest of me to point this out, but the Bellevilles are one of England's oldest families," he said as they came full circle into the great hall. "Our ancestor, Sir Simion de Belleville, came over from Normandy with William the Conqueror. Apart from myself, Simon is the only living Belleville male left to carry on the direct line. Unless he marries and sires a son, the line will die."

The back of Christine's throat knotted. While she had no particular wish to see the Bellevilles wiped from the face of the earth, the prospect of Simon marrying and starting a family made her chest ache.

Somewhere in the house, a grandfather clock tolled. At the fourth chime, she said, "I thank you for your hospitality, but I really must be getting back."

His lordship nodded. "Very well. I'll have Jamison send to the stables for one of the groomsmen to accompany you home."

That house, you are never to go near it. Simon's order, the fierce look on his face, came back to her in a rush.

Christine shook her head. "That is kind of you, but you mustn't. If one of the servants were to see me ride in with your man, Simon would know I'd disobeyed him."

The earl scowled. "You aren't afraid of him, are you?" He hesitated, one brow edging upward to his peaked hairline, bringing to mind his grandson. "He doesn't mistreat you, does he?"

The notion was so preposterous that Christine was hard put not to laugh. "Mistreat me? Heavens, no. Simon is the gentlest man I've ever known. He wouldn't so much as stomp on a bug if he could help it, though I expect he'd not appreciate my saying so. It's only that he's been so good to me, I hate to disappoint him. Staying away from your house is the one thing he's had me promise him since he brought me here."

Belatedly realizing how that must sound, she hastened to apologize. "Forgive me. My mouth runs away with betimes."

He lifted a hand and ran it through the abundant white hair that grew low on his forehead, and Christine was reminded of how Simon often did the same. Only the earl's hand shook.

"There is nothing to forgive, at least not of you, my dear girl." He cleared his throat. "Nor have I any right to ask you to disobey my grandson. Even so, should you happen by in the near future, we shouldn't take it amiss, should we, Jamison?"

Christine hadn't realized it, but the butler had come up behind them. He turned to Christine and *smiled*. "Indeed not, milord. Miss Christine shall be made most welcome."

Lord Stonevale's eyes regained their twinkle. "Splendid. Then it's settled. You'll come again, on Thursday next, for tea. No, not tea." He grinned. "Milk and biscuits."

"I'll try." Dividing her gaze between the two old men, Christine asked herself just when *happening by* had become an appointment.

Yet, despite his lordship's overbearing manner—and the obvious feud between him and Simon—she rather liked the earl. It would be no hardship to visit him on occasion.

Provided Simon didn't find her out.

Thirteen

April Noddy's past and gone,
You're the fool and I'm none.

—April Fool's Day
folk saying, British

Wanting to be alone with his thoughts, Simon remained in the library long after Harrison had left. He stood at the window, brooding out onto his gardens. Gardens that were just now beginning to bloom with April's lush promise, thanks to Christine's having taken his under-gardener in hand. Lost in thought as he was, his whole body snapped to attention when he saw her coming up the path from the stable. Until now he hadn't realized he'd been waiting for her, but the glad leap of his heart told him otherwise. Then Jem joined her on the path and Simon's heart dove.

He fell back from the window. Lifting the drape no more than an inch, he observed his driver handing Christine a large wicker hamper. She took it, laughing as she sought to accommodate its obvious weight. The basket pressed against her chest, she mouthed what had to be an exclamation of delight, then leaned over to plant a kiss on Jem's jaw. Through narrowed slits, Simon watched a silly grin spread over the boy's suddenly flushed face. The pair exchanged conspiratorial looks, then separated, Jem starting back toward the stable and Christine continuing on toward the house.

No longer able to bare it, Simon turned his back on the view, suspicion and something dangerously close to hatred twisting his gut. In the two years Jem had been in his employ, he'd never given cause for complaint, never gotten a girl in trouble nor taken something that wasn't his. Whether washing Simon's carriage or tending the horses, he went about his work quietly and without grumbling. If it weren't for his whistling, Simon might forget he was even there.

But suddenly, inexplicably, Simon didn't trust him.

Not with Christine.

His whistling, that was it. Always the same silly ditty, again and again—and *again*. The habit had never bothered Simon before but now just thinking about it set his teeth on edge. How could anyone trust a man who was always so bloody cheerful?

Pacing, he forced himself to evaluate the situation objectively. Perhaps he was looking a gift horse in the mouth? Were Jem and Christine to make a match of it, her future would be settled once and for all. Given her shady past, Christine could do far worse. Jem was a hard worker, a steady sort. Like Christine, he'd grown up on a farm and, of course, they were of an age.

Simon, in contrast, was five and thirty. It was hard to believe. He ran the fingers of one hand through his hair. Barring the stray silver strand, the color remained the same bluish black as his mother's had been. When he'd left for India, Lilith Belleville had been about his age now. She'd seemed an old woman.

The tap outside his door startled him, drawing him back into a present that seemed every bit as bleak as his past.

"Come in," he called out, falling into the chair behind his desk. He picked up a stock report and pretended to study it just as the door opened.

Even before looking up, he knew it was her. Christine's soft footfalls and light lavender scent were imprinted on his mind, but then so was everything about her. He sensed the precise moment she stopped in front of his desk. Composing his features, he looked up from the columns of meaningless figures and, in a single sweeping glance, took in her bright eyes, mussed hair, and stained gown. All the signs of young love—and a lusty midday tumble—paraded in front of his very eyes. He wouldn't have been surprised to see a stem of straw sticking from her hair.

His gaze dropped to the hamper she held against her chest, her left hand supporting the bottom. Whatever was inside, it must be a substantial load. The gentlemanly response would be to rise, round the desk to unburden her, and then offer her a seat. Instead Simon remained in his chair. If she'd come to tell him she and Jem were eloping, if what the basket contained was a hasty assemblage of her worldly belongings . . . If that scenario proved to be the case, he wasn't at all certain his legs would support him.

Queasiness settled into the pit of his stomach. Fighting it, he seized on brisk cheerfulness. "Back already. Where did you ride?"

Was it his imagination or did the color in her wind-whipped cheeks deepen? "Oh, here and about," she hedged, biting her bottom lip.

"Here and about?" He tossed the report aside and forced a stiff smile. "Tell me, did you traverse 'here and about' alone or with a companion?"

Pupils huge, her eyes appeared poised to spring from their sockets. "Sar?"

He shrugged. "I just wondered if perhaps you might have encountered someone along the way to share your wanderings?"

She shook her head resolutely. Too resolutely. "Oh no, sar. No one. Just me and Cinnamon."

"Hm," he answered, not believing her for a second. His gaze focused on her white knuckled hands clutching the basket. "What have you in there, bricks?"

"No, not bricks." Beaming, she set the hamper atop the desk and worked her right arm. "It's a *secret*. I've been keeping it for weeks now. Nearly a month."

Simon's heart leapt into his throat. Lodged thus, it made breathing a complicated matter, but somehow he managed. "Nearly a month?"

Good God, was the deed already done? His regard flew to her left hand. Relief rushed him when he saw that the ring finger remained bare, then fled just as quickly when he considered that Jem could hardly afford a gold band.

She had the audacity to smile, stretching that amazing

mouth of hers even wider until he yearned to wipe the smile from her lips—with his own. "Jem didn't think we should wait, but I told him I wanted to save it."

Oh, God. Head reeling, he opened his mouth to ask when she meant to leave just as a plaintive whimper caught his attention.

His gaze fell to the now swaying basket, then back up to Christine's amused face. "What the Devil—"

"It's your birthday present. I hope you like it. *Him,* I should say."

Shock brought him to his feet. "A birthday present . . . for me? But how did you know? Who told you? How can a present be a . . ." He stopped when he realized he was babbling.

"I hounded Mrs. Griffith until she told me the date. As for what it is, you'll just have to see for yourself." She reached across and lifted the hamper lid. A little mongrel pup poked its head and shoulders out. A cross between a spaniel and a border collie, the beast was the most improbable-looking dog Simon had ever seen. One floppy ear was sable; the other was equal parts brown and black. Bracing its white front paws on the basket's edge and black button nose working, it leaned out to take olfactory stock of its surroundings.

Simon looked from the puppy to Christine. "A *dog!*" he said stupidly. "You got me a *dog?*"

Uncertainty stole over her features. Her smile fell and her eyes dimmed. "Why, yes, sar. You've given me so much—" She reached up and touched the amber pendant at her throat. "—I wanted you to have something to remember me by after I'm gone, only I couldn't think what. Then I thought back to that talk we had when I was laid up and you read *Wuthering Heights* to me. You do remember, don't you?"

Indeed, Simon remembered only too well, both the discussion and the naked embarrassment he'd felt afterward for having revealed so much of himself. Christine had been lying on the study sofa with her ankle propped atop a bank of pillows. To keep her entertained, he'd read aloud, although Emily Brontë's bleak tale of doomed love would have hardly been his choice for an afternoon's diversion. He'd just come to the passage where Nelly Dean rescued her mistress's spaniel from the garden gate upon which the villainous Heathcliff had hung it. Deciding to close the book on what constituted a high point, he found himself confessing, "All my life I've wanted a dog."

Christine lifted her head from the tasseled cushion. "You've never had a dog? Why not?"

Focus fixed on the closed book in his hands to avoid having to meet her all-knowing gaze, he admitted, "My parents were . . . not as well off as we could have wished to be. And we lived in the city. A dog would have been impractical." *Considering we could barely afford to feed ourselves.*

"No, I mean now. Why don't you have one now?"

Jarred by the question, he thought for a moment. "My schedule. I've not really had time for . . ." In the midst of his floundering, he caught her rolling her eyes. "Why not, indeed?" he'd finally allowed, and they'd both ended up laughing.

Looking at her now, he felt awed and humbled that his sad little admission had so imprinted itself on her mind. But then Christine was far more complex than most women. Or most men, for that matter. At times she seemed hardly more worldly-wise than a newborn babe and yet she had a canny wisdom, a way of looking at life that both delighted and discomfited him.

Shamed by the ignoble thoughts he'd entertained about her and Jem, he repeated, "You got me a dog," and let his head fall back against the chair.

Her watchful gaze monitored his every movement. "Jem asked around and found that the blacksmith's bitch had delivered a litter. He drove me over last month to see, and I picked out this little lad, but we wanted to wait until he was weaned before we took him. Jem went to get him last night after he got off work. He's been a wonderful friend."

A wonderful *friend*. Christine and Jem were friends only. Jem suddenly rose in Simon's estimation. He was a good lad, a hard worker. And his whistling was really rather uplifting. He made a mental note to raise Jem's salary.

But not so high that he could support a wife.

Nibbling on her bottom lip, Christine looked down at the basket. "He's all right, isn't he?" She twisted her hands in front of her. "What I mean to say is, if you don't like him, I suppose they'll take him back. If not, Jem said he'd—"

She broke off as the dog sprang free. Tail wagging, he

skidded across the desktop, scattering Simon's papers to the four winds.

"Oh dear, I expect he's restless." Chuckling, Christine reached out and scratched behind one floppy ear. The dog's black lips pulled back and a little pink tongue lolled out one side.

"I've been calling him Jake after one of my brothers, but he's yours now. You should name him." She hesitated. "That is, if you mean to keep him."

Her regard fixed on his hands, the fingers laced over his waistcoat. He still hadn't touched the dog who, along with Christine, watched him closely. *What kind of monster won't even pet a puppy?* they both seemed to ask, and Simon had to wonder the same.

"Of course I mean to keep him." Like a string being drawn on an open purse, the back of Simon's throat seemed to close so that it was an effort to squeeze out his next words. "He's splendid." *You're splendid.* "And Jake is a fine name." Swallowing against the strangled feeling, he added, "A fine name for a fine fellow." *It's a fine thing you've done for me.* "It's just that I don't know much about dogs. Anything, frankly. I'll need you to help me take care of him at first, show me what to do. He'll have to be house-trained if he's to stay indoors." He combed both hands through his hair, not because it was in his eyes but because it was something to do. "Good Lord, I don't even know what dogs eat."

She brightened. "You can rely on me, sar." He was surprised when she didn't salute. "Though he does look a bit foolish with the bow." She reached across the desk to the plaid tied in a floppy bow about the puppy's neck.

Simon remembered seeing it in Christine's hair just the other day. "No, don't," he said, fingertips brushing the top of her hand. "Let's leave it for now. He only has this evening to be a birthday present. After midnight, he turns back into a regular dog."

She smiled, unearthing the dimple on the left side of her chin. "I hadn't thought of it that way."

Simon managed to smile back but behind his eyes, the pressure was building. It had been years and yet he knew what the sensation signified.

Clearing his throat, he cast his gaze to the door. "For now I think young Jake and I need some time to get acquainted."

Christine took his less than subtle dismissal with good grace. "All right. I'll see you at supper then." She turned to go.

It was folly but Simon couldn't resist calling her back. "Christine."

She circled around. "Sar?"

"I presume Jake will need a walk after he's fed?" At her nod, he ventured, "Perhaps you'll come with us for an after-dinner stroll?"

Her broad smile pulled at his heart. "I'd like that."

She pulled the door closed just as the first tear trickled down Simon's cheek. Elbows on the desk, he stuffed a fisted hand in either eye to stem the tide, but it was no use. Tear upon tear fell, and soon he tasted salt on his lips. Head bowed, he felt something cold and wet nuzzling the back of his hand. He lifted his head, and the pup thumped onto his lap.

Swiping the back of his hand over his streaming eyes as he had when he was a boy, he looked down at the dog, who'd settled in and was licking imaginary dirt from his pristine white paws.

"Cheeky little fellow, aren't you?"

But dogs belonged on the floor. Simon was about to set him down when Jake's big, brown, *pleading* eyes fastened on his face. Like Christine's, they were wide and open and earnest. *Love me,* they both seemed to implore, and Simon was at a loss to explain how he'd become too twisted, too locked up, too dead inside to ever love anyone again.

Especially himself.

I wanted you to have something to remember me by . . .

Christine's bow about Jake's neck was coming undone. Simon finished untying it, then tucked it inside his breast pocket. Next to his heart.

As if attuned to his new master's misery, Jake nudged Simon's palm until he'd maneuvered his little head beneath it.

Hand trembling, Simon stroked the dog's silky crown. "What are we going to do about her, Jake?"

And, more to the point, what am I going to do about me?

* * *

May Day, the annual welcoming of summer on the first of the month, was a time-honored tradition throughout rural England that dated to pre-Christian times. Simon was unschooled at being a country squire, but he'd done his homework on the holiday. Between descriptions of the upcoming event in Maidstone's local gazette and inquiries of Mrs. Griffith, he'd learned that the daylong celebration would take place on the common, beginning at daybreak with choristers from the local parish and culminating with a bonfire at dusk. Bowing to custom, he'd given his servants the full day with wages. As for himself, he'd stay only long enough to hear the mayor's midday address, deliver his own speech, and sit through that of the opposing candidate; as soon as the formal part of the program was concluded, he'd make his escape. When he'd offhandedly mentioned his plans to Christine at breakfast on the morning before, her disappointment had been palpable.

Fork poised in midair, she'd looked over at him, expression stricken. "You mean you're not going to stay for the dancing nor even the ram roast?"

Slipping Jake a morsel of sausage underneath the table, thereby breaking his own rule of no animals at meals, he admitted, "I hadn't thought to. Why, were you thinking of going?"

The question slipped out before he'd properly considered it. A moment later, he was hard-pressed not to smack a hand to his forehead. *Moron. Oaf.* Christine was from the country. Of course she would want to attend. For all he knew, she'd been dancing around the maypole since she'd been out of leading strings.

She shook her head as though giving him up for the lost cause he obviously was. "No matter," she said around a sigh. "I suppose Jem might take me."

That settled it.

Bristling, he said, "*I'm* taking you, and that's final. We'll stay the whole day and half the night if you've a mind to, dance about the maypole and the bloody bonfire 'til our heads spin and our feet bleed if it suits you."

"Hm. As lovely as that sounds, aren't you afraid you'll be bored?" she shot back, clearly unimpressed with his sacrifice.

He shrugged and took up his newspaper. From behind its shelter, he fed Jake his last bite of sausage. Distracted by the pup licking grease from his fingers, he said, "I'll manage." Nudging the drooling muzzle from his pant's leg with a sternly whispered "No more," he added, "Indeed, Harrison will be delighted to learn I'm going." *Although not necessarily delighted I'm taking you.* "It will do my campaign no end of good to be seen mingling with the locals."

Reaching over, Christine batted his outstretched paper until he was forced to close it again. "But how do *you* feel about going?"

He yawned into the back of his hand, already weary at the thought. "I suppose it won't kill me to hit a few croquet balls, judge a pie contest or two."

Or so he told himself the next morning as he dressed with particular care in a collarless shirt of indigo blue, braces, buff breeches—and for once no tie. "You need to appear less standoffish, more a man of the people," Harrison had counseled at their last meeting. As Simon slipped on his linen jacket and set the straw bowler at a cocky angle atop his head, he told himself he was only acting on the party agent's counsel, but the grin he glimpsed in the dressing mirror gave the lie to that particular self-delusion. He had dressed to please one person and one person only. Christine.

But when he went below, the front hall was empty. Nor was she to be found elsewhere in the house. At wit's end, he shoved his folded speech into his pocket and went in search of Mrs. Griffith. He cornered her in the pantry. The housekeeper recalled seeing the young miss a half hour before when Christine had come into the breakfast room, tucked two scones into a napkin, and then hurried out. She'd been wearing her bonnet.

So, the little minx had given him the slip and gone on without him. Gone on with Jem, more than likely. Feeling like a dupe, Simon rushed out a side door and marched down the path to the stable. He knew a moment of confusion when he looked into Cinnamon's stall, expecting Christine to have taken her, and instead found the mare pawing the ground, head tucked. Heart pumping, he headed into the tack room.

It had been years since Simon had saddled his own horse. Haste and anger combined to make his fingers clumsy, but finally he cinched the girth beneath the beast's belly and mounted. Muttering every foul sailor's curse he could recall, he dug in his heels and tore out into the yard and down the drive.

He caught up with Christine more than a mile down the hedgerow-bordered lane. Making brisk time on foot, she ignored him when he hailed her.

Easing his horse to a walk, he drew up beside her. "Why the Devil didn't you wait for me?"

Shielding the sun from her eyes, she glanced up. "I didn't want you to think you had to dance about the 'bloody bonfire' on my account."

"I changed my mind." Reining in, he held out his hand. "Take hold and climb up."

Beneath the sheltering brim of her chip straw bonnet, she eyed his outstretched hand as though it were a snake. "No, thank you. I believe I'll walk."

Chin pointed to the blue sky, she lifted the skirts of her white muslin frock over the heels of her sturdy half boots and continued on.

Following, Simon finally allowed there was no help for it. He drew in his horse and climbed down. He looked up in time to see Christine turning the corner onto the main road. Infernal woman. Taking firm hold of the reins, he set off after her, the horse at a lazy trot behind him and the sun warming his back.

When he caught up, perspiration dampened his forehead. "What the Devil do you think you're doing, tramping about the countryside with not so much as a 'by your leave'?"

Her half-moon eyebrows lifted. Beneath them her eyes were all innocence. "*Tramping*, am I? And here I thought myself to be walking on the two good legs God gave me."

He opened his mouth to return a heated response, then he saw that her scowl had lifted into a saucy grin. As for his own mood, he found it next to impossible to stay angry when she looked at him as she was doing now, eyes mischiefdarkened, the dimple showing at the left of her ripe, upturned, utterly *kissable* mouth.

"Limbs," he corrected, throat dry as he found himself imagining hers. Taking his handkerchief from his pocket, he dabbed the back of his neck. Sun and exercise were only partly responsible for his spiking temperature. "Why didn't you ride Cinnamon?"

"She had a touch of colic yesterday." Tilting her face to

the side, she regarded him, expression disconcertingly knowing. "I thought I'd ask Jem if I might ride in with him, but he's been so busy of late I didn't care to trouble him on his holiday."

Was the reproach in her voice real or a product of his own guilty imagining? he wondered, ignoring the horse sniffing his pockets. Following the incident with the dog, Simon had doubled the lad's wages—along with his duties.

Disregarding the tiny twinge of remorse, he asked, "Did you ever stop to consider that it's more than six miles to Maidstone—and six more back?"

Tapping a finger to her cheek, she pretended shock. "Twelve in all, is it?" She eyed his perspiring face, and the corners of her mouth turned up. In her thickest country accent, she said, "Then ye'd best take off that jacket, or I mid have to carry ye all that long way."

Breaking into a grin, he answered, "I have a better idea. Why don't we *both* ride. Save the soles of our feet for that bonfire dance, hm?"

She cast him a sidelong glance that was so artlessly seductive he found himself shivering despite the heat. "Are you certain you want to encourage we common folk in our pagan ways?" Reaching over, she flicked an imaginary speck from the lapel of his jacket. "You might get a spot of soot on that fine coat of yours."

Didn't she know by now that he'd walk across a bed of hot coals for an excuse to hold her close? Finding his smile, he said, "I believe I'll risk it, Miss Tremayne, if you will."

Fourteen

Come woo me, woo me; for now I am in a holiday humour and like enough to consent.

—William Shakespeare,
As You Like It, Act IV,
Scene 1, 1599

They rode the rest of the way in strained silence, their easy banter having vanished the instant Christine took her place in the saddle across Simon's thighs. Her left arm anchored to his trim waist, she tried not to think about what might happen were she to tilt her face upward and brush her mouth over her companion's square chin. The high plane of his cheek. That moist, firm mouth.

You're a rum fool, Christine, and spooney into the bargain.

Like a lovesick dolt, soon she'd be sneaking up behind him and kissing his shadow if she didn't guard her heart. Determined to take herself in hand, she trained her gaze on the fields and farms they passed and tried not to think about the bittersweet torture of her left breast chafing his chest.

It was both a blessing and a curse when they reached the town. Carriages and carts clogged Maidstone's High Street, prompting Christine to say they were lucky after all to have only one horse to worry about. Echoing that sentiment,

Simon slid out from under her, dismounted, then helped her down.

He handed over the reins to a damp-faced ostler and then turned back to Christine. Frowning down at his timepiece, he said, "The opening ceremony is to begin in twenty minutes. We'll have to hurry if we're to find you a seat."

They joined the others filing down a roped-off path, following the sounds of the brass band to the center of the common. By the time they reached the pavilion where the mayor and parliamentary candidates would deliver their addresses, most of the seats were taken except for those in the cordoned-off section in front. Taking Christine's hand, Simon started down the center aisle. He bypassed several vacant chairs, not stopping until they came to the end of the very first row. Looking about her to the smartly attired ladies and gentlemen taking their seats, Christine felt her stomach knotting. She'd chosen her simple gingham frock out of consideration for comfort, not fashion. Only now did she realize just how grave an error in judgment she'd made.

"Simon," she whispered, tugging on his sleeve. "I can't sit here." When raised eyebrows were his only reply, she jerked her chin toward the sign swinging from the rope. "These seats are *reserved*."

This time he grinned. "Indeed, reserved for the family and friends of the speakers. Meaning you, cousin dear."

The teasing reference to their bogus blood tie sent her heart lurching. If they were only playacting at being cousins, could it be they were only playacting at being friends as well? If that were the way of it, then what was she to make of those dangerous, electrically-charged moments when they'd looked deeply into each other's eyes, and Christine had felt a connection so profound, so divine, she'd wanted to weep over the beauty of it?

Before she could even begin to sort out her thoughts, let alone her feelings, Simon used the edge of his boot to push the stanchion aside. The obstacle removed, he started down the row. Christine had no choice but to follow, begging the pardon of the seated men and women whose feet she sidestepped. At last they stopped in front of a choice seat in the center. Ducking her seatmates' scowls, she sank gratefully into it.

Standing in front of her chair, Simon began buttoning his

jacket. "There's to be a small reception afterward. Join me?"

Simon was actually inviting her to an outing! Stunned, it took the span of several seconds before she found her tongue. "All right, if you like." She dipped her chin and pretended to study the stitching on her white wrist gloves, hoping he hadn't seen how much the invitation meant to her.

But instead he lifted her chin and smiled. A real smile that reached his eyes as they settled on her face. "I would . . . very much."

Melting beneath the warmth of his gaze, it was all she could do to mouth the words "good luck" before he turned to go. Watching as his brisk stride led him to the planked stage steps, then through the curtained-off area in back, she told herself not to read too much into the invitation and yet . . .

Oh, Simon, if only . . .

The sensation of something crawling down her spine caused her to break off before completing her wish. Following her instincts to the source, she found Fanny Albright, resplendent in a silk green carriage dress, glaring at her from the end seat across the aisle. For Simon's sake, Christine summoned a smile. With a smirk, Fanny turned away and tapped her mother on the shoulder. After a hushed consultation, Mrs. Albright shifted to whisper into the ear of her seatmate, Mrs. Priestly. Mouth fixed into a flat line, the squire's wife bent her head to the daughter sitting nearest her who, in turn, nudged her twin. All at once, the entire row turned to stare at Christine.

So this is what it meant to be on the receiving end of *the cut direct*. Digging her nails into her palms, Christine hoisted her chin and turned her attention back to the stage just as the curtain parted. Simon, a bull-necked man in an ill-fitting pinstriped suit, and a gray-whiskered man whom Christine recognized as the mayor walked out onto the platform.

Stepping up to the lectern as the two candidates took their respective seats on either side, Mayor Albright began: "Ladies and gentleman, today we come together to herald not only the arrival of summer but of a new era of peace and prosperity . . ."

It seemed an eternity but at last the mayor introduced Simon. Pride swelling her heart, Christine leaned forward in her seat, forgetting every discomfort, every embarrassment, as Simon stepped up to the podium.

He spoke well, scarcely glancing down at the written speech he'd obviously committed not only to memory but also to heart. Whether the topic he held forth on was the price of corn or manhood suffrage, his gaze continued to connect with the crowd. Once or twice his regard came to rest on her. Heart warmed, she smiled back her encouragement, grateful to be even a small part of this special moment.

He was drawing to a close when from somewhere in the audience a surly voice rang out, "Down wi' Disraeli and the Establishment. Long live the Radical Party."

Looking over her shoulder to the back of the pavilion, Christine glimpsed three men standing in the back. All were shifty-eyed, unshaven, and sporting slouched caps. The speaker, barrel-chested and thick-necked, held a banner that read, "Remember the Hyde Park Martyrs."

Heart thumping, Christine snapped her gaze back to the platform—and Simon. To his credit, his expression registered nothing beyond a tolerant half smile.

Holding up his hand for silence, he spoke above the crowd. "Please, I'm only too happy to respond to this gentleman's remark."

He proceeded to do just that, parlaying the disruption into an opportunity to expound upon the Progressive Conservatives' position on parliamentary reform.

"So you see, *gentlemen,* by extending the franchise to compound-ratepayers, the Conservative Reform Bill actually surpasses the relatively modest reforms put forth by Mr. Gladstone and the Liberals."

One of the ruffians tried again to interrupt, but this time the audience took it upon themselves to shout him down until he and his two mates had no choice but to depart.

Tucking his speech inside his jacket's breast pocket, Simon stepped back from the lectern amidst wild applause. Christine clapped until her palms stung, and Simon turned to shake the hand of his opponent as the latter lumbered forward.

By the time Mr. W. C. Bullworth had finished speaking—or rather, shuffling his papers—Christine almost felt sorry for the man. His halting and rambling oratory, coupled with the prodigious droplets of perspiration falling from his fleshy face, did little to recommend him to the yawning, shifting audience. By the time he concluded, half the seats were vacant.

Simon was clearly the victor of the day. Well-wishers thronged the stage step and, in seconds, he was the center of an ever-expanding circle. Caught up in the enthusiasm, Christine rose and hurried to join him. At the foot of the steps, she found herself face-to-face with Fanny Albright. Taking advantage of the crush, Fanny jabbed her elbow into Christine's ribs, then cut in front. Holding her smarting side, Christine watched her rival mount the platform and sweep across to smoothly slip inside Simon's inner circle.

I'll not shame you, Simon, no matter what promise I gave.

Blinking back tears, Christine made an about-face and joined the crowd heading up the aisle. She was almost to the exit when a strong hand descended on her shoulder.

"Christine, why didn't you come and join me?"

Looking back over her shoulder, she caught a glimpse of Simon's face, distinctly displeased, and turned about abruptly. "I didn't care to be a bother is all."

"Balderdash." His exasperated sigh filled her ear as he steered them through the exit. Once outside, he gestured to the striped tents and stalls dotting the lawn. "Hungry?"

"Yes," she admitted, relieved when he didn't pursue the subject of her broken promise. And then it struck her. "Oh, Simon." She whirled and stared up at him. "What about your reception? The mayor, all those people—"

"I told them I had a previous engagement as I do." He smiled and Christine felt her heart turn over on itself. "With you."

It was the laziest afternoon they'd ever spent together and yet it flew by as though time itself had sprouted wings. They strolled amidst the food stalls, munching from plates laden with fair delicacies—gingerbread, junket, and pickled eggs. Christine was skeptical when Simon suggested the smoked oysters but, after her first hesitant nibble, she polished off not only her portion but most of Simon's as well.

Reaching for her empty plate, his mouth lifted in a grin. "I hesitate to imagine the damage you'd do if you'd actually *liked* them."

"Wretch." Laughing, she handed him her plate and he disappeared to search out a rubbish bin.

The minutes stretched on. Shifting from one foot to the other, Christine was almost at the point of setting out in search of him when she spied him striding across the green toward her. Eyes dancing and arms tucked behind him, he drew up in front of her.

"Simon, you're hiding something behind your back, aren't you?" she asked in the same tone she used when prying a confession from one of her brothers.

Peering at her from beneath steepled brows, he answered, "Am I? Oh, do you mean this?" With a flourish, he held out what had to be the most splendid flower garland Christine had ever set eyes upon. "You can hardly be the May Queen without a crown."

Cowslips, kingcups, tulips, wallflowers, and early roses blurred into a profusion of colors as her eyes filled. The dear, foolish man didn't know a thing about country customs, but he certainly knew his way around a woman's heart.

Fingers on her bonnet strings, she sniffed back her tears. "If there is a queen, it will be one of the senior schoolgirls."

"Not in my kingdom." He lifted off her bonnet and settled the wreath atop her head.

Christine could find no reply to that. They wandered along in silence for a few minutes more until, striking up her courage, she asked, "Why did you really decide to stay for the dancing?"

Jacket slung over one shoulder, Simon shrugged. "Harrison thinks I should mingle more. I believe his precise words were 'cultivate an image.'" Responding to her frown, he added, "He's concerned my being a bachelor will hurt me in the election and wants me to take every opportunity to demonstrate my outstanding citizenship. You know, shake more hands, hold a baby or two, tip back a tankard at the tavern now and again."

She thought of poor Mr. Bullworth, sweating through his too-small suit, and said, "It doesn't seem as though you've much in the way of competition."

"If Bullworth were my only opponent, I'd find myself agreeing."

"He's not?"

He shook his head. "Nathan Oglethorpe is the incumbent and a Tory from the old school. As such, he abhors the progressive direction the party is taking. I wouldn't be surprised if he didn't detest Disraeli and all he stands for even more than those three Radical agitators we heard from earlier. He would have been here today only his wife went into labor last night. Next time I'll not be so fortunate."

"I'm sure you'll best him too," she said with absolute conviction, then blushed when she saw amusement flickering in his eyes.

"We shall see."

He took her arm, and they walked over to the section devoted to booths displaying the local crafts. Knowing how generous he was, Christine took care not to show too much interest in any one item for fear he'd think she was hinting.

But when they came to a stall filled with hobbyhorses, she couldn't resist lingering. Horses of every size, shape, and variety lined the workbench, table, and patch of lawn in front. Her gaze came to rest on a black-and-white hobby that, despite its fresh paint and elaborately carved bridle, had the look of the one her little brothers had played upon. Even though they'd outgrown "Chester" years earlier, they'd wailed like babes when she'd told them they wouldn't be able to take the toy with them. Throat thick, she stooped to give the rocker a push.

"Slight as you are, I think you'd outweigh it."

Feeling foolish, she straightened. "I was just thinking of my brothers."

Gaze watchful, he said, "You told me one of their names—Jake, like the dog?"

She made a quick nod. "The other is Timothy but, other than the times he's in trouble for making mischief, we all call him Timmy. Their birthday is in another two weeks. They're twins, you know."

"Actually you never told me that." He hesitated. "I'd be very happy to purchase this if you think they'd fancy it. I can have Jem drive it to the post office tomorrow."

"Oh no," she said with a shake of her head. "They're going to be ten, you see, and far more interested in riding a real pony than a wooden one. But thank you anyway. It was good of you to think of them . . . and me."

Casting about for a less awkward topic, she found herself recalling Lord Stonevale's remark about Simon being the last of the Belleville line.

Unless he marries and sires a son, the line will die.

Against her better judgment, she asked, "Do you want children?" Simon's widened gaze flew to hers, and she immediately regretted having "opened Pandora's Box," as he would say. "I'm sorry," she rushed on, "that's none of my affair."

He shook his head. "You needn't apologize. It's a reasonable question." Fingering the bright gold braiding on another of the carved ponies, he finally answered, "Like most men, I'd like a son to carry on after me, but I can't say what kind of father I'd make. My own died when I was thirteen and, when he was alive, we weren't close. Why do you ask?"

It must be the oysters for suddenly she couldn't seem to think about anything beyond how very much she wanted to kiss him. Gaze on his mouth, she murmured, "No particular reason. Just curious."

"Hm, I can tell. The way you're looking at me, I was beginning to wonder if I'd missed a spot shaving or perhaps grown a third eye."

Like a mouse who'd followed the hunk of cheese straight into the trap, she searched in vain for an escape route. "Oh no. That is, I couldn't say. Why, was I staring?" she asked, knowing the answer all too well.

He grinned. "Yes, Miss Tremayne, you most assuredly were, while sporting a smile as enigmatic as that of the Mona Lisa. Not that I mind. I'm just *curious* as to what thoughts are wending their way through that head of yours."

I think I'm falling in love with you.

Shocked to her toes by her soul's rallying cry, Christine hurried to conjure some answer—any answer—that might put the subject to bed. Make that to *rest*. "I was just thinking you look different today. Your hair, I've never seen it when it wasn't all wet and shiny."

With the sun striking the top of his uncovered head, the blue-black strands shone as sleek as a raven's wing. In that moment, Christine would have surrendered her place in heaven—assuming she hadn't done so already—for the right to run her hands through his hair.

"I usually apply macassar oil. It keeps my hair from falling into my eyes—" He swept a self-conscious hand through the thick locks tumbling over his brow, then added, "—precisely as it's doing now."

"Oh," she said, feeling stupid. Macassar oil—one more

thing she didn't know. "You look handsomer without it," she added on impulse, then felt her face flame.

This time she wasn't the only one to blush. Simon had undone the top button of his shirtless collar, and a telltale pink climbed his neck.

"You think so?" He swallowed, and she saw his Adam's apple rise and fall. "In that case, perhaps I'll consider adopting a new style." A shadow fell over his face as he added, "It's considerably easier to alter one's appearance than it is one's personality."

"Why would you wish to change your personality?"

He shrugged. "Harrison says I'm perceived as aloof. Cold. I suppose he may have a point. The truth is I'm shy."

Simon, shy? Certain he must be "tweaking" her, she searched his face. "Simon, how can you say so? After you gave your speech in front of all those people earlier—and those hecklers."

"It's one thing to stand barricaded behind a podium and address an amorphous crowd; quite another to converse with a person face-to-face. I'm afraid I'm far more comfortable with the former."

Preoccupied with her own failings, Christine had never before considered that Simon might suffer from self-doubt. Handsome, brilliant, and wealthy, to her he'd often seemed more of a god than a flesh-and-blood man. That her god had feet of clay—or, at the very least, an Achilles' heel—both frightened and excited her.

Still struggling to accommodate the strange notion, she shook her head. "A shy politician. We're going to have to do something to remedy that."

"*We* are, are we? I'm almost afraid to ask, but what precisely do you have in mind?"

Looking about for inspiration, she sighted the striped ale tent, specifically the red-cheeked duo swaying just inside the entrance. Arms flung about each other's shoulders like long lost brothers and feet fighting for purchase on the ground, Mayor Albright and Squire Priestly looked to be in high spirits.

"Come along." Wrapping one hand firmly about Simon's wrist, she tugged him toward the tent.

"Where are you dragging me?" he protested, pulling back on his arm.

"You'll see soon enough."

"Christine, you can't go in the ale tent," he said, digging in his heels when he saw where they were headed. "Ladies aren't allowed."

Coming up on the entrance, she gave him a shove. "It's not me that's going."

His eyes widened. If she didn't know better, she might think he was actually afraid. "But, Christine, I'm not thirsty."

"A pity that, for it seems your *constituents*—including the mayor himself—have worked up a powerful thirst. If we hurry, you can stand for a round before they fall flat on their faces."

"Eighty-eight pints of ale on the wall, eighty-eight pints of ale. If one of those pints should happen to fall . . ."

It was eighty-seven, actually, but Simon wasn't about to correct the mayor or the squire either, for that matter. Sandwiched between them on the bench, he struggled to recall whether the pewter tankard in front of him contained his third or fourth since Christine had all but shoved him through the tent flap. Frozen with terror, he'd been helpless to stop her when she'd announced to all and sundry that Mr. Simon Belleville, Maidstone's next M.P., would be standing for not one but *three* rounds. Coming out of his stupor, he'd whisked around just in time to catch her wink before she'd darted outside.

Looking through the open tent flap, he wondered where she'd gone off. The sudden image of her flitting about the maypole with a bevy of fresh-faced swains was all the encouragement he needed to make his excuses and leave. Amidst slurred protests, he started up. Relieved when the ground beneath him shifted only slightly, he skirted the row of packed trestle tables, fielding raised tankards and back-slaps as he made his way to the door.

Once outside the smoky tent, he paused long enough to draw a head-clearing breath, then started off to search the grounds. Dodging children blowing tin trumpets and conch shells, he came to the center of the common where an eighty-foot maypole had been erected for the day. A dozen or so young men and women twirled about the beribboned stave, but Christine wasn't among them.

Relief gave way to concern when he scanned the footpaths branching off the green and realized she might be any number of places. Determined to find her before twilight fell, he tore off. After exploring several of the walks, he finally sighted her sitting on a vacant bench. Bonnet in her lap, her thoughtful gaze fixed on a group of youngsters passing a ball through a suspended garland, she didn't blink when he hailed her.

Spent, he sank down beside her. "Do not *ever* do that to me again."

Grinning, she turned to him. "Why, sar, you've been drinking," she said, merry gaze belying her chiding tone.

"I'm four sheets to the wind, and you know it, so try not to look so blasted pleased with yourself."

"Your cheeks *are* bright as berries and your hair's all mussed." She reached out and, bold as brass, mussed it even more.

He made a show of shrugging her off but, in truth, her fingers on his scalp felt wonderful. "What I am is muzzy-headed, not to mention clumsy as a new colt. Walk with me until my head clears?"

"All right."

She was on her feet in an instant, bending to slide a steadying arm about his waist as he rose. Cad that he was, he leaned on her just enough to justify her keeping it there as he led her away from the fairground.

Suspended above a trickle of a stream, the old wooden footbridge was a favorite spot of his, perfect for viewing both the sunset and the fireworks that would begin soon after. The seasoned wood creaked as they started across. Stopping in the center, Simon leaned his forearms on the rail and peered out. Inhaling deeply of the spring-scented air, savoring Christine's nearness, he closed his eyes and gave himself up to the unaccustomed peacefulness enfolding him.

"Feeling better?" she asked, touching his sleeve.

Lifting his eyelids, he turned toward her. Hiding a smile at her worried look, he said, "If you're asking whether or not I'm about to lose my lunch, the answer is 'no.' " He touched the pit of his restless stomach and amended, "At least I think not. In fact, I may even rally for that dance I promised you."

She shrugged. "Oh, that's all right. I don't really care

about the dancing or the fireworks either, for that matter. We can leave anytime you like."

Feeling as though he'd failed her, he searched her face in the waning light. "Christine, you're not having a good time. It was selfish of me to leave you alone for so long. I should have held firm and left after the first round. Instead I..." He stopped when she reached over and laid a light finger across his mouth.

"Why, sar, how you do go on when you're in your cups." Smiling, she released a theatrical sigh. "What I started to say—and will say if only you'll let me finish—is I don't much care how we spend the evening...so long as we spend it together."

"Oh." Lifting her hand, he turned it over in his, contemplating her small, callused palm while he collected his scattered thoughts. "Then why do you persist in fleeing me at the first available opportunity?" She started to demur, but this time he wasn't about to let the topic drop. "This morning you set off without me and then again this afternoon." He paused to gather breath—and *courage*. "Christine, if you don't care to be with me, you have only to say so. I won't force my company on you, you've my word on it."

She shook her head so violently that she knocked her wreath askew. "It's not that, truly it's not."

He'd been the one drinking, yet it was Christine who wasn't making any sense. "Then what is it? Tell me... please."

She looked up at him with suddenly bright eyes. "I didn't want to shame you." He started to protest, but she cut him off. Lips trembling, she said, "This dress, these boots, were the last things I should have worn. When I saw how those women looked at me, I tried to bear it but..."

His confusion gave way to anger. "What women? Tell me their names. Whoever they are, I promise you today will be the last time you suffer their snubs."

Expression forlorn, she said, "You can't fight the whole world on my account. Even if you could, I'm not worth it."

"You're worth ten of any woman in this town, in this whole bloody county. I'll not have you disparage yourself just because some pack of provincial biddies frowned upon your frock."

Her soulful sigh rose above the crickets' chirping. She

turned to look out over the side. "In a few months, it won't matter anyway. I'll be gone."

She spoke no more than the truth yet somehow hearing the words from her own lips brought home how imminent, how bleak, was this course he'd chosen for them both. Laying hands on her shoulders, he turned her back to him and rested his forehead against hers.

Voice hoarse with emotions he wasn't yet willing to own, he said, "Don't speak of leaving. I can't bear to think of it."

"My, my, but ain't we chummy."

Simon swung around to see two of the three hecklers from that morning blocking the mouth of the bridge. Unshaven faces stretched into ugly sneers and shirtsleeves rolled up to knobby elbows proclaimed them to be hungering for a fight. He'd seen them earlier in the ale tent where they'd glared at him between quaffs of brew but had dismissed them from his mind. Only now, reading the blood lust in their too-bright eyes, did he comprehend the depth of his stupidity. Was he forever destined to repeat ancient history?

Heart pounding, he whirled to Christine, fighting the terror welling inside him as past and present melded into one. "Run!" he shouted, shoving her toward the foot of the bridge as the duo stopped a few paces in front of them.

The taller of the two said, "Ye and us got a score to settle, *Mister* Belleville."

Simon stared down the twosome. "Then we'll settle it . . . as soon as the girl leaves."

Turning determined eyes on his face, she shook her head. "I'm not leaving you." In a low voice, she added, "If it comes to it, I can kick and claw with the best of them."

He loved her for her bravery but now wasn't the time. "Christine, do as I say!" When she still didn't budge, he muttered as an inducement, "I need you to fetch back one of the constables patrolling the green." He'd say anything, absolutely anything, to remove her from harm's way.

She paled a shade, then snatched up a handful of her skirts and took off toward the far side of the bridge.

And plowed head-on into the broad chest and doughy belly of a third man, the ringleader from that morning. "Where d'ye think ye're off too, sweet'eart?"

Simon died a thousand deaths when he saw the oaf's beefy arms wrap about her, lifting her against his barrel chest.

Pinned, she looked up into the fleshy red face towering over hers. "Sod off!" She brought up her right knee and slammed it between her attacker's thighs.

Simon saw his opportunity and seized it. Hands clenched into fists, he barreled past his two startled assailants. He reached her just as her attacker let out a loud yelp and reeled forward, releasing Christine to cup his groin. Freed, she darted to the side, leaving him just the opening he hungered for. He caught the big man as he came down, his fist smashing into the bulbous nose. The crunch of cartilage beneath his knuckles was a wondrous thing, second only to the sight of him falling backward over the side of the rail.

A dense splash announced his arrival in the water below. Shouting over it, Christine called, "Simon, mind your back!"

He swung about to see the other two lumbering toward him. Logic told him to grab Christine's hand and make a run for it, but the demon driving him demanded to be fed. He charged, fists raised, a deep, primal growl breaking forth from his lips. Two pairs of bleary eyes shot open. The men exchanged terrified glances, then turned tail, tripping over each other in their haste to gain the bridgehead.

But Simon wasn't finished. Not nearly. He sprinted after them, catching up with the slower of the two before the steps. Simon caught him by the collar and dragged him back to the center of the bridge where he hefted him over the rail.

"Rats belong *beneath* the bridge."

Flailing feet fighting for purchase on the air, the man cried, "Please, sir, lemme go. Me and Sam, we was just out for a lark. Waylayin' ye and the lady, that was all Jack's idea."

"And a bloody bad idea it was. You have my leave to tell him I said so when you meet up with him. By the by, you might try avoiding those rocks below. They look devilish sharp." Simon dropped him another notch.

"Simon, leave him be."

It was Christine. She'd followed behind him. Looking back over his shoulder, he glimpsed her horrified face and saw the beast he'd become reflected in her eyes.

He swung his head back to his captive. Tears and sweat rolled down the bristled cheeks. Looking beyond the stubble, Simon saw he was no older than Jem. Likely no older than the university bullies who'd ravished Rebecca. Only about four or five years older than Simon had been when he'd fought—and failed—to rescue her.

Just a boy. I was just a boy. Inexplicably he felt the fury and self-hatred he'd nurtured for nearly twenty years begin to wither.

Simon hoisted him up and over the rail, the wretched little coward clinging to him like a kitten scooped from a well. "If I lay eyes on you again, I *will* kill you, understood?" At the boy's desperate nod, he set him down, then shoved him toward the bridgehead. "Off with you."

The youth took off down the footpath like a hare.

Simon turned back to Christine. Arms clasped about herself, she asked, "Are you angry with me for interfering?" In the fading light, he glimpsed the uncertainty in her gaze, and it tugged at his heart.

He walked toward her, pausing only long enough to retrieve the crown of flowers that had fallen from her head. Handing it to her, he said, "For saving me from doing murder? I think not."

Her beautiful mouth fell open. "You don't mean to say you would have actually *dropped* him."

"In a heartbeat." Weighing his words, he sought to explain without revealing too much of the shocking truth. "Watching someone you care for suffer is a singular sort of torture, a nightmare you replay over and over again in your mind. When I saw that brute lay hands on you, when I thought he might do you harm, something inside me snapped. I'm sorry if my actions distressed you."

She looked at him as though he'd suddenly sprouted a second head. "As if I give a fig for that lot. 'Twas you I feared for. If he'd died in the fall, they might have hung you."

Simon felt the corners of his mouth kick up. "Christine, you are a rare treasure." *My treasure.*

Sluggish movements sounding from below drew his attention. He dragged his gaze away from Christine's adorably flustered face and peered over the side of the bridge. Dusk was settling, but it was still light enough for him to make out a man's stocky figure crawling out from the water and up the embankment.

Simon turned to Christine, who had joined him at the rail. "It seems I'm not to rendezvous with the hangman after all.

He may not be exactly *kicking,* but he is most definitely alive." He exhaled as he felt the unwelcome tug of responsibility. "I suppose I should search out a police officer, make a report."

"Must you?" Odd, but she looked more afraid now than she had when they'd found themselves confronted.

He hesitated. If he filed a report with the authorities, the episode would be certain to find its way into the next installment of Maidstone's gazette. Who knew but by the time the journalists finished with him, Simon might even appear to be the aggressor in the attack. And then there was the little matter of Christine not really being his cousin.

"Perhaps I'll leave well enough alone," he conceded. "I don't think those three will be bothering us again."

She relaxed visibly and once again he asked himself why the thought of speaking to the police filled her with such dread. Then a fledgling smile touched her lips, and all he could think of was how much he wanted—needed—to kiss her.

He stretched out a hand toward her.

She gasped. "Sar, you're bleeding!"

He glanced down to his right hand, the knuckles split wide and weeping, the swollen fingers as purple as plums. Physically he felt as though he'd been run over by a coach and four, yet he couldn't recall ever being so content in all his life.

Joy was both a potent opiate and a potent aphrodisiac. Tucking the offending hand behind him, he met Christine's concerned gaze and shrugged. "It's nothing."

"Nothing?" Facing him, she looked almost indignant. "We have to bring the swelling down at once. There's a man selling shaved ices not far from the entrance. I'll pack your hand, then go to fetch the horse."

He moved closer. "You'll do no such thing, Miss Tremayne." Wrapping his left arm about her shoulders, he drew her against him. "For the past nineteen years I've walked about with the equivalent of a basket of bricks strapped to my back and a short while ago the straps were severed and the weight released. The relief is . . . indescribable. You'll have to forgive me if I insist upon taking a moment or two to savor it."

She looked up at him, brow furrowed. "I don't understand you."

"I know you don't." Using the heel of his injured hand, he tipped her face up to the waning light. "Suffice it to say that not only have I found myself, but I've found you too. Given that both discoveries are long overdue, I believe a celebration is in order."

And then Simon did what he'd dreamt of doing ever since that first evening in London when he'd tossed Christine into the bath. He leaned forward and settled his mouth over hers.

Against her mouth, he whispered, "Kiss me, Christine."

Cradling the back of her head in his palm, he ran his tongue along the seam of her closed lips. Slowly, like the petals of a rose unfurling beneath the early morning sunshine, she opened her mouth and matched her lips to his.

But when he touched his tongue to hers, she pulled back and turned her face away. "I don't know how."

Could it be that kissing wasn't a service on which Madame LeBow's customers had been willing to spend their coin? It must be so, for he'd learned over these past months that Christine didn't possess a single teasing, flirtatious bone in her body.

Flicking his tongue over the delicate inner canal of her ear, he whispered, "Then let me show you."

With a low moan, she turned her face up to his. She tasted of honey and sunshine and the peppermint confection he'd purchased for her earlier. At the first tentative touch of her tongue to his, electricity bolted from the base of his skull to the tip of his spine.

"Hm, you learn fast."

"Only because you're such a good teacher."

Simon wasn't about to argue. He'd gone hot and hard even before she'd kissed him back. Now that she was doing so—quite expertly, in fact—he felt himself approaching the limit of his self-control. At this rate, it would be only a short descent into madness, into shoving up her skirts and taking her there and now on the open bridge. He should stop—he would stop—before he reached that stage. Just another moment . . .

When the first droplet struck him on the bridge of his nose, he told himself it was merely dew from the trees . . . until a second, then a third fell.

Bloody hell, it was raining.

He pulled away from Christine to find that twilight had slipped into night. The lamps dotting the various paths branching off from the common were lit. In the center of the green, red-orange flames danced, and a fiddle's plucky chords mingled with the pounding of feet as the revelers ran for cover.

He turned back to Christine. "Might you be persuaded to accept a *rain* check for that dance I promised?"

Laughing, she wove her arm through his, then raised up to kiss his cheek. "Let's go home."

Home. Pulling her close, Simon decided he'd never before heard a sweeter word.

Fifteen

> Though I am not splenitive and rash,
> Yet have I something in me dangerous.
>
> —William Shakespeare,
> *Hamlet*, Act V,
> Scene 1, circa 1602

Midway back, the heavens opened. Within minutes the dirt road leading from town was a brown river. Lightning burst overhead, slicing through the black canvas of sky. Taking advantage of the flash of light, Simon dismounted. He took a moment to settle the spooked horse before helping Christine down.

Holding up fistfuls of her sodden skirts, Christine sloshed along the grassy roadside beside him. "When we get back, let's have a picnic in the gazebo."

"A picnic! But Christine, it's *raining*, not to mention thundering."

"So it is," she acknowledged, slanting her face upward as if seeing the lightning and rain for the first time. "An indoor picnic then, in the study. We can spread a blanket on the carpet and have our supper before the fire." In the darkness, her eyes sparkled like stars. "Only we'll pretend it's a *bonfire*."

"A carpet picnic. How very civilized."

She swatted his arm. "You're making fun of me."

"No, no, I'm not. But I am having fun. Oh, Christine, you bring me such joy, such..." At a loss, he pulled her to him and brought his mouth down hard on hers. Their front teeth met with a crack. He drew back, feeling like an oaf. "Oh, God, that was clumsy of me. Are you all right?"

She tapped a finger against her top teeth. "I'm fine. Right as *rain*." She chuckled. "I have very strong teeth."

"Yes, I know you do," he answered, and they both laughed, remembering.

They walked the rest of the way in companionable silence, the horse ambling behind them. By the time they reached Valhalla's private drive, Simon's stocking feet swam inside his shoes, the brim of his hat ran water, and his right hand throbbed like the very devil. He couldn't remember ever enjoying himself nearly so much.

"I'll see to your hand as soon as we get inside," she told him as they passed the shingled gatekeeper's lodge.

"No, you won't, at least not until you've changed out of those wet things. I'll not have you contracting an ague on my account."

Inside his head, a warning bell clanged. Fussing over each other like an old married couple, what did it signify? He pushed the uncomfortable question—and the warning it sounded—aside. But Simon being Simon, he couldn't help but start making plans.

"Have you ever been sea bathing?" he asked when they stopped for Christine to retrieve a pebble that had worked its way into her shoe.

"Simon, I've never even *seen* the sea." She gripped his arm, steadying herself as she stepped back into her boot.

"Well, then that settles it. Tomorrow, provided the weather's cleared, we'll rise early and take the morning train to Whitstable. We'll bathe before the heat of the day, then search out a place for luncheon." Watching her bend over to lace her boot, sodden skirts molded to her narrow hips and long legs, he thought of how delectable she would look clad in only a thin woolen bathing costume—preferably wet. Mouth dry, he added, "There's a lovely little restaurant overlooking the water. The cook there serves the most amazing whitebait."

She knotted her laces, then straightened. "Will I like it?"

Imagining himself peeling off that very wet bathing costume, he answered, "The fish? I rather think you will, but we'll have to wait and see."

"No, silly. I mean the sea."

"Oh yes, Christine. Everyone loves the sea."

They fell silent when the house came into view. Reaching the circular front drive, Simon was relieved to see that his servants had returned as well. A footman hurried down the front steps, lantern in hand and umbrella aloft.

"You're a bit late, my friend." Waving aside the umbrella, Simon handed over the horse's reins and went to help Christine up the slick steps. At the top he lingered, suddenly, inexplicably loathe to enter. Swiping his thumb over a spattering of mud on her cheek, he said, "Despite the unpleasantness on the bridge, today has been very special to me."

Eyes downcast, she nodded. "To me too."

The urge to steal another kiss from her sweet lips almost overpowered him. Almost. Before matters between them went any further, he needed to decide what place, if any, she might safely occupy in his life.

Mrs. Griffith opened the front door and ushered them inside. The door had scarcely closed behind them when she announced, "Sir, there is a *person* to see you."

Attention focused on the charmingly drenched woman at his side, he said, "A person, Mrs. Griffith? How mysterious you are this evening." He paused to smile at Christine, adorable in her self-conscious—and doomed—attempts to tidy herself. "Can you be a bit more specific?"

The housekeeper shifted her gaze to Christine as well. "He says he's a friend of yours, miss."

Simon felt Christine stiffen beside him. His gaze darted to Christine. *Who is he?* he silently implored.

I don't know, but I'm afraid, her eyes seemed to say. She gave an infinitesimal shake of her head and looked away.

A chill stole up his spine. He turned back to the housekeeper. "Where have you put him?"

Mrs. Griffith studied her liver-spotted hands, laced in front of her. "In the front parlor, sir, though it hardly seemed the

Tempting 215

place for him." She lifted her eyes. "Shall I tell him you'll be down after you've changed?"

"You need tell him nothing. I—" He glanced at Christine, who was making short work of her bottom lip, and added, "—*we* shall see him directly."

The parlor set to the right of the staircase. The pocket doors stood open as if Mrs. Griffith didn't trust the visitor not to steal anything. On the threshold, Simon took Christine's trembling hand. It was cold as ice.

In a low voice, he said, "Don't worry. Whatever—whoever—it is, we'll face it together."

She lifted her pale face to his. "Thank you for today. No matter what happens, it was the happiest of my life."

Reading the raw fear in her eyes, Simon felt the last of his newly acquired peace crumbling about him. Before he could press her for an explanation, she stepped into the room, leaving him little choice but to follow.

Mud-caked boots propped on the tea table and face buried in Simon's open newspaper, their *guest* didn't trouble himself to rise as they entered.

Simon cleared his throat. "I am Simon Belleville. How may I help you?"

The newspaper inched downward. Straw-colored hair framed a gaunt, clean-shaven face, pale as paste except for the spotty forehead and chin.

And the livid red scar slicing across the jutting brow.

Ignoring Simon, the man settled his insolent gaze on Christine. "Why, Chrissie, luv, ye look a treat."

"Hareton!"

Simon turned to Christine just as she took a step forward and swayed.

Hareton dropped one boot at a time from the table and stood, a slow uncoiling of his narrow frame that had always reminded Christine of a garden snake. Tugging down the too-short sleeves of his ivy-green jacket, he announced, "I've come to fetch ye 'ome, poppet. Now run along and pack your things."

Simon gave her hand a reassuring squeeze. "You aren't taking her anywhere."

Warmed by his loyalty, she found her voice. "He's right,

you know. You can't force me to go with you."

Hareton snorted. "Now there's a fine greeting after all I've gone through to find 'ee." He ran his thumb along the thick ridge of red scar that ran from his left eyebrow into his scalp. "I'm still a bit cross wi' ye for knockin' me o'er the head wi' that poker, but at least I'm prepared to let bygones be bygones."

Out of the corner of one eye, Christine studied Simon. Now that he knew the truth, what must he think of her? But, other than the tensing of his forearm beneath her fingers, he betrayed no sign of shock or even of surprise.

Confidence bolstered, she slipped free and faced Hareton. "How did you find me?"

He broke into the broad, gap-toothed grin that she'd learned to loathe. "I was in Rosie's Pub a few weeks back when I bumped into Tommy Fielding, 'ome from London to visit 'is sick mum. The lad were fair near to burstin' with the news that Christine Tremayne was in London studyin' to be a *lady*. 'Studyin' to be a lady?' says I, sure ole Tom must be drunk as David's sow. But then 'e told me how 'e saw ye outside the bakery on Oxford Street."

Christine recalled the incident only too well. At the time, she'd thought herself to be a murderess on the lam and had feared Tommy would give her away. Lord, but how right she'd been.

Clearly enjoying himself, Hareton continued, " 'E hallooed for ye to stop, but ye'd moved on. So 'e threw down his broom and followed—right to the front steps o' the Mayfair Academy for Young Ladies." His gaze hardened. "I bought my railway ticket the very next day. One o' your schoolmates told me ye'd left for Maidstone in Kent wi'—" He paused to glare at Simon. "—*'im.*"

A muscle ticked in Simon's jaw; otherwise he appeared unmoved. "What is the market rate for forgiveness these days?"

Hareton picked at a fat pimple on his chin. "Hm, well, let's see. First I'll have to reckon on 'er almost killin' me. I lost a lot o' blood, Chrissie, and I still 'ave muzzy spells."

Now that the worst was over, Christine felt her strength returning along with her hopes. She wasn't a murderess. The authorities weren't hunting her. She didn't have to hide any longer. She was free.

She took a step toward Hareton. "If you're muzzy, it's on account of the ale and gin you pour down your throat."

Hareton stared past her to Simon. "Then there's the three months I lay abed, too sick to work."

Hands on her hips, she glared at him, marveling she'd ever allowed this miserable scrap of a man to terrorize her. "As if the likes of you would know what an honest day's work was."

He had the gall to smile. "Then, o' course, I had to hire workers to replace the ones 'ee made off wi' in the middle of the night. By the by, where are the brats?"

It was perhaps one of the hardest things she'd ever done, but Christine found a way to clamp down on her fear. "Liza and Jake and Timmy are somewhere safe, somewhere you'll never lay hands on them."

"Oh, I wouldn't be so sure of that."

Nausea plowed into her stomach like an unseen fist. Had he found them? But no, she told herself, he wouldn't be here if he had.

Simon came up behind her. Laying a warm hand on her shoulder, he said, "We can let the courts settle this if you prefer." His tone was calm but standing so close Christine felt the tension teeming from him in molten waves. "I have some very good friends who sit on the magistrate's bench. I'm certain they'd be more than curious to know how your cousin came by the scars on her back."

Determined not to let her shame show, Christine kept her chin up as she studied her very much alive cousin. Was it only her imagination or had he shrunk? He looked less imposing, smaller. Or was it she who had grown?

He lifted his thin shoulders in a shrug. "No matter," he finally said. "What do I want wi' a parcel of brats anyhow?"

Christine released the breath she hadn't realized she'd been holding, but it was Simon who spoke her thoughts aloud when he asked, "Then what do you want?"

Hareton shoved his hands into his pockets and rocked back on his heels. "I'm not a political man myself, but I'm given to understand that voters frown upon a bloke lyin' to 'em." Bypassing Christine, he ambled over to Simon. "What d'ye think the fine folk of Maidstone would say if 'twere to come out that Christine ain't really your cousin?"

"How much?"

Christine swung about to Simon. "Simon, no. If you give him money, he'll only come back for more. I'll leave. I'll leave tonight, only don't—"

Features as hard as chiseled stone, Simon said, "Christine, be silent."

"Listen to the man, Chrissie. 'E's a sharp shaver." Sucking on his bottom lip, he sent his appraising gaze over the well-appointed room. "Five hundred pounds should settle it."

"Five hundred pounds!" Christine felt as though the breath had been knocked from her lungs. "You must be—"

"Done." Simon's tone made it clear he would brook no argument. Helpless, she followed him with her eyes as he walked over to the small writing desk. "I presume a bank draft will be acceptable?"

Hareton's thick lips slipped back in a triumphant smile. "Aye, I suppose ye're good for it. If not, I know where to find 'ee."

Silence descended, broken only by the sliding of the desk drawer, the slashing of Simon's fountain pen across paper, and the thundering of Christine's heart.

Simon rounded the desk and held out the note. Hareton snatched it and frowned down at the paper. It was then that Christine remembered her cousin couldn't read.

Simon must have surmised as much for he said, "It's legal tender, so I'd advise you to take it and be off before I change my mind about introducing you to the magistrate."

Glowering, Hareton stuffed the note into his coat pocket. "Ye think ye're better than me wi' your fine 'ouse and fancy ways, but ye're not." Eyes glittering, he turned on Christine. Finger stabbing the air, he hissed, "At least I'm canny enough to know a lyin' bitch when I see one."

Wondering what mischief Hareton was about now, Christine looked to Simon just in time to see him lunge. Before she could move to stop him, he slammed his left fist into Hareton's jaw. Blood and saliva whooshed from Hareton's slack mouth. He staggered back, catching himself on the edge of the desk.

He swiped his coat sleeve over his bloodied mouth and straightened. "She's played 'ee for the fool, Belleville, pretendin' to be nice and sweet, when all the while she's been cozyin' up to your grandfather behind your back."

Christine spun toward Simon. Stunned, she opened her mouth, but no words came out.

"Cat got your tongue, Chrissie?" Grinning through his split lip, Hareton nodded toward Simon. "Go ahead, mate. Ask 'er where 'tis she rides off to Thursday afternoons."

"You're lying!" Face afire, Simon threw himself at Hareton, fists raised.

Christine flung herself between the two men. Holding on to Simon's raised arm with both hands, she screamed, "Stop it! Stop it! It's true."

Simon slowly lowered his arm and turned to Christine. The amber-brown eyes, delicately molded nose, and lush mouth were the same he'd spent the past four and a half months memorizing, yet he felt as though he were looking upon a stranger. Worse than a stranger. His betrayer.

Stiffening his jaw, he asked, "What did you say?"

" 'Tis true, I have been calling on Lord Stonevale—" She jerked her head toward Hareton. "—But it's not as he makes it out to be."

"Really?" He stared down at her small hands clenched about his sleeve. Slowly, methodically, he pried each of her clinging fingers from his arm, then turned back to Hareton. "Leave. Leave now before I throw you out myself."

"Oh, I'll leave a'right." Patting his coat pocket, he started across the carpet. "I've got what I want. Pity ye can't say the same, eh, Belleville?"

Whistling, he stepped out into the hallway. Simon stood still, stiff. Waiting to hear the main door open, then close. Only after it had did he move. Numb, he walked over to the parlor doors and drew them together. He'd always scoffed at the notion of zombies, the walking dead of West Indian lore, but now he was less smugly sure. True, his lungs took in breath, his heart continued to beat, his legs carried him forth and yet he felt . . . nothing.

"Simon?"

Slowly, very slowly, he turned about. "How long?"

She wrung her hands. "I can explain, truly I can."

"Can you?" He walked over to the drum-top table set in the room's center. A Dresden china shepherdess presided over the tooled leather top. Curious. Until now he'd never noticed how much the shepherdess' pure features and reed-slim figure resembled Christine.

Simon didn't recall raising his hand let alone sweeping the edge of his arm over the table, but he must have. He heard the thud, heard Christine's gasp at his back. Dumbfounded, he looked down to the shepherdess, lying in bits on the Oriental carpet.

Not a zombie after all. He tossed back his head and... laughed.

"Simon?"

Sensation—*pain*—ripped through him. He whisked about. Gaze scouring Christine's face—the stricken eyes, the trembling mouth still swollen from his kisses—he repeated, "How long?"

"Simon, please." Tears slipped down her cheeks, cheeks that not an hour before he'd likened to rose petals.

Disgusted with his own weakness, he stalked toward her, heels crunching on shards of glass. *"How bloody long?"* he shouted, rage crashing down on him like molten rocks spewed from a volcano.

She had courage, he'd give her that. When he drew up in front of her, she didn't try to move away. "Only a few weeks. Since your birthday... The meeting with Mr. Harrison."

"You're good, I'll give you that." He shoved his hands into his pockets to keep them from her throat. "All this time you've been consorting with *him,* spying on me beneath my very roof, and I never suspected. Never."

She shook her head, the wet tresses lashing the air about her head. "No, you have it all wrong. It isn't like that. We talk, have tea. Sometimes I read to him."

He felt his top lip curl upward. "How... *cozy.* And are reading and talking *all* you do for him?"

"Of course. What else..." She broke off, face reddening. "He's old, he's lonely. I think he's sorry for the quarrel with you."

It was the last straw. "Sorry, is he! Let me tell you about sorry." Seizing her by the shoulders, he shook her hard. Fingers biting into flesh-veiled bone, he hissed, *"Sorry* is seeing your mother go down on her knees to beg the landlord not to put her children out on the street." He shook her again and this time he fancied he heard her teeth clacking together. *"Sorry* is hauling barrels and sacks until you're certain your back is broken, then climbing into bed at night and breathing in your body's foulness, too exhausted, too hungry, to care." He paused to gulp more air into his strangled lungs. "*Sorry* is being beaten and trussed, then made to watch your sister subjected to the vilest act that can befall a woman. Believe me, my grandfather—you—can't begin to know what it means to be sorry."

He released her and backed away, amazed to find he was shaking, not only his hands but his whole body. Sweat trickled down his temples, between his shoulder blades. An invisible vise torqued his chest, driving the air from his lungs, leaving him fighting for breath.

And yet somehow he found breath enough to go on, "If I hadn't been denied my birthright, I could have protected her. Damnation, there would have been nothing to protect her from. She—I—we would have been tucked away in some town house on the West End of the city—pampered, adored, *safe*."

"Simon, I had no idea. I thought you must have always been as you are now—rich. Perhaps your grandfather believes the same? How can you be certain he knew of your family's plight?"

Baring his past was tantamount to stripping his soul, yet how quickly she leapt to the old man's defense. He stabbed a swollen finger into the air between them. "Oh, he knew all right. After Father's death, we wrote to him. He never answered any of our letters." His gaze honed in her face, daring her to dispute him. "You see, my father committed the unforgivable. He married outside his faith and beneath his station. A Jewess. A housemaid. Just one step above a dairymaid. No, perhaps not even that." He backed away, bitter laughter burning a path up the back of his throat.

"Simon. Please, don't do this!" She threw herself at his chest, flinging her arms about his neck. "I love you."

But it was too late. He shoved her away. "You miserable little liar!" Desperate, he swiped the back of his hand across his slick forehead. "Those men on the bridge, they're mates of yours, aren't they? Tell me, Christine, was the plan to get my purse, stick a knife in my ribs, then back to Nantwich to roost with coz and the kiddies? Only your plan fell short, and so you dallied with me on the bridge, just long enough to give Hareton time to get here."

Mouth agape, she stared at him. "You don't mean that. You can't really think that of me. Not after we . . ."

Did he believe it? He didn't know anymore. All he knew was that he had to escape from Valhalla, from Christine. Over the past months, she'd steadily chipped away at the sturdy, protective shell it had taken him twenty years to form. If he allowed her to go on, she'd crack him like an egg, expose the small, shivering embryo huddled inside. The Simon that no one, *no one,* was ever allowed to see.

He started for the oak doors. "I'll set out for Maidstone at first light, take rooms in town while you advertise for a situation." Not daring to look back lest he weaken, he grabbed for the knob. "Tell Mrs. Griffith to send word as soon as you've gone."

Sixteen

> O, call back yesterday; bid time return.
>
> —William Shakespeare,
> *Richard II*, Act III, Scene 2, 1597

Good-bye, Kent. Good-bye ... Simon. Perched on the edge of the tufted leather carriage seat, Christine turned her face to the window, welcoming the honeysuckle-scented breeze drying her tear-tracked cheeks. Had it only been yesterday that she'd stood on the park bridge enfolded in Simon's arms and watched the sunset? Since he'd looked into her eyes and whispered, *Don't speak of leaving. I can't bear to think on it.*

It felt like ages, but then so much had changed since they'd set foot in Valhalla's drawing room. She'd gone from believing herself to be a murderess to knowing that she was a free woman. And Simon had gone from begging her to stay to ordering her from not only his home but his life as well.

Tell me, Christine, was the plan to get my purse, stick a knife in my ribs, then back to Nantwich to roost with coz and the kiddies?

Even now, when her aching head still rang with the terrible things he'd said to her, she couldn't bring herself to hate him. That's what love did to a person, turned you all soft and gooey inside. She loved Simon. With all her heart. With all that she was and had yet to become. As far as she was concerned, the man with the flinty gaze and the arsenic-laced tongue was a stranger. An impostor.

That morning she'd stood at her bedchamber window and watched through tear-blurred eyes as he'd accepted his horse's reins from a groomsman and climbed into the saddle. Briny tears salting her cheeks, she'd silently begged for a look, a nod. Something, *anything,* to show he didn't despise her.

But he'd turned his stallion and ridden down the drive without sparing her so much as a glance, making it abundantly clear there would be nothing more between them.

Not even good-byes.

That was when she'd made up her mind to leave Valhalla immediately. A wiser woman would have done as he'd bid and stayed on until she found a situation either as a governess or lady's maid. But, where Simon was concerned, Christine had never been wise. And she had too much pride to remain in the house she'd driven him from. The sooner she left, found her own place in the world, the better it would be for them both.

"Whoa." Jem's drawl carried downward from the driver's box as the carriage slowed to a halt.

Jolted, she realized they'd arrived at the railway terminus. Gilded by the late afternoon sunshine, the station's façade—in the Italianate style, she'd since learned—was an impressive sight. The first and last time she'd seen it, the day had been bleak and rainy. Yet in spite of her worries for her family, her anxiety over living under the same roof with her moody and all-too-attractive mentor, she'd sensed she was setting out on a grand adventure. If she'd known how tragically that journey would end, would she have chosen a different path, dug in her heels, and refused to leave London?

It took all of a second to admit that no, she would not have. Like a miser hoarding gold, she wouldn't part with so much as a day of her time with Simon any more than she'd consider selling the amber pendant that still hung about her throat.

Her wardrobe was another matter. Pride had tempted her to leave all but a few of the simplest frocks behind, but practicality had won out. The hollow ache of an empty belly was not a feeling she was eager to repeat nor was she foolish enough to believe that starvation would be balm for a broken heart. She'd sell off the richest gowns one by one until she found work; what remained would go in Liza's hope chest.

The carriage creaked, then dipped as, above her, Jem climbed down to lower the carriage steps and open the door. "Valhalla won't be the same wi'out ye, miss." He reached up to take Puss's carrier from her.

Relinquishing it, she stepped down. "I'm going to miss you too, Jem. And Mrs. Griffith, and Janet, and well, everyone."

Especially you, Simon. Feeling her eyes begin to fill with fresh tears, she retrieved the basket and went to find a bench to gather herself while Jem finished unloading her luggage. Her time in Kent had been nothing short of magical, a memory she would forever cherish, but it was time to let go.

Time to look ahead to the future.

God, Margot, you look old.

Margot set down her silver-backed hairbrush—a gift from which of her former lovers she neither remembered nor cared—and leaned into her dressing table's gilt mirror. Was that a new line cracking the right corner of her mouth? Had it been there last month? She'd need her spectacles to be sure, but she didn't think so. Tamping down a jolt of fear, she reminded herself that her face was no longer her fortune. She was the headmistress of a flourishing young ladies' academy. In another few years, she'd be able to sell the school and retire to anywhere she fancied.

But it was London that suited her. London she loved. A seaside cottage in Brighton or Bath might be someone else's idea of paradise, but she adored living in the eye of the storm. She might be on the shady side of forty, but inside she felt young, gay. She wanted to dance, be admired, make love.

Pulling back from her reflection, she admitted, *What I need is a man.*

Someone neither too young nor too old—the balding, bespectacled admirers gathering in her parlor these days only depressed her. No, she needed someone handsome, intelligent, sophisticated . . .

Someone like Simon. Her heart gave the familiar lurch. Dear Simon. Would there ever be another like him?

The sound of heavy footfalls shuffling down the hall toward her door interrupted her maudlin thoughts. Marie, her maid, was late in coming to help her dress for dinner, but Margot didn't have the heart to chastise her. She had an inkling the girl had found herself a lover, an action of which Margot heartily approved. Judging from Marie's sluggish approach, her young man must have quite worn her out.

Smiling at the thought, she called out, "You're late, *chérie,* but I love you anyway."

Her bedchamber door swung open. In the mirror, she glimpsed Simon standing in her doorway.

"Late? D-didn't even know I w-was expected."

He stood too far away for her to make out his features without her spectacles, but she thought he sounded odd. She took a second to secure the sash of her silk dressing robe, then rose and hurried across the room.

Reaching him, she drew back in shock. "Good Lord, you smell like a gin palace." She'd seen him drunk only once before: ten years ago when he'd barged into the Claridge's supper room, a brash young man hell-bent on self-destruction.

He scraped the back of his swollen hand across his stubbled jaw. "Port, act'lly, though I lived above a g-gin shop once." Gripping the doorpost, he leaned forward and confided, "Stunk dreadfully."

"You don't say."

Unshaven, rumpled, and reeking, he released his hold and staggered forward. With a groan, she caught him against her. Casting her gaze out into the hallway, she saw Mrs. Fitz, red-faced and mortified, rounding on them. Motioning the housekeeper to silent retreat, she propped her burden against the wall. She pinned a steadying hand to his chest while, with the other, she reached around him to close her door.

She took a moment to catch her breath, then asked, "I thought you were in Kent courting your constituents and playing at country squire?"

Back flattened against the flocked wallpaper, he lifted his broad shoulders in a languid shrug. "I was ...'til this m-morning. Now I'm h-here." Shoving away, he brushed by her, his weaving footsteps bringing him to the bed. The mattress dipped as he made himself at home on the edge of her silk coverlet.

Thankful that her spring term had ended the week before, Margot followed and took a seat beside him. "You're really quite drunk." She lifted his right hand to scrutinize the scabbed knuckles and swollen fingers. "Not to mention you look as though you've just returned from the wars."

"I was in a f-fight. T-two of 'em, a-actually."

Liquor and fisticuffs. What—or rather, *who*—could have brought her dear, solemn Simon to such a pass? Money troubles? She thought not. Simon was a bold investor, but he never gambled more than he could lose. That left only one plausible explanation—a woman. And not just any woman, she ventured.

Fishing, she said, "I trust Christine didn't rough you up? How is she, by the by? Her last letter came more than a month ago."

He gave his head a vigorous shake, then lifted a hand to it as if checking that it hadn't toppled off. "D-don't want to t-talk about h-her. She's a l-liar. All w-women are liars." He lifted his storm-dark eyes to hers. " 'Cept you, of course." The dark hair spilling over his brow made him look far younger than his five and thirty years.

Resisting the urge to comb back the straying strands with her fingers, she started up. "Of course. I'll just ring for coffee, and then we can talk about it."

He tugged her back down beside him. "Don't want c-coffee. Don't w-want to t-talk."

She was about to ask what he did want when he reached over, fumbling the front of her robe. Good Lord, but he must be even drunker than she'd thought.

Gazing down on his bent head, she asked, "To what do I owe this unexpected honor?"

He cocked his head and looked up at her, eyes wounded. "W-what h-happened t'us, Margie?"

He hadn't called her *Margie* in years. Not since . . .

She cleared her throat, doing her best to ignore his finger tracing the opening of her robe. "Well, as I recall, we were having a perfectly smashing time of it, fucking like two randy rabbits, when I made the mistake of declaring I'd fallen in love with you. The next day you told me you thought it would be best if we were simply friends."

He touched her cheek with clumsy fingers. "I h-hurt you, didn't I? D-didn't mean to."

She sighed. "I know you didn't, dearest. I suppose it was no more than I deserved for being a dirty old woman and robbing the cradle."

"You're not old." His palm found her breast.

Pushing his hand away, she struggled for strength. "Simon, you really are quite foxed."

"Uh-huh." He tugged her robe the rest of the way open and took each of her breasts in his hands.

His thumbs found her nipples. She bit her lip as the warm, delicious sensations trickled through her. It was too bad of her to take advantage of his drunken state, but she was only human, and it had been so long. Too long.

"Lovely," she murmured, arching against his hand.

He shuddered, then slumped against her. She waited for him to stir, but he didn't. Had he passed out? Then she heard a muffled exclamation, felt something warm and wet trickle between her breasts.

Pulling back, she looked down onto broad, shaking shoulders. "Oh dear." She covered herself as best she could, then put her arms about him and drew him close until his hot cheek rested against her shoulder. "There, there," she soothed, rubbing his back as though he were one of her homesick students. "Have a good cry, dearest, because after you're through, I mean to hear all about it. And I do mean *all*."

Two hours, two chamber pots, and six cups of strong black coffee later, Simon sprawled on the silk-covered settee in Margot's drawing room. Grimacing, he dutifully lifted his china cup from its scalloped saucer and downed his last bracing swallow.

"Care for another?" Perched on a peach-and-cream striped armchair across from him, Margot reached for the silver coffeepot on the Queen Anne style tea cart set between them.

He shuddered and set down his empty cup down. "God, no."

Port was another beverage he heartily hoped never to touch again. The two bottles' worth he'd vomited earlier would likely last him a lifetime. Even in the midst of swilling, the sweet wine had only fortified the sharp stab of misery he'd first felt when Trumbull had arrived at his hotel bearing an overnight bag and the news that Christine had left for the railway station earlier that day.

The urge to go after her had been strong indeed but pride and some other indiscernible emotion had held Simon back. Even so, he'd known he wasn't yet equipped to return to his empty house. Nor did continuing to swill port while pacing his rented rooms like a caged beast strike him as a lasting solution. Telling himself that a change of scene would provide the cure, he sent his horse back with Trumbull and hired a hansom to take him to the railway station. Only now did he admit that he'd harbored the secret hope he'd find Christine waiting on the platform. But he hadn't. Ignoring the titters and curious stares of his fellow travelers, he'd staggered up to the ticket agent's counter and purchased a one-way ticket. By the time his train pulled into London Bridge Station, his mind was as empty as the pocket flask he'd brought along. Vision bleary, sour mouth sheathed in cotton wool, he'd followed the flow of disembarking passengers. It was a minor miracle that he'd managed to make his way through the turnstile and out the front gate; a major one that he hadn't met his death when, without a glance, he'd lurched out into the busy street. Cockney curses and horses' shrieks sliced through his stupor. He'd snapped up his head in time to see metal shod hooves bearing down on him. Fortunately for Simon, the hansom driver at least had his wits about him. He reined in and, after some persuasion, conceded to let Simon crawl inside the cab. Simon's crowning humiliation had been to forget where he lived. Slumped on the cracked leather seat, the only direction that had come to him was Margot's.

Flashing him a mischievous smile, she set the pot down. "Well then, now that you're back among the living and passably coherent, perhaps you'd care to tell me what happened between you and Christine?"

"Not really." He let his heavy head fall back. "Perhaps." He sighed. "Very well."

In as few words as possible, he recounted the events of the previous day. Deliberately he skimmed over the episode on the bridge—the kiss especially—to focus on Hareton Tremayne's appearance at Valhalla.

Margot's gaze sharpened. "Don't tell me, a seedy, bug-eyed little chap with a nasty slice out of his forehead?"

He hoisted his heavy head. "Yes, that's him exactly. Now that I recall, he admitted to coming here."

"Oh, Simon." Eyes anguished, she nodded. "He turned up a few weeks ago, asking after Christine. I told him I had a strict policy of not releasing personal information on former students, but he persisted until finally I had to ask him to leave. He did, but later I saw him loitering outside, head to head with Maddie Johnson. I considered calling the constable to give him the shove off, but I was afraid I might be bartering trouble given Christine's background." Her shoulders dipped. "I kept meaning to telegraph you, but . . ."

Simon exhaled heavily, feeling as though the Fates had conspired against not only him, but Christine as well. "It's not your fault, it's mine."

"Yours? How so?"

Painful as it was, he slogged through the remainder of his tale, not sparing himself when he came to the part about Christine's secret visits to Lord Stonevale—and his own furious reaction to the news. Throughout Margot listened in sedate silence, sipping from her cup of hot chocolate.

When he finally finished, she said, "Is that all?"

Desperate to convince both of them that he'd been in the right, he took refuge in indignation. "What do you mean 'is that all?' She deliberately disobeyed me, went behind my back. God only knows what mischief the old man put her up to."

To his chagrin, she only shook her head. "Really, Simon, you sound like Bluebeard. It seems to me that Christine is guilty of little more than girlish curiosity and a soft heart. Even knowing how you feel about Lord Stonevale, I have difficulty imagining you striking out at an innocent. Whatever induced you to behave in such a beastly fashion?"

It seemed the Fates had decided to be merciful, if not kind, for he was saved from answering by the appearance of Margot's housekeeper, Mrs. Fitz.

The old woman poked her head and shoulders inside the open doorway. "So sorry to disturb you, mum, sir, but there's—" She hesitated, glancing at Margot. "—*someone* to see you."

With a sigh, Margot set down her cup and rose. "A caller, at this hour?"

Rather than elaborate, the housekeeper cut a warning look in Simon's direction. He obliged by looking away but not before he glimpsed the two women exchanging speaking glances.

Margot turned back to Simon, the Mona Lisa's own smile playing about her lips. "Excuse me for a moment?"

Wondering what the mystery was, he said, "Of course."

She followed Mrs. Fitz out into the hallway, pulling the door closed behind them. Doing his level best to close his ears to the whispering taking place on the other side of the closed door, he rose and drifted over to the window overlooking the street. Palms braced on the sill, he stared out to the hansom stationed curbside outside Margot's front gate. Dodging raindrops, the driver labored to unload a substantial-looking portmanteau from the cab's boot. Two more trunks, equally bulky, dangled from the arms of Margot's footman as he hurried back toward the house. A new student?

But no, now that he'd sobered, he remembered that Margot's spring term had concluded. No new students would be arriving for at least a fortnight.

Had Margot found herself a lover? The quantity of luggage suggested that the newcomer certainly meant to stay for some time. Simon turned away from the window, happiness for his friend turning to chagrin as he brooded on how he'd barged into her bedchamber earlier, the ham-handed liberties he'd taken. Pushing aside his personal humiliation, he resolved to be happy for her. Margot was a lovely woman and despite the pride she took in the success of her school, she'd been lonely. He was glad she was getting on with her life. If only he might find a way to do the same.

That wistful thought led him back to her parting question. What *had* possessed him to order Christine away? Anger, to be sure, over a trust betrayed, but was taking tea and cakes with his estranged grandfather really so great a crime?

And was it only yesterday that he and Christine had shared those soul-shattering kisses? Even the muddy, rain-soaked trek back to Valhalla that had followed had been marked by a kaleidoscope of intimacy that had shifted from passionate to playful, teasing to somber. But then there were so many facets to Christine, it would require a lifetime to explore them all.

A lifetime. *His* lifetime. At some point on the walk home, he'd realized he wanted to spend it with Christine.

Good God, was that when the panic had set in? The terrible festering fear that, once they crossed Valhalla's threshold, the fantasy plans he'd begun formulating might suddenly become . . . real? Had Hareton Tremayne's revelation served as a convenient excuse for him to push Christine away, to *run away,* before his feelings for her could take root?

The staccato pounding in his temples, the bile burning holes in his stomach, the cotton multiplying inside his mouth—all were small discomforts compared to the scathing agony of self-reflection. He knew a pathetic relief when he heard the chamber door open and saw Margot standing on the threshold.

The bustle filtering in from the front hallway reminded him that, unlike him, she had someone waiting for her. Deciding he'd likely exhausted his allotment of selfishness for the next decade, he started for the door. "I should be going."

"Oh no, you don't." Stepping inside, she pulled the door closed behind her. "We aren't finished yet, not nearly. *Sit.*" She pointed him back to the sofa.

After a moment's hesitation, he gave in and retraced his footsteps to the sofa, only too glad to face away from her too-knowing eyes. Their violet hue had dimmed over the years, but the insight had sharpened. Margot understood him better than anyone, including himself.

Collapsing on the cushion, he confessed, "God, Margot, I thought I had it all figured out—M.P. by thirty-five, a cabinet post by forty." *A pretty, biddable wife to serve as my dinner hostess.* He shook his head, suddenly appalled at his own shallowness. "The truth is I don't know what the hell I want."

Resuming her own seat, she lifted one pencil-darkened brow. "Don't you?"

He ran a hand through his hair, wincing when his bruised fingers caught in the tangles. At one time he might have been content with a conventional marriage but now he doubted it. If the past months with Christine had taught him anything, it was that there was a great deal more to want, to *feel.*

"What I do know is that ever since I found Christine in that blasted attic, my life has become . . . complicated."

She leaned toward him, her proud smile that of a teacher whose problem pupil has finally solved a difficult mathematics problem. "Simon, dearest, life *is* complicated. Love especially so. Regardless of the outcome, you have to face your feelings and that means facing Christine."

"How can I?" He fitted a hand over his throbbing brow. "She told me she loved me. I called her a liar and all but threw her out of the house. And now she's gone."

"I shouldn't wonder." She paused and then added, "I suppose you'll just have to find her." She gave his shoulder an encouraging pat. "Surely you must have some clue as to where she might go?"

He lifted his head from his hands and sighed heavily. "Her family's dairy is in Nantwich but, with her cousin alive and still in control of the property, she'd never go back there." He racked his brain, wishing he'd paid more attention in those early days. "Her sister and brothers are working on a farm somewhere in Shropshire, but I don't even know what parish it's in, let alone the name of the establishment."

All true, for Christine had posted the money he'd sent rather than give over their direction. At the time he'd not given a great deal of thought to why she was so secretive, but now he understood. She hadn't trusted him, at least not entirely. As much as that hurt, given his recent actions, how could he blame her?

"Before I return tomorrow, I'll see about engaging a detective to locate her."

In the course of his tenure as vice commissioner, he'd had occasion to enlist the aid of one or two such firms. Not that he imagined for a moment that, once he found her, she'd care to have anything to do with him. But, selfish bastard that he was, he needed to assure himself that she was safe and well; otherwise, he'd go lunatic. And, after the vile way he'd treated her, the least he could do was to make certain that neither she nor her siblings suffered from want.

Margot's violet eyes glowed like twin Chinese lanterns. "Who knows, but perhaps a detective won't be necessary after all."

Wishing he might share in her optimism, he said, "Perhaps not but I won't take that chance." Thinking her other *guest* must be growing impatient, he started up, this time determined. "I've monopolized your time far too long."

Her placid expression transformed into alarm. "Leave, in this storm? Don't be ridiculous. It won't do Christine any good if you're struck by lightning or your coach is overturned in a ditch."

He turned and glanced back at the window to where a steady rain drove against the glass panes. Mired in his own misery, he'd scarcely registered the gathering squall. Blackening skies and waving treetops confirmed that a storm was indeed brewing. Praying that Christine was sheltered somewhere safe and dry, he turned back to Margot. "And your other, uh, ... guest—"

"Shan't mind a bit. It's a large house and depressingly deserted now that the girls have all left for holiday. You can have the third floor entirely to yourself. I've already sent Mrs. Fitz to prepare the room."

Margot's bedchamber was on the second floor so, presumably, he'd not be invading her privacy or that of her *guest* either. And she was right—there really wasn't anything he could do for Christine tonight. A crack of thunder sealed his decision.

"Very well. Thank you." He rose. On his way to the door, he stopped by her chair. "You're a good friend, Margot. Far better than I deserve." He laid a hand on her shoulder. It wasn't the touch of a lover but of a friend. "After tonight, I wouldn't blame you if you never spoke to me again only I hope you will accept my apology. Not just for my earlier behavior, which is beneath contempt, but for all the times I've given you so much less than you've given me. So much less than you deserved."

Reaching up, she covered his hand with her own. "Oh, Simon, there's nothing to forgive. You can't help *not* loving me any more than you can help loving Christine." Eyes watery, she waved him toward the door. "Now go on before I change my mind and decide to have my wicked way with you."

Feeling his ears heat, he was only too glad to turn away and head for the door. One foot planted in the hallway, he couldn't resist turning back. "Do you really think I'll find her?"

The chair's high wing hid Margot's profile from view, but he fancied he heard the smile in her voice. "I feel certain of it."

Tempting

Simon entered the front hall to find Mrs. Fitz waiting at the foot of the stairs. Now that the effects of the port had worn off, a bone-deep weariness enveloped him as he followed Margot's housekeeper up the cantilevered staircase. His mind, he felt sure, would remain far too active for sleep, but it would feel wonderful to stretch out full-length on a bed and close his eyes for a few hours. To give Margot and her *friend* their privacy, he'd make sure that he was up and gone before the household stirred. Odd that she hadn't volunteered his name, for it wasn't like her to keep secrets from him. Then again, knowing Margot, she had her reasons.

Pondering the identity of Margot's mystery man was his best defense against his darker musings: Was Christine truly safe? Would he really find her? Before he knew it, they'd stepped off the third-floor landing and were moving down a narrow corridor, their way lit by the domed gaslights flanking the wainscotted walls at regular intervals.

Mrs. Fitz drew up at the closed door at the end of the hall. Turning slowly back to him, she said, "Well, I'll just er, . . . leave you to your rest. Have a . . . a good night." Cheeks mottled, she made a beeline for the stairs with a haste that belied her mature years.

Reaching for the knob, Simon asked himself whether or not the old girl might have joined him in hitting the port that day. The door fell open, spilling shadows out into the hall. Blast, but the fool woman hadn't thought to leave him a light. Cursing to himself, he propped open the door to allow the light from the hallway to trickle inside, then began edging his way toward the shadowy shape of a four-poster.

"Blast!" He reached down to massage his smarting shin.

Straightening, he circumvented the unspecified, but exceedingly solid, square shape he'd just bumped into and continued on at a half crouch. His outstretched hand met the polished edge of the bed's footboard. Skimming it, he edged his way toward the head of the bed. Next to it there was certain to be a bedside table and, atop it, a lamp. His hand dropped to the mattress. Beneath the covers, something warm and rounded and very much alive stirred beneath his palm. One of Margot's Persians, burrowed beneath his bedsheets?

In no mood to share, Simon swooped, intent on scooping the beast into his arms and then onto the carpet. "Oh no, you don't. It's the floor or nothing for you, my friend."

A clap of thunder joined with the unmistakable shrillness of a woman's scream.

Seventeen

Be shy of loving frankly; never tell all you feel or (a better way still) feel very little.

—William Makepeace Thackeray,
Vanity Fair, 1848

Simon released the female's derriere and stepped back. Bemused, he registered more riffling sounds from the bed, then the click of the lamp. Light flared, then slashed through the darkness, illuminating the bed and its occupant.

"You!" Propped up on one elbow, the sheet pulled up to her chin, Christine regarded him through slitted eyes.

Was he drunk still? Asleep? He blinked, half expecting her to disappear in the fraction of a second it took him to lever his eyelids. But no, she was here. She was real. She was *safe*. Simon knew such relief, such blinding *gratitude* to The Powers That Be, he could have kissed not only Christine but also her cat curled up on the pillow beside her.

Except that Christine didn't look like a woman who wished to be kissed. Scowling, she ripped free of the covers and swung bared legs over the side of the bed.

She thudded to her feet, her white cotton night rail fluttering about her slim form like a sail. About her slender throat, the gold chain of the amber pendant sparkled like starlight. Not only had she kept the necklace but she'd worn it to *bed.* Surely that must count for something?

She planted a fisted hand on either slender hip, tapering the garment to her waist. A waist he could easily span with his two hands . . . assuming she ever let him touch her again. "I thought you'd let rooms in Maidstone."

Realizing she awaited an answer, Simon struggled to find his tongue. "I did . . . that is, I was at the hotel there until this afternoon. When Trumbull arrived with my luggage, he told me you'd left. And now I find you . . . here." *Safe, sound, and still wearing my keepsake.* Fresh relief came to him in a dazzling rush far more potent than the port he'd quaffed. Arms open, heart full, he started toward her, closing the distance separating them in two long strides. "Thank God you're safe."

"Thank Him indeed, for 'tis no thanks to you." She hauled back and slammed her fist into his solar plexus.

Simon might have chalked up the swift flash of motion to the interplay of light and shadow if it weren't for the sharp, cramping pain knifing his gut. Coffee and sourness bubbled up the back of his throat and for a terrifying moment he thought he might shame himself by falling down on all fours and retching at Christine's feet. Holding a hand to his roiling stomach, he concentrated on mastering the nausea. Only when he was once more in command of his body did he venture a gaze in Christine's direction. Two crimson spots colored either cheek; otherwise she appeared remarkably composed.

Straightening, he managed a tight smile. "If I'd known you could hit like that, I would have enlisted your aid on the bridge the other day."

Eyes firing arrows, she opened her mouth to reply but it was Margot's voice that sounded from the open doorway. "Lovely, I see you two are catching up." Standing on the threshold, she wore a smile that would have put the sun to shame.

And suddenly Simon understood. It was Margot who had orchestrated this humiliating little tête-à-tête. Grateful as he was to have found Christine, he was prideful enough to balk at being bested by a woman. Make that *two* women.

Jaw clenched, he jerked back to Christine. "You planned this, didn't you? Somehow you knew I'd end up here."

"You think I followed you!" Amazement, then anger brewed in the coffee-colored depths of Christine's eyes. "Why, 'tis plain as the nose on your face that I'm as shocked to see you as you are to see me." She started toward him, hands curled at her sides. "Or at least it would be if you weren't such a stodgy snob, such an arrogant *arse!*"

That did it. "Is that so?" Simon started forward, only too willing to meet her halfway. "It seems to me as if *someone's arse* is in dire need of a sound spanking."

"Stuffy snob. Arrogant ass." Margot entered the room and deftly inserted herself between them. "Marvelous alliteration, don't you think, Simon?" Planting a restraining hand on his chest and another on Christine's shoulder, she divided her gaze between them. "And of course, Christine is quite right . . . at least about her being as surprised as you. She had no more of a notion that you were in the drawing room than you did that she was outside in the hallway. That said, I am terribly glad that you each felt you could turn to me."

Venting a snort in Simon's direction, Christine turned to Margot. "When I left this morning, I meant to go directly to Shropshire and fetch Liza and the twins but then I realized I couldn't, not when I haven't so much to offer them as a roof over their heads. Then I remembered what you said to me before I left school, about how I was to come to you if—" She hesitated, voice faltering. "—If things didn't work out. So I bought a ticket to London instead and came here in the hope that you'd let me stay on until I find work."

The plaintive admission brought a fierce ache to Simon's chest. Delicious thoughts of turning Christine over his knee drowned in the rush of shame he felt. For the first time, he understood, *truly* understood, the full ramifications of his actions. In giving way to his petty pride, his overblown anger, he'd not only cut off Christine but also the family that relied on her for sustenance. From the corner of his eye, he glimpsed Margot watching him. Perhaps it was the lingering effects of inebriation, but he fancied her gaze held a silent appeal. *This is your chance. Your final chance. Don't muck it up.*

Before he could be sure, she broke eye contact and turned to Christine. Lifting her hand in a breezy gesture of dismissal, she said, "Let us talk about this in the morning. I for one have always found that the future appears a good deal rosier after a night's rest." Patting away a yawn, she started backing into the hallway. "Which is what we all seem to be in dire need of."

Simon turned to Christine. "You've already settled in. I'll find another room."

She replied with a resolute shake of her head that sent her thick braid swinging like a bell rope. "No, you stay here. I can sleep on the cot in my old room."

Blast, would the stubborn woman not cede him an inch? "I *said* I'd . . ." He let the rest of his argument die as it struck him that Margot was being uncharacteristically quiet.

He whirled in time to see the bedchamber door close behind her. Rushing forward, he made a grab for the knob but too late. The lock clicked into place.

"Damn it, Margot, this isn't a game. Open this blasted door at once." Heedless of his sore right hand, he raised it into a fist and began to pummel.

Christine joined him at the door. "Margot, please. You can't mean for me to stay in the same room with . . . *him*." With a strangled exclamation, she too laid into the door.

Ever patient, Margot waited until their pounding and pleading had petered before announcing, "You two are going to stay put until you settle your differences once and for all even if it takes all *night*. By morning, I shall expect you to have come to an understanding. If not . . . well, my new term doesn't begin for several more weeks."

Rubbing his bruised knuckles, Simon shouted back, "This is outrageous. You can't lock us in together as though we were quarreling children."

"On the contrary, if you two persist in behaving like children, I am simply going to treat you as such. *Bonsoir, mes enfants.* Sleep well."

Another chuckle, then Margot's fading footsteps. Disgusted, Simon turned away from the door lest he cede to the impulse to bash his head against the hard wood. He braced one shoulder against the panel and directed his attention across the room to where Christine appeared to be conducting an exhaustive excavation of the top dresser drawer.

Folding his arms across his chest, he asked, "What the deuce are you doing?"

Without pause, she pushed the drawer back in place and yanked out the one below. "Searching for a skeleton key."

Embarrassed he hadn't thought to suggest doing so himself, he grunted a reply.

This time her busy hands stilled long enough for her to look back at him over her slender shoulder. "You could help, you know, unless you'd rather stand there all night feeling sorry for yourself."

"I am not feeling s—" He broke off, realizing that was exactly what he was doing. Caught, he shoved away from the door, stripping off his jacket as he stalked across the room.

Together they made a thorough search of the rest of the chamber. They shared a brief, heady triumph when Simon located a likely looking candidate in a Sevres porcelain dish atop the mantel shelf. Triumph dashed to defeat when they discovered that the key fit the lock on the wardrobe door, but not that of the chamber. At Christine's insistence, they joined forces to turn over the mattress only to discover a great deal of lint, several hairpins, and a copper penny but no key.

The mattress once more in place, she slumped down on the side of the bed. "This is hopeless."

Dashing the back of his hand across his damp forehead, Simon sat beside her. Transferring the found coin from one hand to the other, he said, "Cheer up, you haven't that much longer to bear my company. It's already half past midnight. Morning."

Following his gaze to the clock on the fireplace mantel, she released a sigh. "So it is."

For the first time he noticed how tired she looked, how drawn. Wishing he might smooth away the bruised crescents beneath her eyes with the pads of his thumbs, knowing he hadn't the right, he tossed the copper onto the bedside table. "We should try to get some rest." He reached down and started on his right riding boot.

It thudded to the floor. Christine sprang to her feet. "W-what do y-you think you're d-doing?"

Without looking up, he worked on freeing himself from his other boot. "Preparing for bed." He set the footwear by the bed as was his custom then began stripping off his stockings.

Christine's gaze swiveled from the mussed bed, to the

boots *beneath* the bed, and then back to Simon's face. "B-but . . ."

Annoyed that he'd given her ample cause to think him less than a gentleman, he snapped, "You needn't look at me as though I mean to ravish you. I fully intend on sleeping in a chair." He glanced to the brace of Chinese Chippendale chairs, both heaped with her clothes, and amended, "Make that the floor."

"Oh." Fiddling with the lace edging her sleeve, she conceded, "I suppose that will be all right."

He had it on the tip of his tongue to point out that, short of him climbing outside to sleep on the roof, they hadn't a choice. Stifling the sarcasm, he rose and stomped to the washstand to wash up before *bed*. Then it hit him. "Damn!"

Christine paused from pacing the vicinity of the bed. "What is it?"

"I left my bag in the front hall." Running his tongue over his fuzzy top teeth, he cast a longing look at her tooth powder and brush set out on the marble stand. Watching her in the mirror, he asked, "Mind?"

"And if I do?" She folded her arms across her breasts. Her small, firm, breasts. Breasts that, the other evening, he'd discovered fit his palms perfectly. As if she were made for him.

Feeling less than charitable himself, he shot back, "Then I might be tempted to remind you that a mere twenty-four hours ago I had my tongue in your mouth."

That silenced them both. Cursing himself for venting his frustration in temper, he dumped water into the basin, dampened the brush, and applied the tooth powder. Amidst savage brushing, he conceded he was making a hash of this reunion. And that, if he didn't turn things about and soon, he might not get another chance. Ever.

Holding on to that dire thought, he finished, then crossed the room to the two clothing-piled chairs. Stripping off his cravat, he did his level best to ignore Christine's silk stockings and—good God—garters dangling from the chair's back. He'd just added his waistcoat to the mounting pile when a sudden prickle of awareness shot through him. He looked up to find Christine watching him, gaze riveted to the triangle of flesh revealed by his open shirt collar. Despite the chilly, rain-scented air wafting in from the half-open window, he felt his flesh heat. And his pulse quicken.

Holding her gaze, he said, "Christine, we have to talk."

"There's nothing more to say." She turned abruptly away. Giving a fierce tug to the bedclothes, she said, "You'll need a blanket."

He came up behind her. "On the contrary, there's a great deal to be said and I mean to say it."

"I won't listen." She whipped about and shoved the armful of coverlet at his chest.

He took it and dumped it back on the bed. "Damnit, I'm trying to apologize if you'll but give me the chance."

Brows shooting upward, she asked, "The same chance you gave me when I tried to explain how I came to be calling on Lord Stonevale?"

The hard words vibrated with a strong undercurrent of hurt. She wouldn't forgive him easily. Quite possibly she wouldn't forgive him at all, yet he had to try.

"*Touché*. Now, will you hear me out?"

She studied him, her mouth pressed into a flat line. For a moment he feared she would tell him to go to the Devil, then stomp away. Instead, she inclined her head. "Go on, then."

Relief rushed to anxiety as he struggled to make his start, his tongue suddenly grown too big and clumsy for his mouth. "Last night, the vile things I said. I was angry. Furious." *Afraid.* "I'm not a man who trusts easily. When I thought you'd betrayed me to Stonevale—"

"I never betrayed you."

"I know that now but, at the time, I felt as though my world were collapsing. It's a poor excuse, no excuse really. I wish I could take back every word, erase them from both our memories, but I can't. All I can do is to apologize, beg your forgiveness. Will you give it?"

Hands on her hips, she hoisted her chin. "That depends."

In need of an anchor, he wrapped his hand about the bedpost. "On?"

She drew a heavy breath, then released it in a sigh. "On whether you're only sorry for hurting my feelings, sorry that I left, or truly sorry for what you said."

Simon was about to ask if there was a difference, but he wisely bit back the question. Obviously to Christine there was. "All of the above."

She looked at him askance. "Spoken like a true politician."

Damn but she was as implacable as a boulder. Desperate,

he let go of the post and poked a hand through his hair, fingers catching on the tangles. "Is there nothing I can say, do, to move you?"

Beneath her night rail, her breasts rose and fell with each rapid, rushed breath. "You all but accused me of . . . of lying with your grandfather. Of going behind your back to scheme with not only him but Hareton too. With *Hareton,* of all people." She turned her face up to his. "Of everything, I think that hurt me the most."

Seeing the pain darkening her eyes, Simon felt as if a razor slashed at his heart. "And yet you still wear the necklace I gave you." He lifted the gold chain on a single finger, warmed by its contact with Christine's flesh. "Why?"

Her mouth trembled but her gaze never wavered. "You know why."

Such honesty deserved to be answered in kind. He let the chain drop. "Ah, Christine, I've spent the past decade pretending to be something, *someone,* I'm not. Hearing you say you loved me, telling you about my past, I felt as if all the masks I'd accumulated over the years were being stripped away at once." Unable to meet her steady gaze and still go on, he walked over to the fireplace. "I've never met anyone like you before. When I'm with you, I catch glimpses of the man I might have been. A better man, a *feeling* man." He turned away and gripped the mantel shelf with clammy hands. "I want to become that man, not so much for myself as for you. And that . . . that terrifies me. *You* terrify me."

There, he'd said it. As spent as if he'd just run a footrace, he rested his forehead against his forearm and waited. Outside the storm had muted to a few murmured rumblings. Above his head the ormolu clock ticked on, its beats maddeningly rhythmic, regular. A sharp contrast to the choppy, uneven rapping of his heart.

Footsteps whispered across the carpet toward him. And then he felt it. A light hand warming his back. And Christine's voice, a bare whisper, saying, "All right, then. It's all right. I forgive you."

He released the wood and turned to face her. "You do?" Afraid to believe, he searched her face for some sign of subterfuge.

But Christine's eyes never lied. Forgiveness shone from their amber-brown depths as clearly and as brightly as the tears welling there. She reached up and touched her hand to his cheek. "Yes."

It was then that Simon knew he still possessed a soul because he felt it soar. Joy so intense it skirted pain flooded him. He grabbed for her hand and carried the palm to his lips. "You won't regret giving me this chance. I promise you."

"No promises." She laid a hand on either side of his neck and turned her face up to his.

His hands found her waist. How small she was, how delicate. Like a wood sprite. A wood sprite with the lush mouth of Venus. A mouth he could no longer wait to claim.

But wait he must. With trembling hands, he held her from him. "God help me, I want you, Christine. I don't know if you're my poison or my cure, but you've wormed your way inside my soul and now I couldn't cut you out even if I wanted to." He drew a barbed breath. "I'm aching to make love to you, to be inside you. But before I touch you I need to know that you want it too."

Christine used her tongue to moisten her lips. "I want you too, Simon. And I'll lie with you . . . if you truly want me."

Simon stared down at her, amazement etched on his every feature. "*If* I want you? Christ, Christine, I spend my days and nights doing little else but wanting you."

Christine managed a wobbly smile. "Then, sar, we are of a mind."

She wrapped her arms about his neck and pulled his face down to hers. Standing on tiptoe, she matched her lips to his, her body to his, her *passion* to his, until it was no longer possible to tell where he ended and she began. Until the kiss had become much more than a kiss. Until he'd ferried them across the floor to the bed. Until she felt the rock-hard length of him against her belly and realized, in a flash of cold panic, that he was more than ready to claim her.

She couldn't help herself. She shoved at his chest.

He released her in an instant. "Christine?"

She turned away before he could see the shame branding her cheeks. *Damn you, Hareton, must you steal tonight from me too?*

Still facing away from him, she said, "Everything is moving so fast." Immediately she hated how lame she sounded, how weak and unsure. Determined to smooth the tremble from her tone, she tried again. "I want you, I do, only..." Hating Hareton, hating herself even more, she let the explanation trail off.

"Only you've had a bad experience and now you're afraid." His hands descended on the tops of her shoulders. "I won't hurt you, you know." Instead of drawing away, he kneaded the tautness from her muscles with knowing thumbs. "I only want to give you pleasure." He brushed her braid aside and skimmed her nape with butterfly light kisses that scattered her fears and sent her soul soaring. Minty breath teased her ear, the back of her neck. "But promise me, no pretending. You've only to tell me—show me—what you want."

Leaning back into his solid warmth, Christine searched her muzzy brain for the response he seemed to expect. Aside from Hareton, there had been only Tommy Fielding. Last August during haymaking, Tommy had finally found the courage to steal a kiss from her behind a hayrick. Poor Tommy, his slippery tongue had reminded her of jellied eel, and the leeks he favored hadn't helped matters.

Glad Simon couldn't see her face, she admitted, "I can't say. I don't know what it is I want."

"Then let me help you find out." He slipped his arms about her, lightly cupping her breasts in his palms.

Through the fine cotton of her night rail, his clever fingers found her nipples. She tensed again, remembering how once Hareton had used his big hands to hurt her there.

Simon's hands were big too, but his touch was gentle as he rolled her between his thumb and forefinger. She hardened. She heated. She shook from head to toe.

Knees as weak as her head, she sagged against his hard chest. "Oh, Simon, I feel so queer."

"I'll accept that as a compliment." His throaty chuckle floated above the top of her head, reminding her that she probably ought to do something more than droop against him like a storm-battered vine. "But I suspect you'll like it even more without this nightgown in the way. I know I will."

Reaching around her, he started on the queue of buttons that closed the front of her night rail. One by one, the little seed pearls popped free of their holes until the gown gaped open to her waist. Damp air brushed her flushed breasts, the top of her belly. A second later, fresh panic plowed into her as he pushed the garment down over her shoulders. He mustn't see her and certainly not in the light.

She made a grab for the gown. "*No,* please."

He stilled his hands. "Why not?"

Clenching the cloth, she racked her brain for an excuse he would accept. "Because it . . . it isn't decent."

He started to laugh, then stopped when she didn't join him. "You are a true enigma, Christine Tremayne." He took hold of her wrists before she could manage to rehook even the first button. "But let's have done with secrets, shall we."

He slipped her night rail off her shoulders, pressing a kiss atop each one even as she tried to wriggle away. A moment later, the garment whispered down her hips and legs to land in a pool about her ankles. Chilly air—and Simon's regard—pricked her bared backside. She bit her bottom lip hard, for she knew only too well what he was seeing. Scars. An especially ugly one snaked from just below her hairline to the nape of her neck, a permanent reminder of the time Hareton had used his belt buckle to punish her. She felt Simon's breath feathering the back of her neck. Then his mouth, as warm and wet and hungry as when he'd kissed her before, settled between her shoulder blades. And then—dear Lord, the shame of it—she realized he was following the ridge of raised tissue with his tongue.

A tear splashed her cheek. "Don't," she pleaded, her voice a raw whisper as she tried again to pull away.

But he had her about the waist and he showed no sign of letting go. "Am I hurting you?"

She considered lying, knowing he'd stop in an instant if he thought he were causing her pain. But, whatever tonight was, she didn't want to taint it with lies. "No," she admitted.

"Then why won't you let me kiss you here?"

As if she could stop him. His arms, stronger than the heaviest of hemp, pinned her against him, and he was already licking another fat scar that curled, like a serpent's tail, over her left shoulder.

Fresh tears trailed her cheeks. "Because it's ugly." *I'm ugly.*

"No, it's not. Not to me."

She looked back at him over the shoulder he still nuzzled,

expecting to see pity, even disgust. But there was no mistaking what she found in his gaze. *Desire.*

He wanted her. Even now. Her back might be as badly flayed as those of the Roman galley slaves she'd read about in their ancient history lessons, but it didn't matter to him. Not a jot.

Throat knotted, she slowly turned in his arms. Hands on her shoulders, he held her at arm's length while he sent his gaze on a slow, thorough journey that began and ended with her eyes.

When she would have looked away, he raised her chin on the edge of his hand. "You can't know how many times I've imagined us like this. You like this. Even so, you're a hundred times lovelier than you were in my fantasies."

The breadth of his smile sent her heart somersaulting. So it was true. He'd wanted her all along! It was too much. He was too much. More tears—of gratitude and relief—stung her eyes. He'd given her body back to her. She didn't know what to say, how to thank him.

Or perhaps she did. Dropping her gaze to his chest, she said, "You're still dressed, and here I am risking lung fever." She shivered, although she'd never been so hot in all her life.

He carried her hands to rest on his breastbone. The warmth of him filled her palms. "Then help me with *my* buttons, and we'll risk it together."

Christine had dressed and undressed her little brothers many times. Unlike those two squirming imps, Simon stood perfectly still, his entire attention focused on her. Christine swallowed hard. Willing her clumsy fingers to cooperate, she worked at the queue of cloth-covered buttons fronting his shirt, then slipped her fingers beneath the waist of his trousers to free his shirttail. Slowly, reverently, she slipped the cambric over his shoulders, then off.

Christine stared. Never before had she considered that a naked man could be beautiful. Simon was that and more. Roped with muscle, his upper arms were thicker than those of the blacksmith back home, his stomach washboard flat and rippling with sinew. Dark hair dusted his chest; beneath his breastbone, it narrowed to a queue that disappeared inside his trousers.

Where more buttons wanted undoing. Behind them, what promised to be a truly magnificent erection strained to be free. She froze. Her hands turned to blocks of ice even as her face and throat went up in flames.

"No matter," he murmured, then turned away to shed his trousers. When he turned back to her, he still wore his knee-length cotton smallclothes.

Sensing he'd kept on the undergarment to spare her sensibilities, she felt tears of gratitude and regret prick her eyes. "You're so grand," she whispered, wishing the stock of words inside her head were large enough to describe all that she felt.

Determined to banish the past once and for all, she threw her arms about his neck and pressed against him, skimming the sandpaper roughness of his jaw, his neck, the hard plane of his chest with mouth and hands. She closed her eyes, the better to savor the ragged sound of his breathing, the musky scent of sweat mingled with Windsor soap, the way his skin shivered beneath her touch.

The sensation of being swept off her feet prompted her to open her eyes. Simon had lifted her into his arms and was carrying her to the bed. Brushing the balled-up blanket aside, he laid her on the crumpled covers, then came down atop of her. Obviously in no mood to share either her mistress or her pillow, Puss hissed, then dove off the bed.

"I don't think your cat likes me much." Chuckling, Simon found the crest of Christine's right breast with his mouth.

She gasped as a stream of bittersweet bliss rippled from her nipple, pebble-hard and aching, to the reservoir of liquid heat brewing between her thighs. "Well, I like you." She laced her fingers through his thick hair and arched against him, wanting more.

He obliged, transferring his attentions to her other breast. "I'm glad to hear it because I like you too. Very much."

He moved slowly down the length of her, exploring her with mouth and hands, tongue and fingers. "You've the body of a ballet dancer. Long-boned and lean. A sublime combination of curves and angles."

His praise warmed her heart even as it resurrected her shyness. Hiding behind a light laugh, she said, "A ballet dancer, am I? I've two left feet. Two *large* left feet."

Smiling, he shook his head. "You're perfect right down to the tips of your toes." He skimmed the contour of her left leg from calve to ankle to arch, ending by hooking her foot atop his shoulder.

She pulled herself up on her elbows as his hand wrapped about her other foot. "Simon, what are you about?"

His answer was a meltingly wicked smile. "Helping you to discover what it is you want."

Legs splayed, she was completely open to him. Completely vulnerable. Embarrassed, she tried to squirm farther back on the bed, but his hands held her knees, holding her fast against him.

"This?" Bristle from his unshaven jaw grazed the inside of one thigh, then the other. "Or perhaps this?"

When his mouth, moist and warm, descended to cool the sting, Christine fell back against the pillow, dimly aware that she wanted his lips somewhere else. Beyond shame, she whispered, "Please," in a stranger's voice, not entirely sure what she'd just asked for.

But Simon knew. He let go of her legs, now locked about him of their own accord. With his fingers, he found her inner lips. Slowly, carefully, he spread them and slid one long finger inside. "Am I getting warmer?"

Christine sucked in her breath. She certainly was. A warm stickiness dampened the inside of her thighs, and she wondered for a frantic few seconds if her monthly had started. But no, it was too soon in her cycle. And this steady, humming ache was unlike any sensation she'd ever known.

The stretching, the stroking, the murmured endearments—it was all too much. Perspiration filmed her forehead, the crease of her breasts, the backs of her knees. Liquid pooled in her belly, between her legs. Clutching great fistfuls of covers, she started to beg him to—she wasn't sure what—when his head disappeared between her thighs and he found her with his mouth. His tongue swept over her, parting, exploring, suckling. Heaven and hell, pleasure and pain, folded into one. The throbbing grew until she could feel herself swelling, her inner muscles hammering in time with her heart.

Then he found it. Something small and tight and sheathed by folds of flesh like an oyster-sheltered pearl. He touched it with the tip of his tongue, then circled once, twice ...

Christine's release was as swift as it was unexpected. Like a covey of morning doves suddenly set free, she took flight, leaving her earthly body far below. She soared, dipped, then soared again, each time calling out her pleasure.

When she finally landed, limbs weak and trembling, she realized Simon had joined her at the head of the bed. "Welcome back." Smiling down on her, he brushed her cheeks with the pads of his thumbs.

She realized she was crying again. Before she could focus her fuzzy thoughts to answer why, he planted a knee on either side of her. Glancing downward, she saw that he'd unbuttoned his underdrawers. His swollen sex surged forward, longer, thicker, and more formidable even than the mental image she'd conjured.

He fitted himself to her and pressed forward. "Ah, Christine . . ."

Panic seized her as the blunt pressure built, *deepened*. She tried to close her legs, but he was wedged between her thighs, his weight pressing her into the mattress. "Simon, I'm not . . ."

The rest of her words were lost in a gasp as pain, sharp and searing, stabbed into her.

Eighteen

> And see! the lady Christabel
> Gathers herself from out of her trance
> Her limbs relax, her countenance
> Grows sad and soft; the smooth thin lids
> Close o'er her eyes; and tears she sheds—
> Large tears that leave the lashes bright!
> And oft the while she seems to smile
> As infants at a sudden light!
>
> —Samuel Taylor Coleridge,
> "Christabel," Part I, 1797

Simon felt the cobweb-thin inner barrier break even as Christine's gasp filled the chamber. One hand braced on either side of the pillow upon which she lay, he fixed his gaze on her terrified eyes. Slowly, carefully, he withdrew and edged his gaze downward.

Oh God, no, it can't be.

But the dark inky wetness on his penis didn't lie.

He'd just deflowered a virgin.

The ugly reality of what he'd done, of what he'd taken, hit him like a fist in the gut. He rolled onto his back and fitted a hand over his brow. "You should have told me."

She snapped the sheet up to her chin. "How was I to know you thought I wasn't?"

He cast a sideways glance to her profiled features. "In case you've forgotten, I did find you in a brothel." A second later, he would have surrendered his last farthing for the chance to take back those scathing words.

Clenching the sheet in one white-knuckled hand, she sat

up. Mouth trembling, eyes betrayed, she answered, "I told you before, I didn't know what kind of a place it was when I agreed to work there."

"Yes, but I thought you had . . . worked there, I mean. That in the end they'd forced you. Good God, you were in your night rail when I found you. I just assumed . . . Well, never mind."

Color rushed her cheeks. "You might have asked me."

Stifling a groan, he slid his legs over the side of the bed and rose. He found his trousers on the floor and jerked them on. With some difficulty, he managed to button the front flap, then stumbled over to the washstand. Feeling as though he were living a nightmare, he poured fresh water from the pitcher into the basin, dunked a facecloth, and wrung out the excess. Damp cloth in hand, he returned to the bed.

Knees steepled, Christine sat watching him, the sheet tucked demurely about her. Seeing the white linen molding the curves of her small, firm breasts, Simon couldn't help but recall how perfectly they'd fit his palms. Even now, his mouth watered at the thought of laving her coral-colored nipples, of plundering the musky treasure between her thighs, not just with his mouth but with his sex, still rock-hard and throbbing.

He sat on the edge of the bed and reached for the discarded blanket. Laying it across his lap, he offered her the cloth. "I thought you might want to . . ."

She hesitated, then took it from him. "Thank you."

Bracing his shoulder against the headboard, he twisted away, pretending interest in a pair of French watercolors hanging from the opposite wall. When he sensed she'd finished, he said, "Perhaps you should tell me the whole of it."

For the span of several minutes the only sound in the room was the ticking of the mantel clock. Patience had never been Simon's strong suit but, sensing how hard this must be for her, he steeled himself to let her tell her story in her own time.

Finally she said, "I'd been in London going on a fortnight when I met Madame LeBow. She was mates with the woman who owned the lodging house where I'd taken a room. Truth be told, I didn't care for the looks of her, but when she offered me work I told myself beggars couldn't be choosers." Loosened hair streamed from the plait hanging over her bare shoulder. She shoved the toffee-colored strands behind the shell of her ear before continuing, "When I got there and saw just what kind of house she ran, I told her straightaway I'd be on my way. She took it well, or so I thought. Said it wasn't the life for every girl, and I had to follow my conscience. To show there were no hard feelings, she'd give me a hot meal before I went." Her fingers flexed on the covers. "It was stupid of me, I know, but I was so hungry."

Simon had never forgotten what it was to be hungry. The gnawing bellyache, the terrible hollowness, were sensory memories that would stay with him the rest of his life.

He wrapped a shielding arm about her shoulders. "I don't think you were stupid. Desperate perhaps, but not stupid."

She settled her head into the curve of his shoulder, and he leaned back against the headboard. "She must have put something in the stew. When I woke up, she was standing over me with a candle. I'll never forget her face, her *eyes,* when she told me I belonged to her now, that I'd stay in the attic and on bread and water until I gave in, starved, or went raving. I'd been there around a week when you found me."

Simon thought of how close he'd come to *not* climbing those attic stairs, and a shudder shot through him. He gathered her more tightly against him. "Hush, love. It's over. You're safe."

Safe from everyone but him. Inside his trousers, his manhood felt like a firearm poised to explode, stretching the fabric so taut he feared at any moment he'd send buttons popping.

Regretfully, he slipped his arm from her shoulders. "I'm glad you told me, but what you need now is rest." He started to swing his legs over the edge.

Eyes incredulous, she grabbed for his arm. "I've told you and now you want nothing more to do with me?"

He shook his head. "No, no, it isn't like that. You're tired, it's late. I'm . . . Christ, Christine, I'm trying to be considerate."

"Considerate?"

He nodded, inadvertently cracking the back of his head against the headboard. Almost grateful for the distraction of pain, he said, "I've taken your virginity and with all the finesse of a rutting bull. The very least I can do is leave you to your rest."

"And if I don't care to rest?" She cut a knowing look to the blanket bunched over his lap. "What's more, I don't think you do either."

Wearing only a bedsheet, her toffee-colored hair spilling free from the braid, her brown eyes dark with desire, she was temptation personified. Steeling himself to be strong yet sensing he was doomed, he said, "You've no intention of making this easy on me, have you?"

Her amazing mouth tilted upward. "None at all." She took his hand and laid it, palm-down, over her left breast. "If you won't listen to your own heart, then listen to mine. It's beating for you. Can you feel it?"

Like a trapped bird beating its wings, he thought, feeling each desperate flutter as though it came from within his own chest. Hand resting still on her breast, he turned toward her. "If I were a better man, I'd find the strength to resist you."

"You're the only man I want."

That sealed it.

He slipped his hand down to her waist, taking the sheet with it. Tearing off his blanket, he buried his fingers in her hair and angled her face to his. "Christine, sweet Christine," he moaned, licking her closed eyelids, sucking at her bottom lip, nipping the soft skin of her throat. "This time I'll make it good for you. I swear it."

"No promises," she said for the second time that night, her mouth moist against his heated ear.

The promises, even the ones he'd made to himself, drowned in the rush of pleasure he felt when she dipped her head and her mouth descended on his right nipple, tracing hot, wet circles.

Not even Margot's practiced touch had ever brought him this excitement, this *rush*. He fell back against the pillows, taking Christine down on top of him. This time he didn't have to ask her to help him with his buttons. She found his trouser flap, her fingers trembling only slightly as she moved down the queue. It wasn't until she took him into her hand, stroking a single curious finger down the length of him, that he remembered whom was supposed to be initiating whom.

He snatched her hand away and pressed a kiss into her palm. "Tonight is for you." As much as he ached to bury himself deeply inside her, his every instinct screamed that, for Christine to relax enough to enjoy the experience, she would need to feel as though she were in control. "Ride me," he rasped, part command, part plea.

Her eyes widened, whether in shock or desire he couldn't tell. "Ride you?"

"I will be your stallion, completely at your command." He stroked a coaxing hand from her breasts to her waist, setting the taut, satiny flesh quivering. "As my mistress, it will be for you to set the pace."

Sprawled on top of him, a knee planted on either side of his torso, she held still as a statue. "But I don't know what to do."

He bit back a frustrated groan. "Take hold of the headboard to steady yourself."

She obeyed, rising above him to grip the curved edge with both hands. He reached down between them, his thumb slipping in her slickness. Simon smiled. Her mind might be undecided but thankfully her body was resolved. Holding one hand on her waist, he used the other to guide himself to her and then flexed upward with his hips. She was so hot, so wet, so slick that he filled her in one thrust.

A choked sound escaped Christine's open mouth, but this time the utterance held no hint of pain. She stared down at him. "Oh, Simon." She flicked her tongue over her full bottom lip, and he was almost certain he would explode inside her.

Reining himself in, he said, "As with riding a horse, you must establish your seat. Now spread your legs wider, lean forward, and hug my sides with your knees."

He cupped her buttocks, his fingers sliding inside the curved juncture between the moon pale lobes. The intimate caress had the desired result. She let go of the headboard to take hold of his shoulders, her newly grown fingernails scoring his skin.

And then she started to move. Awkwardly at first, but with increasing confidence. Simon met her stroke for stroke, licking the delicate bone of her clavicle, laving the pink points of her breasts with his lips and tongue. Soon they were moving in a unison so sublime that it was impossible to tell where he ended and Christine began. Nor did he care.

Looking up into her flushed face, he knew the exact moment when her climax came upon her. Her feverish eyes flashed even as her kiss-swollen lips parted on a gasp. She let out a keening cry, and Simon didn't care who heard them. He lashed his arms about her damp back and thrust upward, letting the clenching and unclenching of her inner muscles trigger his own release.

When it was over, he sank back against the pillows, more sated than he could remember ever being. Moist and quivering, Christine seemed to melt into him. He wrapped an arm about her and held her close, content to share the silent peace of the moment. When he finally shifted to look down upon her face tucked into the curve of his shoulder, it was to see the half-dried tears tracking her cheek.

Inside him, remorse rose like a tidal wave. "I was too rough. I've hurt you again."

Against his chest, she shook her head. "No, not a bit."

He stroked the damp hair back from her temple. "Then why are you crying?"

"Because it was so beautiful." She turned her face into his shoulder. "Because I love you so much."

She still loved him. Even as his heart leapt at the miracle of it, the old fears clawed their way to the surface. What if she came to depend on him? What if he came to need her?

What if he failed her too?

He'd only just made peace with the fact that he wanted Christine in his life. He couldn't imagine taking any other woman into his bed. Listening to all she'd suffered was akin to having his heart ripped from his breast. The sight of her scarred back had made him want to hunt down Hareton Tremayne and murder him. Slowly. Painfully. With his own two hands. But was that love?

Even as he asked himself the question, desire rose. He shifted so that Christine lay beneath him. Despite her earlier tears, she was as eager as he was. She slid a hand down to his waist, then beyond. Simon sucked in his breath as her fingers curled about his shaft, guiding him into her. This time their coupling was fast, frenzied. Each time he returned to her, she arched to greet him. Her name was the single sweet word he called out as he surrendered to his satisfaction.

Desire he understood.

* * *

In the hallway, Margot set Simon's bag just outside the bedchamber, then reached into the pocket of her silk wrapper for the key. She bent and slid it under the door.

Straightening, she pressed two fingers to her lips, then laid those fingers gently against the locked door. *"Bonsoir, mes enfants."* Smiling, she turned and quietly retraced her steps to the stairs.

Margot wasn't the only person to spend the night in silent vigil. Leaning against a lamppost across the street from the school, Hareton tipped back his gin flask and drew a greedy gulp. He savored the burn wending its way downward even as he savored his cleverness over the past weeks since he'd first run Chrissie and Belleville to ground.

Watching the two of them together at the May Day Fair, it had been plain the sot fancied her. As for Chrissie, the mooncalf look she'd worn when Belleville set the wreath of flowers atop her head had nearly been Hareton's undoing. He'd barely been able to hold back from rushing forward to rip the trifle off her head. Later, when he saw them wander off into the park, he'd been tempted to follow, stick his knife into Belleville's back, and then carry Chrissie off. But there'd be no money in that and too many possible witnesses. So he'd held in his temper and made his way back to Belleville's estate. There he'd waited. And plotted.

Belleville might be rich as a king but like any man he had his weakness; in his case it was the old man, his grandsire. The rift between the two must cut even deeper than the gossips claimed. When Hareton had announced that Chrissie was visiting the codger, a secret he'd stumbled upon after following her one day shortly after his arrival in Kent, Belleville had been even angrier than Hareton had hoped for. Instead of pocketing his bribe and leaving, he'd hidden in the garden. The bank draft for five hundred pounds had warmed his pocket even as he'd shivered on the hard wood of the gazebo bench. But the sacrifice had paid off. Early the next morning, he'd seen Belleville ride out, a substantial-looking saddlebag strapped to his horse's girth. But it was Christine's comings and goings that concerned him. He held on, waiting. His patience was rewarded that afternoon when he'd spotted her leaving in a carriage loaded with traveling trunks. He'd helped himself to one of Belleville's swifter-looking horses and set off after her. He wasn't really surprised when her carriage turned into the railway station. Once there, he'd only to slip the ticket agent a fiver to learn her destination: London. He'd purchased a ticket on the next train out. Trailing her back to the Mayfair Academy had been child's play. Where else had she to go?

The one thing he hadn't counted on was Belleville showing up at the school. He'd lay odds they were holed up together right now, banging their bleedin' brains out while he, Hareton, hunkered in the drizzle with only Mother Geneva to take the chill from his bones.

Draining the flask, he jammed it back into the pocket of his rumpled suit coat. Five hundred pounds might be a fortune, but it didn't begin to soften the sting of Christine's betrayal. Even more than money, it was her he wanted. Fortunately for him, he was cannier than most people gave him credit for and patient when the occasion warranted it. With a bit of brains, of patience, he'd walk away with the money *and* Chrissie too.

With a bit of patience . . .

Christine awoke to the golden sunshine of late morning streaming the room. Rolling onto her side, she reached for Simon. When her hand met empty space, she pushed up on one elbow, heavy-lidded gaze scanning the room until she spotted him at the washstand, lathering his whiskered jaw.

He caught her gaze in the mirror and smiled. "Good morning, sleepyhead."

"Good morning." Not entirely certain how to behave with him now that the bright light of day was upon them, she tucked the sheet carefully around herself before sitting up to watch.

Her father had worn a beard. Hareton, because of his skin condition, would often go days without shaving before the patchy growth prompted him to take up his razor, not that she'd ever cared to watch *him*. But this was Simon and she was eager to learn everything there was to know about him. Even so, she had to look away when he took up a truly wicked-looking razor and held the blade against his cheek. It was then that she noticed the leather bag at his feet.

"Your bag. However did you get it?"

He scraped an unerring swath from cheek to jaw before

answering, "I found it in the hallway outside our door." Wiping the blade's edge on the towel about his shoulders, he added, "The key was beneath the door when I awoke."

"So we're free," she said, hoping she didn't sound as disappointed as she felt.

"As birds." He finished shaving, then doused his face with water and dried it on the towel. A freshly ironed shirt lay draped over the back of a chair. Slipping it on, he came toward her. "Before we fly the nest, may I claim a good morning kiss?"

"I think that might be arranged." Feeling her shyness evaporate in the face of his easy intimacy, she let go of the sheet to wrap her arms about his neck.

A searing kiss ensued, even more intoxicating than the early ones they'd shared for now she was as familiar with the terrain of his body as he was with hers. Being pressed against him skin to skin now felt as natural as breathing.

Against her lips, Simon said, "I could become used to this."

"I think I already have." Wondering if he might be tempted, she took a gentle nip from the side of his neck, tasting bay rum and soap and warm, warm male.

"Minx." He pulled back to study her. "You should rest. You didn't get much sleep last night."

She slipped both hands inside his shirt. "Neither did you." She glanced at the mantel clock. "Besides, it's after ten."

He shivered as she caressed him from pectorals to abdomen, springy hair making her palms sing. "And you must be sore."

"Not *that* sore." Laughing, giddy, she slid her fingers inside the waist of his trousers.

He caught her hands and pressed a kiss into each palm. "I have to go, love, but I'll be back." Leaning down, he stifled her fledgling protests with his lips. "There is an important matter I must attend to."

"Business." She made a face even as she tried to draw his hand to her breast. "Can't it wait?"

"I'm afraid this particular matter will brook no delay." He kissed the tip of her nose, then stepped back. "But if all goes well I should be back by early evening. You and Margot can visit while I'm gone. I suspect you'd like that?"

Grudgingly she admitted that she would. He crossed the room to finish dressing.

Christine followed him with her gaze. "Simon?"

He paused in slipping on his waistcoat. "Hm?"

She girded herself, then blurted, "When we return to Valhalla, will I live as your mistress?"

He finished buttoning the garment before asking, "You would consider such an arrangement?"

Fearing she'd offended him, she twisted the blanket in one hand even as she admitted, "If that is the only way we can be together then yes. Yes, I would." She looked up to search his face. "If you wouldn't mind."

"Mind?" In three long strides, he closed the distance between them. Swooping down beside her, he lifted her onto his lap. Between exuberant kisses, he said, "I don't know what I ever did to deserve you but, whatever it was, I'm glad."

This time it was Christine who found the resolve to push him away. "Off with you. The sooner you leave, the sooner you'll come back to me." Grinning, she pointed him to the door. *"Go."*

With a groan, he set her aside and rose. "You're a hard taskmistress, Miss Tremayne." Shrugging into his coat, he walked over to the door. Hand on the knob, he turned back. "You didn't see much of London the last time you were here. Think about what you'd like to do this evening."

Christine broke into a broad grin the moment the door closed behind him. As diverting as it would be to have him squire her about town, there was only one thing she wanted to do when he returned and it wouldn't require a carriage. Or clothing.

Hugging her steepled knees, she let her wicked mind imagine all the many ways that one glorious act might be expressed. In one night, she'd gone from innocent girl to fallen woman. She should feel shame, remorse, perhaps even a bit of fear.

What she felt was wonderful.

After her first, shaky initiation, they'd made love two more times before dawn. Each encounter had ended with her feeling as though she were soaring, connected to her physical self yet separate. New as she was to sexual congress, she was certain that what she'd experienced with Simon had been more than mere physical satisfaction, although certainly she'd experienced that in abundance. No, there could only be one explanation. Simon must be her soul mate.

Soul mate or not, she knew he could never marry her. Loving him as she did, she wouldn't dream of asking him to make such a sacrifice. Even if they were lucky and no one ever learned of her time at Madame LeBow's, she was still a dairymaid. And Simon, despite the poverty of his childhood, was a gentleman. By rights, he should be a peer.

Being his mistress might not be ideal but, after last night, parting was unthinkable. And someday if he decided it was time to sire a legitimate son to carry on after him? She would face that when and if the time ever came. If her past troubles had taught her anything, it was that only a fool bartered the surety of the present for the shadowy future. Happiness could be snatched away in a heartbeat.

And she *was* happy. Gloriously so. Bursting with energy, she suddenly couldn't wait to share her news with Margot, the woman responsible for her and Simon each setting aside their stubborn pride. She slipped out of bed and all but skipped over to the washstand. Unless Margot had changed her morning routine, Christine would find her still lingering over breakfast below.

Simon was halfway to the main door when the aroma of bacon and eggs reminded him that he hadn't eaten since breakfast the day before. As he followed the tantalizing smells to the breakfast parlor, he found himself hoping that Margot had breakfasted earlier. As much as he wanted to express his thanks, a part of him wasn't yet prepared to forfeit his and Christine's privacy.

Poking his head inside the open doorway, he realized he'd have no choice. Tucked into a shield-back chair at the head of the table, Margot bent over an open copy of the *Times*.

"Good morning." Choosing to brazen it out rather than starve, he entered and walked briskly toward the sideboard.

She whipped off her wire-rimmed spectacles and slipped them into her pocket. "Good morning."

Laying silent bets on how long it would take her to begin her inquisition, he took his time in making his selections.

When no room was left on his plate, he carried it to the table and took the seat opposite hers.

Smile innocuous, she reached for the coffeepot. "Care for a cup?"

"No, thank you," he answered, so quickly that she laughed. Recalling, as surely she was, the six cups he'd quaffed the night before, he turned over his coffee cup and reached for the pitcher of orange juice.

Idling tapping the side of her spoon against the shell of a soft-boiled egg, she asked, "I trust you slept well?"

He topped off her juice glass, then filled his own before admitting, "I scarcely slept at all."

"Even better." Smile wicked, she indicated his brimming plate. "It appears you mustered quite an appetite."

"A fishing expedition, at this hour? You might as well give it up, for you'll get nothing more from me." Resolute, he picked up his fork and delved into his food.

She released a put-upon sigh. "A gentleman to your very core. How tiresome." Perking up, she asked, "Christine, will she be making her appearance anytime soon?"

"I don't know," he admitted around a mouthful of biscuit. "She was, uh . . . still abed when I left her." Despite himself, he broke into a very broad, very un-Simon-like grin.

She reached across and snatched a fat sausage from his plate. "Ah, memories." Wriggling her brows, she slid it between her lips.

He shook his head, laughing even as he felt his ears heat. "Margot, you're incorrigible."

"Entirely." Eyes dancing, she took a delicate nibble from the very tip of the link, then set the rest aside. Dabbing the corners of her mouth with her napkin, she asked, "Am I safe in assuming that you and Christine have, er, . . . *reconciled?*"

Simon felt his light humor begin to give way to the press of responsibility. Swallowing a bite of shirred egg, he admitted, "She's said she'll become my mistress."

Was it his imagination or did his friend look less than pleased? Settling the napkin back on her lap, she said, "Well, that ought to settle everything rather tidily."

No longer hungry, he pushed his plate away. "It ought to only it doesn't." He drew a deep breath and dared himself to confess what he'd known ever since he'd awoke to see Christine's sweet face on the pillow next to his. "I love her."

Beaming, Margot clapped her hands. "What did Christine say when you told her?"

He traced the rim of his juice glass. "I haven't . . . not yet. But I will, this evening when I propose."

"Propose! Can you mean—"

"To marry her, of course." There, he'd said it and, in doing so, made it *real*. Relieved, he confided, "Christine believes me to be meeting with a business associate this afternoon, but in truth I'm off to see about a special license."

A frown line appeared between her brows. "This is splendid news, of course, but aren't you putting the cart before the horse? I mean, shouldn't you *ask* Christine to marry you *before* you see about the license?" A wistful expression whispered across her features. "After all, a woman marries but once in her lifetime. For all you know, your bride may have a very different sort of wedding in mind."

He shrugged aside the feminine objection. After last night, a conventional courtship was out of the question. And Christine—*his* Christine—was far too practical to crave a fuss. "A small, quiet ceremony will suit Christine."

"Perhaps." Margot studied him. "And you, Simon? Will a small, quiet ceremony suit you as well?"

The thinly veiled criticism acted like a bullet striking bone. Wounded more by the truth underlying it than her obvious censure, he shoved away from the table. "And what if it will? Is it wrong of me to want to keep the news out of the papers until after the election? To want to salvage something of a career for which I've spent the past decade preparing?" When her only answer was silence, he rose and stalked over to the window.

As he looked out onto the quiet, elm-shaded street, Disraeli's words from the preceding winter came back to him: *Get yourself a wife . . . who will be a credit to you—and the party.* Were the prime minister to discover that Simon's intended was not only a dairymaid but also a former brothel inmate, he'd be certain to withdraw his support. But if the discovery were to come *after* Simon won his seat, thereby bolstering the Conservatives' dwindling minority, well, that would be a different matter entirely.

Margot broke in on his thoughts. "So you mean to hide Christine? Conceal your marriage until after the election?"

Turning away from the window, he said, "What choice

have I? The opposition will do anything to discredit me. You know as well as I that Christine's past won't bear their scrutiny—or that of Fleet Street."

She shook her head. "If that's how you truly feel, I wonder you don't merely make her your mistress. At least in that arrangement there would be *honesty.*"

The blunt words cut Simon to the quick. He resolved to be equally candid. "Last night Christine was a virgin, this morning she's not. If I'd known, I never would have touched her, but I did and now it's too late. There is only one honorable course of action and that is to marry her."

"How noble of you." The corners of Margot's mouth dipped farther downward. "Only do try and muster a bit more romanticism when you approach Christine tonight; otherwise you may well find yourself still a bachelor."

Simon opened his mouth on a sharp retort, then closed it. Margot might be his oldest friend, perhaps the wisest person he'd ever known, but she was still a *woman.* And women were essentially creatures of sentiment . . . especially where weddings were concerned.

Mustering a smile, he walked toward her. "This evening, I shall be so charming, so dashing, so utterly *romantic,* that Christine will be helpless to utter any word save *yes.* You may take that as a promise." He dropped a kiss atop her golden head and started for the door.

Margot shoved her spectacles back onto her face and reached for her newspaper. "Don't make promises it isn't in your power to keep."

As he stepped out into the hallway, it occurred to Simon that Christine had given him almost the identical warning.

Christine drew back from the half-open door, feeling as though she'd been struck. So that was how Simon thought of her—a burden to be shouldered, a dirty secret to be hidden away. She girded herself to charge in and tell him in no uncertain terms just what he could do with his notions of duty and honor, his plans for special licenses and rings.

She stopped just short of doing so. Flattening her clammy back against the papered wall, she asked herself did she really wish to repay Margot's kindness with an ugly scene? Especially when, if she bided her time until evening, she'd have the far sweeter satisfaction of answering his proposal with a resounding *no!* Of crushing his precious special license into a ball and throwing it back in his smug face along with his ring and anything else he might give her. Starting with...

Trembling, she reached up and yanked at the gold chain about her neck. She pulled harder, the links biting into her flesh until the chain finally snapped. The amber pendant, still warm from her skin, dropped into her palm. Enclosing it in a tight fist, she marched back through the front hall. At the stair landing, she flung the necklace, chain and all, into the base of a potted palm, then started up. Midway to the second floor, she stopped to wait.

Before long, Simon's footsteps sounded from the hallway below. Dashing away a renegade tear, she started back down as if for the first time that morning.

He caught sight of her and smiled. "This is a nice surprise. I hadn't thought to see you again before I left." Meeting her on the stair landing, he moved in for a kiss.

"I-I've just come down." Turning her face away, she offered him her cheek.

Frowning, he drew back to study her. Odd that he hadn't noticed earlier how pale she was nor how pink her eyes. "Is something amiss?"

"Of course not," she snapped. "I'm only tired."

Could this be the same passionate, playful nymph he'd made love to not once but *three* times the night before? Wondering what accounted for the change, he asked, "Are you certain there is nothing more? You don't seem yourself."

She answered him with a chilly smile. "But then I'm not myself, am I? I'm a fallen woman, or had you forgot?"

His puzzlement over her peevishness dissolved into tenderness as all at once he understood what must be ailing her. Feeling guilty that he hadn't exercised more restraint, he strove for delicacy.

"And perhaps more tender than you thought yourself to be?"

She blushed but didn't look away. "Yes. That too."

Rather than kiss her, which she didn't seem to want, he touched her cheek in a glancing caress. "Have one of the maid's draw you a hot bath after you've breakfasted. It will help."

"Yes, I'll do that. Thank you."

As he backed off the landing and made his way toward the main door, he found himself unable to shake the sense that something was fundamentally *wrong*. On the threshold, he surrendered to the impulse to turn back one final time.

"Christine, are you certain—"

"Yes, Simon," she answered from her place on the stairs. "I've never been more certain of anything in my life."

Nineteen

How quick the old woe follows a little bliss!

—Petrarch,
Canzoniere, 1360

The main door closing behind Simon sliced through the fragile ribbon of Christine's self-control. She folded onto the landing, limbs shaking with delayed reaction. Hugging her knees, she let the hot, fat tears run fast and free down her cheeks.

It was thus that Margot found her. "Christine, dearest, whatever is the matter?"

Looking up into her friend's concerned violet eyes, Christine found herself unable to dissemble. "I was on my way into breakfast when I overheard..." The remainder of her confession broke off in a sob.

"Ballocks." Margot hiked up her skirts and sat on the step beside Christine. She withdrew a frilled handkerchief from her pocket and handed it to Christine.

Christine paused to blow into the rose-scented folds. "I could have been his mistress and still held my head up because I love him and I thought... I hoped... he might feel the same about me. But I'll not be his charity bride, a shameful secret to be hidden away."

Margot's arm, just heavy enough to be comforting, wrapped about Christine's shivering shoulders. "Then that is precisely what you must tell Simon when he returns."

Christine crumpled the soggy hankie into a tight fist. "I shall tell him that and more. Toss his precious special license and ring back at him and then..." Her shoulders slumped. "And then I shall leave."

Margot answered with a *tsk-tsk*. "Running away never solved anything. If you love Simon as you say you do, then you must stay and fight for that love. Let him see that you won't settle for anything less than a marriage of minds, a full and equal partnership. Make him see that if he wants you for his wife, he's going to have to court you. Woo you. *Fight* for you."

Christine sniffed back fresh tears. "How can you be certain he would accept such conditions?"

Margot slid her arm from Christine's shoulders. "He hasn't any choice. He loves you." At Christine's disbelieving snort, she persisted, "He does, Christine, and far more deeply than I suspect even he realizes." Eyes afire with purpose, she popped up from the step. "Before you make your decision, there is someone I want you to meet."

Guarding her heart against false hope, Christine slowly rose. "Who?"

"Simon's sister."

A *half an* hour later, Christine sat across from Margot in the latter's pitching town carriage. Although she'd yet to see what difference her meeting Simon's sister could possibly make in her decision to leave, she'd allowed herself to be persuaded. In truth, she suspected she was only putting off the inevitable and, in doing so, prolonging her pain. She almost welcomed the choppy ride. At least the jostling provided some distraction from thinking too much on her future, a future that once again stretched before her, flat and bleak.

One hand clutching the lavender velvet squabs, a shade lighter than her eyes, Margot frowned. "I can't imagine what the devil has gotten into that driver of mine. From the jostling he's giving us, one would think he'd never before handled the ribbons."

"Perhaps it is only the poor condition of the roads?" Christine offered. Venturing a glance out the window, she added, "But are you certain we are headed in the right direction?"

Although Simon had said he'd been poor, she still found it difficult to reconcile herself to the idea of him growing up amidst the squalor and wretchedness through which they now passed. Great hulks of decaying buildings slouched forward from either side of the narrow street, their gabled roofs blocking all but a trickle of sunlight. A variety of foul odors wafted from the rubbish running freely down the open gutters to mingle with the heavy pall of coal dust thickening the air.

Margot nodded. "Indeed, I have visited Mordechai and Rebecca many times over the years, although I have been somewhat remiss of late. My driver, Freddie, knows their direction by heart."

Mordechai, Christine had learned in the course of their journey, was Simon and Rebecca's stepfather. Their mother, Lilith, had succumbed to the typhus while Simon was still in India. Rather than uproot Rebecca after his return, Simon had left her in Mordechai's care, although he called regularly when in town.

Drawing on her thoughts, Christine asked, "Has Rebecca never recovered from the attack?"

"Her body is sound enough. It is her mental faculties that are in question."

"She is mad, then?" Christine felt a shiver ripple through her. During her imprisonment in Madame LeBow's attic, starvation and ravishment had been real fears but neither could match the terror that day after day of nothing but darkness would rob her of her wits.

Examining the stitching on her gloves, Margot seemed to be weighing her words. "Most people would deem her as such for soon after the rape, she retreated into a fantasy world. She believes herself to be a little girl and behaves accordingly. Whether she is truly deranged or simply chooses to live within her safe cocoon is a question that not even the finest physicians have been able to answer."

Christine shook her head. More to herself than to Margot, she said, "He never told me." How could she even think of plighting her troth with a man who trusted her with neither his confidences nor his heart?

"I'm sure he will someday... once he overcomes his guilt."

"Guilt?"

Margot nodded. "Simon was but fifteen at the time of the attack and, characteristic of boys that age, he'd taken Rebecca somewhere they ought not to have been. He blames himself for the consequences."

Indignant on Simon's behalf, Christine blurted, "Surely not!"

"I'm afraid so. You see, Simon and Rebecca's father had died a few years before. Despite his tender age, Simon assumed the dual role of provider and protector. He has never forgiven himself for placing Rebecca in danger in the first place and then for failing to fend off her attackers. I suppose that is why he finds it difficult to forgive others." Margot's somber gaze settled on Christine's face. "Or to express his true feelings."

Christine tried to gird her heart against softening, but found she couldn't. Poor Simon, to have shouldered such guilt for all of twenty years! Inside her breast pity surged, as much for the frightened, angry boy as for the bottled-up man.

Regarding her tightly laced hands, she said, "In telling me this, you've broken faith with Simon, haven't you?"

Margot didn't deny it. "On this occasion, betraying a friend's confidence seemed the lesser of two evils when compared to letting the woman he loves walk out of his life."

Christine was spared having to respond by the carriage jolting to a halt. She peered out to a queue of brick town houses, fronted by postage stamp-sized patches of lawn. A thin ribbon of crumbling sidewalk was all that stood between the houses and the busy street.

"This is where Simon grew up?"

Margot paused in wrapping against the carriage roof to reply, "Mordechai married Simon's mother not long after the attack on Rebecca and moved the family here." When neither driver nor footman materialized to lower the steps and open the door, she muttered an oath and reached for the door handle. "Simon lived here only a few months before he left for India." She yanked open the door and gingerly stepped out.

Negotiating the gap between carriage and curb, Christine followed her down. "And before?"

Margot shrugged. "An assortment of tenement houses, a loft above a gin shop, once even the street itself." Leaving Christine to make of that what she might, she glared up at her driver, slouched on the box, and next to him the new footman. Voice laced with cynicism, she called, "Rough night, lads?"

Face pale, Freddie answered with a mute nod.

"Aye, 'twas the *vewy* Devil." The footman pulled his powdered wig low over his brow and settled back for a snooze.

"What cheek," Margot muttered beneath her breath.

Christine was too busy absorbing Margot's latest disclosure to pay Freddie or the footman much heed. Her proud Simon had lived on the street! It didn't bear thinking of. Wishing he'd told her himself, grateful that someone had, she fell into step beside her friend. Silent, they walked up the cracked pavement leading to Simon's past.

Rebecca sat cross-legged on her bedroom floor, her lap divided between Miss Lucy and her Persian kitten, Phoebe, when from the front parlor she heard her stepfather. "My dear friend, how good it is to see you."

Normally the noise from the workshop below would have made eavesdropping difficult if not impossible but today was Saturday, the Hebrew Sabbath. The downstairs was as silent as it was empty.

Setting aside her doll, she pricked her ears in time to hear a familiar silky voice reply, "We're not intruding, I hope?"

Recognizing it as belonging to Simon's friend, Margot, Rebecca leapt up. She devoted a precious moment to situating Phoebe on her shoulder before darting out the bedroom door.

As soon as she reached the parlor, the burning question tumbled from her lips. "Miss Margot, Miss Margot, did you bring it?" When she spotted the slender young female hanging back by the door, she skidded to a halt.

Margot smiled. "Rebecca, dearest, you have a memory like an elephant. But I'm afraid my maid, Marie, is not quite finished sewing Miss Lucy's new ball gown." Dividing her gaze between Rebecca and the interloper, she added, "In the meantime, I've brought something even better. My friend, Christine Tremayne."

Rebecca greeted the stranger with an open glare.

The girl, Christine, came forward, her gentle-golden brown eyes intent on Rebecca's face. "I am so pleased to finally meet you, Miss Belleville." The high forehead beneath the chipped straw bonnet lifted. "Or would you prefer I call you Rebecca?"

Pointedly Rebecca ignored the question.

Christine reached out a slender gloved hand to Phoebe, still perched on Rebecca's shoulder. "May I?"

Rebecca hesitated, then nodded.

Stroking the cat, Christine said, "I have a cat too. Her name is Puss."

Reassured by Phoebe's appreciative purr rumbling in her ear, Rebecca volunteered, "Hers is Phoebe."

Margot stepped forward to scratch Phoebe beneath the chin. "You might recognize her, Christine. She's the pick of Pompie's last litter."

The corners of the girl's almost too-wide mouth lifted in a soft smile. Addressing herself to the cat, she said, "I thought you looked familiar. You've grown, haven't you, pretty girl?" With two fingers, she gently scratched Phoebe's silken ears.

Relaxing another fraction, Rebecca let her gaze rove over the newcomer. Wispy, almost fragile, Christine looked to be around nineteen or twenty, not much older than Rebecca had been when . . .

Without warning, the black balloon began its descent. Caught in the riggings like a rabbit ensnared, Rebecca felt herself being dragged down, down, *down* to the craggy abyss.

Desperate to free herself, to claw her way back up to sunshine, blue sky, and fluffy white clouds, she backed away even as she opened her mouth to chant the antidote. "London Bridge is falling down, falling down, falling down—"

"Rebecca." Mordechai's voice was not unkind but it was firm. "It is not mannerly to sing aloud when we have guests."

Christine spoke up, "That's all right. I rather fancy that tune. And you have a sweet voice, Rebecca. Mine isn't nearly so nice but, oh well . . ." She opened her mouth and—amazingly—began to sing.

Rebecca hesitated, then joined in. They concluded their singsong to Margot's enthusiastic "Brava!" and Mordechai's more reserved nod.

If Christine was aware of Margot and Mordechai exchanging uneasy glances, she gave no sign of it. Gaze fixed on Rebecca, she hinted broadly, "Margot tells me Miss Lucy has quite a collection of gowns."

Rebecca hesitated, weighing the risks against the reward. Christine wasn't asking only for permission to enter her bedroom to see her doll's dresses. She was asking to be admitted to Rebecca's private world. The inner sanctum that no one, not even her beloved Simon, was allowed inside of. Ever. And yet it had been a long time—years—since she'd had a human playmate. She could always evict the newcomer once she tired of her.

It was Rebecca's kingdom after all.

"Come." She did an about-face and started back down the hallway, confident that Christine would follow.

"Your Miss Tremayne is good with her," Mordechai observed as soon as Christine and Rebecca's footsteps faded down the hallway. Gesturing Margot toward an overstuffed armchair, the room's finest, he asked, "Is she equally good at gentling my stepson?"

With a sigh, Margot subsided onto the worn horsehair cushion. "As always, you say little but see much."

"Ah, I but strive to heed the wise words of the American philosopher, Mr. Emerson, who tells us 'the eye of prudence may never shut.'" Mouth quivering with suppressed amusement, he ambled over to a scarred oak sideboard. Lifting the stopper from the chipped crockery wine decanter, he said, "Now we will take some wine and, while we drink it, you may tell me all that my stepson has been up to since last I saw him."

Christine spent the next hour sitting cross-legged on the floor of Rebecca's room, fitting Rebecca's doll into a variety of ensembles only to have Rebecca become disenchanted in favor of yet another costume.

Glancing up from the miniature velvet bonnet she'd just set atop Miss Lucy's buttercup-yellow hair, she quipped, "It's comforting to finally meet a female who possesses an even greater number of gowns than I do." Even if that "female" was a doll.

Rebecca hesitated, then her mouth lifted into a lopsided half smile. For an instant she looked so like her brother that Christine felt her heart squeeze over on itself.

"Yes," Rebecca agreed, eyes bright. "Miss Lucy is quite the clotheshorse—" She hesitated, then added, "For a doll."

Caught off guard by the canny statement, Christine laughed. She was more than half convinced that Simon's sister wasn't so much mad as she was choosing to live in a world of her own making. Thinking of the hard choice she herself faced later that evening, Christine almost envied her. Almost.

Pounding outside the flat's main door caused both women to look up. A guarded look replaced Rebecca's placid expression.

Sensing that Rebecca was closing in on herself, Christine schooled her voice to sound light and cheerful as she said, "It seems you have yet another visitor." Half hoping, half dreading it might be Simon, Christine set Miss Lucy on her miniature chair and uncrossed her legs to rise. "Shall we go in and greet them?" She stretched out a hand, willing Rebecca to take it.

Rebecca shook her dark head. "I'll wait here."

Christine bit back her disappointment, reminding herself that they'd made tremendous strides. Dropping her arm to her side, she said, "Very well, then. But if it's Simon, I shall be back to fetch you."

Reaching for the doll's miniature brush, Rebecca didn't trouble herself to look up. "If it's Simon, you won't have to."

Mordechai headed through the alcoved foyer just as Christine stepped into the parlor. She threw Margot a questioning glance. "Simon?"

Coward that she was, she wished Rebecca had come with her. She could use all the allies she could muster and certainly Simon wouldn't stage a confrontation if his sister were present.

Margot sighed. "If it is, I don't imagine he'll be very pleased with me for bringing you here. Or with you for accompanying me."

A crash, then a strangled groan, cut off Christine's reply. Heart drumming, she took off toward the entrance.

Mordechai lay in a crumpled heap just inside the half-open door. Swallowing a scream, Christine dropped to her knees beside the old man.

Margot drew up behind her. "Is he . . ."

Christine looked back at Margot's ashen face and shook her head. "No, he's breathing." She slipped a hand beneath his head only to find it slick with blood.

Margot stepped forward and peered out into the hallway. Turning back inside, she reported, "Whoever attacked him must have lost their nerve and run off. I'll send Freddie for a doctor . . . and the constable."

"I'm afraid dear Freddie's indisposed."

Hareton, dressed in Margot's livery, stepped out from behind an ornamental teakwood screen. Pistol in hand, he shoved Margot inside and moved to block the door.

"Don't look so surprised, Chrissie girl. Ye should've known I'd come to fetch ye sooner or later." He flashed her a gap-toothed smile. "I decided on sooner."

Margot's gaze moved over the purple and gold livery hanging on his spare form. Taking a step forward, she demanded, "What have you done with my driver?"

He used the flat of his arm to shove her back. "I've no call to answer to ye, slut. Get back inside." His gaze narrowed to Christine. "That goes for you too." He cocked the pistol hammer and trained it on Mordechai's thin chest. "On your feet and march or I finish off the old man."

Forcing a calm belied by her pounding heart, Christine gently laid Mordechai's head on the bare floor and rose on wobbly legs. "You'll never get away with this," she said in a voice meant to carry to the back of the house. Praying that Rebecca would overhear and have the sense to hide herself, she added, "Even if you do, Simon will see that you hang for it."

"Shut up! No one's 'angin', least of all me." The vein that split Hareton's scarred forehead had begun to pulse, a telltale sign that she'd gotten to him. "If ye knows what's good fer ye, ye'll not speak that devil's name in my presence again." He hauled back and caught her cheek in a stinging backhanded slap.

She might have fallen if not for Margot, who caught her at the last moment. Arms intertwined, the two women walked back into the parlor, the pistol pointed at their backs.

Inside the parlor, he waived his pistol between Margot and a spindle-backed chair. "Sit." Christine started to follow, but his sharp voice stayed her. "Not you, missie. Ye're comin' wi' me."

Folding her trembling arms across her breast, Christine stared him down. She was afraid, oh yes she was, but she'd also learned that there were worse things than death. "Shoot me if you like, but I'm not going anywhere with you."

He shook his head as though she were a tiresome child. "Chrissie, Chrissie, d'ye honestly think I'd put myself in 'arms way these past weeks only to off ye? 'Tisn't ye I'll shoot." He swiveled toward Margot, the pistol cocked. "I believe I'll start wi' her."

"No!" Christine launched herself between them.

Grinning, he lowered the pistol and turned toward her. "A change o' heart. Well now, that's just the spirit ye'll need to make it in the New World."

The New World! Could he really take her out of the country and get away with it? Distracted, her heart nearly stopped when he shoved his free hand into his coat pocket.

But instead of another weapon, he pulled out two lengths of cord. Shoving them into her hand, he ordered, "Tie 'er 'ands and feet." His gaze narrowed. "And mind ye make the knots good and tight."

Mind spinning possible escape plans, Christine walked over to Margot. They exchanged desperate glances. Margot offered her clasped hands and, after a moment's pause, Christine began winding the cord about the other woman's wrists.

Concentrating on making the binding tight enough to satisfy Hareton without cutting off the blood supply, she asked, "Where are you taking me?"

He hesitated but, in the end, he couldn't resist boasting. "I've booked passage for two to Virginia. Just ye and me, coz, and Belleville's blunt to set us up proper and prime."

Virginia. She and Margot exchanged charged glances.

He tore off his neck cloth and walk toward them. He handed the soiled rag to Christine and said, "Muzzle the bitch."

Christine hesitated, then stepped behind the chair.

Margot opened her mouth and, hands shaking, Christine inserted the rolled cloth. "I'm so sorry," she whispered, then reached behind to tie it firmly, comforting herself that Hareton wouldn't bother to bind and gag a woman he meant to shoot.

And Rebecca? With any luck, Simon's sister listened from her hiding place. Was it too much to hope that she might come out from hiding to untie Margot once it was safe?

As if on cue, Rebecca drifted into the parlor, dashing Christine's fledgling hope. "Simon, is that you . . ." Her gaze alighted on Hareton, pistol in hand, and she backed away.

"Well, well, who's this?" Watching Hareton saunter toward Rebecca, Christine felt her entire body begin to shake. She left Margot to rush to Rebecca's side.

Pinning Rebecca's chin between his thumb and forefinger, he jerked her face up to his. "Ye're a pretty peach. What's yer name?"

Mouth trembling, Rebecca struggled to reply. "R-Rebecca." Holding her breath, Christine prayed she'd leave it at that but no such luck. The past hour had drawn her out of her shell sufficiently so that she found sufficient voice to say, "Rebecca Belleville."

Hareton's gaze widened. "Then ye must be kin to my mate, Simon?"

Teeth chattering, Rebecca ground out, "H-he's my b-brother."

"Is 'e now?" Releasing her, he turned to Christine. "In that case, I think I'll take 'er along to bear us company."

"Hareton, please! Leave her be. She's not . . . she's not in her right mind," she added, hoping to sway him.

"Jealous, pet? There's no need." His face darkened in a scowl. "*I* knows what it means to be faithful." Easing into a crooked smile, he added, "I'll only keep 'er long enough to get us to the docks . . . as security in case her brother gets the itch to come after us." Reaching into his pocket, he produced yet another cord and looped it around Rebecca's wrist, then Christine's. "Cozy as two peas in a pod," he clucked, tying them together. To Margot, he said, "Tell Belleville that, if 'e's a good chap and leaves off, I'll turn his sister loose before we set sail. If he don't, then 'e can look for 'er at the bottom o' the Thames."

"What do you mean they've gone visiting?" Simon demanded of Margot's housekeeper later that day. Shoving a hand into his coat pocket, he fingered the amber lump he'd just dug out of the planter.

Troubled all day by Christine's odd behavior that morning, he'd decided to return early. By pure chance, he'd spotted her gold chain dangling from the leaf of the potted palm and, upon further investigation, the pendant in the base of the stand.

Mrs. Fitz lifted a Dresden china figurine from the mantel shelf of the drawing room and batted at it with the duster. "I don't know as it's my place to say, Mr. Belleville."

"Your place or not, you'll put that bloody thing down and talk to me." He snatched the duster away.

She made a grab for it, but he only held it higher. "Now Mr. Belleville, I've no time for your mischief."

Ordinarily the sight of Mrs. Fitz, short and stout as a beer barrel, dancing on her toes to retrieve her duster would have brought a smile to even his lips. But there was nothing ordinary about this day.

Something was wrong. Very wrong.

Holding the feather duster aloft, he demanded, "Where?"

Red-faced and panting, Mrs. Fitz settled back onto her slippered soles. "Oh very well. To see your stepfather, sir, and . . . and Miss Rebecca."

Damn. This time Margot had gone too far. It was for him and him alone to decide when—or if—Christine met his sister. Until now, he'd managed to sort the various aspects of his life into neat compartments. Introducing Christine to his sister—to his past—was tantamount to sending the walls of Jericho toppling down on his head. Simon did not appreciate the demolition.

Stiffening his jaw, he demanded, "When?"

"Late morning, sir, not long after you left."

He handed her the duster. "I believe I shall join them."

"Go on, get in."

Hareton shoved Christine and Rebecca toward the open coach door. Inside, Margot's driver sat trussed and gagged. Poor Freddie looked very young and very afraid. But then Christine suspected so must she.

Visibly trembling, Rebecca dug in her heels. The vein in Hareton's forehead started to pulse anew.

He tore off his wig. "I said get inside the blimey coach."

Christine bent to Rebecca and, as calmly as she could, said, "Come along, Rebecca. Climb up. It's going to be all right."

Praying that were indeed the case, she climbed over the gap, gently tugging Rebecca with her. Inside, she took care to position herself nearest the door before falling into the seat across from Freddie.

Holding the door, Hareton hissed, "Unless you want to be flattened beneath coach wheels, ye'll stay put." He slammed the door, leaving them to contemplate that grim image.

The coach dipped as he climbed up onto the box. The whip hissed and, with a terrified shriek, the horses shot forward.

"Courage, Rebecca." Christine reached over to clasp Rebecca's untethered hand. It was cold as snow, but then so was hers. "You're going to have to be very brave because, when I give the word, I want you to jump out that door." She looked over to the driver and whispered, "We'll send for help as soon as we're able. And your mistress, Miss Ashcroft, is unharmed, so you needn't worry for her."

Tears filling his eyes, he nodded.

Rebecca's gaze swerved from the closed door to the window where city blocks whizzed past like painted scenery in a diorama. Eyes popping, she turned back to Christine. "Jump?"

In a firmer tone, Christine repeated, "That's right. When I tell you to, you and I are going to jump out that door. And we're going to be *fine*."

She searched Rebecca's waxen face and glazed eyes for some sign that she'd understood. Slowly, she moved her head up and down in a nod.

Relieved, Christine turned back to the window. Steeling herself against the sickening rush of motion, she watched for her opportunity, praying it would come before they reached the docks.

Opportunity knocked before they'd cleared the second street block, for Hareton was no horseman. Having whipped the lead horse into a frenzied gallop, he was in no position to slow when a dray loaded with fruit pulled out from a side street. He swerved sharply left, sideswiping the dray and scattering apples and oranges to the four winds. Dodging the overturned cart, he crashed his team up onto a sidewalk lined with costermongers. The impact pitched Christine and Rebecca onto the coach floor though Freddie managed to keep his seat. Pulling herself up on bruised knees, Christine peered out the window to see a profusion of foodstuffs fanned across the narrow street. Children of all ages spilled out onto the street as well, cramming food into pockets, shoes, and mouths even as they dodged the costermongers who took off after them. Shrieking horses, Cockney curses, and applause from the gathering crowd added to the confusion.

Christine leapt up, bringing Rebecca with her. "It's time, Rebecca." With her free hand, she reached for the interior handle and jerked open the door. She used her foot to kick the door the rest of the way open, then swung back to Rebecca. "On the count of three. One, two, . . . *three!*"

Twenty

Perils commonly ask to be paid in pleasures.

—Francis Bacon,
"Of Love," *Essays,* 1625

Christine and Rebecca landed side by side on the cobbles. Feeling as though her brains had been tossed into a mixing bowl, Christine turned her head to Rebecca and whispered, "Are you all right?"

Mouth trembling, Rebecca lifted one bloodied palm from the road. "S-stings."

"I know it does, but we can't think about that now." Peeling her own skinned palms from the road, Christine lifted herself up. "We're going to run to that street at the end. I believe it will lead us back toward Fleet." And, pray God, to a constable or someone who could help them.

She started up, bringing Rebecca with her. Rebecca's left leg folded beneath her. Christine caught her before she dragged them both down.

"My ankle, I twisted it." Rebecca's face puckered. "Oh, Simon, what are we to do?"

Heart racing, it took Christine a moment to realize by what name Rebecca had addressed her. Not that it mattered. What did matter was that her planned flight would never work now. That left them with only one option: They would have to disappear. And quickly, while Hareton was still busy trying to calm the terrified team.

She swung her gaze back to Rebecca. "We're going to have to hide in that alley just ahead."

She pointed to a slim side alley less than a yard away. Sandwiched between a brewery and a glass factory, it was piled high with crates, casks, and bins brimming with rubbish.

Teeth knocking together, Rebecca shook her head. "I-I c-can't."

With her free hand, Christine reached across and gave Rebecca's a reassuring squeeze. "Yes, you can. You must."

Rebecca stared, eyes wide and mouth agape. Christine braced herself for the scream that would surely give them away.

But the moan that emerged was no louder than a pebble slipping into a placid stream.

Simon rode hell-for-leather to Goodman's Fields. Reaching Leman Street, he saw that Margot's carriage was not stationed out front; however, the two piles of fresh droppings on the street near the curb post suggested that a horse-drawn vehicle had been there not long before. A man's wig festooned with a purple ribbon such as he'd seen Margot's male servants wear lay discarded in the gutter. Not certain what to make of that, he swung down from the saddle and quickly tied the mare, lathered and panting, to the post. A cold wariness cooled his earlier anger, and giving in to impulse, he took off running.

Mordechai's shop door stood open, the Closed sign stirring in the slight breeze. Simon stepped inside and hurried down the aisle of silent machines and empty cutting tables to the stairs. Taking the steps two at a time, he reached the second floor landing and strode through the open hallway.

The door to Mordechai's private apartments also stood ajar. Senses on the alert, Simon stepped over the threshold. As he did, the heel of his right boot slipped in slickness. He looked down. Fresh blood, a great deal of it, coated the waxed floorboards.

Oh God, oh God, oh God.

Rivers of icy sweat rolled down his back, causing his shirt to cling. He withdrew the small pocket pistol from his coat before following the scarlet stains into the parlor where he found Mordechai and Margot.

Lowering his pistol, Simon rushed to where Mordechai knelt at Margot's feet, struggling with the bonds that lashed her ankles to the chair. In a single glance he registered the blood drying in his stepfather's grizzled hair and the pink indentations branding the sides of Margot's face—evidence that, until recently, she'd been gagged. Relief that neither of them looked to be seriously hurt was almost immediately displaced by darker, deeper fears.

He swallowed hard. Pocketing the pistol, he asked, "Are you all right?"

Margot gave a quick nod. "More or less. But Christine and Rebecca . . ." She broke off on a sob.

Mordechai looked up, eyes stricken. "Taken, both of them."

Margot held out her joined wrists. "It was Christine's cousin, Hareton. He disguised himself as one of my footmen and must have held my driver, Freddie, at pistol point on our way here. And now he means to use Rebecca as a hostage long enough to get Christine to the docks."

Mouth dry with fear, Simon handed Mordechai his pocketknife to finish slicing through her bonds. "The docks?"

Simon had never known Margot to cry but looking at her now he knew she was perilously close. "Oh, Simon, he means to take her with him to Virginia."

Panting, Rebecca staggered toward the dark alley, the jagged cobbles cutting into the thin soles of her slippers. The bad men were after them—or was it only one? She couldn't remember why, but she knew she had to run. Run for her life. Sweat streaked down her brow, salting her eyes. Did blurred vision explain why, instead of her little brother, Simon, a slip of a girl with hair the color of toffee appeared to be tugging her along?

Leaning on the slender arm to which she was bound, she limped toward the passage. Foul smells of stinking garbage and rotting lumber rose up as they entered.

"Behind that pile of lumber and quickly!" The girl—Christine, Rebecca remembered suddenly—pressed her toward the large heap.

They ducked down behind. An irate squawk, then something small and white scrabbled over their feet. Rebecca stared down into beady black eyes and gasped, "Mouse!"

Christine motioned her to silence. "Hush," she whispered, "I think I hear something."

"Chrissie, luv, 'tis no use. I know ye're here."

Rebecca's heart leapt into her throat. It was the bad man. He'd found them! She turned to Christine, who only held a finger to her lips.

Whistling, he started down the alley, heels clicking on the slick stones. Rebecca broke out into a cold sweat that sent her teeth chattering, the sound reminding her of the organ grinder's monkey she'd watched as a child. Mere months ago or had it been years?

She clamped her free hand over her mouth to mute the *clack, clack, clack,* which seemed to increase in volume with every passing second. God, she was going to give them away. Just like she had that other time . . .

Suddenly the whistling stopped and so did the footfalls. She and Christine exchanged frightened glances and pressed back against the slimy stones of the wall. The girl was obviously striving to appear calm, but Rebecca knew that deep down she was every bit as frightened as she was.

Suddenly Christine's eyes widened. Rebecca followed her companion's frozen upward gaze to the man's evil face.

"There ye are, my poppets." Looming over them, he clamped rough hands on Christine, dragging her to her feet and with her, Rebecca.

He grabbed Christine's chin in a bruising hold and jerked her face up to his. "It's nice and private 'ere, and we've loads o' time before the ship sails."

"Go to hell!" Christine struck out at him with her free hand but, hampered as she was, he easily evaded her blows.

He turned to Rebecca, an ugly leer twisting his mouth. "Fancy a watch? No? Well then, mum's the word." Cackling, he swung back to Christine. "We're not shy, are we, sweeting?"

From the locked storehouse of Rebecca's memory, a more

cultured but equally cruel voice stole out, *We're not shy, are we, sweetheart?*

Rebecca's right wrist was still joined to Christine's but, inside her, an invisible bond snapped. The black balloon burst, the whoosh near deafening. Black bits of rubber rained down like chunks of coal but this time Rebecca resolved not to be buried.

"Leave her be!" Clawing her way back to the light, Rebecca lunged, gouging fingers sinking into the bad man's face.

"Ahhhh!"

Simon was struggling to sort through the muddled accounts of several irate costermongers when he heard the scream echoing from the alley across the street. Rebecca or Christine? Heart pumping, he tore off.

The alley was dark as twilight and foul as a draining ditch. Drawing his weapon, he started down. Equal parts blessing and curse, the darkness obscured not only him but also the shadowy trio at the other end.

"I just decided I don't need a 'ostage after all." It was Hareton Tremayne, one hand pressed to his bloody cheek. In the other, he held the butt of his pistol against Rebecca's breast.

"Then you'll have to kill both of us." It was Christine, struggling to block Rebecca's body with her own even as she struck out at her cousin with fist and foot.

Sweat running in sheets down his back, Simon edged closer. Everything he loved, everything that mattered, lay just a few paces ahead. What if he missed and Hareton shot Christine or Rebecca in retribution? What if he missed and hit Christine or Rebecca himself!

I won't miss. I mustn't miss.

He cocked his pistol's hammer and took aim.

The pistol's report roared through the narrow passageway, a near-deafening salvo bouncing between the walls of the two buildings. Certain she'd been hit, Christine scrunched her eyes closed against the sting of gunpowder and waited for the searing pain to overtake her. When none came, she opened her eyes and turned to Rebecca. Simon's sister was pale, but the only blood on her was beneath her fingernails.

She shot her gaze downward to where Hareton writhed at their feet, clutching his bloody shoulder. "Chrissie, 'elp me." Rivulets of blood threaded through the splayed fingers of the hand he stretched out to her.

She tried to feel pity but, in that moment, the only emotion she could claim was a blinding relief. Kicking the pistol out of his reach, she said, "I'll be back as soon as I find a constable."

Turning away from him, she took hold of Rebecca's elbow and steered them toward the alley entrance. As she did, she caught sight of a man's silhouette breaking through the smoky haze.

"Simon!" Waving wildly with her free arm, she started toward him, Rebecca running beside her.

They met up with him halfway. Strong arms enfolded her and Rebecca. Simon's arms.

Face half buried in her hair, he whispered, "You're safe. I'm here. You're safe."

Christine closed her eyes and put her free arm about him, hugging him back as hard and as close as she could. Beyond words, she pressed her cheek against the side of his damp neck and let the tears stream.

They were safe. He was here.

For the moment at least.

Much later that evening Christine found Simon in Margot's library, an open book lying ignored in his lap, a brandy snifter cradled in one hand. Standing in the doorway, she allowed herself a moment to admire the stark beauty of him. The lamps atop the mantel were the room's only light, playing upon the sculpted planes of his profiled features. With bruised crescents etched beneath his eyes and midnight black hair combed neatly back from its widow's peak, he reminded her very much of the first time she'd laid eyes on him in Madame LeBow's attic. Then she'd likened him to a dark angel. Her dark angel, if only . . .

He turned his head to the open door and greeted her with a weary smile. "There you are." He moved the book off his lap and patted the vacant sofa cushion next to him. "Sit with me?"

"All right." Seizing on small talk, she started toward him. "It seems Margot and that nice Chief Inspector Daniels have taken quite a fancy to each other. Before we left the police station, he asked her to supper. They just left."

By sheer accident, her shoulder brushed against his as she took her seat next to him. The heat radiating from the brief contact struck like a burn.

His mouth eased into a smile. "Good, I'm glad." He hesitated, smile fading. "And Rebecca?" The raw vulnerability in his eyes was like a razor slashing at her heart.

"Mrs. Fitz made her a posset and she's slumbering like a lamb. She's still overset, of course, but very much in her right mind."

He shook his head. "To think that all these years the cure lay in reliving the harm. Such a dreadful waste."

"What matters is that she's on her way to being well." It was folly to touch him, but she couldn't resist reaching over to give his hand a squeeze. "I do truly believe the worst is over for her, that she will recover now. But you must be patient."

His mouth quirked in a self-deprecating smile. "Patience. Yet another of my many great virtues." His gaze honed in on her face. "But enough of everyone else. How do you fare?"

"A few scrapes and bruises but none that won't mend." She managed a wobbly smile. "We Tremaynes are a stout lot." Her smile fell. "Simon, what will happen to Hareton?"

He shrugged. "As soon as he's recovered, he'll stand trial. Kidnapping is a capital offense."

She swallowed hard. "Meaning they'll hang him?"

"Assuming he's found to be guilty, which surely he will be." His gaze narrowed. "Don't tell me that after all he's put you through you feel some sympathy for him?"

"Not sympathy exactly. It's more that . . ." Oh dear, how to explain it? "I've spent the better part of a year believing that I'd done murder. Even knowing that I struck out at him in self-defense, it was a heavy burden to live with. Hareton may deserve to hang, but I can't help hating that in a way I'll be responsible for it."

"Some men are born for the gallows and your cousin is

one of them. His fate is of his own making." His gaze softened. "But if it will set your mind at ease, I'll see what I can do. As a former vice commissioner, I still have some connections. Perhaps I can pull a few strings, request that his penalty be transmuted to life imprisonment, although personally I'd rather meet a swift end at Jack Ketch's hands than spend a lifetime picking oakum and wearing prison stripes."

Christine drew a relieved breath even though his generosity in going against his principles for her sake only made it that much harder to say what she'd come to say. "Thank you."

"You're welcome. Now that's settled, I've something to give you." He released her hand to reach for a small velvet box set on the table beside him.

In a flash of panic she saw that it was a ring box. And that her moment of truth was at hand.

He flipped back the velvet lid. She steeled herself not to look, but the sudden flash of fire drew her eyes. A large diamond surrounded by finely cut rubies winked at her from its cream satin nest. Wishing for numbness, anything but this bruising pain, she admitted, "It's lovely."

Grinning, he reached for her left hand. "Don't mind if the band is overlarge. The jeweler assures me we can have it altered in time for the wedding."

The wedding. Inside her guilt surged, but she struck it down, reminding herself that it was only his pride at stake, not his heart.

Withholding her hand, she said, "I can't wear this. I'm sorry."

His smile stiffened. He snapped the box closed and dropped it into his lap. "Then we'll go together tomorrow and select a ring suited to your taste."

"Simon, it's not the ring."

He frowned. "I don't understand."

She drew a shaky breath. "It's you, or rather your reasons for wanting to marry me. The truth is you don't." He started to protest, but she cut him off. "This morning, on my way downstairs, I heard the things you said to Margot."

He regarded her, expression wary. "I take it that explains how your necklace came to be in the plant stand? Exactly what did you overhear?"

"Enough to know that because of what passed between us

last night, you feel duty-bound to marry me. But Simon, you're not. You didn't *take* my virginity. I gave it to you as I gave you my heart, freely and without obligation."

He expelled a weary breath. "Can you not trust me to do what is right for us both?"

She shook her head. "I won't take your name knowing I haven't your heart. Nor will I live with the fear that my past will be your undoing and that—" Feeling as though steel bands encircled her lungs, she paused to draw breath. "—That you will come to hate me for it."

"I could never hate you." Light and shadow limned the muscles working his throat. "As for the other, I'm a businessman, not a poet. It's not always easy for me to voice my feelings, but that doesn't mean I don't have them." He reached for her. "Believe me, Christine, I do have them."

She moved away. "That's not good enough, Simon."

His gaze darkened. "You mean for us to part, then? After all we've been through, all we've built?"

"All we've built!" The sudden flash of anger was a welcome but all-too-brief respite. "These past months, I've let you make a pet of me. Mold me into your notion of a proper lady. I've worked so hard to please you, to win your favor, that I've lost sight of who I really am. Christine Tremayne, the dairyman's daughter, and proud to be so."

Cupping her shoulders in his palms, he drew her toward him, the ring case falling onto the carpet at their feet. "You're so much more than that. You can be anything you set your mind to."

Even now, faced with the prospect of losing her, he wasn't willing to accept her for who she was. Grief settled like a brick in her breast, firming her resolve.

She pulled back. "I am who I am. Until you can accept me, value me, for who and what I am, there can be no future for us."

She started up but he caught hold of her and drew her down onto his lap. "Christine, I can't let you go. I *won't* let you go." None too gently, he took her face between his hands, angling it to his. "If you won't be persuaded by reason, then be persuaded by *this*."

He crushed her mouth beneath his, the kiss hard and bruising even as he gentled his hold. For a terrible moment, her will weakened and she melted against him.

"Oh, Christine." He slid one hand down her front, branding her breasts, her belly, the curve between her thighs with his heat even as he sought to bend her to his will.

Somehow in the midst of the tumult, she found the strength to tear her mouth from his. "Stop!" Breathing hard, she flattened her palms against his chest and pushed. "If you go any further, it will be rape."

Rape. Christine knew it was the ugly word, and not her feeble shove, that caused him to slacken his hold. His hands fell away but his wounded gaze still held hers. "Is there nothing I can say, do, to change your mind?"

She grasped the sofa arm to steady herself and stood. "No, I don't believe there is."

Simon leapt up from the sofa. "Christine, I love you."

Tears stinging her eyes, she shook her head. "But not enough, dear Simon. Not nearly enough."

Having instructed Mrs. Fitz not to wait up, Margot fumbled in her reticule for her key, fingers made clumsy by the nearness of her handsome escort, who stood on the doorstep just below. He'd insisted upon walking her to her door, not that she'd protested overmuch. Attractive, intelligent, and charmingly old-fashioned, Chief Inspector Drew Daniels was the most promising man to have crossed her path in some time. Years.

Key clenched in one damp hand, she turned back to him. "Thank you for a lovely evening, Chief Inspector."

Hat in hand, he climbed the final step to stand beneath the domed lights bracketing her door. "Drew, please." The flickering glow played over the rugged planes of his face and the liberal silver streaking his wavy brown hair.

"Drew." She smiled even as she asked herself whether or not she dared invite him in.

They certainly seemed to be compatible. Over supper at Paddy Green's Song and Supper Rooms, he'd asked interested, intelligent questions about what was involved in directing a successful young ladies academy. Charmed by the novelty of a man expressing interest in *her* work, she'd soon found herself chatting freely as if to an old friend. The London underworld, he'd insisted when she'd first tried to draw him out, wasn't a fit topic for a lady's ears. Eventually she'd worn him down, although she suspected he'd greatly downplayed his bravery as well as the danger involved.

Intense hazel eyes settled on her face. "I should very much like to kiss you. May I?"

He really was dear not to mention quite dashing. Margot moistened her suddenly dry lips, heart tripping in anticipation. "Yes."

He wasn't quite as tall as Simon, but he still had to bend down to kiss her. He settled his mouth over hers, his neatly trimmed mustache a pleasant tickle on her upper lip. A moment later she forgot all about the mustache as his mouth began to move over hers. Strength sheathed in gentleness, passion seasoned with patience, his kiss conveyed the certainty of a man accustomed to command by mastery, not force. That he kept his hands respectfully at his sides only brought home how very much she wanted to feel them on her breasts, the insides of her thighs, *everywhere*.

When he stepped back, her pulse was pumping and her knees felt as wobbly as the orange custard she'd had for dessert. "That was—"

"Magic?" he suggested with a knowing smile, though his eyes were uncertain. Vulnerable. "I know we've only just met, but would tomorrow evening be too soon to call on you again?" He stroked a single, blunt finger down her cheek, drawing a shiver.

She hesitated, trying to find her breath. "You're not a man who believes in wasting time, are you?"

In truth, tomorrow evening wasn't nearly soon enough. She wanted him now, this minute, but she also feared to offend him by seeming overeager.

He dropped his hand, expression contrite. "Forgive me. I don't mean to press you. It's only that . . . Well, blast it, I'm fifty years old." He shoved his hands in his coat pockets and stared down at the step. "I've been alone since my wife died last autumn and content with my memories until . . . until I set eyes on you earlier today." He looked up at her, expression earnest. "It occurred to me then that perhaps I haven't all that much time to waste."

Margot couldn't resist. Sliding her gaze slowly over him from broad shoulders to trim waist, she said, "You appear hale and hearty to me, Inspector."

A telltale pink crept along the contours of his whiskered

jaw. "It's late. I should leave you to your rest." He turned to go.

Inside her, panic flared. Had she, in her boldness, just chased him off? Hoping she wouldn't seem too desperate, she reached out to touch his shoulder. "Tomorrow evening would be perfect."

From the bottom step, he turned back, a broad smile crinkling the corners of his eyes. "I shall count the hours."

Simon spent the rest of that long, lonely night alone in the library. Sometime after midnight he heard Margot come in, but he stayed put, too despondent to seek out sympathy or even wise counsel. Besides, he suspected he already knew what she would tell him.

He'd been a bloody fool.

Polishing off his port, he acknowledged that he'd gone about this marriage business all wrong. Not once had he entertained the notion that Christine might refuse him. Now that she had, quite emphatically, he was at a loss as to where to go from here. Once he might have stooped to bullying or cajoling her, but now such mean tactics seemed unworthy of them both. Christine had grown up over the past months and so, he realized, had he. He couldn't force her to marry him any more than he could retract the callous words he'd tossed off so effortlessly only that morning. Taken out of context, his concerns about honor, duty, and reputation must have sounded damning indeed.

It wasn't until the wee hours that he found the nerve to climb the stairs to the bedroom they'd so briefly shared. By then he was decided. *Hang honor, hang duty, and hang pride, too.* Whatever it took to change her mind, to keep her with him, he was prepared without compunction to do it. Whether that meant tying her to the bedpost with rough gentleness until she saw reason or going down on his hands and knees to grovel, he scarcely cared. He not only loved her, but he needed her. He wanted her. For now. For always.

Putting his pride behind him, he drew a deep breath and entered only to discover that he'd found his resolve too late.

Christine was gone.

Twenty-one

> Love rules the court, the camp, the grove
> And men below, and saints above
> For love is heaven, and heaven is love.
>
> —Sir Walter Scott,
>   "The Lay of the Last Mistrel,"
>   Canto iii, Stanza 1, 1805

LONDON, TWO MONTHS LATER

Simon sat at his desk and, for the fifth time that morning, struggled to concentrate on the mounting piles of parliamentary transcripts and personal financial reports. He hadn't returned to Valhalla since Christine's departure; instead he'd sent for Mrs. Griffith and Trumbull to reopen his London house. At first he'd told himself he stayed on for Rebecca's sake. Although she grew better by the day, she still wasn't ready to venture far from Mordechai's house. Simon's daily visits were a definite benefit of his staying on, but they were hardly the main reason. In truth, he was hiding out. Sweltering in London during the late summer heat was preferable to returning to an empty country house replete with bittersweet memories.

Pushing aside the report he'd pretended to read for the past half hour, he reached for a slender but well-thumbed document. The latter confirmed that the celebrated London detective agency of Grayson, Kent, and McFabish had lived up to its reputation. Within a week of Christine's departure, their detective had assembled a detailed dossier of her whereabouts. Unable to resist, he skimmed its contents yet again.

The *target,* one Miss Christine Elizabeth Tremayne, had quit London for the Oates Farm, a small dairy property in southern Shropshire. There she'd reunited with her siblings, Miss Eliza Tremayne and Messieurs Jacob Edward and Timothy David Tremayne. After a day's sojourn involving an alfresco luncheon, several matches of hide-and-seek, and copious episodes of group tickling, the foursome had boarded a train bound for Cheshire. Disembarking at Chester, they'd reached their destination, a dairy farm in Nantwich, on foot.

A whine, then a telltale scratching, drew Simon's attention to the study door. Jake paused in his labors to fix Simon with a soulful glance.

Simon set aside the report and rose. "You're getting more spoiled by the day, old chap, but I suppose I could do with a walk myself." He grabbed the leash off a chair seat and opened the door. "What the deuce . . . Who let *you* in?"

Leaning heavily on his walking stick, Lord Stonevale said, "Your housekeeper made a valiant effort to convince me you weren't *at home,* but I insisted otherwise."

"I'm not at home, at least not to you." Simon might have said more but just then a flustered Mrs. Griffith drew up behind the earl.

"I'm that sorry, Mr. Belleville, truly I am. One moment he was beside me and the next . . ." The housekeeper's apology lapsed into a fit of hand wringing.

Having no desire to air his family's dirty linen before an audience, he waved her off. "No harm done. You may leave us."

Looking relieved, she curtsied and scurried off.

As soon as she'd turned the corner, Simon dropped the smile. "You, sir, may depart as well."

"In due course after I've said what I came here to say."

"You and I have nothing to say to each other." Simon moved to slam the door in his lordship's face, but the old codger was nothing if not cagey.

He inserted his foot in the doorway. "On the contrary, there's a great deal to be said and I mean to say it. I can either shout through the closed door or you can invite me in."

Bested, Simon had no choice but to step aside and allow his grandfather entry. As soon as the old man cleared the threshold, Simon pulled the door closed with a resounding slam.

His lordship didn't so much as flinch. Calmly he removed his hat, laid it atop a pedestal table, and walked toward the desk. All eagerness, Jake followed, then plopped down on his hindquarters at the earl's feet.

With a chuckle, Lord Stonevale reached down to scratch the dog's head. "Never seen a dog like this one before. What kind is he?"

Disgusted by this display of canine treachery, Simon hedged, "A new breed, extremely rare." He eyed the ebony cane upon which his lordship's right palm rested heavily. "I suppose I should offer you a seat, although you won't be staying long enough to warm the cushion."

"Don't trouble yourself. I'll stand."

Shrunken with age, Stonevale stood several inches shorter than Simon, but the gray eyes he lifted to take his grandson's measure were just as piercing as they had been five years before when the two had chanced to meet in London. En route to their respective clubs, grandfather and grandson had returned only stiff nods as they'd passed each other on the streets of St. James.

At length his lordship remarked, "You don't much favor your father."

Simon snorted. "I take that as a compliment."

The old man scowled. "It's apparent you've a damnable temperament."

Simon glared back. "And I wonder where I got *that*."

Stonevale wagged a crooked finger. "I've kept my eye on you over the years, my boy. Hadn't pegged you for a soft touch. That gel you're passing off as your cousin, Christine Tremayne, she's your mistress, isn't she?"

Simon clenched his jaw until it stood in peril of popping. "None of your bloody business."

"Ah-ha." Triumph lit the old man's eyes. "Just like your father. The apple doesn't fall far from the tree."

Simon stepped forward, hands laced behind his back to

keep them from the old man's throat. "If that were true, then I'd be *marrying* her, wouldn't I?"

That pronouncement seemed to douse most of the old man's fire. In a milder voice he asked, "Why don't you?"

The wound was too raw to bear much probing. "I asked her. She turned me down. End of story." Wondering why he was confessing to the earl of all people, Simon stalked toward the study door and opened it.

Refusing to take the hint, his lordship remained rooted to the spot. He squared his shrunken shoulders. "You're so proud, you're pea-witted."

That was it, the very last straw. Simon whirled on him, no longer caring whether or not they were overheard. "And God knows *you're* not proud? Too bloody proud to acknowledge your own son's death let alone to lift so much as a finger to keep his widow and children from the workhouse... or worse."

The earl blanched. "What are you saying."

"The letters. After Father died, Mother wrote you. She was that desperate. God, even I wrote you once, thinking—praying—it might move you to put aside your hatred and help us."

The earl swallowed hard. "My wife was ill. I'd taken her to Bath in the hope that taking the waters might do her some good. It didn't. When she passed on, I left England for a time. Toured Italy and then France trying... trying to make some sense of it all. By the time your letters found their way to me, they were more than a year old. I tried to track you down, even hired a detective, but it was as if the three of you had vanished."

Simon snorted. "A necessity when one is evicted."

"And then years later, after you'd returned from India, you made it clear you didn't care to know me. I'd already promised the title to... Well, bother it, if you'd come to me then, I would have made things right."

Fury firing his blood, Simon rounded on him. "Come begging, you mean. Well, old man, by then I'd done with begging. And you're correct on one count. I didn't... I don't care to know you."

"Does your sister feel about me as you do?"

"If anyone has cause to hate you, it is Rebecca. Of all of us, she suffered the most."

"What . . . what do you mean?"

It was all Simon could manage to keep his hands from his grandfather's throat. "We were out late. I'd had the opportunity to earn a few extra quid. Oh, I know that mustn't sound like a great deal of money to you but to us it was a small fortune, the difference between having a bit of meat for supper or not. It was Rebecca's birthday, and she was very fond of goose. We were on our way to fetch one from the cook shop when we ran into . . . There were three of them, one a big Irish fellow, a bully they'd hired to do their dirty work. I tried to fend them off, to protect her. But the Irishman, he held my arms, while the other two . . ."

"Oh, God. Oh, dear God. Is she . . ." The earl looked away but not before Simon saw the single tear slipping down his weathered cheek.

Had the earl been a stranger, the sight of him teary-eyed and slump-shouldered would have roused Simon to pity. But this was Stonevale, the man he'd spent most of his life learning to hate.

Ruthless, Simon went on, "Dead? Well, yes, in a manner of speaking. She's spent the better part of twenty years trapped in a little girl's mind. It wasn't until two months ago that she began to come back to us. Christine . . . well, it doesn't matter now."

"She's left you then?"

It seemed that Simon's silence was all the answer the earl required. "Some things are worth more than pride. The love of a good woman, for one. If you love this gel, then go after her. And when you find her, don't be too proud to beg her to take you back."

Simon surveyed his grandfather. Now that the storm within him had broke, he felt curiously calm. "Odd advice coming from you."

"In case you haven't noticed, I'm not so proud anymore, only now that I've owned my mistake, it's too late to make it right. I'm an old man holed up in a moldering pile of stones with only my butler and a barn cat for companions."

Simon folded his arms over his chest. "My heart bleeds."

Stonevale slammed the butt of his stick onto the carpet, prompting Jake to edge away. "Spare me your sarcasm so long as you think on what I've said. Don't *you* be too proud to forgive someone you love for disappointing you . . . or to ask them to forgive you."

Mordechai's words came back to Simon. "*Love, Simon. It is the greatest gift life can offer us.*"

Schooling his features to impassivity, he asked, "Is that all?"

The old man nodded. "For now."

"For now? What is that supposed to mean?"

Stonevale turned to retrieve his hat. "It means that don't suppose you've seen the last of me. I've been an absentee grandfather for thirty-five years. I can't say how many years I have left, but however many I do, you can count on me being around. And that goes for your sister too."

Hat in hand, the earl hobbled out. Feeling as though he'd aged a decade within the last ten minutes, Simon closed the study door and turned back inside. Regarding the room, empty save for his dog, he felt the terrible truth of his life rise up inside him, bitter as bile, final as death. Christine hadn't left him, not really. He'd driven her away. Just like he drove everyone away.

Oh, God, Christine.

He shuffled back to the desk, limbs leaden. Slipping into his seat, he looked down upon the functional, impersonal business of his life's work. His blotter resembled a clock's face: the unread reports set to his right at three o'clock; his fountain pen and ink bottle occupied the nine o'clock position. In the bottom center at six o'clock was his latest correspondence sorted according to content into neat stacks. His appointment book presided over all the other articles at twelve o'clock. His desk might have been a metaphor for his soul. Meticulous in its order. Sterile. Trapped.

"*Enough!*" He swept the edge of his arm over the top, scattering paper and pens to the four winds.

Elbows on the desktop, he buried his face in his hands. The anger—the *hurt*—mounted inside him, scraping his breastbone, blocking the back of his throat until he thought he would explode or suffocate. On the left side of his chest, a great gaping hole gushed with grief.

It was almost a relief when the tears spilled into his palms. A low sob followed, building to crescendo until he was beyond shame, beyond caring who outside his door might bear witness to his pain. For a time the regular ticking of the clock and his ragged wails were the only sounds to stir the silence.

Finally he drew his hands away and looked up. His chest hurt and his throat felt as though it had been scraped with a razor, yet he felt lighter, more at peace. Straightening in his chair, he took a deep breath, his first in many years. Curious, he glanced over at the clock. Nearly an hour had passed. Incredible.

He pushed back from the desk and stood. For the first time in years—in his entire existence, really—he felt well and truly *free*. Free to live his life as he chose. Free to forgive not only his grandfather but also himself.

Free to love Christine.

Squatting on the three-legged milking stool, the meadow grasses tickling her bare ankles, Christine pressed her temple to the cow's flank and reached beneath the beast's belly. A bit out of practice, she was gradually regaining her touch. She began to hum softly, and Tilly relaxed under the gentle pressure of her mistress's kneading fingers. Soon enough the cow's milk began pinging the pail, the rhythmic *tap, tap, tap* reminding her of the rain pellets beating against window glass the night she and Simon had made love.

Oh, Simon. Determined to shake her melancholy, she fixed her gaze on the meadow ahead, but instead of tall grasses, buzzing flies, and wildflowers stirring in the faint breeze, it was Simon's face she saw. It had been two months and a day since she'd put London—and him—behind her, but at times such as this it felt more like a lifetime.

Fortunately, since reuniting her family under one roof, her opportunities for brooding on the past were few and far between. The sorry state of their property had cast an undeniable pall over their homecoming. Hareton had sold off the prime milchers to pay his gaming debts and keep himself supplied in drink. Only old Tilly and a handful of her offspring remained, their ribs sticking out from their sunken sides. The dairy and other dependencies had fared just as badly, victims of leaking roofs and general neglect. As to the cottage, it had taken the four of them days to make it decent. Once they'd settled in, Christine had forced herself to put aside sentiment and survey the situation with a dispassionate eye. It would take years to bring Tremayne Dairy up to what it once had been, not to mention money she didn't have. Her conclusion had been as agonizing as it was obvious. She would have to sell.

So she'd engaged an agent to carry out the transaction. Just the other day Mr. McFabish had ridden over, broad face beaming with the glad news that he'd procured a purchaser! Emotions mixed, Christine had invited him inside the cottage. Over tea and cakes, he'd told her that the prospective buyer was prepared to pay *triple* the amount Christine had asked. The only stipulation was that he was to remain anonymous until the sale was finalized.

Christine had readily accepted both the generous offer and its puzzling condition. How could she possibly refuse when it meant that Timmy and Jake would have some legacy after all? To keep the family together, she and Liza would find work on one of the dairy farms dotting the vale at least until the boys finished their schooling. A dairymaid's life was a backbreaking one, but it had its rewards. At least she'd have the chance to carve out a life for herself among decent folk. Aping the grand lady had earned her nothing but misery—and a few fleeting moments of bliss—yet not for the world and all its riches would she trade those blissful memories.

The warm stickiness striking her leg snapped her attention back to the present. She stared down in horror at the precious milk running down the sides of the pail. All at once, the spillage seemed to stand as a symbol for everything, *everyone,* she'd ever loved and lost.

Eyes filling with angry tears, she tore off her bonnet and threw it to the ground. "Bloody, *bloody* hell!"

A familiar *tsk-tsk* sound caused her to snap her head around. "Language, Miss Tremayne."

She whirled to see a tall figure striding toward her from the far end of the field. Her mouth opened on a gasp.

A single word spilled out to fill the silence. "Simon!"

Simon handed Christine her bonnet. Hiding his nervousness behind a grin, he said, "Surprised you, did I?"

Gaze shuttering, she took it and crammed it into the pocket of her calico pinafore. "You could say that." She picked up her stool and an empty pail and moved to the next cow.

Determined, he trailed behind her. "I've missed you. Is it wrong of me to hope that you might have missed me too?"

Rather than answer him directly, she plopped down on the stool. "I'm working. Or at least trying to."

He folded his arms across his chest and stared down at her. She was stubborn but then so was he. "Then I'll help." When her head shot up, gaze disbelieving, he only shrugged. "If I have to milk cows to speak with you, then so be it."

He picked up an empty pail and walked over to another milcher grazing contentedly nearby. Christine's appeared to be the only stool, so he positioned the pail beneath the area of probable flow and squatted. Casting her a sideways glance to make certain she was watching, he flattened his cheek against the cow's side as he'd seen her do and shoved his hands beneath.

The beast balked as soon as Simon grabbed hold. She kicked out with her hind legs at the bucket. Startled, he fell back, landing in a clod of something far too soft to be dirt.

"Bloody hell!" Feeling like a clown, he lifted himself off the pile of dung and stared up into Christine's amused face.

Standing over him, she offered him her hand. Telling himself it was tantamount to an olive branch, he took it gratefully and pulled himself up.

Keeping her hand, he asked, "How the devil do you do this? I can't see a blasted thing."

She pulled free and set her stool next to the cow. "You see with your hands, not your eyes. Here, let me show you." Settling in, she took hold of the teat and began to demonstrate.

Watching the deft movements of her hands, he remarked, "You make it look so simple."

"It is . . . with practice. The same notion behind your making me repeat 'Hairy Harry Hastings asked his aunt Hannah to Hold His Handsome Hat for Him while He went to Hail a Hansom' again and again until I finally got it right."

He hunkered down beside her. "A not entirely unpleasant memory, I hope?"

"Not entirely." Cheek pressed to the beast's flank, she asked, "How is Jake?"

"Big. He's grown into those paws of his and then some. He misses you." *I miss you.*

"And Mrs. G? How is her rheumatism?"

"Better, I believe. There's a new remedy she's tr—" He broke off, exasperation getting the better of him. In another moment, they'd move to comparing notes on the weather. "Mrs. Griffith, Jem, Trumbull, the dog—they're all fine. They all send their love. They all miss you." *They're all counting on me to bring you back.* "But I didn't come here to talk about them nor to learn how to milk a cow, delightful as that has proven to be."

She stopped milking and turned to face him. "Why did you come?"

Her steely look tested his courage, but he reminded himself that nothing worth having was ever won easily. "To tell you that I love you with all my heart." He drew a long breath, filling his tight lungs with the still, fragrant air. "That I've loved you from the first moment I clapped eyes on you in that attic, only I've been too bloody proud and stubborn and stupid to admit it." He sank down on his knees. Ignoring the dew seeping through the knees of his trousers, he said, "I've only one heart to give you, Christine. Please, I beg you, tell me that it is enough."

Her gaze softened. "Simon, I don't know what to say."

With his fingertips he brushed back the damp tendrils of hair curling at her temples. "Say you'll marry me. I want you for my wife, my helpmate, my *lover*."

A shadow fell across her face. Eyes miserable, she shook her head. "Nothing has changed."

"Everything has changed. *I've* changed." He caught her hands and carried them to his lips. New calluses thickened the palms, a fresh blister split the juncture of her left thumb, and the nails she'd worked so hard to grow were broken off. Hers weren't the hands of a lady, but they were the only ones he cared to hold.

"I've even made strides toward reconciling with my grandfather, difficult though it's been." He laid her work-roughened hand over the left side of his chest, bringing it to rest over his rapidly beating heart. "I'm not the same man who drove you away. If you can't see that, can you at least *feel* it?"

She shook her head, eyes brimming. "Oh, Simon, even if you have changed, can't you see I haven't? You can dress me up, teach me to behave as a lady, but you can't change who I am. I'm Christine Tremayne, the dairyman's daughter. 'Tis who I am, who I'll always be."

He shook his head, desperate to make her see. "I was wrong to try to change you, a pompous idiot to even consider hiding you away. Please, say you forgive me and that you'll marry me, or at least consider it."

Mouth trembling, she shook her head. "We both know I'm no fit mate for a future member of Parliament, let alone the heir to an earldom. Sooner or later you'll come to regret shackling yourself to a country mouse who still can't be trusted to know one fork from another."

"Shall I regret marrying my heart's desire, the one person on earth who has the power to make me smile and laugh? I think not. The only thing I'll ever regret is letting you go. If you were to say yes right now, I'd shout it to the rooftops, have the banns read in every bloody parish in London, hire the biggest, gaudiest carriage I could find and parade you through the streets in your bridal gown, right up to the Houses of Parliament." He gained his feet, bringing her with him. "Can't you see that having you say you'll be mine is the only dream that matters, that growing old with you *is* my life's ambition. The only question that remains is whether or not you'll have *me*. Will you, Christine? If you say yes, I'll promise to spend the rest of my days thinking of ways to make you happy."

She was going to accept him! He could feel it in the way her body relaxed against his, could see it in the sudden easing of tension from her features.

Nibbling her bottom lip, she said, "Simon, before I answer, there's something I need to tell you. Something more you need to know."

Eager to put to rest whatever worries she still harbored, he urged, "Then tell me quickly, for whatever it is can only make me love you more, not less."

She smoothed a hand over the flat plain of her stomach. "I think I may be . . ." Her voice trailed off.

Their gazes met and held. Without another word passing between them, Simon *knew*.

Pulling her into his arms, he lifted her until they were on eye-level, her feet dangling. "A baby, Christine!" He twirled them both around and around until, laughing, she begged him to set her down. Drunk with joy, he complied, bracing a steadying arm about her. "You'll marry me, then? Say it quickly, otherwise I'll think I'm dreaming."

She tilted her face up to his. The warmth of her smile dissolved his last gnawing doubt. "Yes, I'll marry you." A steely look sharpened her gaze. "But not because of the baby, mind you, but because I love you so very much."

The cow flicking her tail beside them, the birds chirping, and even the meadow itself faded into a distant and only marginally real world. All that existed for Simon was Christine: her fresh springtime scent, the sleek strength of her as she wrapped her slender arms about his neck and pulled him close, the sweetness of her kiss as she matched her lips to his.

If it hadn't been for the sounds of giggling and small, stamping feet running toward them, Simon might have gone on kissing Christine until nightfall. As it was, he cracked open an eye and peered over his beloved's shoulder to the tall, dreamy-eyed girl and the two little towheaded boys watching them with rapt interest.

Cheeks stained a charming pink, Christine pulled out of his arms and turned to greet the interlopers. Taking his hand, she started, "Simon, I'd like you to meet—"

"Liza, Timmy, and Jake," he finished for her. "We met at the cottage when I first arrived. It was your sister, in fact, who took pity on my wanderings and directed me here."

Liza dipped her head in acknowledgment, her shy smile reminiscent of her older sister's. It was obvious that the twins, however, hadn't a trace of shyness in them. Like rambunctious pups set loose from their kennel, they bounded forward.

"Chrissie, Mr. Belleville says we're all to come and live in 'is 'ouse. And me and Jake are to each 'ave a pony of our *wery* own."

Jake elbowed him. "And a puppy. Don't forget about the puppies."

Liza, silent until now, spoke up. "And I'm to train for a teacher."

Eyes sparkling with tears, Christine turned back to Simon. "Is this true?"

"Of course." Moved beyond measure, he reached down to ruffle Timmy's curls. "Having this lot about will be splendid preparation for when our child comes, don't you think?"

Christine's answering smile was more precious than a trunk full of gold. "We'll start packing this afternoon." For a flicker of an instant, her smile dimmed. "I had to sell the dairy. I'll join you in Kent as soon as the new owner arrives to take possession."

Caught up in the thrill of having Christine agree to be his wife, Simon had as good as forgotten. "Well, as to that . . ." He reached into his trouser pocket and withdrew the flattened square of vellum. He handed it to her.

Taking it from him, she asked, "What is it?"

Feeling like the cat who'd swallowed the canary, he said, "Read it for yourself."

A hush fell over their small party as Christine unfolded the paper and began to read. A moment later, her head snapped up.

Clutching the bill of sale to her breast, she stared at him. "*You're* the anonymous gentleman, the new owner of Tremayne Dairy!"

He was smiling so broadly that his jaws ached, yet he couldn't seem to stop. "No darling, *you* are. Consider it my wedding gift to you along with whatever funds you require to set the property to rights."

"Oh, Simon." She flung herself at his chest, the paper crushed between them as she sprinkled his face, his jaw, his throat with sweet kisses.

Impervious to his new family's giggling and feet shuffling, Simon claimed Christine with a searing kiss. When they finally broke apart, it was to clapping hands and wild cheers.

Above the raucous, a tiny voice piped up, "Oh, Chrissie, ain't life goin' to be grand?"

Beaming up at Simon through the happy tears, Christine answered, "Yes, darling, life is going to be wonderful indeed."

Epilogue

Simon and Christine's long life together was indeed wonderful. Their more than fifty-year union resulted in five children, thirteen grandchildren, and thirty great grandchildren. Even Valhalla with its many rooms became a bit crowded when the Belleville clan, including Christine's sister and brothers and their respective families, took up residence.

The young Mrs. Belleville divided her busy days between caring for her growing brood and planning the conversion of her family's dairy into a vocational academy for former prostitutes. Over the years, Tremayne Dairy Farm Academy became a national model for progressive—and profitable—social reform, drawing investors throughout the British Empire and beyond.

As for Christine herself, despite her shaky start, London society soon clasped her to its bosom. Dubbed an "original," she found her quaint mannerisms and sayings copied by ladies from the royal princesses on down. Hostesses who wanted to ensure that their charity events were a *veritable crush* were wont to pen "Mrs. Simon Belleville will attend" at the bottom of their invitations. Even so, Christine was never happier than when she could spend a quiet evening at home with her handsome husband by her side, a book in her hand, and a child or cat snuggled on her lap.

Although Gladstone ousted Disraeli as prime minister in the general election of 1868, Simon won his seat in a landslide victory. The swearing-in ceremony took place in December of that year. Even though Simon had waited more than an hour to hear his name called, when he finally did he hesitated. Wanting desperately to share this special moment with Christine, he slanted his gaze up the Perpendicular Gothic walls and along the gallery until he sighted her. Looking proud and exceedingly pregnant, his new wife was joined at the rail by Margot, Rebecca, and Mordechai. Heedless of the countless spectators watching them from the cockpit floor as well as from above, he caught her amber-brown gaze and mouthed the words it had taken him far too long to say. *I love you.* Only then did he turn away and step forward. He repeated the oath in a firm voice, yet his hand shook when he signed his name to the Test Roll's parchment page, for he was as much moved by the great love he'd found as by the honor of his new office.

Revered by his constituents and respected by his rivals, Simon served in the Commons for the next fifteen years. On more than one occasion he crossed the House floor to throw his support behind a Liberal bill concerned with the welfare and protection of women, children, and even London's homeless cats and dogs!

Jake, Simon's dog, lived a long, happy, and excessively spoiled life. When Parliament was in session, he never failed to accompany his master to both morning and evening sittings. Shamelessly partisan, he was wont to thump his tail and release a happy howl whenever Simon rose from the bench to address his fellow members. By the same token, he kept a baleful eye on the opposition and was not above growling at one or two especially contentious members, from whom he frequently won the floor. His several successors, all of them mongrels, carried on the happy tradition, and

Simon often said he didn't feel entirely dressed to go out without a dog's leather leash in hand.

Over the years, Lord Stonevale was a frequent and welcome guest in Simon and Christine's home. According to his physician, the joy he took in bouncing his great grandchildren upon his arthritic knees was largely responsible for him living into his nineties. Upon his death, Simon resigned his seat in the Commons to assume his rightful place in the House of Lords. The new Lord and Lady Stonevale were presented at court with all due pomp and ceremony—and only one minor mishap. *Her ladyship,* nervous about making her bow before the queen, dumped her feathered headdress at the royal feet, prompting the stone-faced Victoria to break into a broad smile.

Rebecca eventually recovered not only her mental faculties but also her ability to smile. Although she continued to live with Mordechai until his death, she made frequent visits to Kent, dividing her stays between Valhalla and The Priory. Remarking that country life obviously agreed with her sister-in-law, Christine asked her to oversee the dairy school as its headmistress. Rebecca accepted with alacrity. With the assistance of Nantwich's village physician, a gentle widower whom she later wed, she expanded the school's curriculum to include a special program for women recovering from sexual assault.

Margot and Chief Inspector Daniels married a mere month after Christine and Simon took their own vows. Despite the lateness of their union, the couple was blessed with a daughter, whom they named Arielle. Having at last achieved the domestic bliss she'd craved for so long, Margot closed down her finishing school and converted her Mayfair town house back into a private residence, which she shared exclusively with her husband, daughter, and multitude of cats.

As for Hareton, after several years spent cooling his heels in a Newgate Prison cell, he was released on the condition that he leave England for good. He set sail for Australia the very next day and, to everyone's supreme relief, was never seen or heard from again.

Dear Readers,

The evolution of Britain's parliamentary oath has a long and fascinating history. Members were at one time required to take three separate oaths: the oaths of supremacy, allegiance, and abjuration. Religious restrictions embedded in these oaths effectively barred Jews as well as Roman Catholics, Quakers, and atheists, from entering political life on the national level.

Until 1858, the oath of abjuration concluded with the words, "on the true faith of a Christian." Some Jewish aspirants, notably the future prime minister and earl of Beaconsfield, Benjamin Disraeli, surmounted this obstacle by becoming nominal members of the Church of England. But others held firm.

It was not until 1858, with the passage of the Jews Relief Act, that Jewish M.P.s were permitted to take a modified version of the oath. On July 26, 1858 the Jewish baron, Lionel Nathan de Rothschild finally took his seat in the House of Commons—eleven years after he'd first been elected for the City of London in 1847.

But it would take nearly three more decades before the first Jew would be admitted to the House of Lords. In 1885, Nathaniel Rothschild, son of Lionel, took his seat in the Lords.

Sometimes progress takes time.

Until next time . . .

Wishing you fairy-tale dreams and a never-ending supply of fabulous romance fiction,

Hope Tarr
September 2002

USA Today **Bestselling Author**

LYNN KURLAND

"Kurland out-writes romance fiction's top authors by a mile." –*Publishers Weekly*

Kurland's own stunning novels...

THE MORE I SEE YOU	0-425-17107-8
ANOTHER CHANCE TO DREAM	0-425-16514-0
VEILS OF TIME	0-425-16970-7
THE VERY THOUGHT OF YOU	0-425-18237-1
THIS IS ALL I ASK	0-425-18033-6
A DANCE THROUGH TIME	0-425-17906-0
STARDUST OF YESTERDAY	0-425-18238-X
IF I HAD YOU	0-425-17694-0
MY HEART STOOD STILL	0-425-18197-9

And her anthologies with other fantastic authors...

CHRISTMAS SPIRITS   0-515-12174-6
Anthology with Elizabeth Bevarly, Casey Claybourne, and Jenny Lykins...magical stories celebrating the miracle of love.

A KNIGHT'S VOW   0-515-13151-2
Anthology with Patricia Potter, Deborah Simmons, and Glynnis Campbell...four magnificent Medieval romances.

To order, please call 1-800-788-6262

(B739)

National Bestselling Author
JULIE BEARD

ROMANCE OF THE ROSE
0-425-16342-3

Lady Rosalind Carberry is determined to rule Thornbury House—her inheritance—as a free and single woman. But when her childhood nemesis, the handsome Drake Rothwell, returns to claim the estate as his rightful inheritance, the Rose of Thornbury is ready to fight for what is hers...

FALCON AND THE SWORD
0-515-12065-0

People whispered about Ariel. For a young woman in the Middle Ages, she was anything but common. She was beautiful, independent, and the most skilled falconer anyone at Lonegrine Castle could remember. Still, she longed for something she'd never known...

A DANCE IN HEATHER
0-425-16424-1

Lady Tess Farnsworth bitterly accepted the royal decree to wed the man whom she detested above all. The gloriously handsome Earl of Easterby had failed her in a desperate time of need, and her only solace in wedding him was the promise of vengeance...

LADY AND THE WOLF
0-425-16425-X

Lady Katherine swears to her dying brother that she will spend the rest of her life in a convent. But her father betroths her to cold-hearted Stephen Bartingham, the son of an earl. She embarks on a journey to join her future husband, determined to remain chaste...

THE MAIDEN'S HEART
0-515-12515-6

A dashingly handsome knight errant agrees to marry a baron's daughter...sight unseen. But his new bride is determined to stay innocent. Her plan, however, will drive them both to the edge of desire—and danger.

MY FAIR LORD
0-425-17481-6

Regency England will never be the same when gaiety and ghosts combine in this captivating romantic novel.

VERY TRULY YOURS
0-515-13039-7

When some mysterious letters are delivered to Jack Fairchild's law office, he sets out to find the young lady who wrote them—and rescue her from a frightful predicament.

TO ORDER CALL:
1-800-788-6262

(AD # B195)

MIRIAM GRACE MONFREDO

brings to life one of the most exciting periods in our nation's history—the mid-1800s—when the passionate struggles of suffragettes, abolitionists, and soldiers touched the lives of every American, including a small-town librarian named Glynis Tryon...

SENECA FALLS INHERITANCE	0-425-14465-8
NORTH STAR CONSPIRACY	0-425-14720-7
BLACKWATER SPIRITS	0-425-15266-9
THROUGH A GOLD EAGLE	0-425-15898-5
THE STALKING HORSE	0-425-16695-3
MUST THE MAIDEN DIE	0-425-17610-X

The Seneca Falls series continues into the Civil War with Glynis's niece Bronwen Llyr, who goes undercover and behind enemy lines in the service of Pinkerton's Detective Agency.

SISTERS OF CAIN	0-425-18092-1
BROTHERS OF CAIN	0-425-18638-5

Available in hardcover:
CHILDREN OF CAIN	0-425-18641-5

Available wherever books are sold, or to order, call:
1-800-788-6262
B511